RED WEB

RED WEB

Through the Canvas: Book Two

NINIE HAMMON

STERLING & STONE

Chapter One

SHE HEARD his footsteps crossing the wooden slats of the back porch and thought of horses' hooves, clattering loud and purposeful. When Brice appeared in the kitchen, his jaw was set, his eyes narrowed, the smile of greeting that bloomed on her face drained away. This was not the big man who'd volunteered to haul junk out of Bailey Donahue's attic so she could sell the not-junk at a yard sale. This was Kavanaugh County *Sheriff* Brice McGreggor.

"Dispatch just got a call from Corruthers Elementary School," he said as he strode past her. "A first-grader is *missing.*"

It was his day off and he was out of uniform. He ran to his cruiser, tore out of the driveway and raced off down the street, light bar flashing and siren wailing.

Bailey felt gooseflesh break out on her arms. She stood for a long time at the door, looking at the empty place at the end of Sycamore Street where Brice's cruiser had turned and gone out of sight. She listened until the wail of his siren faded, then thought she could still hear the echo of it, but that was just in her head.

Sparky sat down in front of her in his *pet-me-now* pose and she reached down and absentmindedly scratched the little golden doodle behind his ears. Then she straightened and slowly climbed the stairs to the second floor. At the end of the hallway was a smaller staircase that led to the huge attic resting atop the whole length and breadth of the historic Watford House.

T.J. Hamilton was there and he spoke over his shoulder.

"Was that an ambulance sittin' in the front yard or is the house on fire?" He didn't turn around. "You ever heard of a shoebox fetish? I ain't. But somebody who lived here once musta had one 'cause I done counted thirty-seven of 'em. Think anybody'd buy a shoebox at a yard sale?"

"The siren was Brice's. There's a child missing from the elementary school."

T.J. stopped what he was doing and turned toward her, a tall, thin black man with a head of wooly hair the color of a gun barrel and red suspenders holding up his trousers.

"That all you know, a child's *missin'?*"

"Uh huh."

She turned away and began mindlessly stuffing a pile of tangled-up coat hangers into a junk box, trying to get her head around how horrible it must be for your child to be *missing.* She knew the anguish of being separated from her child, the everyday throbbing pain that sometimes reached out with a white-hot saber and seared a hole in her heart. But she knew where her child was. She knew Bethany was *safe* — and would remain safe as long as Bailey stayed *dead.* To wonder if your child was in danger, though, in pain. To wonder if someone was … *hurting* them … Bailey couldn't stand that.

Then she burped out a grunt of acknowledgement. Couldn't stand it — right. She'd once have said there were all manner of things she "couldn't stand." As she and Aaron drove down the rain-sodden streets toward the airport that day, she had cried out to him that she missed Bethany — the baby they had deposited in Bailey's sister's arms less than fifteen minutes before. Bailey had told him she *couldn't stand* to be away from Bethany for a whole week.

A whole week.

She hadn't seen the child in twenty months, eleven days and — she looked at her watch — five hours, not that she was counting or anything. She had withstood that breath-stealing pain and loneliness, not because she was strong or brave or even stoic but because she didn't have any choice.

"It's a little boy named Riley Campbell." T.J.'s voice startled Bailey back to the present. "A first-grader. That's what the news says." He held out his phone to her, but she didn't look.

"Says he's seven years old and that he went outside for recess but never came back in."

"He probably just wandered off, chased a butterfly or saw a rabbit. They'll find him."

Chapter Two

BRICE DROVE 10-60, lights-and-siren, to the elementary school, and didn't stop by the station to change into his uniform. On the way, he talked to his chief deputy, Raleigh Fletcher, "Fletch," who was at the school, and got the basics of what had happened. Fletch had texted the boy's picture to every officer in the county, both on and off duty, and he gave Brice the bad news right off the top.

"The Cottonwood Festival is setting up in that field next to the school. I locked it down as soon as I got here, but it's got more leaks than a dog-chewed garden hose." Meaning there were no "entrances and exits" to close off, just a wide open area where people could come and go at will.

Brice's heart sank. The festival wasn't a surprise. He'd scheduled officers to patrol it during its weekend run. But he hadn't yet put it together that people were there *now* setting up, a random-grab of unvetted strangers within rock-throwing distance of an elementary school.

The festival featured dozens of booths hawking all manner of merchandise. Local artists brought their pots and paintings, added to flea market junk ranging from fake switchblades to not-so-fake nunchucks, handmade quilts and fresh-baked brownies, a petting zoo, pony rides, even a carnival.

Fletch told him that the missing child, a student in Melody McCallum's first-grade class, had last been seen on the playground during recess. But his desk remained empty after the bell rang.

Brice instructed the dispatcher to alert the sheriff's departments in the adjoining counties, a heads-up that he might be requesting assistance, depending on how things went. A clock was ticking. If the boy'd been kidnapped — and that was a call Brice was *nowhere near* ready to make — the first seventy-two hours was crucial. Although stranger kidnappings were very rare, statistics painted a bleak picture: sixty percent of kidnapped children who didn't survive were killed less than three hours after they were taken, eighty percent within the first two days. If he found his fifteen-man department couldn't cover all the bases, he'd ask for help. The West Virginia Highway Patrol had already been notified.

The scene was controlled chaos when Brice arrived. There were five units from his department, plus two patrol cars from the Shadow Rock Police Department, which was manned by officers whose sole professional responsibility was writing parking tickets and being a uniformed presence outside Shadow Rock's historic homes to corral the tourists. The real law enforcement in the county was provided by Brice's sheriff's department. There was even a West Virginia State Police cruiser — Trooper Charles Richards, a man who had surely gotten all F's in the "plays well with others" column of his own elementary school report card.

Officers were posted around the perimeter of the festival beside the school, with sight-lines to each other so anyone attempting to enter or leave would be spotted. Fletch had said that two teams of officers had already searched the handful of campers, RVs and camper-trailers used by those setting up the festival — the livestock trailers that had brought the menagerie for the petting zoo and the trucks that hauled carnival equipment.

Deputy Fletcher met Brice as he stepped out of his cruiser, appearing to read from his report. In truth, Brice knew Fletch was operating on memory, an incredibly good one that took up the slack for his limited mental acuity. Reading, though, not so much.

"The K9 unit is en route. The teachers double-checked their classrooms to confirm Riley is the only missing child."

Before Fletch had a chance to continue, a car pulled up in the parking lot and three people leapt out of it, two women and a man, and rushed toward the front door of the school. Brice intercepted them.

"Are you Mr. and Mrs. Campbell?"

"Where's Riley?" cried a slender woman with red hair. The little boy in the picture Fletch had sent out had red hair. "They called and said he was missing? How can a child be *missing* from school?"

The second woman had her arm around the shoulder of the first. Mr. Campbell, bearded, wearing glasses, said nothing, just ignored Brice and headed into the building. Brice blocked his way.

"I'm sorry, but we have the school on lockdown right now. Nobody's going in that building and nobody's coming out of it. Please understand and let us do our jobs. Let us find Riley."

"You're telling me I can't go into my own son's school?" Fear was making the man belligerent.

"Yes sir, that's exactly what I'm telling you." Brice turned to Fletch. "If you'll take the Campbells over there ..." He indicated one of a handful of benches in front of the building. "We need some information from you."

"You have to find my little boy — *find him!*" There was an edge of incipient hysteria in Mrs. Campbell's voice.

"The best way to help us find your son is to answer Deputy Fletcher's questions."

Fletcher took Mrs. Campbell's arm and began to guide the couple toward the table, speaking calmly.

"Ma'am, I need to know what your son was wearing when he left for school this morning."

Fletch didn't need to know any such thing. The officers had been on the scene long enough to gather all the identifying information they needed. Fletch was keeping the Campbells occupied and out of the way. He'd gather information, too, of course, find out from the couple if the boy had ever run away, if he had any favorite haunts where he might go, the names of his best friends … things like that.

Brice strode into the building and found Trooper Richards questioning the principal, Samuel Bergman.

As Brice approached, the trooper snapped his notebook shut. "That's all for now, Mr. Bergman," he said. "I'm sure I'll have more questions for you later."

Bergman turned to walk away but Brice stopped him.

"Actually, I have a few questions of my own. Will you excuse us for a moment?" He motioned and the trooper reluctantly moved a few steps away.

"Appreciate your help, Charlie." His voice was level and controlled. "But we got this."

The officer bristled. "At least I'm in uniform. And I was first on the scene—"

"I've already notified your post, confirmed that they'll dispatch *detectives* if I need more help." He smiled. "But we could sure use you in crowd and traffic control. The word's out and parents are—"

"I don't report to you, McGreggor." The trooper walked away and Brice turned to the principal.

"I know you've already explained what happened, but I need to hear it firsthand. His teacher was the last person, the last adult who saw Riley, right?"

"Yes, sir, Melody McCallum. And several children say … we haven't had a chance to talk to all of them—"

"Would you please get Ms. McCallum? I'd like to talk to both of you in your office in five minutes. And would you ask someone to gather up all the children who might have seen Riley today — I know there are probably a lot of them, but we need to talk to each one individually. Is there a gymnasium or auditorium where you could put them?"

"Certainly, Sheriff. I don't know what could possibly have … how … we've looked every—"

"I'm sure you have, Mr. Bergman. Your office, five minutes, okay?"

The man hurried away down the hallway.

Brice nodded at the deputy who had taken up a post at the front door of the school. Fletch had gone by the book. That was his strong suit. Almost in the manner of a savant, Raleigh Fletcher knew police procedure and protocol inside and out and was unerringly dedicated to dotting every i and crossing every t. Just don't ask him to spell a word with more syllables in it than mayonnaise. Fletch had been only a couple of blocks from the school when the 911 call came in and he'd immediately secured the building, stationing officers at all the exits. Nobody in. Nobody out. No exceptions. He had also set up a perimeter, a circle out about a hundred yards from the school where officers allowed no one in or out. When the K9 unit arrived, the dog would be taken immediately to the parking lot to inspect every vehicle. The animal wouldn't be trying to track scent in such a scent-polluted environment, but a trained dog could hear a human heartbeat in the next room with the door closed. They'd take him past every car trunk. If the kid had somehow gotten into the trunk of a car — unlikely as that was — he was in grave danger. It was a cool day for the middle of August but the temperature was eighty degrees and climbing. A child in a car trunk in that kind of heat couldn't survive more than a couple of hours — maybe less.

After the parking lot was cleared, the K9 officer would give the dog the kid's gym shoes from his locker and then walk the animal slowly around the school inside the perimeter — but outside the playground where scents would be too confusing. If a lone child walked away from the school in any direction, the dog would cross the child's path and could follow the scent from there.

The building had been divided into quadrants and four search teams were formed, each consisting of a deputy and a teacher or counselor or administrator, someone on the school staff. The teams had combed their quadrant. Then they switched quadrants and by the time Brice arrived, the whole building had been searched four times by a total of eight different people.

While he waited for the teacher and principal, Brice gave the school property a quick walk-through, not as if he expected he'd suddenly stumble upon the missing child but to refamiliarize himself with the layout of the facility. He knew every school building in the county, had been to each of them dozens of times for various reasons, in addition to taking every new officer on a schools tour, so they'd know the layout in any emergency — though that was more about responding to a school shooting or bomb threat than to a missing child.

It just happened that this building was particularly familiar to Brice. It was the building where he had gone to elementary school. The old facility had been maintained well through the years, though like every other building in the county, it had been "maintained" as it had always been rather than being renovated, or — *heaven forbid!* — bulldozed and a newer, more modern facility built in its place. Shadow Rock was, after all, a historic community with an economy based on tourism — on water sports enthusiasts at Whispering Mountain Lake and tourists who came to see the elegant homes that'd been built by the uber rich friends of Andrew Carnegie in the early 1900s. The Historical Society Nazis had done their dead level best to freeze history in the whole of Kavanaugh County, to keep every building "as-is" — even the buildings that clearly post-dated the historic homes the tourists paid to explore.

Taking long, brisk strides in the hallways, Brice could hear a murmur of voices behind the closed classroom doors, but it was subdued. The school secretary and another woman he didn't recognize in the office only nodded as he passed. They'd both been crying.

He stuck his head into the janitor's supply closet and the boiler room in the basement, and stepped out the back door at the end of the Grades K-3 hallway onto the playground. The playground equipment he remembered — monkey bars, seesaws, swings with wooden-slat seats and a merry-go-round that was already squeaking and wheezing its way around in circles when he was a boy, had fallen victim to safety restrictions. Swings had plastic seats. Everything else was stationary. He reflected that his generation had somehow managed to survive the hazards of a moving-parts playground, but quickly dismissed the mental rant he might some other time have indulged. He was just glad he wasn't a kid, grateful he wasn't a parent either.

And never would be a parent.

Instantly pulling a mental lever, he shifted his train of thought onto another track before it could pull up at stations where he never stopped anymore. But he wasn't quite quick enough and a lone rogue thought made it into his consciousness.

Brice McGreggor would never have children because *he didn't dare.*

Chapter Three

BRICE GLANCED at the big clock on the school office wall as he stepped into the principal's office — 2:37 p.m. Riley was last seen at 1:20 p.m.

Tick. Tick. Tick.

He took a seat in one of two chairs facing the principal's desk, feeling a wave of "principal's office anxiety" wash over him. In some ways, you never grew up. Bergman sat behind the desk. He was an older man, surely circling the drain of mandatory retirement, with white hair and a neatly trimmed white beard and mustache. He was dressed in a suit and vest. A gold watch was visible in the vest pocket that put Brice in mind of Dobbs's pocket watch that had never kept time. It had helped him rescue a family from a flood, though, so it had earned its keep.

Each of the three elementary schools in the county was unique, in part due to the different characters of the schools' principals. In East Point Elementary School, the principal was what Brice called a "hangly-dangly" kind of woman, who had paper mobiles made by the children decorating her office and the school hallways. The principal of Madison Elementary School was into Precious Moments figurines — along with ceramic Winnie the Pooh and Harry Potter characters ... plus hobbits, dwarves, elves, gnomes, fairies, and other small, unidentifiable creatures. Bergman was a motivational-posters kind of guy. In *National Geographic*-esque pictures, inch-high saplings stood beside California Redwoods above the word *Determination*, the Golden Gate above the admonition to *Be the Bridge* and a photo of a single drip of water hitting the surface of a pond, above the words *Attitudes are ripples. Change your attitude and you change your world.*

Melody McCallum sat in the seat beside Brice, looking like a child herself, a petite woman with delicately beautiful features. Her hair was striking — thick and an unusual caramel shade of brown, hanging in loose curls that framed her face. She was seated in a shaft of sunshine, and he could see reddish copper highlights — either natural or skillfully colored — that caught and reflected the light, giving her hair a glossy, sparkling sheen. Her complexion was very pale and he suspected she could sunburn from the picture of a beach on a postcard.

She wore a neck brace.

"Whiplash," she told him when she saw him notice it. "I was in a wreck six weeks ago. I get the brace off tomorrow afternoon."

"Melody downplays the accident," Bergman said, giving her a paternal look. "A pickup truck driven by an illegal ... oh, no, that's not politically correct." He almost ground his teeth. "There were three Hispanic men in a pickup with no license plate or vehicle registration and without a speck of identification — a driver's license or anything else — among them. The driver blew past a huge sign that said "right lane closed" like perhaps *he couldn't read English.* Ran Melody right off the road." He didn't smile, but you could hear lightly veiled satisfaction in his voice when he continued, "All three of the men were killed."

That was odd. Why were there fatalities in the other vehicle when Melody's was the one run off the road?

"The side of her car was ripped open, but she was thrown free, thank God. Found her unconscious beside the road."

She dismissed his concern with an "I'm fine" and focused on Brice. "Please, you have to find Riley! I don't know where he could have gone. He was there and then …"

"Start at the beginning, please." She looked down at her hands, clasped in her lap. She was trembling. No, make that vibrating.

"I can't remember *anything* that was different—" Her voice broke. She was desperate to recall every detail and the sheriff knew from experience that such effort usually had the opposite effect.

"Please, Ms. McCallum—"

"Melody."

"Melody, I'm Brice. I know you're upset but I need you to relax. If you try too hard to remember everything, you won't remember much of anything. Just tell me what you *do* remember. If you think of some other detail later, you can give me a call."

That helped to relax her.

"When did you see Riley for the first time today?"

"Before school started. I'm at my desk half an hour before the bell rings and the doors open so I'm always there when the children arrive. The first bell rings at 8:15, the final tardy bell rings at 8:45."

"Classes start at 8:45," Bergman said. "First recess is short, just fifteen minutes, at ten o'clock. Lunch is 11:20 to 11:50. Second recess is longer for the younger children, K through third grade — they have more energy to run off — a full half hour between 1:15 and 1:45. The busses start running at 3:15."

"What do the children do when they first get to school, before the tardy bell rings?"

"This morning, Riley came in right after Beth Singletary. Corey Warren was the last of today's feeders."

Brice looked quizzical.

"My classroom is a bit of a zoo and the children take turns feeding — it teaches them responsibility. I have a parakeet named Frodo, two gerbils named Frick and Frack, an aquarium full of fish and a terrarium on a table by the window. The children are most fascinated with Bambi."

She answered his unasked question.

"Bambi is a tarantula spider almost as big as a saucer. He lives in the terrarium."

Brice was horrified. He wasn't arachnophobic, but spiders totally creeped him out and he would not willingly get near one.

"You have a hairy black spider in your classroom?"

She almost smiled at his surprise.

"In many cultures spiders are revered as gods. But in our culture, we're scared to death of them, *prejudiced* against them. First-graders are so impressionable and I want them to understand that prejudice, in any form, is unacceptable, that it's not okay to *pre*-judge something — or some*body* — you really know nothing about. A spider is the perfect object lesson."

Brice thought he could have come up with a less horrifying object lesson but he didn't say that.

"I let the students name him. They chose 'Bambi,' which shows you how they felt about him. None of my students is afraid of him."

Her smile faded. "No, that's not true. *Riley* was still a little bit ... I knew he'd get over it, though. School only started a week ago. It was his job this morning to feed live grasshoppers to Bambi. He did it, but he didn't want to watch ... you know, he didn't want to see the spider kill the grasshopper, so I let him feed the fish." She looked stricken. "You don't suppose that's why, that he ran away—"

"We don't know that he ran away. Please continue."

"That's one reason I let him help me. He seemed to still be a little upset over feeding Bambi this morning, so I picked him as one of four boys to help me load up the paperbacks into my car at the beginning of second recess." She gestured toward her neck brace. "Carrying things is awkward."

Melody explained that the children had been bringing in their parents' old paperback books as a class project. The bargain bookstore paid a quarter apiece for them and last year's class had raised more than thirty dollars to donate to the county animal shelter. She was supposed to deliver the books today to the bookstore, which was only two blocks from the school, so she and the children carried the boxes from her room out to her car parked in front of the building and put them into the trunk.

"Were the children ever alone when—?"

"*Never.* I never left them alone. *Not for a second.* With the boys' help, it only took one trip, maybe five minutes. Then I told Riley and the other three — Danny, Corey and Damien — they could go on out to the playground to play. I *watched them* go into the building and down the hall toward the play-ground door. The last time I saw Riley, he was going into the boy's restroom and the other boys were going outside. Then I left, drove to the bookstore and unloaded the books. I was seated at my desk before the bell rang for the end of recess. But Riley never came back into the room. I asked one of the boys to go see if he was still in the restroom. Maybe he had gotten sick and stayed in there. But he wasn't."

"There are four teachers on the playground at all times during recess," Bergstrom said, with an edge of defensiveness beginning to creep into his voice. As soon as the shock of the boy's disappearance abated a little, everyone would naturally slip into CYA mode. It would eventually occur to the whole staff, from the custodian to the librarian, that they might somehow be held responsible for the boy's disappearance.

"I will want to talk to those four teachers," Brice said.

"Certainly, but I already talked to them. Gwen Ragland —
her classroom is the first one on the right when you come in
the building — distinctly remembers seeing Riley playing, said
he was on the slide with some other boys. But the other three
can't specifically recall seeing him at second recess, though two
of them remember seeing him outside during first recess."

"I should have walked them all the way out to the playground." Melody's voice quavered like a grieving child. "But
my car was in the bus lane *right in front of the building*. And I *saw*
them go down the hall."

There were windows in the front doors of the building and
floor-to-ceiling glass panels on both sides of the doors. Anyone
in the hallway could have seen her car. The view from the
window in the principal's office on the left side of the front
doors was partially blocked by shrubbery, but nothing
obscured the view from a whole room full of windows in the
classroom on the right side of the doors.

"What did you do after the boys went inside the building?"

"I delivered the books to Twice Told Tales."

"Immediately?"

"Yes." She paused. "Well, no. I remembered the grocery
sack of books — Megan Magee brought it in this morning
and left it sitting beside the door in my room. So I went back
inside and got it, took maybe two minutes, then drove to the
store, dropped off the books, was back here before the end of
recess. But Riley, I saw him walk down the hallway … and I
never saw him again."

A bell outside rang loud and long.

"That's the first bell, 3:10. The busses start running at
3:15," Bergman said.

"Not today, they don't," Brice said. "The last children who
saw Riley, the three little boys, I'd like to see them now, one at
a time."

Chapter Four

WHILE BRICE SAT ALONE in the principal's office, waiting for the first little boy, he stared down at the photo of Riley that Fletch had texted to all the officers. It was a school picture and he was wearing a plaid shirt with the sleeves rolled up to his elbows and a white t-shirt underneath. He had curly red hair, not carroty red, but not a deep wine color either. An attractive red. His skin was so pale it was almost translucent, with red freckles, little ones, like he'd been dusted with chili powder, and red eyebrows that almost vanished into his face. His eyes were a clear blue, the same color blue as the blue in his plaid shirt, and Brice wondered if his mother had done that on purpose, matched the blue in his shirt to his eyes for his school picture. He was not smiling but not frowning either. If Brice had to guess, he would suspect that the solemn look on the boy's face was his face in repose, his natural look. He appeared to be a serious child, perhaps sensitive, as evidenced by his reluctance to watch the tarantula spider eat the grasshopper he'd put into the terrarium.

Brice shuddered. A tarantula. Fragile little Melody McCallum owning a pet spider was glaringly out of character. It was noble, he supposed, to use a spider to teach tolerance, but Brice suspected that more than a few of those children were at least unsettled by Bambi. Spiders were inherently scary creatures. The author Stephen King once said that the true embodiment of evil was a spider. Brice couldn't have agreed more.

Mr. Bergman escorted a boy into his office and introduced him to Brice as Corey Warren. The boy had brown hair slicked up with "product" into a faux hawk, and there were strips of no hair on both sides of his head like racing stripes. He hadn't yet grown into the incisors that had so recently replaced the blank space in front and his mouth seemed too full of teeth to talk.

Brice was glad he'd been called to the school out of uniform. He suspected the sheriff's uniform would have been intimidating, and his size alone was intimidating enough. He was seated when the child came into the room, and didn't rise. Six feet, five inches was a long way up for a kid to have to look to make eye contact.

Corey sat in the chair beside Brice and he noticed that the boy's feet only barely touched the floor.

"You know what's happening, right? That Riley is missing."

"Uh huh, Miss McCallum said so but we already knew because she got real upset when she couldn't find him after recess. Where'd he go?"

"I was hoping you might know."

"Me and Riley ain't friends. We play together sometimes, but he's not my BFF or anything like that."

Brice smiled. BFF. The boy was clearly proud of owning that word and grateful for the opportunity to use it.

"When was the last time you saw him today?"

"We were helping Miss McCallum load boxes of paperbacks into her car and then she sent us back out to the playground for the rest of recess. Riley stopped to go to the bathroom and I didn't see him after that."

"Do you think Riley would have run away?"

"Naaa, not Riley. He's not the type."

"What type is he?"

"The type that wouldn't run away."

Damien House was the next child, a black boy with a fro half again as big as his head. He was wearing a Pittsburgh Steelers t-shirt.

"You a Steelers fan?"

"My dad says he bleeds black and gold."

"You play?"

"No, you have to be eight. My dad played in college, though. He was a blocker, and when he lined up, he'd chant, 'I am da house and da house don't move.'"

Brice smiled.

"You know Riley Campbell is missing. When did you see him last?"

"On the playground at recess."

"After you and the other boys helped Miss McCallum haul the books to the car?"

"Uh huh. When we were finished, Me and Danny and Corey went back outside for the rest of recess."

"Corey said Riley stopped to use the restroom and the rest of you went on outside."

"Yeah, I guess. But I saw Riley later on the slide."

"So you know Riley came out of the building to the playground after you helped Ms. McCallum?"

"I saw him on the slide." The boy paused. "I think."

"I need you to think real hard. Did you see him or didn't you?"

"I saw him on the slide, at the top, and he yelled something, you know just hollered out like 'woo-hoo,' like that, before he went down. I remember. But maybe it was at first recess."

Danny Keeling had a mop of blond hair and dimples deep enough to eat pudding out of.

It was clear he did not want to talk to Brice. He fidgeted in the chair and refused to make eye contact, answered questions with one- and two-word replies.

"Did you see Riley out on the playground after you boys loaded the boxes into the trunk of your teacher's car?"

"I don't know."

"Think about it — was he on the swings or the slide?"

"Maybe."

"Are you … afraid of something, Danny?"

The boy looked stricken.

"No!" But every syllable of his body language was screaming, "Yes!"

"Because you're not in any trouble. I just need help finding Riley. If you were lost, you'd want your friends to help the police find you, wouldn't you?"

"I won't get lost. I don't want to get in trouble."

"What do you mean?"

The boy squirmed and said nothing.

"In trouble with your teacher?"

He shook his head, still not looking at Brice.

"With your parents?"

"I'm not allowed to go out of the yard by myself or I'll get in trouble."

Brice decided not to pursue the subject, but he made a mental note to do a little nosing around. This child was more scared than he ought to be of "getting in trouble."

"Did you see Riley go into the bathroom as you boys were leaving the building?"

He nodded his head.

"Did you see him come out?"

He shook his head.

"Do you know anything about Riley that might help me find him?"

He said nothing, then, "He doesn't like Bambi. He's afraid of Bambi."

"So am I," Brice said, and the kid's head snapped up and he looked Brice in the eye for the first time. "Did having to feed that grasshopper to Bambi this morning bother Riley?"

"I guess. I know he asked to be moved out of the row of desks by the window so he wouldn't have to be so close to Bambi."

"Do you know any reason why Riley might run away?"

"I don't think he ran away. I think somebody took him."

Brice froze, then forced himself to ask the next question casually.

"What makes you think so?"

"There are lots of bad people in the world."

"Do you know who took him?"

He shook his head. "But if you're not careful, bad people will take you away and make you do terrible things. I don't think Riley was very careful."

None of Brice's questions managed to pry any more information from Danny.

After Brice interviewed the children, he talked to the four teachers who'd had playground duty — Wanda Phelps and Roger Dunlap, third grade; Angela Reed, second grade, and first-grade teacher, Gwen Ragland. None of them remembered seeing Riley on the playground during second recess. Mrs. Ragland had told the principal she did, but when the sheriff questioned her, she admitted that perhaps that had been at first recess, not second. All the teachers stressed that with more than a hundred children running around, chasing each other, squealing, they could have missed a quiet boy like Riley.

When the last teacher left the principal's office, Brice sat for a moment, looking over his notes for a pattern. He saw nothing. He looked at his watch — 4:15. Children would already be at least an hour late getting home from school today, and even though he'd had Fletch make announcements on the local radio station, and post notices on the school's website, the sheriff's department's website and on both their Facebook pages, he knew parents' anxiety was growing by the minute.

He stepped out into the empty hallway, walked down it and out the front door of the school, and saw exactly what he expected to see. News had spread of the child's disappearance and other parents had panicked and come rushing to the school. He was sure that despite the best efforts of his deputies and the state police, traffic was gridlocked for blocks leading away from the school. Concerned parents had likely abandoned their cars in the streets when they weren't allowed to get close to the building and now an anxious crowd of several hundred people stood uneasily outside the yellow-and-black police line perimeter.

Buses couldn't move until the traffic mess was cleared.

He went to his cruiser and pulled a megaphone out of his trunk. Then he went out toward where the crowd was gathered outside the police tape and climbed up into the back of a pickup truck parked there. He knew he made an imposing figure standing there like that, even out of uniform. And that was his point.

"I completely understand that all of you are concerned about the welfare of your children," he said into the megaphone, which delivered his words after a set-your-teeth-on-edge screech of feedback. "They are all perfectly safe. One little boy, a first-grader named Riley Campbell, is missing and we are doing everything we can to locate him. But every other child in this building is sitting perfectly safe at their desks in their classrooms."

"We heard there were several children missing."

"The radio said it was a little girl, not a little boy."

"Are you looking for a van? My neighbor said she saw a woman dragging a little boy toward a van in front of the furniture store this morning. The boy was crying."

Other questions fired at him out of the crowd but he ignored them and held up his hand for quiet.

"I need you to listen to me and believe what I'm telling you. I don't know or care what you *heard*. Reality is that one little boy is missing and we're hoping to locate him very soon, but ..."

He let that word hang out there in the air, then repeated it.

"But ... *your* children — all of them *safe* in their classrooms right now — are going to be stuck in those classrooms in that building unless you go home! We've delayed the buses for more than hour already, and you've blocked the streets so they can't run now. If you want your children to be delivered to your door safely, go home!"

A few people peeled out of the crowd and started walking away. The vast majority remained resolutely where they were. Their children were in that building, after all, their *babies*. They were *staying*.

"I have instructed my officers to begin towing away every car that is parked illegally in the street — *or legally at the curb* — on any side street leading to this school." That was a bluff, of course. He had nothing like the manpower it would take to tow away all the cars blocking the streets. And there were only a handful of tow trucks in the whole county. But these people weren't thinking logically right now. If they had been, they wouldn't have rushed here in the first place and remained here after he instructed them to leave.

"Unless you want to walk home, and then get a ride to the impound yard tomorrow so you can wait in line with all these other people to pay the two-hundred-dollar towing fee and the fifty-dollar overnight storage charge, you need to leave. Now."

That got them moving. Nothing like threatening to tow someone's car to put the fear of God into them.

He got out of the back of the pickup truck and looked at his watch. The last time the child had been seen was at 1:20.

It was 4:25. He'd been missing for more than three hours. He motioned Deputy Fletcher to him.

"Issue an Amber Alert for Riley Campbell," he said.

Fletcher paused for a beat, looking at him, then nodded.

In less than a minute, every police department in the state and in neighboring Ohio, Kentucky, Pennsylvania, Maryland and Virginia would receive Riley's picture and description, an alarm would sound on hundreds of thousands of cell phones and his face would start popping up on electronic interstate signs all over the five states.

Amber Alerts were wonderful tools. But you couldn't overuse them or the public would start to ignore them. Law enforcement officers used their own discretion about the circumstances under which they would proclaim a child missing on that network. You didn't do that if there was any hope that a child had just wandered off.

Issuing that alert gave voice and substance to the conclusion Brice had reached after talking to the witnesses.

Riley Campbell had not merely wandered away from the playground three hours ago.

Somehow, the boy had been taken off the school property. Kidnapped.

Brice made the next call himself, keyed in the number for the Pittsburgh field office of the Federal Bureau of Investigation.

Chapter Five

AFTER THE LAST of the school buses pulled out of the pickup lane in front of the school, Brice took a few moments in the mostly empty building to walk the route the little boys had taken from the front door, down the hallway toward the bathroom, then out to the playground. He didn't take big steps, studied sightlines — who could have had eyes on them. The room on the right of the front door with the only unobstructed view of the front of the building was Gwen Ragland's room and she had been on playground duty. The room would have been empty. Anyone in the hallway could have seen—

"Sheriff McGreggor." The voice was soft but it carried. He turned to see Melody McCallum standing in the doorway of her classroom.

"Brice, remember."

"I don't want to take any more of your time, but ..." She stepped out into the hallway and held out her hand. In it was a plastic baggie with a photograph inside, a snapshot of Riley. "I just wanted you to have this. I take pictures of all the children for the bulletin board." He could see a small hole in the top of the photograph where a stick-pin had been removed. "I know you already have his school picture. But it's so ... serious. He's smiling that sweet little crooked smile of his here." She pressed the baggie into his hand. "*This* … is the little boy you're looking for."

She whirled around quickly, sucking back tears, hurried into her classroom and shut the door behind her. He could hear her inside crying as he slipped the picture into his shirt pocket.

Shortly before five o'clock, the dispatcher notified Brice that the FBI had arrived at the sheriff's department — Pittsburgh to Shadow Rock in under an hour. They'd made good time. He was out with other officers, canvassing the neighborhoods surrounding the school, going door to door, showing pictures of Riley and asking if anyone had seen the boy, and questioning them about any vehicles they might have seen today that they didn't normally see in the neighborhood, any strangers hanging around, anything at all out of the ordinary. The problem was that there were precious few people at home in those neighborhoods to see anything. Stay-at-home moms had not totally gone the way of the homing pigeon and the white rhino, but sightings of them were more and more rare. In this working class neighborhood, most of the houses held families in which both parents worked. If there was a father at all. In many of them — not most, it would have been most in the Regis Hills area of town but this neighborhood wasn't that poor — there was only one parent and she had been away at work all day.

The sheriff's department took up much of the first floor of the Kavanaugh County Courthouse — an ostentatious white stone building constructed long enough ago that the Historical Society Nazis wouldn't allow the county clerk's office on the second floor to install a window air conditioner.

He had left instructions that the department's conference room be turned over to the agents for their use. The sheriff's department had been the command center in July for the manhunt for Derrick Osbourne, the man who shot Deputy

Fletcher and blew up the dam on the sludge impoundment lake at the top of Turkey Neck Hollow. Brice had coordinated that operation out of his office. The FBI would need more room than that.

The sheriff made sure all his men got the message that the FBI agents were to be extended every courtesy and given *full cooperation*. As a general rule of thumb, outside agencies — particularly federal ones — were not particularly welcome additions to a local investigation. It was a crap shoot. He'd worked with Drug Enforcement Agency agents who acted like they should be provided gold-plated urinals, and conducted their affairs to the absolute exclusion of his department. "We got this," one of the smug senior agents had informed him condescendingly, then proceeded to screw up not only the investigation but the arrest, so the meth dealers they caught walked on technicalities.

He had only worked with one other FBI agent in his nine years in law enforcement and it wasn't a total catastrophe, but neither had it been a particularly enjoyable or mutually beneficial relationship either. He was girding his loins in anticipation of meeting this contingent of investigators.

The dispatcher informed him that six agents were setting up shop, installing computers and commandeering phone lines and internet access in the conference room, and that the senior agent wanted to meet him.

When Brice got to the station, he changed from street clothes into his uniform, then stepped into the office marked Sheriff Brice McGreggor in gold lettering on the door to find a man seated in his desk chair rather than on the sofa or in either of the other two chairs provided for visitors to his office. Goody.

He was Asian, Japanese. He looked up and immediately rose to his feet. He was probably five-foot-six or seven, roughly a foot shorter than Brice.

The agent was obviously making the same comparison.

"Your grandfather would have fit right in on the deck of the battleship Missouri in Tokyo Bay," he said.

Brice had heard the story — that Admiral Nimitz had commandeered the biggest sailors in the fleet to be present when the Japanese contingent came aboard to sign the peace treaty ending World War II. The agent said it pleasantly, and Brice understood that most Asian humor was delivered deadpan. Still, he didn't know the man. The remark was either a good-natured reference to his size or the words of a man suffering a raging case of Little Man Syndrome.

"I'm Senior Special Agent Haruto Nakamura." He extended his hand. "I will be in charge of the investigation."

"Brice McGreggor, Kavanaugh County Sheriff." Brice shook the man's hand. Firm handshake, though formal — once up, once down — and he looked Brice in the eye.

Nakamura sat back down in Brice's chair then. He didn't apologize for commandeering Brice's office, just said he needed fast computer access and the command center wasn't completely operational yet.

"I'm almost finished here, then we need to talk. Five minutes."

He returned his attention to the screen and only shook his head when Brice offered to bring him coffee or a soft drink.

Brice left to get himself a cup of coffee. He stepped into the once conference room that was being transformed into a — he hated the words "command center" but that's what it was. Three coat-and-tie-clad male agents and two female agents in dark pantsuits were working feverishly with equipment they'd obviously brought with them in the black van parked out front. Its only identifying marks were the federal plates, no FBI insignia on the side. He introduced himself and they reciprocated, with brief perfunctory handshakes or nods, clearly totally focused on the task at hand.

Agent Tom Hardesty, a big black man whose shoulders strained at his suit coat, hauled in a piece of electronic equipment Brice couldn't identify and set it on the former conference table in front of Agent Ashok Arya, an Indian man wearing round, rimless, Gandhi glasses. Agents Nikki Trimboli, who wore her brown hair in a spiky boy cut and Emma Gomez, whose hair was pulled back in a bun so tight it might have pulled her eyebrows up, were setting up keyboards and monitors.

When Brice asked if they needed anything, a skinny bald man who'd introduced himself as "Elijah Gascoyne, but Eli will do," said, "Tommy could use a whiteboard." His thick Pittsburgh accent turned Tommy into *Twommy*.

Brice went into the dispatcher's office and instructed a deputy to get the whiteboard and stand that was set up in the city council's chambers on the top floor of the courthouse, and anything else the agents might need, then asked to hear the recordings of two 911 calls that had come in after the news hit that the boy was missing. He'd been told their content; one was a hysterical mother who was certain her child in nursery school was in danger and would the police please send a unit to pick him up and bring him home.

The other was from a well-meaning citizen who had seen someone dragging a crying child toward a car in the parking lot in front of Hollingsworth Furniture Store — likely the same woman seen by the neighbor of the man in the crowd outside the school that afternoon. Deputies had already checked it out. The boy was being dragged by his mother because he'd thrown a tantrum in the store and refused to leave. He was five years old and black, and the incident had taken place before Riley had gone missing.

"Sheriff McGreggor." Brice looked up and saw the senior agent in the doorway. "May I have a moment of your time, please."

Though Brice was sure this man was several generations removed from immigrant ancestors, the culturally polite flavor was still there.

They went into Brice's office and the agent sat this time in the visitor's chair facing Brice's desk. Brice decided to forego his office chair, ensconced almost throne-like behind the big cherry desk, and sat down instead in the chair beside Agent Nakamura.

"Let's get the elephant out of the room first thing, Sheriff McGreggor. I am here to find that little boy — and find him alive." He looked at his watch, likely doing the math. Riley had last been seen at 1:20. He'd been missing now for more than four hours. "That is my single-minded pursuit and I have no tolerance for petty jurisdictional rivalries that get in the way. This isn't my first rodeo. I know how local authorities feel about the FBI. I welcome your input and your help. You know things about this place and these people and I don't have time to learn. Just make no mistake about it. This is *my* investigation and *I will run it.* If you get in my way, I will freeze you out and you'll be directing traffic outside my crime scene. Are we clear?"

"I understand who crows in this chicken house and who lays eggs, Agent Nakamura."

The agent smiled a small smile.

"I can help you find Riley Campbell, and I don't give a Fig Newton who gets the credit when we do. I don't want to butt heads."

"Good." A one-beat pause. "I'd need a ladder."

Brice's smile was bigger.

The agent stood.

"I'd like you to brief me and my team, tell us what measures you've taken, what you have discovered."

The two adjourned to the conference room/command center and while deputies moved in a portable white board, affixed a borrowed cork board to the wall and the agents continued to install and check equipment, Brice filled them in on the case, what had happened and everything that his department had done from the moment the school notified them that a child was missing.

He described cordoning off the building, using tracking dogs, quadruple searches, and containing the restroom for an FBI forensics team as the last place the child was seen. He'd instructed the school staff — teachers, administrators, janitorial staff and lunchroom staff — to remain on the premises, available for questioning by the FBI.

"The biggest horsefly in our buttermilk is the festival that's doing setup." He described the Cottonwood Festival and explained that its presence had turned a firehose of unvetted people loose on the property next to the school.

"There were approximately fifty people there when we arrived and sealed the area. But the boy was last seen almost an hour before we were summoned and anybody and his Uncle Hurl could have left the area and been across the river into Ohio before we got there. My officers detained everybody and took down ID information before they were allowed to leave the property."

"And those people were …?" Hardesty asked.

"The carpenters and other construction people assembling the bandstands and the portable stage for the festival, the vendors setting up booths—"

"What kind of booths?" Gascoyne wanted to know.

"Local craftspeople sell their wares at the festival, anybody from Sue-Sue Bentley, who looms her own wool, dyes it and makes hats and scarves to Ancil Brunswick, who carves miniature train sets. Potters, jewelry makers, artists, homemakers' circles who make quilts, sculptor wannabes who make duck lawn art. The Kavanaugh County Craftsman's Association sells small furniture items, end tables and Adirondack chairs." Like the one that'd saved the life of Macy Cosgrove six weeks ago, but not because she grabbed it in the water while she was drowning. "Those people are predominantly local, but there were a few Away-From-Heres."

"Away-From-Heres — an interesting way to put it," Naka-mura mused, unsmiling.

"That used to include anybody who couldn't trace their ancestry back at least three and preferably four generations. But in the past twenty years or so the population has exploded. Shadow Rock has become a tour-bus destination. Whispering Mountain Lake is a watersports mecca. The Carnegie-and-Friends historic homes draw tourists in droves. And since the opening of the Nautilus Casino and adjacent hotels on the other side of the lake, this place isn't a small town anymore where you'd necessarily notice an unfamiliar face."

"Anybody else besides craftspeople?" asked Emma Gomez.

"Food vendors — those might or might not be local people. Some of them are food trucks from Charleston, drove down here to make some extra money during setup and at the festival this weekend."

"When does it start?" Nakamura asked.

"It doesn't officially open until Friday noon. All the schools in town are scheduled to let out early. There'll be live enter-tainment Friday night, a Bluegrass band from Kentucky — carpenters are building a small stage — contests and kids' games and a kiddie parade down Whitlow Street on Saturday. A disc-jockey dance on Saturday night. The Knights of Columbus have a license to sell beer, so it'll get rowdy. Festi-val's not officially open today, but gawkers, lookie-loos and bargain hunters always show up early."

Nakamura hung his head and shook it. "A festival."

"*And* pony rides, a petting zoo and a small carnival." Nakamura actually winced. "The basic el-cheapo carnival with about half a dozen rickety rides, and games. This one seems to be legitimate, if not thriving. Wasuski Brothers Carnival. They were here for the Fourth of July and did pretty well so they came back for the festival. My men patrol the carnival as well as the festival open to close, repeatedly check the games, and we've never caught anybody with weighted teddy bears ... yet."

"And all those people are still here, in town?" Gascoyne asked.

"I got the contact information for anybody with a pulse who was on the school property today, and I told those who were transient to settle down and get comfortable, they weren't going anywhere for a few days."

Brice sat back down on the edge of a desk and spread his hands.

"But as you can see, that is a mountain of information to sift through, names to check for criminal records, basic background information on everybody. I don't have the manpower for that."

"Our job, Sheriff McGreggor," Agent Arya said, pushing his Gandhi glasses up on his nose. "If you'll get your deputies to bring us lists of names and addresses, we'll start with the NCIC computer databank, see if anybody pops, start running background checks."

When Brice's report was complete, Nakamura stood and took over. He assigned tasks to the various agents, then turned to Brice.

"I'd like you to accompany me to the school, please. I want to talk to the teacher, the principal and the last children who saw Riley." He had sent agents Gascoyne and Trimboli to the Campbells' house to talk to the boy's parents. "Then I want to meet the Campbells."

They continued to talk on the way to Brice's cruiser.

"Have you spoken to the boy's parents? Do you know them personally?"

"No and no. They came barreling down to the school — along with the parents of at least half the children in the building — and were so upset they were no help at all. I told them the FBI would want to spend some time with them."

He got in behind the wheel of the cruiser and Nakamura got in on the passenger side.

"I don't know them personally. They've been married twelve years. Riley is the oldest of their two children."

"Nasty divorce in either one's past? Custody fight?"

Brice pulled away from the curb and flipped on his bar lights but used no siren.

"Divorce, yes, but appears garden-variety nasty. Mrs. Campbell — Jeanette — was married before, and we need to look closer. Her ex-husband lives in Maryland. I don't know anything about the current Mr. Campbell, name's Norman. He's a broker for a local firm, Waterhouse Securities, and Jeanette is a legal secretary in Bill Stanley's office — McNutt & Stanley. My records show no reports of domestic violence at the Campbells' address and from what my deputies have been able to gather from the neighbors, they're good people."

Nakamura looked at Brice appraisingly but said nothing. Clearly, the man was keeping score.

Brice looked at his watch. Riley Campbell had been missing for—

"Five hours," Nakamura said, without looking at his own watch, "and fifteen minutes."

Chapter Six

BAILEY FIGURED Brice wouldn't even bother to go to bed that night, but *she* at least tried. She climbed in between the cold sheets and when the image of the school picture of a little freckle-faced boy filled her mind, as she knew it would, she replaced it with the only image powerful enough to banish it. Bethany.

In the beginning, when she'd first been exiled from everything and everybody she knew and loved, Bailey would sometimes pretend it wasn't so. She'd imagine all was right with the world, conjure up the sound of Aaron's joyous laughter and the baby-giggle of her little girl, a sound so unutterably precious that it stole Bailey's breath. She never did that anymore, though. Bailey had quickly learned that the illusory happiness of make-believe was not worth the agony when the delicate fantasy she'd so carefully crafted suddenly burst with a little sparkle like a soap bubble. The blow of reality afterward was staggering.

So no, she didn't pretend that Bethany was asleep in her bed just down the hall. But to banish the face of the freckle-faced little boy who'd vanished yesterday afternoon off a school playground, she *did* allow herself to tiptoe through a minefield of real memories.

THE WHOLE FRONT of Aaron's shirt is covered in a fine dusting of fragrant baby powder, but his smile is so bright she hasn't the heart to tell him he'd put the diaper on backwards.

Bethany is looking in wonder at sand draining through her fingers as Aaron empties another fifty-pound sack of it into the other end of the sandbox he's building for her.

She's splashing happily at the bubbles popping to the surface from the dislodged patch in her blow-up baby pool while Aaron tries to keep it inflated with a bicycle pump.

The smell of baby-shampooed hair.

The dimple in Aaron's chin.

Tiny high-top sneakers.

Little handprint smudges on the chrome front of the refrigerator.

Lazy Saturday mornings in bed.

THE TROUBLE with allowing yourself to remember was that other images lurked in the darkened shadows behind memories, prowled there. And if you weren't vigilant, they'd jump out and bite you.

A RAIN-DRENCHED STREET.

The stench of a homeless woman's wet clothes.

A firecracker pop.

A Rockport filling with rainwater.

A dumpster.

Rats in the mud.

. . .

IMAGES from the nightmare five minutes that'd destroyed her life took her mind hostage then, rumbled through it and destroyed every good thing in savage brutality.

A boy in one of the foster homes where she'd been parked for a time by Child Protective Services when she was a kid had been enormously proud of his "washboard abs" and used to invite the other kids to punch him in the belly. All they got for their trouble were sore hands until the day the new kid sucker-punched him and he doubled over and couldn't breathe.

This was that. Prepared, Bailey had finally grown strong enough to withstand the razor-edged assault of the *uglies*. But sitting up in bed in the midnight dark, stroking Sparky's stuffed-animal-soft fur, she'd been sucker-punched.

Sparky whimpered and she realized she was squeezing him too tight. That broke the spell, and she shook horror out of her head, got up and padded barefoot into the kitchen for a glass of orange juice. And, of course, a dog biscuit for the too-cute-for-words pup.

She didn't bother to go back to bed, just curled up on the sofa with an Amish quilt and a soft dog and surrendered. She didn't want to think about the missing ... *kidnapped* boy, but there was no help for it now.

Riley Campbell. His face had been all over the news.

In the self-absorption of the past two-and-a-half years of personal misery, Bailey had believed there was no worse fate a mother could endure than being separated from her child. She'd been wrong. Somewhere in Shadow Rock, Riley Campbell's mother could testify to that error.

Bailey snuggled Sparky closer and thought about Macy Cosgrove, the gap-toothed little girl whose portrait Bailey had painted, been *compelled* to paint — because of Oscar, the bullet she'd put in her own head. Or maybe it had nothing to do with Oscar at all. Whatever the reason, Bailey had awakened in the hospital after her attempted suicide with a strange "gift." Just like T.J.'s mother, who'd also suffered a head injury in the same Watford House kitchen almost sixty years ago, Bailey could paint "what hadn't happened yet."

Six weeks ago, she had painted a portrait of Macy Cosgrove — *dead*. Drowned. *And Bailey had drowned with the child as she painted the picture* — a horror so awful Bailey had sworn she would never, *ever* paint another portrait like that again.

But Macy Cosgrove was home safe in her own bed right now — and maybe that was because of Bailey's painting.

Riley Campbell was not home. And he was not safe.

Time drained away. Bailey stared out the big window on the front of the house at black sky with impossibly bright stars, watched the color begin to dissolve into deep blue with fading twinkles and soft pink/gold edging — what passed for sunrise in a valley where the sun didn't actually crest the mountain to the east until mid-morning. She faced it then, acknowledged the conclusion she'd been trying all night *not* to reach. Maybe her "gift" could help the police find the missing little boy.

Could she do that — again? She'd sworn she couldn't. *Wouldn't.* Sucked into another reality that was unutterably awful. Just that part was a life experience nobody'd want to repeat. But that wasn't the worst part. T.J.'s mother'd painted portraits of encounters with the black underbelly of human existence — death and dismemberment in its ugliest forms. A man whose hand was chopped off. A little girl who was stran-gled. A family burned to death in a fire.

And his mother had lived those experiences as she painted. *Lived them.* Felt the terror, the panic, the desperation, the pain of all those people. *Died* with them, as Bailey had died with Macy Cosgrove.

Was Bailey willing to do that *on purpose* — to slide into someone else's head and … yeah, and what? What had happened to Riley Campbell? If Bailey painted his portrait, she'd find out! If he'd been … go on, brutal honesty here — if he'd been murdered, Bailey would be murdered right along with him.

Murdered.

But what if he hadn't been killed — *yet?* What if he was still alive? What if Bailey could see something out his eyes that would help Brice find him *before* ... find him and *save* him?

That really was the only thing she should consider here. The ultimate bottom line: could Bailey save Riley Campbell's life? She had no idea, didn't even know if she could simply decide to paint a "future" portrait and make it happen. She didn't know—

Oh, stop it!

It didn't matter what she did or didn't know, whether she could or couldn't do it. If there was any possibility, even the slightest hope that she could save a little boy's life, Bailey had to try. Of course, she did.

She was standing in the front yard waiting for Sparky to make a deposit when Brice pulled into her driveway eighteen hours after Riley Campbell vanished off a school playground. He got out of his cruiser and came to stand beside her. Clearly, her guess had been correct. He probably hadn't even gone to bed.

"T.J. out of town?" he asked, nodding to Sparky.

"No, just a doggie playday." About once a week now, she invited the mini golden doodle with the perpetual smile to spend the night at her house because she so enjoyed his company. And no, she did *not* intend to get a dog of her own. That was ... that felt too much like having a child, and the emotional fallout from entertaining such a thought was too painful to endure. "I took him with me for a run this morning, and it raised an interesting question."

Sparky was batting at the fuzzy top of a dandelion and when it exploded into thousands of wispy flying seeds, he snapped at them, then tried to catch them as the wind carried them away, barking furiously. "Those are meanies." She indicated the dandelion seeds. "It's his job to protect me from meanies and he takes his work very seriously."

"The interesting question?" Brice prompted.

"Oh, that. It occurred to me to wonder ... I ran six miles, on two legs. Sparky was right beside me, on four legs. So does that mean he went twice as far as I did, since he has twice as many legs? Or did he go half as far as I did?"

Brice merely looked confused, clearly not completely certain whether or not she was serious. And actually, she wasn't sure either.

"Did you even go to bed last night?" he asked.

She started to run a bluff but was too tired to bother.

"That's the pot calling the kettle black, don't you think?"

"*It's my job*." There was a one-beat pause. "I know why you texted me, asked me to stop by for coffee. And the answer's no."

"You're not allowed to say no until I ask the question."

Turning back toward the house, Bailey patted her leg to summon Sparky, saving from certain death the hump-back beetle he was pawing at in the grass, and tossed words over her shoulder. "And no offense, *Sheriff* McGreggor, but I don't need your permission." She stopped at the door and turned to face him. "The decision isn't yours to make; it's mine."

She opened the screen and stepped back with a sweeping come-in gesture. "And stop looking so fidgety. I know you're in a hurry. I'll put your coffee in a to-go mug."

He stood looking at her. "Five minutes, then." He took the stupid-looking, flat-brimmed sheriff's hat off as he stepped inside.

She'd set out a to-go mug on the counter beside the coffee pot that filled the room with wake-you-up aroma. He didn't sit at the table. A man the size of Brice McGreggor standing tall could be intimidating. She knew he used that to his advantage when he needed to. Well, it wouldn't work today.

Pouring his coffee with her back to him, she opened her mouth to recite the speech she'd constructed in her head as she'd stared into the darkness. Then gave it up and just blurted it out.

"I want to paint a portrait of that little boy, Riley Campbell." She turned and extended the cup of coffee. "I might paint some detail that would help you find him."

"No."

She couldn't help a surprised look.

"After the portrait of Macy Cosgrove, you said you didn't ever want to paint another picture like that ever again."

"I don't *want* to paint a picture of Riley Campbell!" She hadn't meant it to come out with such revulsion. But there it was. "I *have* to."

"*Have to?*"

Bailey set the cup of coffee down on the countertop and tried to think how to explain.

"Sometimes, I wake up in the middle of the night and think — this can't be real. I've even gone to look at the portrait T.J.'s mother painted of me and tried to come up with some other explanation for its existence than ..."

Than the supernatural. Than ... what? Magic?

"*Thirty years before I was born*, the woman painted a portrait of my face in perfection, down to the moles on my neck, and the mosquito bite on my forehead I got five minutes before T.J. showed up with the painting! And, oh, by the way, she knew I was going to ..." She hesitated. Bailey didn't like talking about that part, about trying to kill herself. "And I can't come up with an explanation, an answer to the central question — *how?*"

She stopped, turned and looked him in the eye.

"While I was wide awake all night, I finally gave up. Surrendered. Ran up the white flag. I don't know *how*, never will know. Or why *me?* But I've finally made my peace with that part, I know where I stand. I'm committed now, like I got hired, like I was the one millionth customer at the grand opening of a Walmart and the prize was a paranormal ability.

It's been given to me. *That's just the way it is!* And because it has, that somehow … obligates me to use it, to … oh, I don't know, do the right thing with it, I suppose."

She almost reached out and took his hands, but didn't.

"I just know that little boy's gone, Brice, and if there's a chance, even the most slender thread of hope that I could help find him, I have to take it."

Brice said nothing.

"Come on, it's just a shot in the dark, probably won't even work." His face was impassive. "Trying to paint one of *those* portraits instead of being compelled to … I don't imagine T.J.'s mother ever tried anything like that, so there's no reason to believe I could do it."

"You think you can, though, don't you?"

"I have no reason to believe …" Hadn't they agreed not to play games with each other? No, actually they hadn't, but Brice had claimed they had an "unspoken agreement" to that effect and that it was "the most binding kind." "Yeah, I think maybe … what's the harm in trying?"

"The harm?" Now, he held up *his* hand to silence *her.* "I know you don't want to go there, but Oscar——"

"My bullet, my brain, my problem," she snapped. Her suicide attempt two months ago had left a bullet Brice named "Oscar" lodged in her head that could kill her if she sneezed too hard. Or might sit snug as a bug in a rug if she went over Niagara Falls in a barrel.

She was about to launch into the speech about not letting a little piece of metal become the hall monitor of her life, when he said quietly, "It's just … I've seen what painting these pictures costs you."

"Macy Cosgrove is alive now because I paid that price. I painted her *drowned.* And we saved her before that happened. You sorry I did?"

He leaned back against the counter and took a long drink of coffee.

"As I have already made abundantly clear, I don't need your *permission,* but I'd like your *help.* My plan, such as it is, is to take the picture of Riley that's in this morning's newspaper, and see if that will ... will *whatever,* make whatever it is that happens happen. But if you have an actual photograph ..."

Brice gave it up.

"We're holding a handful of nothing, Bailey. Checked out parents, family members and friends, neighbors, the people who live near the school ... The FBI ran background checks on every human being who was on that property when the boy was taken. Nothing. There are no registered sex offenders in Shadow Rock. We've gotten the usual number of bozo calls on the Amber Alert. Otherwise, zip. And every hour that boy is missing makes it less likely that we'll find him ..."

"You think he's still alive?"

"*If* he is, the clock's ticking."

Bailey set down her own cup of coffee.

"Can you get me his picture?"

He said nothing, just looked at her. Then he let out a breath.

"I have his picture." He patted his shirt pocket where a plastic baggie stuck out over the top. "Off the bulletin board in his classroom."

"Then let's do this before I change my mind."

Bailey started out of the kitchen.

Brice stopped her, turned her around and put his hands on her shoulders.

"Are you—?"

"Sure? No."

She pulled free and headed down the hallway toward the studio.

A picture rested on the easel set in the middle of the room's perfect northern light. No work of great art with emotional power and psychological punch. Just a colored illustration.

"It's a gall bladder." She held up a medical textbook with a photograph of an actual gall bladder, moved the gall bladder painting off the easel and set it in front of the window to dry.

"How do you plan to replicate a process you don't understand?" Brice asked.

"I have no idea." She went to the far side of the room where several blank canvasses were leaned against the wall, selected a large one, maybe three feet square. "T.J.'s mother didn't know why it happened to her, or how the process worked — or if she did, she never told T.J. And she painted — what? — dozens of paintings. It's only happened to me once so I'm certainly no expert."

She set the canvas on the easel.

"All I could think was that when I touched the Adirondack chair, I was 'connected' to Macy Cosgrove — *after* I'd painted her portrait. So even if the painting's no help, maybe I'll connect ..."

Brice pulled the baggie out of his pocket and handed it to her.

"Riley's teacher gave this to me."

Bailey opened the baggie, took out the picture and stared at it. The photo in the newspaper had been Riley's school picture. This was a snapshot of a red-haired little boy with a crooked grin, holding up a finger painting with hands still covered in paint. She studied it. Then she set the picture aside and picked up a paintbrush, dabbed it in white paint. She cast a single sideways glance at Brice. His face was stern. Then she touched the brush to the canvas.

Chapter Seven

BAILEY'S STUDIO vanished in an eye blink the instant she touched the paintbrush to the canvas.

STATIC. Music. More static. Then a male voice warbles, "… takes my breath away, the way you look tonight …"

"Oh, wait — stop there, turn it up," a woman says. "I love Elton John."

The music plays louder, but the sound's muffled coming out the speaker of the baby monitor lying beside the little girl. But Mommy wouldn't allow her to ride in the camper hooked to the back of their car unless Daddy figured out a way for them to talk. He said muffled was better than nothing.

The little girl lies on her back on the camper seat and watches the world fly past the porthole in her castle. Castles in stories have names, but she can't call her castle "Burro," which is the name on the outside of the little camper. That's a dumb name for a castle.

The as-yet-unnamed castle — so tiny, like a dollhouse — is the best birthday present she ever got, only it's not really her present. It's just borrowed. But for now, she pretends it belongs to her.

She sucks her thumb happily, with her index finger hooked over her nose. Mommy and Daddy say she's way too old to suck her thumb and they don't like it, especially Daddy. He says if she keeps doing it she will mess up her front teeth and he'll have to pay for something called "braces." She likes riding back here in the camper so she can suck her thumb and they can't see.

The green of the passing trees smears the gray clouds. The sky is all one color. Not blue with white clouds that look like cotton candy, but solid gray. It looks like one of those smooth rocks she finds in the creek that runs behind her great aunt's house, where she's not supposed to play because she'll get dirty and her aunt doesn't like for her to get dirty. She plays there anyway, sneaks out of the yard, but she's careful, takes her shoes and socks off and leaves them on the rocks beside the creek. The rocks that are the same color as this sky.

She wonders what the sky is made of. Is it a rock, only a great big one, so big you can't see the edges of it? If it's a rock, what holds it up there? Can it fall down, maybe, if whatever is holding it — like tape or glue or something, lets go? Even Superglue lets go sometimes. Daddy glued the broken horn back on her unicorn with Superglue but it came off again anyway so maybe the rock sky could come off and drop on the world and crush it.

She takes her thumb out of her mouth, leans over and speaks into the baby monitor.

"Mommy, if the sky fell down would it smash us?"

Mommy isn't listening. She's singing along with the song on the radio.

"… in the moonlight you just shine like a beacon on the bay …"

"He just released that song," Daddy says. "How do you already know all the words?"

The little girl asks the question again and she hears her mother's muffled voice through the speaker.

"No, Katydid, the sky isn't going to fall down." Mommy and Daddy call her Katydid. Nobody else does. She likes the name because katydids are a kind of cricket and they make pretty sounds at night. Then she hears Mommy tell Daddy, "A child who thinks the sky could fall down is too young for this."

"Oh, come on. We've already—"

"You're telling yourself she's old enough but you know better."

"You agreed that—"

"I did not *agree. I just gave in. It's not safe for her to ride back there."*

Mommy *and Daddy had an argument about that when she begged Mommy to let her ride in the castle instead of in the car. Daddy won the argument, but Mommy stayed mad about it, even after Daddy rigged up the old baby monitor so they could talk.*

"Oh, that. I thought you were talking about the whole trip, and you did sign off *on that."*

"In principle, yes. But I didn't know you'd come home two days later with a camper."

"I didn't start this — you did. I wasn't the one who read that every family should go camping together even if all they've ever done is roast marshmallows in the back yard."

"That's what I mean. In principle, *I believe that, but—"*

"Oh, the trip will be a disaster, you said, but years later, everyone will talk about the time Daddy got tangled up in the tent cord and—"

"Family bonding will cancel out the chigger bites, right, but—"

"Borrowed camper equals no chigger bites. Well, not as many chigger bites, but definitely no tent to assemble. It lets us ease into the camping experience."

"I had in mind easing into the camping experience with sleeping bags in the back yard! And on her ..." She spells a word the little girl doesn't know. "B-I-R-T-H-D-A-Y."

"You packed the P-R-E-S-E-N-T, didn't you?"

"Of course, I did. Don't change the subject. A wilderness *area isn't a back yard. There could be, oh, I don't know—"*

"Bigfoot?"

"I'm serious, who knows ..."

"Afraid the forest meanies will mistake us for sardines, jammed into that little silver box?"

They keep talking but she isn't listening because she's trying to figure out how not to get crushed when the sky falls down. She's sure the glue's not going to hold it where it is forever. Should she crawl under her bed or—?

Her mother screams, "Look out!"

There is a terrible whump sound and the castle jerks violently sideways, throwing her off the cushioned seat onto the floor. Her mother keeps screaming and everything starts spinning. The camper tumbles like a carnival ride. Her mother's screaming is cut off and everything goes black.

BAILEY BLINKED, smelled Brice's aftershave and felt his hands on her shoulders. She became aware of her own body then, standing, leaning with her back against him. He wasn't holding her upright, just steadying her.

"Bailey?"

She relaxed her arms and heard a clatter, opened her eyes and saw a completed portrait on the easel in front of her. The clatter was the brushes dropping out of her hands onto the floor.

Two brushes.

It was all crazy, everything about it — unbelievable. But for some reason, out of all the things that couldn't possibly happen but did, the fact that she could paint a portrait *with both hands* was the most singularly amazing.

"Bailey, can you hear me?"

She didn't respond because the air to form words was stolen from her lungs by the image on the canvas, the paint wet and shiny.

It was fundamentally what she expected to see — a still life. The painting T.J.'s mother had painted of her with a bullet hole in her temple had featured a table with a bowl of fruit. In the one she'd painted of Macy Cosgrove, there was a vase of daisies instead of fruit. This one had a bouquet of roses. But in all three pictures, the still life was just suggested, inconsequential. The focus of the work of art was the oversized, out-of-proportion window behind the table and flowers or fruit. A face had taken up the whole window in the one T.J.'s mother had painted. *Her* face. Macy Cosgrove, lying on her back in black mud, her whole body slathered in goo, had been in the window she'd painted. Bailey expected, *hoped*, to see in the window of this painting Riley Campbell — *still alive.* That's not what she saw.

The image in the window was not a little boy with curly red hair and serious eyes. It was a little girl with long hair in braids, so pale blonde it was almost white. Only her body from the waist up was visible. There was a huge lump on her forehead, greenish purple, and red splotches on her left cheek, at the base of her right thumb and on both arms. Bailey thought of the mosquito bite shown on her own forehead in the portrait T.J.'s mother had painted, and these splotches looked like that. Bigger, though, brighter red. Stings, not mosquito bites. Her face and hands were dirty. What Bailey could see of the Buzz Lightyear t-shirt she was wearing was stained and wrinkled. She wore little-girl jewelry, bracelets — stretchy bands with colored plastic beads, a locket, and earrings in the shape of tiny yellow flowers.

The little girl's eyes were the color of a robin's egg. A striking pale blue. Staring. Sightless. *Dead* blue eyes.

"Who is this little girl?" Brice asked. "And why didn't you—?"

"I don't know and I don't know. But this little girl wasn't kidnapped ... or murdered. She died in a car accident."

Bailey turned out of his grasp, away from the still-wet portrait, didn't want to stand there gawking at it, hooked to it, staring. She headed toward the kitchen. "I need coffee."

Seated a few minutes later at the table that looked out over the immense back yard of the Watford House, where huge oak, walnut and maple trees painted dappled puddles of shade on the grass, Bailey idly stirred her coffee. Just habit. There was nothing in the coffee to stir. She had once in another life — *literally in another life* — taken her coffee so full of cream it was the color of khaki pants. Now, she took it black. And not because she wanted to be different, to remove herself from the small things that connected her to that life and that time. She genuinely preferred it black now, hadn't just made some decision to cultivate the taste. That was one of a host of small things that had just … changed after she woke up in the hospital with Oscar in her brain, the bullet that could drop her in her tracks if she banged her head on a door frame, or sneezed too violently. Maybe it was the presence of the foreign object. Obviously, brain cells had been destroyed by the bullet plowing through tissue and maybe that had changed her. Or maybe she was a totally different person now than she had been in her other life — changed by circumstance, by growing and having to become someone she'd never expected she'd be.

Not only did she drink black coffee, but she loathed onions when once she'd smothered her hamburgers with them. She'd once loved beets, couldn't stand guacamole. It was the other way around now. She had always run, but now it was no longer the natural activity of a former athlete. Now, she hated every step. Now, it was a self-discipline, a defiant "I hate this but I am *by golly* going to do it anyway!" She didn't care about fashion, though she'd been something of a — what was it her sister, María, had called her? — a "coat hanger" before. Now, t-shirts and jeans and running shoes were her normal attire, her black hair pulled back in a ponytail instead of coiffed in the latest style.

She really was an entirely different person.

"What happened to that little girl?" Brice asked.

"I'm not sure exactly, but I think maybe her father hit a deer. She was in a camper, apparently a very small one, pulled behind the car. Talked to her parents through a baby monitor. Then the car wrecked, rolled and she was killed. Maybe they all were, the whole family."

"So I give you the picture of a little boy who's been

kidnapped and you paint the picture of a girl killed in a wreck."

"I don't think this is a what-hasn't-happened-yet picture, either." Bailey spilled a drip of coffee on the table, plucked a paper napkin from the holder and blotted it up. "I think this happened a long time ago."

"T.J.'s mother never painted things in the past, did she? I never heard him say she did. Why do you think—"

"Because I don't feel any connection to this little girl — Katydid. That's what her mother called her. It's like I'm holding the phone but there's nobody on the other end of the line. Macy Cosgrove … as soon as I painted her, I *felt* her. She was there, alive. The little girl in this painting isn't."

"T.J.'s mother felt no connection to you when she painted your portrait because you hadn't been born. Think maybe this little girl is so far out in the future—"

"No, her parents were listening to a *radio*, not an iPod or a playlist on their phone. I heard her father surfing stations. Then his wife told him to stop, she wanted to hear Elton John. It was 'Something About the Way You Look Tonight.'"

"Maybe they were tuned in to an oldies station."

Unconsciously, Bailey began to fold the damp napkin into smaller and smaller squares.

"No, her father was surprised she knew the lyrics because it'd just been released."

Brice pulled out his phone and punched the Google app.

"The album came out in January, 1997. So you think this car accident happened in 1997, eighteen years ago?"

"What else could it mean?"

"The little girl looks like she was about the same age as Riley Campbell, a first-grader, about seven. So why did you paint a portrait of a first-grade girl killed in a car wreck eighteen years ago instead of a first-grade boy missing in 2015?"

"I have no idea." She paused, thought for a moment. "Maybe it's because I 'tried' to paint this picture, wasn't compelled to. Maybe the whole process—" She stopped and barked out a sardonic laugh. "Right, like we understand the 'process' of going into some kind of trance and painting a portrait with both hands."

"There is some kind of process involved, though, even if we don't know what it is. And maybe when you tinker around with the process, all bets are off."

"Maybe that's it. Still, it just … feels like there's some *connection* between the children." She noticed the tiny square of damp napkin in her hand and got up to put it in the trash. "If we knew the identity of the little girl, maybe we could find it."

Brice set his empty *to-go* coffee mug on the table and started to put his cellphone in his pocket, but it rang in his hand.

When he answered it, the look on his face told Bailey something bad had happened.

Chapter Eight

CALLER ID on Brice's phone identified Deputy Fletcher.

"Folks in town have started listening to police scanners and a bunch of them know the codes so I didn't want to send out a 10-26."

Brice's heart leapt into a gallop and the solid ball of lead in his belly swelled to take up his whole midsection, fit so tight his diaphragm hardly had space to take a breath. Fletcher filled him in on the call the 911 dispatcher had just received.

"What?" Bailey asked as soon as he hung up.

"We got a sex offender in the wind." He dropped the phone into his pocket and got to his feet.

"*Sex offender.* Why would you go looking …?"

"The sex offender registry's full of child predators."

Every state required offenders to register. All 850,000 names were viewable online. Most states required them to appear in person at regular intervals to local law enforcement.

"We just got a call claiming there's an offender in Shadow Rock who's not registered here."

"What does that have to do—?"

"He was one of the carpenters working on the Cotton-wood Festival grandstands yesterday."

Brice pulled out of Bailey's driveway and flipped on his lights and siren. When he got to the courthouse, he met Agent Nakamura coming down the broad front steps with agents Hardesty and Gascoyne. Nakamura hadn't informed him about the lead. Intended exclusion? Or did he assume Brice would be notified because the call had come in to the sheriff's department dispatcher?

"You got here fast," was all he said.

"In this town, you can get anywhere fast."

"All right, bring a couple of deputies, then. We have an address — what do you know about 3496 Beech Grove —?"

Brice stopped in front of Nakamura.

"I need to make the initial contact."

Gascoyne bristled. "Take care of traffic control, Sheriff, and we'll handle—"

Brice ignored him, spoke to Nakamura.

"You want to question this guy or spook him so he runs?"

Nakamura stopped and looked at Brice, saying nothing in a blank-faced, definite way.

"Samuel Kent's married, did you know that?" As he drove to the courthouse, Brice had called Ancil Spencer, a man who owned a lot of low-end rental property in and around Beech Grove Hollow, asked if anybody named Kent was one of his tenants. "Wife's name is Marcy. She works at Best Buy Supermarket as a checker but she called in sick today."

That stopped Nakamura cold.

"I buy my groceries at Best Buy. She knows who I am."

"What's your point, McGreggor?"

"FBI shows up on your porch — flashing guns and badges — scared people do dumb things. But just one guy, a familiar face you've seen around, maybe not so much."

He looked deep into Nakamura's eyes.

"And what I 'know about the address' is that it's at the very end of Beech Grove Road where it cuts back into the mountain. That hollow's barely wide enough for a house, the road, a creek and a prayer. I know the mountains around there and if this guy's a hunter, so does he. He runs and gets loose in those woods — you'll need an army to flush him out."

"And you're suggesting?"

"There's an old logging road half a mile this side of the end of Beech Grove. Stop there, let out two of my deputies who'll go up and over the ridge and come down in the woods behind the house. He bails, we got him. Everybody else stay out of sight."

"Listen, we—" Gascoyne began.

"I'm *not* trying to be the star of my own movie here," Brice fired back at him. "*Are you?*"

Still no expression. Nakamura must have been a killer poker player.

"All right, Sheriff McGreggor. We'll play this one your way. I'll ride with you … so you can fill me in on what you know about this man that you haven't shared with me."

The address that'd been provided by an anonymous caller turned out to be a double-wide trailer snuggled into a wide spot beside the road. The grass in the small patch of front yard was neatly mowed and a tidy flower garden bloomed beside the porch steps. Set in the woods behind the house was a tin building with two bay doors and a single small door. There were several cars parked around the building — not Appalachian-lawn-art wrecks but late-model cars. One was a pickup truck with the hood up. The bay doors on the building were closed.

Brice stopped so his cruiser was out of sight from the trailer. A swing set was visible behind the trailer and a plastic Big Wheel lay overturned in the driveway.

Once Brice had confirmed that his deputies were in place, he and Nakamura got out of the car, exchanging a glance at the toys. The two FBI agents, Gascoyne and Hardesty, parked and advanced only as far as Brice's cruiser. Brice crossed the small yard alone and stepped up onto the concrete slab porch.

A handprint was visible on the edge, made by a little hand in wet cement beside the date *June, 2013*. He knocked on the door.

The woman who opened the door was about forty and carried an infant on her hip. A little girl, maybe four or five years old, played with toys on the floor behind her. The woman looked tired, sick maybe, and when she saw Brice, her face registered surprise and fear, which she quickly covered with a tenuous smile.

"Sheriff McGreggor, what brings you way out here?"

"Hello, Mrs. Kent." Brice recognized her. She'd even checked out his groceries a couple of times. "I'm looking for your husband, Samuel Kent. Is he home?"

"No," she said, but it didn't appear to be an answer to his question. More denial. She shook her head and said again, "No … please, no. He …"

"Where is your husband, ma'am? I just need to talk to him, that's all."

She scrambled to regain her composure, feigned confusion. "What's this about? Sam's not in some kind of trouble, is he?"

Brice put steel into his tone. "You need to tell me where he is — now."

"Out back. Working on a car."

Brice turned and headed down the steps, speaking quietly into the mic at his shoulder. "Subject is in the garage. Cover the rear exit."

Quickly crossing the distance between the house and the garage, Brice drew his duty weapon, a Glock 22 pistol. Facing the wall beside the door, he moved slowly along it until he was close enough to reach out to the knob. It flashed through his mind that movies and cop shows always depicted officers clearing doorways by placing their backs against the wall beside the door and then suddenly spinning around into the room. Presenting their full body as a target, with no reconnaissance and an unsteady weapon. The only explanation he'd ever been able to come up with for such an absurd distortion of police procedure was that it looked cool, and directors likely placed Tom Cruise with his back to the wall so he would be facing the camera.

Before Brice had a chance to reach for the knob, open the door a crack and peek around the jamb, a voice called out from inside.

"Come on in, Sheriff." The voice sounded worn out. "I knew you'd show up eventually."

Brice opened the door and pushed it inward, then looked carefully around the door frame. A man in greasy coveralls, with a mop of shaggy black hair and a full beard was standing in the middle of a small office. He had his hands up.

"You know perfectly well I'm not Samuel Kent. Marcy's brother called you, didn't he?"

Brice said nothing to the man, but spoke into his shoulder mic and Deputy Fletcher came running out of the woods and joined him outside the garage door. Then the two of them stepped inside the building, both with weapons drawn but pointed at the floor.

"Mr. Kent, you—" Brice began.

"Drop the *Mr. Kent*, okay? You know I'm Joe Goddard or you wouldn't have come." The man held his arms out in front of him, offering his wrists for handcuffs. "I know why you're here."

The deputy holstered his weapon, moved forward and cuffed the man as Brice put his own gun away.

"Mr. Goddard, you are under arrest for violating the state sex offender registration law," Brice said. "You have the right to remain silent ..."

Brice took the man by the elbow and walked him out the door as he continued to intone his rights. Nakamura and the other agents came out from behind Brice's cruiser. Brice caught Fletch's eye and nodded toward the garage where

Goddard had been working and the deputy stepped to the door and scanned the inside of the building — a second set of eyes. Brice had already seen for himself that there was nothing inside the workshop big enough to hold a child.

Goddard's wife was standing on the back porch. She still carried the baby. The little girl was beside her, watching with wide, frightened eyes. When she saw her husband, the woman rushed down the steps and hurried toward him, leaving the little girl on the porch, looking lost and confused. Deputy Tackett intercepted her, "I'm sorry, ma'am, but you have to stay back."

"I'll call Walter," she said. "He'll help—"

"You know he won't," the man said as Brice led him past her. "Not when he finds out." He looked back over his shoulder. "You need to take the girls and go to your grandmother's."

"No! I'm staying right here." She was following along as Brice escorted the man to the cruiser. "I'll be waiting for you. You'll be home soon and I'll be right here, waiting for you."

Agent Hardesty approached the woman then, and asked politely for her permission to search the house, pointing out that if she refused, the agent would wait while another agent secured a court-ordered search warrant. Brice didn't hear what the woman said, if she said anything at all, just saw her nod and gesture toward the house while she remained where she was in the front yard watching Brice load her husband into the back seat of his cruiser. The little girl ran to her and buried her face in her mother's skirt.

Nakamura got back into the car on the passenger side and when Brice got in behind the wheel, the FBI agent turned in his seat to look at the handcuffed man behind him.

"I'm Special Agent Haruto Nakamura with the FBI and we're taking you to the sheriff's office to ask you a few questions."

"Fine. Ask away. It won't matter what I say to you, you're not going to believe me. You people never do."

They rode back into town in silence and parked behind the courthouse. The deputy escorted the prisoner into the building and into what passed for an interrogation room, small with a table and four chairs, the requisite straight-backed kind. No two-way mirror, though. But there was a surveillance camera in the corner.

Nakamura turned to Brice at the door.

"I'd like you to sit in on the questioning, Sheriff McGregor. *Sit in.* I'll be conducting the interrogation. I want you there to watch for inconsistencies in his story — you know the geography, how long it'd take to get from point A to point B. Listen for anything you know's bogus."

Brice nodded and he accompanied the two FBI agents into the room where Goddard was seated in one of the chairs facing the door. The sheriff picked up one of the other chairs and moved it over by the door, swung it around and straddled it, resting his arms on the back.

The two agents remained standing.

"This is Special Agent Elijah Gascoyne, Mr. Goddard — so you do admit that you are Joe Goddard?" Nakamura said.

"That'd be me, Mr. Joseph Alexander Goddard, registered sex offender."

"But you didn't register, Mr. Goddard, and that's why you're here today. The law requires—"

"You think I don't know what the law requires? That I show up and get my picture taken, fingerprinted — like my fingerprints are going to change from one visit to the next for crying out loud! Let you perform a strip search to make sure I haven't gotten any new 'identifying marks' or gotten rid of any old ones, give you my address, my employer's address, and ..."

He'd been on a roll, but the air suddenly whooshed out of him.

"And a pound of flesh. Every six months. Yeah, I know what the law requires."

Chapter Nine

Joe Goddard sat with his head in his hands, shaking it slowly back and forth. He was a big man, made more intimidating by the full head of hair and the long beard, which Brice suspected he'd grown when he'd decided to become Samuel Kent, so his picture as a sex offender wouldn't match his current face.

"Mr. Goddard, you have been advised of your rights, have you not?" Nakamura said.

"I know what rights I have — none. Zero. Zip. Zilch. Nada. As soon as I was convicted of a sex crime I lost my rights as an American."

"How do you figure that?"

"Oh, come on, don't act like you don't know what I'm talking about. There are the rights granted by the First Amendment of the Constitution to all American citizens and then there are the limited array of rights granted to sex offenders. The first list is very long. The second is very short."

The man sounded much more intelligent and articulate than his dress and demeanor would indicate.

"Tell me what you mean."

"Can we just stop this." He looked up, both disgusted and

resigned. "This little game. You know that I am a registered sex offender who has not reported as required by — well, in Kentucky it's Kentucky Revised Statute 402.205, Section 5A, but I don't know the exact statute number in West Virginia. And you know that puts me in violation of some other unnamed West Virginia statute, which is punishable by I-guess-I'll-find-out-what real soon. Can we all just agree to that and move on?"

"I'd like to ask you some questions about where you were and what you were doing yesterday afternoon. You were working on the construction of the bandstands for the Cottonwood Festival, is that correct?"

"You know it is." He cast a glance at Brice. "Your deputy took down my name, phone number and address just like he did everybody else's, probably fifty people in the area where I was. But did you haul the other forty-nine people in here in handcuffs to talk to them or did you just single me out because you figure I must be responsible for that little boy's disappearance, given what a living pond scum of a human being I am?"

"So you know there was a child missing from that school on the day you were working there?"

"Of course I know there was a kid missing."

"Mr. Goddard, would you mind walking us through what you did on that day? Start at the beginning."

He sighed, and sat back in the chair.

"Well, my day started at about three o'clock in the morning when Emily woke up crying. My wife and I take turns with night duty. We both work so it's not fair for one of us to be tired all the time and Emily is … let's just say she's not the most good-natured five-month-old in the world. Colic."

"So you got up at three o'clock?"

"… and I walked the floor with the baby until about four-thirty when she finally nodded back off. But I was afraid to lay her down in her crib because if she woke up again I wouldn't get a wink of sleep and I had to go to work at six. So I just sat up in the recliner with her and dozed until her mother got up for work."

"Where does your wife work?"

"That's none of your business! You leave her out of this. And my kids, too. This is all on me. I violated the registration rules, they didn't. They're innocent bystanders and you have no right to drag them into it." The emotion in his voice was two parts anger and three parts anguish. Add water and stir.

"I can find out without asking you, and it'd be a whole lot easier—"

"Okay, okay, she works as a checker at Best Buy. Has a Masters in accounting and she rings up people's groceries."

"Why would she be—?"

"Oh, come on. She can't claim her education because the diplomas are all in her real name, not the particular alias we happen to be currently using. Just the cost of doing business when you're dodging the law."

"So go on, Mr. Goddard, what did you do when your wife got up?"

"We both got ready to go to work, took the kids to the daycare center and I dropped her off and got to work — Peterson Lumber Company, but you knew that — about seven. We loaded up the truck and went to the school."

"Did you remain on the worksite all day? Did you leave at any time?"

"Yes ... and no. Let's cut to the chase. You want to know if I had anything to do with the disappearance of that little boy. There's absolutely no reason for you to think such a thing except — drum roll, please — I am a registered sex offender. So whenever you need somebody to blame for some heinous crime — bingo, there's my name, right there on the list. Why do you think I changed my name?"

"Why did you change your name?"

"Oh, come on! I couldn't get a job, couldn't pass a background check. I couldn't find anywhere to live, the neighborhoods all had regulations about people with records in sex offenses. I'm looking at Jenny starting kindergarten next year and do you know how far we'd have to drive her — because I can't live within five miles of an elementary school — or of a public park, or a church or ..."

He took a breath.

"My wife and my family are suffering for something they didn't do. Well, Marcy did it, but hey, she was the *victim*, not the perpetrator."

"What does that mean?"

"You read my record, didn't you?"

"Why don't you tell us about it anyway?"

Goddard let out a long breath.

"It's all in the record. I was a history teacher." He fingered his beard and looked at Brice, seated quietly by the door. "Look a lot like a history teacher now, don't I? So I was hot out of college, my first teaching job in an urban high school in Louisville. I was twenty-one years old, on fire to make a difference in the lives of my students. Yeah, right. I made a difference alright. At least in the life of one of them."

He stopped again, continued in a quieter voice.

"Marcy was in my first period class. She was a senior, but she had skipped a grade" — he smiled — "because she was so smart! So she wouldn't turn eighteen until right before graduation. Her mother died when she was nine and she'd been looking after three younger brothers — cooked, cleaned, took them to the doctor, made sure the older ones got their homework. She wasn't your typical seventeen-year-old girl."

He looked almost wistful.

"And there she was every day, sitting in the back row. And ... I was twenty-one years old and should have known better but I was an idiot, okay, just fell for her hook, line and ... ankle bracelet. I tried to keep my feelings to myself, but one day after school, several students and I were working on a history project ... they left and we were alone ... and I found out she felt the same way I did.

"Oh, come on, you know how the story goes. We started sneaking around to see each other. We were in love. Yeah, sounds trite, but it was true. I loved her and she loved me. But then ... enter her father on the scene. He found out about us and went to the authorities and I was arrested, charged with statutory rape, convicted and sentenced to ..."

He took a swallow.

"Eight years in prison." He shook his head. "Eight years."

He glanced back at Nakamura's expressionless face and continued.

"So there went my life. And her life, too. I served five of those years. Five years in prison as a 'kiddie-fiddler.' The other inmates ... those were *hard years*. Then I was paroled. While I was in prison, Marcy went to college, got a graduate degree and was teaching in a junior college. When I got out, we got married. That was seven years ago."

He shook his head.

"If I had it to do over again, I would have refused to answer a single one of her letters while I was in prison. I meant to, intended to, told her to go on with her life and to forget about me. But ..."

He stopped and looked at the men, one at a time.

"When you were seventeen years old, did you believe in love? Did you maybe fall in love? Well, she did. And it was real. Her father was a monster."

His voice took on a hard edge.

"It was such a cosmic joke. After we were married, she admitted to me that he had started sexually abusing her when she was five years old. That's why he went off like a rocket when she and I got together. She was a senior in high school and he had never allowed her to go on a single date! Not to the movies, or the prom. He kept her at home, under his thumb because he was ..."

Brice watched him grab hold of his emotions, lower his rising voice. When he continued, he ground the words out through clenched teeth.

"When I found out, I went crazy. I had *loved* Marcy, wanted to marry her. He had *raped* her — how many times in more than a decade? But *I* went to prison for five years and *he* lived a normal life as an upstanding and upright citizen of the community, on the elder board of the church and ..."

The momentum his anger had granted him failed and he continued in a flat, emotionless voice.

"You don't care about any of this. You probably don't even believe it, but you can check out the facts ... even if you believe I put my own spin on them."

He grew quiet for a moment.

"If I could have, I'd have been guilty of a far more heinous crime than falling in love with a seventeen-year-old girl. I'd have been guilty of murder. When she finally admitted to me what that monster had done to her, I'd have killed him. *Wanted* to kill him. *Ached to put a bullet in his brain.* But by that time there was nothing left of his brain. He was in a nursing home with Alzheimer's. Didn't even know who Marcy was."

He stopped again, looked at Nakamura.

"I didn't have anything to do with the disappearance of that child. Why on earth would I do a thing like that? He's only a couple of years older than my own daughter. I don't have 'a thing for little boys.' I fell in love with an underage girl who had a monster father and I paid for that with five years of my life behind bars at the mercy of the other inmates who ... And Marcy's paying for it now with me.

"She's why I didn't register. Marcy and the girls. I wanted them to have a decent life, a normal life. Now, I'm a suspect in a kidnapping. That's going to go down well with our neighbors. Think they'll let their children play with Jenny once word of that gets out?"

"While you were at work that day, did you at any time go onto the school grounds?"

"No, of course not. What for? I was building a bandstand. And I was trying to get done early so I could go by the deli and get takeout. I wanted to surprise Marcy. She's been fighting a bad cold, feeling rotten, and I didn't want her to have to fix supper. She could curl up on the couch and we could watch some kids' movie with Jenny, then go to bed early. At least, that was the plan. Of course, that didn't happen when you locked down the school property. I wasn't home early, I got home three hours late. And I didn't show up with the surprise of a sub sandwich. I showed up with the news that a kid had gone missing from the elementary school near where I was working ... and the cops were going to blame me."

"You were turned in by an anonymous caller—"

"Anonymous! Right. Marcy's brother, Boyce. When we got married, we left her whole family behind. They were all a bunch of degenerate druggies and alcoholics. But he tracked us down and showed up at the house a couple of weeks ago. Wanted to stay with us, just till he got back on his feet. I threw him out after three days because he was using drugs and probably selling them. The 'anonymous' call was payback."

"So you're telling me you didn't have any contact that day with any of the children? Not even one?"

"Not even one. But I could have had contact with every single one of them and it wouldn't have mattered. I'm not a pedophile. I have never and would never molest a child. Go check my file and you'll see."

He looked up into Nakamura's eyes, and must have been disappointed in the lack of empathy he saw there, because he dropped his head and said softly, "Okay, game over. I'm not going to sit here answering questions knowing you're not going to believe a word. I want a lawyer." He burped out a sour piece of a laugh. "And no, I can't afford one so yes, the court will have to appoint one to represent me before I am questioned. So go find my poor court-appointed attorney. I'm tired. My baby kept me up again last night. Just take me to jail and let me sleep."

Nakamura tried to get the man to answer more questions but he refused to say another word. Finally, Agent Gomez brought in some papers to the senior agent, he read them, and ended the interview.

"We'll talk again later, Mr. Goddard."

"I'll be looking forward to it."

Outside in the hallway, Brice looked a question at Nakamura, who shook his head, holding up the papers Agent Gomez had brought him.

"This is his record. The facts of his story check out. Statutory rape of a seventeen-year-old girl. Eight-year sentence. Served five. That much, at least, is true."

The agent shrugged.

"Whether the rest is bogus or not is immaterial. The profile of the crime he committed doesn't fit the person we're looking for."

Nakamura walked away and Brice stood there, looking through the doorway of the room where Joe Goddard sat chained to a table by his handcuffed hands. The word "crime" was bouncing around in his head, ricocheting like a bullet off a cave wall.

He turned away toward the conference room/command center at the end of the hall and through the open doorway he could see the agents working. And the clock. It'd always been there, a big industrial-sized clock above the coffee machine. After Riley went missing, it had become in Brice's mind the countdown clock, ticking away the passage of minutes and hours like sand out the bottom of an hourglass. The face of the clock looked at him accusingly now. Almost two o'clock. A little boy's teacher saw him walk down the hallway, his friends saw him turn toward the bathroom ... and then he vanished in a puff of smoke *more than twenty-four hours ago.*

His cellphone rang. When he answered, the voice on the other end of the line didn't even say hello.

"The sex offender — did he ... was there—?" Bailey couldn't even get out a complete question.

"Swing and a miss."

He heard a shuddering sigh, then her voice came back strong. "I want to go to Riley Campbell's classroom."

Chapter Ten

THERE'D BEEN no talking Bailey out of her plan, and in truth Brice didn't try all that hard.

"When I touched that chair Macy Cosgrove touched, I was connected to her, I could see out her eyes," she'd said, talking fast so he couldn't interrupt and argue with her. "I didn't connect to Riley Campbell just looking at his picture, but what if I touched something Riley'd touched, like at school … sat in his desk? Maybe …"

It was somewhere on the other side of a longshot. But right now, there were no other leads. And that clock, that accusing clock on the command center wall was relentlessly tick, tick, ticking away the little boy's chances of survival. He'd been missing more than twenty-four hours. With Joe Goddard no longer a person of interest, it felt better to try something, *anything*, than to sit by and do nothing at all.

The school day was over so there'd be no children in the building. He called Melody McCallum to tell her they'd be visiting her classroom and she told him to pick up a key in the office. She couldn't let him in personally because she was at her doctor's office getting the brace removed from her neck. The one she wore because three men in a pickup truck ran her off the road six weeks ago. Three men who died at the scene.

Half an hour later, he was walking down the hallway toward the grades-one-through-three classrooms in the north wing of Corruthers Elementary School, his heavy footsteps and Bailey's lighter ones echoing in the cavernous space. Even as tired and distracted as he was, he noticed the gold highlights in her hazel eyes when she looked up at him — eyes he thought he'd never see when "Sleeping Beauty" lay unconscious in the hospital after she put Oscar in her brain.

"The last time I was in an elementary school, I was a student there," Bailey said.

"I was a student *here*."

"Seriously?"

"Told you I was a homie."

He stopped in front of a door about halfway down the hall. In letters six inches tall, a calligraphy sign proclaimed, "Melody McCallum, First Grade." He fished in his pocket but paused before he inserted the key he'd picked up in the office, remembering the teacher's description of her classroom zoo.

"So … how do you feel about spiders?"

"I don't like them. Who does?"

"Melody McCallum."

"And you know that because …?"

"She keeps a spider in her classroom."

"You're joking."

"Not just any spider, a big black hairy tarantula in a terrarium."

Bailey's face blanched.

"She has other wildlife, too. A parakeet named Frodo, two gerbils called Frick and Frack and an aquarium—"

"Full of piranha?"

"She's growing a potato plant, too, just like my teacher did. Cut off one end of a potato, stick a pencil through it to hold it on the rim of a glass full of water and you can watch roots begin to form—"

"I get fish, gerbils, birds and potatoes ... but a tarantula? Why?"

"She said she wanted to teach the children that bigotry in any form is wrong, that it's not okay to pass judgement on a harmless creature just because it's ugly and scary-looking."

"Harmless? Those babies can bite."

"It's like a wasp sting, hurts but not fatal."

"The *bite* wouldn't have to be fatal. If one of those things crawled up on me, I would die of fright. If I had known there was a tarantula in the room, I ... okay, I'd have come even if I'd known. But I'd have gotten drunk first."

"Wait here. I'll go inside and cover up the terrarium with something, so you won't have to look at him." He unlocked the door. "His name is Bambi, by the way."

"So maybe I'll want to pet him?"

"She let the kids name him."

"This lady must be one weird duck."

Brice opened his mouth to say there was nothing weird about Melody McCallum — then said nothing. There was, in fact, an oddness to the woman that seemed to reach beyond the fact that her BFF had eight legs and ate live grasshoppers. She was too perfect. It was like she'd bought a First Grade Teacher for Dummies manual and reinvented herself in that image. She wore a sweater that somebody'd spent hours appliquéing — maybe she did it herself — with an apple on the pocket and ladybugs flying up the sleeve. Her smile was as beatific as a statue of the Virgin Mary. When she spoke to you, her voice intonation and inflection sounded like she was addressing a six-year-old. And Bambi, of course. There was that.

He crossed the room to the terrarium on the wall and at first saw nothing in it except a live grasshopper.

"You are not long for this world," he told the bug. "You know that, don't you?"

Then he saw the spider and literally jumped back a step. How a room full of children could concentrate with that ... *thing* crawling around just a pane of clear glass away from them was more than he could imagine. It was the epitome of horror. Hairy black legs, moving the way tarantulas walk, the back four legs on both sides working in tandem. It was approaching the grasshopper, oblivious to Brice, but it stopped, turned toward him and he couldn't help a pang of cold dread settling in his stomach. The spider changed course then, crossed the terrarium to a spot just opposite Brice and began to crawl slowly up the glass wall. For a horrified moment, Brice feared the creature would get out of the enclosure. In which case, he would, of course, have responded professionally — he'd have run out of the room and locked the hairy monster inside. Then he noted the roof on the terrarium and relaxed. A little. Not totally. The spider had seen him and crossed to him and was now showing its belly to him through the glass, the horror of a face and the fangs that administered the not-fatal, wasp-sting bite. If Brice had been paranoid, he'd have sworn the creature was trying to be intimidating. It worked.

He tore his eyes away from the beast and looked around for something to drape over the terrarium. He spotted a checked tablecloth on a round table in the corner beside the windows, where there was good light for the plants growing there. He moved the plants off onto the windowsill, removed the tablecloth and then draped it gingerly over the terrarium. There was a hissing sound from beneath the tablecloth.

He thought he heard a small thump, like maybe the spider had leapt off the wall. What? In anger? Pissed because Brice had cut off the sunlight? That was ridiculous.

As soon as it was no longer possible to see the hairy visage of the monster arachnid, Brice's mood immediately brightened, like the presence of the spider cast a darkening pall that made the room gloomy. He'd never allow his kid to sit in a classroom every day with a tarantula spider! He didn't have to worry about that, of course, because he would never have a kid in the first place.

"Where's the spider?" Bailey asked when he opened the door.

He pointed to the checkered tablecloth.

"And it can't get out of there, right? There's no way for it to escape?"

"There's a lid on the terrarium, and wire mesh under the lid."

"*Bambi*." She visibly shuddered. "Let's do this so we can get out of here."

It wasn't hard to find Riley's desk. You couldn't miss it on the far side of the room. Danny Keeling had said Riley'd asked to be seated there because he didn't want to be close to the spider. There was a big yellow ribbon on the back of the chair. Scattered all over the desktop and in a box on top were small items. A miniature Hulk action-figure doll. A rabbit's foot. An old locket. An equally old teddy bear. A threadbare baby blanket.

He answered her question before she had a chance to ask it.

"When I talked to Melody this afternoon, she told me about his desk. She said she'd asked the students to bring in objects that were precious to them. Things that really mattered. Then one at a time, the students set the items on Riley's desk or on the floor around it."

"And the purpose was …?"

"She didn't want the kids looking at where Riley *wasn't*. She wanted them to see something special, something they loved when they looked at his desk. And the yellow ribbon is there until he comes home."

Brice didn't mean for it to happen, but his voice broke a little when he said "home."

Bailey went to the desk, picked up the Hulk doll, then the blanket, touched the tattered ear of the teddy bear and said, "Some little kid is sleeping alone tonight." Picking up the rabbit's foot, she examined the motley fur. "This was a sweet gesture. I take back what I said about Melody McCallum being weird. She's sensitive. She loves kids and understands them."

Then Bailey moved a one-eyed baby doll on the seat of the desk and sat down in it, though she was too big. Brice turned unwillingly to give the terrarium a onceover, making sure the tablecloth hadn't slipped off. When he turned back, Bailey was gripping the sides of the desk so hard her knuckles were white. Her eyes were fixed on something he couldn't see.

He'd seen her look like that before, the day she touched the Adirondack chair at the lake and instantly looked out the eyes of Macy Cosgrove at the carnival. As he watched, Bailey's eyes moved, following the action of images he couldn't see.

The impossibility of it, the insanity of it, that this woman could *paint the future*, could see out the eyes of … it only washed over him briefly and was gone. It'd taken tremendous effort, but he had finally reconciled all that in his head, had finally stopped trying to fit demonstrable reality into the shape of his personal belief system about how the universe operated.

From the look on Bailey's contorted face, it was clear she wasn't watching a Hallmark Channel movie. Brice felt a hole open up in his belly and a chilly breeze blow through. Whatever was happening to Riley Campbell, whatever Bailey was living with him at that moment as she saw the world through his eyes, it was a nightmare.

Chapter Eleven

THE BREATH BAILEY *inhales is full of the most horrifying stench imaginable. It is unbelievably rank and foul. An overwhelming stink, a gasping, gagging kind of reek, worse than anything she has ever smelled anywhere.*

She's looking out eyes that see a small hand with an angry red welt at the base of the thumb, the hand of the little girl in the wreck. Katydid.

The dirty fingers are clasping a pink ribbon.

The little girl is able to blot out the stink right now because of the piece of pink ribbon in her hand. She brings it to her lips and touches them with the satiny softness of it. She squeezes something in her right fist, hugs her fist tight against her chest, but she is lying on her side and she is only holding the object, clutching it, not looking at it. When she looks away from the ribbon, her eyes sweep across a small space, maybe three feet tall and ten feet long. Her eyes pass over a window and there's ... it looks like a tree trunk is jammed up against it. The little girl crawls through the small space and her hand touches something that looks like ... a covered light, like the dome light in a—

It's the camper.

The wrecked camper, upside down. There was a car wreck but she wasn't killed instantly. Katydid survived.

She crawls across the ceiling where there is a wet mass of trash every-

where. There are empty cans of Vienna sausage and flip-top tuna, empty pudding tins and fruit tins. There are soft drink cans, too, and empty bags of chips. She crawls over the trash, digs through it and pulls out a bottle of water. She twists the lid off and looks up to the right, where there is light streaming in through a broken window on the other side of the camper. Woods, trees, the rocks and dirt of a forest floor. The girl then crawls through the trash to a spot where she has made a place for herself. A rolled-up sleeping bag for a pillow and blankets for a bed. There are toys, several small dolls — two or three inches tall, but their long pink-and-blue hair stretches down to their feet, and doll furniture, miniature to fit into a dollhouse. There's a scruffy brown teddy bear, too, and she draws it into her arms when she lies down on her makeshift bed.

But it's wet. Everything's wet.

She has stopped wondering why Mommy and Daddy went away and left her here by herself in this place. She has given up trying to figure out what exactly she did wrong. Whatever it was, it was a terrible thing. At first she cried out to them, screamed as loud as she could so they could hear, promised she would never do another bad thing ever in her whole life if they would come back and get her. She promised she would be the perfect little girl, that she was sorry for whatever it was she did and she wouldn't do it again.

But Mommy and Daddy didn't answer her cries. They didn't come back for her.

A day. Two days. Three. She lost count after that.

Something nearby started to smell really bad a couple of days after the wreck, not all the time but when the wind blew from the back of the camper. It was so bad, it made her want to throw up. That was before the storm.

Two nights ago, it'd started to rain and she was glad at first because she couldn't smell the stink in the rain. But it rained all the next day and night. Water ran down the hillside and into the camper and got everything wet. Then she felt the camper start to move. It was totally dark and she screamed and cried and the water came in and the camper slid down the hillside and she thought she would drown — but it stopped sliding, the camper hit something, some bushes, and stopped.

When the sun came up, she heard the humming, the buzz. A hive of some kind must have been in the tree or bush the camper hit. Wasps — bees and flies, too — came in through a window that broke out in the dark. They flew around and around the soft drink cans and the empty pudding cups. More and more of them.

They stung her and it hurt!

And as soon as the rain stopped, she smelled the stink. Worse than before, all the time now. It filled every breath, so foul she couldn't eat and vomited until nothing came out and her throat was raw and burned.

She tried to cover her nose, but the stink was everywhere. Like the wasps. She cried and screamed and shooed them away, swatted at them. But they kept coming. She couldn't get to the hole in the window to stop it up with something and they kept coming and coming and she got under her sleeping bag to get away from them but it was wet and cold and awful there.

Then it was dark again and there was nowhere she could go that there weren't puddles of water and she was cold and shivering.

This morning, the warrior came out of nowhere and attacked the wasps, killed them! She watched him, the mighty Shannuck, her protector. He kept her safe from the wasps and made them pay for trying to sting Katydid.

But as the day gets hotter and hotter, the smell gets worse. Worse than it has ever been. It is so horrible now she only takes little breaths but that doesn't help and she gags and vomits up nothing — again and again until her stomach and head hurt. Nothing smells this bad. Nothing in all of life or the world or the planet or the universe smells this bad.

She can't stand the stink! But there's nothing she can do to escape it.

Then she remembers the day Mommy was in her bathroom blowing her hair dry and suddenly the electricity in the bathroom and in her bedroom went out and the lights went out. Katydid was playing a video game and the screen suddenly went black.

She went out into the hallway. Mommy had gone to the top of the stairs and called down to Daddy, who was watching a football game in the den.

"Blew a breaker again. Would you go throw the switch? I'm not dressed."

"What's a breaker?" she'd asked.

"Go with Daddy. Get him to show you."

She went downstairs and saw Daddy open the door to the garage.

"What's a breaker?" she'd asked him, but he was mad that he had to leave the football game and not in a mood to explain.

He had opened a gray metal door on the wall and said, "This is a breaker." Beneath the door were two rows of switches. Some of them had pieces of paper taped beside them with words written there. Daddy reached up to the first switch and flipped it off. She was standing in the kitchen and when he flipped the switch, everything in the kitchen went dark, the lights under the cabinets, the clock on the microwave and the one on the coffeemaker and all the bulbs in the chandelier over the dining room table she could see through the archway. The refrigerator stopped humming and fell silent and the fan on the ceiling spun slower and slower.

Daddy flipped another switch and the lights in the utility room on the other side of the kitchen went off.

She realized that every time he flipped a switch, a room somewhere in the house would go dark.

Snap. Snap. Snap.

With every snap, things stopped running. Then the lights in the garage went out and everything was black for a moment before Daddy started flipping the switches back on. When he flipped the first switch, the breaker, everything came back on in the kitchen, except instead of numbers on the clocks on the microwave and the coffeemaker there were just blinking green zeros.

The darkness hadn't lasted long, but for as long as it did last, nothing changed. Everything had remained exactly like it was before the lights went out.

The little girl wonders if maybe people are like that, too. Maybe they have a breaker box with switches. She goes looking for it, inside her head, searching for a way to turn off the world that is all wrong now and smells bad and wasps come and sting.

And she finds it.

She finds a way to make it all go away — just like Daddy did.

She flicks a breaker.

Now she can smell. Flick. Now she can't smell.

She is cheered by her discovery, by the power it gives her. Now that she has discovered the breaker box, the switches she can turn off inside to make the awful go away, she starts flipping them one after the other, flips all the switches and plunges her mind and soul into darkness.

It is dark now and peaceful. She puts her thumb in her mouth and curls her finger around her nose. No more scared. No more stink.

She'll hide here in this place where no light, not even a crack of it, comes. She is safe here.

Holding tight the birthday present she found among the camping supplies, in the box that had been wrapped in shiny white paper and a pink ribbon, she makes herself two promises — that she will keep the present always. And that she will never flip the switches back on. Never see the light again. Never.

Chapter Twelve

BAILEY GASPED AND JERKED UPRIGHT, for a moment was totally disoriented, had no idea where she was ... and wasn't quite sure *who* she was.

She looked around, trying to get her bearings, trying—

Then she was nauseous, so nauseous she wordlessly leapt to her feet, looked around frantically — where was she? A school, a classroom, that little boy's classroom, and she bolted for the door, threw it open and barely made it across the hall to the girls' restroom before she was violently sick. She vomited again and again, then dry-heaved until she was so weak she sank down onto the tile floor that smelled of Pine-Sol and leaned her head back against the wall of the toilet stall, panting, tears running down her cheeks.

"Bailey, are you alright?" Brice called from the door.

"No!" She took a breath. "Yes, I'm okay, give me a minute."

She got slowly to her feet and staggered to the sink where she turned on the tap and splashed cold water into her face. She felt the nausea return, but swallowed it back down. She ripped off a paper towel and slowly dried her hands, looking at her own pale reflection in the mirror and thought she looked as dead as the child in the portrait she had painted.

The little girl. Katydid. *Oh, that poor child!*

Bailey went out into the hallway where Brice was waiting for her and the images struck her again so powerfully she was momentarily weak-kneed. When she staggered, he swept her off her feet up into his arms, carried her as if she weighed no more than a small child down the hall to the principal's office and laid her on the couch in the waiting area, ignoring her pleas to "put me down" and her protestations that "I'm fine."

She sat up immediately. Lying on a couch made her feel like she must be in a shrink's office. She asked Brice if he'd get her a drink of water and he returned in a couple of minutes with a coffee mug emblazoned with the words "If you can read this, thank a teacher" that he had obviously swiped out of the teacher's lounge or off some teacher's desk.

While he was gone, she concentrated on breathing in and out *slowly*, not hyperventilating. But every time the images returned to her mind, she began to pant, gasp in horror and revulsion.

That poor little girl!

Brice pulled one of the waiting area chairs over to the couch and sat down in it.

"Are you all right now?"

"It was ... oh, Brice, I can't tell you ..." She lost her words, looked at him helplessly, unable to speak.

He got up from the chair and sat down beside her, putting his arm around her shoulders. Then she found herself crying. She turned to him and burst into great wrenching sobs that went on and on until her throat felt raw and her chest ached.

When the sobs ratcheted down into sniffles, she was embarrassed that she was doing that thing little kids did after they'd been crying, the hiccupping-breath thing.

She remained in his arms for a time, though, grateful for the feel of them around her. Grateful that he was there and that she felt safe, profoundly *safe*, maybe for the first time since she'd hidden under a dumpster with the rats.

Finally, she pulled back and sat up. He handed her a tissue, which she used to wipe the tears off her face. She took in a deep, shaky breath, drank a swallow of the water out of some teacher's cup and discovered that her hands were trembling slightly.

"Brice, it was so horrible for that little girl. I can hardly describe it."

He reached out and took her hand in his.

"Little girl?"

It was only then that the realization made it through the horror to the higher centers of her brain. She had come here to connect to Riley Campbell, just as she had painted that portrait in an effort to connect to him. But she had painted a portrait of a little girl instead of Riley, and now, sitting in his chair, she had connected not to Riley Campbell, but to the mysterious little girl again. Why?

"What did you see?"

Brice's words brought the images pounding back into her mind, a tsunami that washed away all other thought.

"The little girl I painted, she wasn't killed in the car wreck. She *survived*. But her parents *didn't*. They were killed. And the little girl was trapped in the camper. Not just for a couple of hours. For *days*."

"How did she survive … food, water?"

"They were going camping so they'd packed supplies, food you could eat without having to cook it. There were empty tins all around, tuna, Vienna sausage, candy and cupcake wrappers. Chips and soft drinks."

"So she survived. How do you know her parents—?"

"She could smell them! The stench. Her parents' bodies —" Bailey couldn't say it, couldn't force the word "decay" …

"Oh, dear God."

"The stench. That's why, that's what made me sick. How bad it smelled."

She stopped, afraid she was going to be sick or start crying again.

"Katydid didn't know what the stink was. She thought her parents left her there *because she'd done something bad*!"

Brice patted her shoulder, urged her to take another sip of water. The motion of swallowing was calming.

"I can't imagine anything worse — *drowning wasn't that horrible*. She was stuck there. Alone. Afraid. Confused. It rained and everything got wet. And wasps. There was a wasp nest and they stung … that's what made the red welts on her arms and face. Wasp stings!"

She lost it again, started panting and hyperventilating.

"Breathe slowly." Brice patted her back. "In and out, slow." He rubbed her arm tenderly and she grabbed hold of her emotions.

"I didn't get this part. She said *Shannuck* came out of nowhere and saved her from the wasps. She imagined something, made up something, probably hallucinated some super-hero savior, I don't know. I guess Shannuck was her imaginary protector."

Bailey took in a deep, shaky breath and let it out, slowly, like Brice said.

"The little girl was looking at a ribbon, a pink ribbon. That's the first thing I saw, the pink ribbon in her hand. She had just found it, her birthday present. Her parents talked about packing her present, spelled words so she wouldn't understand. She must have found the present when she was digging around for food."

She paused, gathering herself to get out the rest of the story.

"So she remembered her daddy flipping the breakers once and how everything in the house got still and quiet. And she wondered if people had breakers, too. Somehow she … Brice, this child was going insane and I was in there in her head, with her, watching her, feeling it."

Brice squeezed her hand.

"I don't know how to describe it, but she found a way to ... turn things off, turn off reality. She mentally flipped a switch and she couldn't smell the ... *bodies* anymore. Then she kept flipping switches so she couldn't see or hear or ... being in her head ... it just got darker and darker and darker until ... nothing."

She shuddered again violently.

"That little girl ... just left, checked out. I don't know how she actually died. Thirst, maybe? *Starved* ..." A strangled sob caught in her throat and she couldn't finish the sentence.

"Back up a little. To the beginning. Tell me again what happened. You sat down at Riley's desk and then ...?"

"I was suddenly inside Katydid's head and looking out her eyes. Like with Macy at the carnival, and when she was feeding Jakey. I saw what she was seeing at that moment—"

"At *what* moment? The little girl in the camper has been dead for — what? Almost twenty years. You couldn't have been looking out her eyes in real time like you did with Macy. So what moment in her life ...?" He stopped. "Wait a minute. What was the birthday present she found?"

"I don't know. I never saw it. There were toys lying around. Maybe the present was a little doll or doll furniture. She was holding the ribbon out, looking at it, and squeezing the present in her other hand."

"Like she'd just opened it, the present?"

Bailey nodded.

"Maybe that's it, then. The birthday present."

Bailey didn't know what he was getting at.

"She got something for her birthday and you touched it, here, today, just a few minutes ago."

"I touched it. How?"

"One of the things on Riley's chair. Something there was what that little girl got for her birthday. And when you touched it—"

"I was taken into her head to the moment when *she* first touched it."

"Makes sense to me." Then he stopped, shook his head. "As much as any of this makes sense to me. Ever since" — he waved his hand in a sort of all-encompassing gesture — "I came charging into your house, gun drawn, when you screamed, I've been trying to apply 'sense' to something that's not logical. Reality is, we don't know jack about how any of this works."

He was right, of course. It was all—

"But if it *were* logical, it'd make 'sense' that you connected to that little girl because you touched her birthday present on Riley's desk."

Bailey started to rise, but Brice held her firmly by the shoulder.

"Oh, no you don't. You're not going back in there."

"But I have to. We have to know which one—"

"You are *not* going to touch any of those things."

"I have to figure out which one was her present, trace it to Riley. She has *some* connection to Riley Campbell." Her voice rose a little too high, an edge of hysteria creeping into it, but she couldn't help it.

Brice was silent for a moment. "Okay, I'll grant there must be some connection. Melody told the children to bring in something that mattered to them. Maybe a child brought in a family heirloom."

"How are we going to find out which of those items it was if you won't let me—?"

"I'll talk to the children and ask, tell Melody I need to find out where the children got the items they brought to put on Riley's desk."

"What's your excuse for wanting to know?" She tried to mimic his voice. "See, I have this friend who paints portraits of dead people who aren't dead yet and has visions of live people who've been dead for twenty years and—"

"I'll think of something. But right now ..." He stood up and held out his hand to her. "I'm taking you home!"

Chapter Thirteen

"YOU KNOW you don't have to bribe us with chocolate chip cookies to get us to drop by," Dobbs said, taking another cookie from the proffered plate.

"I had to come by anyway," T.J. said. "I got visitation rights with my dog — one night a week and every other weekend."

Bailey rolled her eyes.

"He's not here *that* often."

"I keep his picture on my mantle to help me remember what he looks like."

T.J. took a cookie, holding his hand under it as he bit in so the crumbs wouldn't fall on the floor where Sparky was snoozing contentedly at his feet. There wasn't much chocolate in a chocolate chip cookie, but it didn't take a whole lot of chocolate to make a small dog sick.

"I'm just trying to grease the wheels." Bailey put the last cookie off the sheet onto the platter and inhaled the delicious aroma. True, she had baked the cookies as a bribe for T.J. and Dobbs, but also because the smell of fresh-baked cookies was a clean, hopeful smell and she needed that after …

She hadn't completely recovered from her nausea until she'd pulled the first baking sheet out of the oven.

"Long's you keep bakin' cookies, Dobbs'll show up to eat 'em."

"You guys are a cheap date."

"Ain't free but we are reasonable." T.J. popped the last little bit of cookie into his mouth, swallowed it, and when he spoke again the bantering quality was gone from his voice. "So, what'd you paint this time?"

Of course, he knew. They both did.

"It's more than a painting this time."

T.J. rose. "Then let's go have us a look-see."

"You look, I'll make coffee. You're going to need it after you see what's in there."

When the three of them sat facing each other at Bailey's kitchen table cradling steaming cups of coffee, she began the story.

"The little boy who disappeared yesterday — I tried to paint a portrait of him."

"On purpose?" T.J. was clearly surprised.

"Brice gave me the picture the boy's teacher gave him, but as you saw, that portrait in there isn't Riley Campbell."

"Who is it, then?" Dobbs asked.

"I'm hoping the two of you can help me figure that out." She took a deep breath. "It's worse than just that portrait. It's …" Even now, the memory hit her so hard she shuddered. "It's unimaginably horrible."

When she finished telling them what had happened at the school, both men sat staring at her in shocked silence. She knew exactly how they felt.

"Told you you'd need a cup of coffee."

"Coffee?" Dobbs shook his head. "I need a drink strong enough to dissolve the swizzle stick."

"That portrait can't possibly be some random child my compulsion pulled out of its bag of tricks and forced me to paint. It has *something* to do with Riley Campbell — it has to.

Why else would I have connected to the little girl when I sat down in Riley's chair in his classroom?"

"And you want us to help you find the connection," Dobbs said.

"Would you? Please."

"Done."

They said the word in unison, then looked at each other and rolled their eyes.

"The first step is findin' out *who* the child is."

"Brice said that finding the record of a triple-fatality car accident wouldn't be all that difficult if it happened somewhere around here."

She turned to T.J.

"Did your mother ever paint something that happened far away … a plane crash in Montana or something like that?"

"Ain't no way to know for sure 'cause sometimes we never did find out who it was she'd painted. She'd paint somebody lying dead in the woods, a bullet hole in his chest and a couple of days later we'd hear that somebody over in Butler County got killed in a hunting accident. But lots of other times, she'd paint things and we never knew what happened. If it was somebody dead, in a couple of days she'd feel the connection snap and we knew the person had died, though we didn't know where."

"Goody. So this wreck could have happened in Bangladesh."

"Could have, I s'pose. But my best guess would be somewhere nearer than that."

He cast a sideways glance at Dobbs before he continued.

"Got to remember, my mama was paintin' portraits sixty years ago. And back in them days … let's just say the gene pool in West Virginia didn't have a whole lot of fish."

Dobbs nodded. "Mountain people had a kind of look to them. I couldn't describe it, one of those things you know it when you see it."

Bailey watched Dobbs reach into his pocket and draw out his watch. He flicked the catch with his thumb and glanced at the watch face. He didn't want to know what time it was, of course. If he had, he certainly wouldn't have looked at that pocket watch, which hadn't kept time since ... maybe it never did. Taking it out and looking at it, that was just something Dobbs did.

"The people in mama's paintings, they had the look of mountain folks."

"There have been more fish added to the pool in the last half century, so you can't tell anymore just by looking that somebody's one of us. But if T.J.'s mama only painted local happenings, why would you be any different?"

"I think there's somethin' ... something about West Virginia or maybe about mountain people that's ... part of the magic."

"So ... I painted that picture either because that child, that family were" — she smiled — "*mountaineers*, or the accident that killed them happened somewhere close around here — is that what you're saying?"

"Sounds right to me," T.J. said.

"I was here in Kavanaugh County in 1997 and if there had been a triple fatality that gruesome, I guarantee I'd remember it," Dobbs said. "The wreck might have been somewhere close around, but it wasn't right here. They were going camping ... the parents didn't say anything about stopping for the night, did they?"

"No."

"Then I'm betting that wherever they were going, it wasn't more than a day's drive from here."

T.J. nodded. "I say we start lookin' for a wreck that happened in an area — I'm just puttin' this out there — no more than a hundred miles from here. Anywhere within a hundred-mile radius."

Bailey watched T.J. drop effortlessly into police-officer mode.

"You check accident reports online, a three-fatality wreck in 1997. Wouldn't think there'd be a huge number in just one year. Check West Virginia, Virginia, Ohio, Kentucky and Pennsylvania. I'll see what I can find out from obituaries online. Pro'ly won't be much. And Dobbs—"

"I'll check local newspapers. If there was a fatal wreck in that county, they'd have the story. The West Virginia Press Association's website will have a list of the weeklies."

Three hours, two delivery pizzas and another batch of chocolate chip cookies later they had all come up snake eyes. The only fatality statistics available were from the state highway departments, which listed the number of fatal accidents in each county — a grand total by year. Obituaries online were a complete dud. The names were listed in alphabetical order by year. In 1997, only two counties showed three obituaries with the same last name, but none of them were adults with one child, a girl about seven years old. And they were listed by county of residence, not where the people died.

Dobbs had made out best. He'd contacted all twenty-three weekly newspapers in West Virginia, along with a dozen weekly newspapers in Ohio and Kentucky that lay near the West Virginia border. All of them had some record of past issues, but the form of those records varied widely. Most had digital records of the actual newspapers dating back five to ten years. Beyond that, though, the newspapers themselves were available only on microfiche — at the newspaper office. Dobbs had figured out quickly that the kind of records he needed weren't always available in such small operations, so he'd taken to asking to speak to "the oldest person in the building."

"A three-fatality accident — that's a big deal in those counties. They'd remember."

To Bailey's surprise, though not to T.J.'s and Dobbs's — he had found a "veteran" of at least twenty years in most of the newspapers he called. Unfortunately, the old-timers remembered the bad accidents where local people were killed. But three strangers … maybe, maybe not.

There were only four newspapers where he couldn't find out anything at all. They were among the smallest of the newspapers, three of them in neighboring counties deep in the mountains. There'd been no old-timers on the premises he could talk to, and the only records of the newspapers from 1997 were bound volumes of the newspapers themselves, stored in the attic or basements of the newspaper buildings.

"I think the newspapers are our best bet," Dobbs said. "I've eliminated all but these four. I vote we take a road trip. We could hit all four in one day — a long day." He cast a glance at Bailey, and merely said "mountain roads" by way of explanation. "It's a total shot in the dark. Anybody got a better idea?"

Nobody did.

They agreed to leave after breakfast the next morning.

Bailey had hardly slept at all the night before so she hoped she wouldn't stare buggy-eyed into the darkness tonight, too. She tried really hard not to keep doing the mental math, but her eyes kept straying to the clock on the dresser as she got ready for bed.

When she turned off the bedside lamp, the digital readout cried out in flashing red letters in the dark.

Riley Campbell had been missing almost thirty-six hours.

Chapter Fourteen

BRICE COULDN'T HELP BEING squeamish about Melody McCallum's classroom, didn't relish spending quality bonding time with Bambi, the saucer-sized tarantula. Though he'd arranged to meet Melody before the start of the school day, there were four children already in the room when he arrived — the "lucky" children whose job it was to feed grasshoppers to the spider.

Melody stood by the window with a bright green parakeet perched on her finger.

"Pretty boy," she said.

"Pretty boy, pretty boy," the bird chirped in bird speak as it paced like a sentry up and down the length of her finger. "Hello. Goodbye. Pretty boy."

When she spotted Brice, she put the parakeet back in its cage and met him at her desk.

"The rest of the children won't be here for another fifteen minutes."

Brice found himself leaning toward her when she spoke because her voice was so soft. He wondered if that was a calculated thing, to get the children to pay attention. She was wearing a different sweater today. No ladybugs on this one, just an apple that had a cute, grinning worm sticking his head out a hole.

"Would you mind explaining to me how talking to the children about what they put on his desk will help you find Riley?"

"Sometimes … no, maybe most times, you don't know what you know. Witnesses know things they never think to tell the police because it doesn't occur to them the information might be important, or because they only remember some detail when they're reminded of it."

He hoped that would suffice. It didn't. She just stood there, watching him.

"It's possible, probably not very likely — that one of these children saw something they didn't tell anyone about, not because they were trying to be secretive but because they just didn't think of it."

She said nothing.

"Yeah, it's a long shot, but we have to chase every rabbit down every hole."

"But how will these things—?"

"For the same reason you had the children bring them in — to put the children at ease. If I can get them to talk to me about something easy, that might serve as a springboard to some other unrelated thing."

Lame. Though she didn't say so, it was clear she thought he was on a fool's errand. T.J. Hamilton would have pointed out "they picked the right man for the job."

The room filled with children, not rowdy, cheerful children, though. Subdued. Quiet. As soon as the final bell rang outside in the hallway, Brice stepped to the front of the room. Before he had a chance to ask his first question, the children began to interrogate him.

"Why can't you find Riley?" asked a bespectacled little boy in the front seat on the first row. "The FBI knows everything.

They find lost kids all the time. My mom said so. Why can't they find Riley?"

"We're doing everything we can and you can help by answering a few questions."

"I don't want to answer questions," said a sour-faced little girl seated beside the terrarium where Bambi was probably chowing down on a still-live grasshopper. "Why do we have to?"

Brice wanted to respond, "Because I'm bigger than you are and I have a gun." Instead he said, "You want to help Riley come home, don't you?"

She nodded.

"Even if you don't understand why I'm asking these questions, you still need to answer them fully and truthfully. Deal?"

The children murmured among themselves. A couple said, "Deal." Most just stared at him.

He picked up a well-worn teddy bear off Riley's desk.

"Whose is this?"

A chubby little boy in the back row reluctantly raised his hand.

"I don't sleep with it," he said, making it clear he wasn't anybody's wimp.

"Why did you bring it?"

"It belonged to my dad. But he didn't sleep with it either! I keep it on my bed to remind me of my dad — he's in Afghanistan. I throw it on the floor when I go to bed at night."

Brice had the same basic exchange with every one of the students.

The little girl who put the china doll on Riley's desk had gotten it for Christmas. Her grandmother made china dolls.

The boy who'd provided the tractor wanted to be a farmer, like his uncle.

The baseball glove belonged to a little boy who — duh — loved baseball.

So it went with the matchbox car, the stuffed Ninja Turtle, the Han Solo light saber, the Hulk action figure doll and the rabbit's foot. Most of the items had been purchased for the children themselves, which ruled them out. Still, Brice took down the name of the child and notes on the item each had placed on Riley's desk.

"When's Riley coming back?" a little boy asked as Brice opened the door to leave. "Me and him, we was gonna play *Angry Birds* tomorrow at my house. We play every Saturday." He sighed elaborately. "It's the only game my mom will let me play. Will he be back by then?"

"I hope so."

His cellphone rang as he was walking out of the building.

"You want to tell me what you're doing at the school?" The condescension in the senior FBI agent's voice was thicker than clabbered milk. How'd Nakamura know where Brice was? Like the little girl said, the FBI knows everything.

"I didn't agree to become lawn art in my own front yard. I'm concentrating on what I can do that you can't."

"And that is?"

"Get the locals to open up to me. You charge in here like" — he caught himself before he said a kamikaze pilot over Pearl Harbor — "Sherman marching through Atlanta and nobody's going to tell you anything. I'm working to get people — children, specifically — to relax and maybe they'll think of something they didn't know they knew."

"And what did you find out?"

"Nothing. Yet."

The beat of silence that followed spoke volumes.

"I'm giving a status briefing in fifteen minutes."

That was it and then the line went dead.

As he drove back to the courthouse, Brice called Bailey and found out that she, T.J. and Dobbs were on their way to Bartlesville.

"There was nothing on Riley's desk that was an obvious link to a child killed in a car accident in 1997."

He didn't like the sound of fatigue and hopelessness he heard in his own voice so he hung up without further comment. As soon as he stepped into the conference room/command center in the courthouse, his eyes were drawn to the clock. There seemed to be more than accusation in the clock face now. Now, he saw condemnation. Riley Campbell had last been seen in the hallway of Corruthers Elementary School Wednesday afternoon. Today was Friday. The percentage of kidnapped children found alive after forty-eight hours was ... miniscule.

It was clear Bailey didn't want him and Dobbs to see how disappointed she was that Brice had found out nothing from talking to the children in Riley's classroom. She'd a'made a lousy poker player.

The first newspaper they tried was the Bartlesville Bee. The building was undergoing renovations. Only a small portion of the front office was visible, with the rest of the interior behind plastic sheeting to keep the clouds of drywall dust at bay.

The microfiche reader was in the part of the building quarantined by dust and the receptionist couldn't be persuaded to let them brave the contamination at their own risks.

T.J. tried to talk her into allowing them to take the files with them to the library —

"No library in town," she said. "And the files are stored back there with the reader. I'm not going to go digging through that mess to find them. Come back in a couple of weeks. No, make that a month."

It took more than an hour to get from Bartlesville to the next community with a weekly newspaper. T.J. thought about telling Bailey that the distance between the two communities "as the crow flies" probably wasn't twenty miles. But driving on the winding roads was already making her carsick and she didn't need the added stress.

Simpsonville's newspaper was located in a small office in the town's only "strip mall" — a single long structure that contained the Dollar General Store and Beddingfield's Insurance Agency on the other end and a vacant space in between.

"Prosperous little burg," Bailey commented when they got out of the car.

"More prosperous than some," Dobbs said. "Looks like the electricity's still on."

It took less than five minutes for them to discover their hour's drive had been wasted. The reason the newspaper was occupying space in the "new building" was because the old newspaper office had burned down a couple of years before. All the records had burned with it.

"You could have told me that yesterday when I called," Dobbs told the bored twenty-something working the front desk.

"You didn't ask."

Half an hour later, the voice from Bailey's iPhone's Maps app instructed her to turn left on Yosemite Road.

"How come you got a British accent on that thing?" T.J. asked, when the voice pronounced the street *Yo-sem-ity*. "Around here, they call it Yo-se-mite."

"I just like the sound of it, so crisp and official. I always wanted to go to England."

"It's one of those nice-place-to-visit-but-I-wouldn't-want-to-live-there destinations," Dobbs pointed out from the back seat as Bailey turned from Yosemite to Baldwin Street.

"And you know that how?"

"I lived there for a couple of weeks. Left as soon as I could. Got tired of hearing dumb-American as a hyphenated word."

As T.J. recalled, Dobbs had closed a financial deal during that "couple of weeks" that had netted the man six figures.

From the front passenger side of Bailey's little blue Honda Accord, T.J. looked out at the little town of Hemphill, which might have had a couple of thousand residents, making it the biggest town anywhere around. It actually looked prosperous, lawns well kept and trimmed, neat brick houses. There was the requisite Civil War Memorial in the town square, dedicated to the soldiers who'd fought on *both sides* of the conflict, which he thought was considerate of them. But this was, after all, *West* Virginia, a state hunked out of Virginia because the residents sided with the North rather than the Confederacy. Maybe more than any other border state, West Virginia had split — literally — down the middle on the slavery issue and maybe more than in any other border state, the conflict had torn families apart.

Bailey pulled into a parking space opposite a row of buildings where the disembodied British voice had directed them. Across the street from the lot was the Crenshaw County Water District Office, the Hair Affair Beauty Parlor, the Hemphill Enterprise and the Hemphill City Police Department.

There was a bell on the door when they entered and a young woman whose smile was so perfect it had to have cost her parents a fortune in orthodontist bills stepped up behind the counter.

"May I help you with something?"

"We called yesterday, asking about a story in one of your old newspapers."

"Yes, you talked to me. You were looking for a traffic accident, right?" When Dobbs nodded, she gestured for them to follow her. She went through a half-swinging door in the middle of the counter and led them to the back of the building. "If a story's more than fifteen years old, we only have the summaries searchable online on the newspaper's website.

We're gradually converting the old files, but anything dating back before 2000 is still in the bound volumes up here."

Before them was an old wooden staircase. The door at the top opened to a cavernous storage space that spanned the width and breadth of the whole building below. It was filled with boxes, crates and old equipment, outdated machinery made useless by computerized technology. T.J. suspected the old printing press in the back corner was a genuine antique and would probably command a good price on eBay.

In the back portion of the room were shelves filled with gigantic books. Each had bound between its covers actual newspapers, six months per volume.

The receptionist walked along the shelves, searching the covers.

"You don't know the exact date the accident happened, right, just the year?"

Bailey nodded.

"We're a weekly newspaper, twenty-six issues in each book."

She walked past the books, reading the spines.

"January to July, 1994, July to December 1994, January to July 1995 …"

When she came to the volumes for 1997, she pulled one large book off the shelf and carried it to a long standing table in the middle of the room.

Dobbs got the other volume for 1997.

"It won't take you long to look through these, I wouldn't think. You won't have to search the whole newspaper. A multiple-fatality wreck in this county — the story would be on the front page."

The woman looked around.

"Sorry it's so dusty up here. You can haul the books downstairs where there's air conditioning if you get too hot, but it probably won't take you long to find what you're looking for."

She turned to go, then turned back. "I hope you don't mind spiders. This place is full of them."

Bailey visibly flinched, looked around like there might be something crawling on the floor near her. She saw T.J. notice.

"I did a certifiably dumb thing this morning; woke up before sunrise, couldn't go back to sleep, and got to thinking about Bambi. So I googled tarantulas."

"And ...?" Dobbs said, as he dusted off the big book and opened it.

"I guess it was 'horrified fascination' that sent me down Google rabbit trails I never should have let myself travel. You know what I mean: 'the ten most aggressive spiders in the world,' or the 'five deadliest spiders in North America.' That kind of thing."

She gave a full-body shudder.

"They's a whole lot of things in life you's better off not knowin'."

"I don't know that I agree with that," Dobbs said. He opened the book he'd set on the table and gestured to the other. "You take January to July. I'll take July to December. Obviously, the wreck didn't happen in the wintertime. You saw green outside the windows in the vision." He continued his thought as he began to page through the book. "What did you find out about spiders that you didn't already know?"

"Nightmare material!" Bailey took a breath and began to rattle off facts rapid-fire. "The jumping spider can jump like fifty times its own body length, the bite from a Sydney funnel-web spider kills in minutes — and it'll come after you and *keep biting*, the wolf spider doesn't have a web, it goes out hunting prey and *leaves puncture wounds* ..." She took a breath. "Okay, I did find out that a tarantula is *not* the meanest dog in the junk-yard, but they'll *all* bite you if you get in their space." She looked around on the floor. "Can we stop talking about this?"

She stepped up next to Dobbs and watched as he began to page through the book.

T.J. opened the first book to the January 3, 1997, issue. He flipped through it to January 10, then to January 17, scanning the pages. The newspapers weren't big, usually an A and B section, about twenty pages each. Though he knew the wreck happened during warm weather, and though the receptionist had said the story would be on the front page, he paged through every month and every page of every issue.

They had been looking for only a few minutes when he paged past the last of the B section on June 18 and saw the front page of June 25. The lead story was about a school board meeting in which the superintendent had obviously been fired. The story below that was about a wreck on US 68 in which two people had been killed.

It wasn't a triple fatality, still …

"Here's something," he said. "Not exactly what we're looking for, but …"

He read the story aloud.

"A squirrel hunter came upon a grisly scene on Friday when he discovered a car that had obviously run off the road and crashed into the woods. Hidden from view, the wreck had gone undetected for some time."

Bailey and Dobbs abandoned what they were doing and came to stand beside him. T.J.'s stomach cinched into a knot as he continued to read.

"There were two people dead in the vehicle and a small camper lay upside down farther up the hillside." He needed a little sip of air to continue. "A little girl was found in the overturned camper — *alive.*"

Chapter Fifteen

SEATED at a table in the command center beneath the accusing clock on the wall, Nakamura was peering into the screen of a laptop.

When he saw Brice, there was no greeting and he simply said, "Don't suppose you've got a monitor around somewhere, do you? A bigger screen?"

Brice shook his head.

Nakamura gestured toward the small screen.

"After a while, this print all runs together."

Brice made a mental note to dispatch a deputy to the library to borrow one of their monitors — two, no, three of them. Then Nakamura stood and the other agents stopped what they were doing and turned toward him. Elijah Gascoyne and Nikki Trimboli were stationed at the Campbells' house to operate the recording/tracing equipment in the less and less likely event of a ransom call. Gomez and Arya were working at computers and Hardesty was posting on the bulletin board the pictures of missing children from the area. Excluding Pittsburgh, there were fewer than half a dozen missing children for a hundred miles around Shadow Rock in every direction. All those children had been missing for a long time; none of them was from Kavanaugh County.

Riley Campbell had the distinction of being the first kidnapped child in Shadow Rock's two-hundred-year history.

"Here's where we stand," Nakamura said and gave a rundown on the developments in the investigation — brief, because they'd spent the past two days eliminating possibilities, hoping to seine out suspects and instead had ended up with a handful of nothing. The FBI, Brice's deputies, the state police and the municipal Shadow Rock police had run background checks through NCIC, the National Crime Information Center, on everyone who had been on the school property at any time in the week before the boy disappeared. Because of the festival setup and the carnival, that list totaled more than 150 people.

The FBI had also run a TLO check on all the names. TLO, a technology for locating, researching and finding the connections between people, had flagged two names.

"One is a carney, his name is …" Nakamura leaned closer to the computer screen. "Edgar Ray Garrison, forty-one. The address on his driver's license is in Cincinnati. He has a rap sheet, but nothing serious. Petty crimes, kiting checks, several misdemeanor theft charges that were plea-bargained from burglary charges. Only violence is one domestic abuse report but the victim refused to testify."

"What was he doing at the school?" Hardesty asked.

"One of the two operators of the Tilt-A-Whirl ride at the carnival." Nakamura sat back and rubbed his eyes and Brice thought to wonder if the senior agent had slept at all since he'd arrived in Shadow Rock. "A carnival came to our neighborhood in San Francisco every summer when I was a kid and I always rode the Tilt-A-Whirl. Made me throw up every single time, but I always went back for more."

That was the first bit of personal information the agent had shared since Brice had met him.

"The other name is Sylvia Marie Douglas, thirty-five, a.k.a. Wanda June Adams, a.k.a. Alisha Marie Williams, last known permanent address is in Buffalo, New York. She runs the arcade booth. She has been arrested for prostitution half a dozen times in as many cities, and for possessing with the intent to sell weed, crack, meth, bennies, roofies ... Tidy Bowl."

"A woman?" Arya asked, shoving his Gandhi glasses up on his nose.

"Doesn't fit the standard profile, but right now we don't have enough evidence to come up with a specific one."

Nakamura pushed his chair back from the table and looked at Brice.

"You and Gomez go have a talk with Garrison. Hardesty and I will pay Miss Douglas/Adams/Williams a visit."

Even after the boy's disappearance, the activities of the Cottonwood Festival had rocked on as scheduled, with what appeared to Brice to be something like an insectile frenzy of cheeriness. But in an effort to distance the festival from any hint of suspicion, organizers had banished the carnival, and the Wasuski Brothers had been forced to move the enterprise and set up the equipment and rides on a vacant lot a few blocks from the boat dock on Whispering Mountain Lake. It was nothing like as lucrative a location as a festival, and when Brice and Agent Gomez arrived, everything was shut up tight. No one was outside the equipment trailers or the campers used by the employees.

"Somebody skipped," Brice told Gomez as he pulled up beside the carnival office in the largest of the camper trailers. "I counted five campers when the carnival was set up next to the school." Now, there were only four.

"Let's find out who bailed and why," she said.

Of all the agents, Gomez alone appeared to Brice to have an emotional stake in the case. He'd caught her looking at the accusing clock, saw her face tighten when the other agents dispassionately discussed the boy's dwindling chances for survival. She was too old for this to be her first kidnapping, but he sensed it had somehow become personal. Maybe she had a kid Riley's age.

Gomez stepped up on the portable porch unit on the front of the trailer and banged on the door.

"This is the FBI, open up."

Nothing.

She banged harder. "I said, open—"

A disheveled man in a dirty wife-beater t-shirt appeared, a cigarette dangling from his lower lip in Humphrey Bogart style. The reek of tobacco and maybe some other burning weed wafted out when he opened the door and immediately launched into a rant.

"You can't keep us here, you know that. We got a right to move on. We ain't making no money with parents scared to let their kids out of their sight. We're moving out!"

"Mister …?" Gomez prompted.

"Bosky, Leland Bosky."

"Mr. Bosky, you're moving out when we say you're moving out," Brice said.

A sly look found fox features in the man's face, highlighted them almost as if he were undergoing a moon-driven trans-formation.

"I got friends in high places, you know, Sheriff. One word from me, just one word and you could lose your badge over this."

"I got friends, too, Mr. Bosky. At the county health depart-ment, the state gaming commission, the West Virginia Depart-ment of Amusement Rides. One word from me … well, actually two words — "surprise inspection" — and you could lose your business license—"

"Okay, okay, we'll stick. What do you want?"

"For starters, who left?" Gomez asked.

"Left?"

"One of the trailers that was at the school isn't here. Whose is it, why'd they leave and where'd they go?"

"Oh, that. It's just the Dentons, Marge and Harry. They run the ring toss. I got up this morning and they was gone. I own all the rest of the trailers but they own theirs, so it ain't up to me where they go."

"What can you tell us about them?"

"I got a file. We require licenses and releases on all—"

"Let's have a look at that file," she said.

"I'll have to find it …" The man looked put out.

"Edgar Garrison," Brice said. "Where's he?"

The man gestured toward the last trailer in the line.

"That's the trailer Ed uses. Don't see his truck, though, so he ain't there right now."

"I'll get the Denton file," Gomez said.

Brice took the handoff. "And I'll go check on Mr. Garrison."

Crossing behind the merry-go-round, Brice went down to the end of the line of trailers. The last one was parked near the edge of the lot next to a fence that gave way to a line of bushes. Beyond the bushes was a warehouse.

Brice knocked on the door, thought he heard movement inside, but no one answered. He knocked again.

"Edgar Garrison, this is Kavanaugh County Sheriff Brice McGreggor. Open the door."

He definitely heard a sound this time — the door on the other side of the trailer banging open.

Jumping off the metal porch, Brice ran around the trailer. He drew his Glock, paused at the end of the trailer, peeked out around it and saw no one, but a battered Chevy pickup truck was parked out of sight there.

Brice took off toward the bushes after Garrison. He had no way to contact Agent Gomez, so he spoke into his shoulder microphone, panting, as he ran.

"Need backup at the carnival by the dock. Suspect fled the

scene. Unit Two, proceed to Taylor Avenue and approach the Bufford Gate Company Warehouse from that side. Unit Five, take up a position at the intersection of Halstead Street and Taylor Avenue. I'm following on foot."

Brice raced around the bushes and still saw no one. Running along the fence line, he came out into an alley. This was the old part of Shadow Rock where streets and alleys had been paved with cobblestones. Weeds grew up between the stones here, though, had dislodged some, making the surface lumpy and treacherous. Following the alley, looking right to left, Brice came to the north side of the warehouse. He ran along the building to the corner and then took a quick peek around it. Again, he saw no one, but there was a door there. Looking up and down the alley, Brice could see nowhere else the man could have gone.

Approaching along the wall to the door on the knob side, he pulled his gun back toward his body. The door swung outward and he intended to shove it open, then back away and shine his flashlight into the dark interior of the warehouse before entering.

But apparently Garrison was waiting just inside the door because as soon as Brice grasped the knob and turned it, the door burst open. Garrison exploded out of it — probably six feet tall, pudgy, with a scraggly blond beard and mustache and a bald head. He held a pipe in his left hand, swinging it with all his strength at Brice's head. A pipe wielded like a baseball bat was a lethal weapon.

Brice dodged backward, but the pipe still scraped his radio mic off his shoulder and slammed into the back of his hand with such force his fingers went numb and the gun flew out, hit the side of the building and clunked to the ground. The mic dangled behind Brice on its elastic cord.

Garrison drew the pipe back for a second blow, but before he could strike, Brice got inside the swing, slammed his left shoulder into the pudgy man's body and with his back to

Garrison wrapped his left arm around Garrison's pipe-swinging arm, hugged it tight to his chest. Now Garrison had no leverage. When he tried to free his arm by lurching forward, Brice used the momentum of the movement to swing the man full circle, slam his back against the side of the building and pin him up against it.

Grabbing Garrison's wrist with his right hand, Brice hammered the side of the man's head with the back of his left elbow, two staggering blows, then wrapped both hands around Garrison's wrist. Shoving upward on the back side of the hand holding the pipe, Brice forced the fingers to open.

The pipe clattered to the cobblestones.

Still clutching the man's wrist in his left hand, Brice slid his right hand under Garrison's forearm and grabbed his own forearm, creating a vice. All he had to do now was lift Garrison's arm *upward*, push his wrist *downward* and the man's elbow would snap — pop outward like a twig.

It would be a devastating injury. Half a dozen repair surgeries and he still might not be able to scratch his own nose. And Brice had every right to deliver it. The man had tried to kill him; Brice was justified in using deadly force to subdue him.

But if he broke Garrison's arm, it would be hours, maybe days before they'd be able to question him. Riley Campbell didn't have that kind of time.

Instead of snapping the man's elbow, Brice stretched out his left leg and used it as a lever to toss Garrison to the ground on his back. He twisted Garrison's hand sideways, causing him to reflexively roll to his stomach, then dropped one knee into the middle of his back. Pulling his left wrist back and then his right, Brice cuffed him, then lifted his cuffed hands off his back to check for weapons in his waistband.

Rising to his feet, Brice stood still, breathing hard, more from the adrenaline dump into his bloodstream than from exertion. The whole altercation had lasted less than thirty seconds. Half-hour-long fight sequences in movies were pure fantasy.

His mic still dangled uselessly behind him on its extending cord, bouncing up and down. Brice grabbed at it, missed, grabbed again, realizing how ridiculous he must look before he finally snagged the cord and pulled the mic to his lips.

"Suspect in custody. Repeat, suspect in custody."

Dispatch acknowledged his transmission and he checked out the back of his right hand where Garrison had hit it with the pipe. It was still mostly numb, but the mother of all bruises was coming up there, the skin turning purple and swelling. Since he could flex all his fingers, he'd apparently suffered no serious damage, though.

Taking two steps to where his gun lay on the ground, he picked it up and holstered it. He reached down and pulled Garrison to his feet by his cuffed hands as two deputies screeched cruisers from opposite directions to a stop in the alley. Agent Gomez approached, trailing the carnival manager behind her like the tail on a kite.

"You alright, Sheriff?" Fletch asked as he got out of his cruiser.

Brice nodded.

Reeling off a string of colorful expletives, Garrison disparaged not only Brice's heritage, but the profession of his mother and the proclivities of his siblings. Brice shoved the man at Fletcher.

"Attempted murder of a police officer. Resisting arrest. He's all yours."

Fletcher began intoning Garrison's rights as he dragged him by an elbow the man was lucky still functioned to the cruiser. Gomez reached out, took Brice's hand, turned it over and looked a question at him.

"Pipe."

She cringed.

"Ouch. That's ugly."

Two more cruisers arrived and one of them carried Haruto Nakamura. Brice nodded toward the man Fletch was loading into the back seat of his cruiser.

"He very much did *not* want to talk to me."

"Wonder why not," Nakamura said. Brice turned to the carnival manager.

"You own these trailers — that's what you said. Do we have your permission to search this one?"

"Of course you can search it. Throw all his stuff out on the ground for all I care. Bringing the law down on me like he done, I hope you find a dead body under his pillow."

There was no mouldering corpse anywhere on the premises, but the contents of a shoebox in the bottom drawer of his dresser explained Garrison's reticence to talk to the police.

Brice edged the lid back with his fingertip, then called out to Nakamura, who was searching the living room while Gomez tackled the kitchen. "Appears the guy has a good-sized collection of kiddie porn."

Gomez entered from the kitchen carrying a plastic sandwich bag full of ice and handed it to Brice.

"Put this on that hand. Too late to stop the worst of the swelling, but it's better than nothing."

Nakamura appeared in the doorway holding a CD in his gloved hand.

"This was in his computer. I didn't watch much of it but I can tell you it isn't *A Charlie Brown Christmas*."

Chapter Sixteen

Bailey gasped.

"The little girl I painted ... she was *alive?*"

T.J. continued to read.

"The child had obviously been trapped when the camper was torn loose from the vehicle, rolled halfway down the embankment and came to rest on the roof."

Dobbs reached over and patted Bailey's hand. She was trembling, her eyes wide and horrified.

"Dead at the scene were David Whitfield, 26, and his wife Susan, 25, from Charleston. Their seven-year-old daughter, Caitlyn, was rushed by ambulance to Crenshaw County Hospital where she was listed Friday as critical. No further information on her condition was available at press time."

"Alive," Bailey said, her voice soft, full of awe and horror. "She was alive when they found her!" She took a breath. "Seven years old." She turned to him then, her voice anguished. "That little girl was seven years old!"

"Is that all?" Dobbs asked. "No more information about the wreck?"

T.J. thumbed through the volume to the next week's issue,

hoping for a follow-up story, but there was nothing. Nothing in the two weeks following that, either.

"The byline on the story is Henry Burkhold, Managing Editor," T.J. said. "Let's see if he's still around."

Bailey took a picture of the newspaper story with her phone, then they returned the books to their spaces on the shelves and went downstairs to talk to the receptionist, who informed them that Henry Burkhold had died in 2010.

"The story quotes Ben Aberdeen, an Emergency Medical Technician who worked the accident," T.J. said. "Do you know where we might find him?"

"Now *that* I can help you with. Ben's the fire chief now. You'll find him at the fire station, the big two-story building at the far end of Main Street."

As they left the newspaper office, T.J. put his arm around Bailey's shoulders.

"You okay, sugar?"

"I thought she was dead. She *looked* dead. I guess she was just unconscious, but … with her eyes open? *Caitlyn Whitfield.* Can you imagine what something like that would do to a seven-year-old? Maybe she's still …"

"Let's not count on that. They might have found her alive, but that don't mean she … You said you wasn't 'connected' to her, remember. So ain't likely she's …"

The firemen were out front of the big building washing the tanker truck when Dobbs and the others pulled up. They directed the three inside, said the fire chief was making dinner for the other on-duty men.

A burley man of about fifty, thick-shouldered and muscular with a bald head and a prominent nose, was pouring the water off a pot of steaming spaghetti when they stepped into the kitchen/dining area behind the front office.

"Excuse me," Dobbs said, and introduced the three of them. "We're looking for Fire Chief Ben Aberdeen."

"That'd be me," he said. "Can you hold on a second?"

He finished draining the water, steam forming a cloud above the strainer, then dumped the mountain of spaghetti into a huge bowl, dropped a couple of dollops of butter on it and began to stir.

"Early lunch," he said. "We were on a run at dawn and worked up an appetite. Grease fire at the McKendricks' place. Smoke damage, but it coulda been a lot worse. You'll have to excuse me while I finish up."

"Let us help," Bailey said, and picked up plates from a stack of them on the counter and began to deal them around the table like playing cards.

The man looked a bit surprised, but smiled. "What can I do for you folks?"

"We're looking for information about someone who was killed—" Dobbs stopped. He wanted to believe that wasn't the case, but wasn't hopeful. He'd seen too many pictures of the dead people T.J.'s mother had painted years ago to believe that this one time would be different. He didn't think the ... magic ... worked that way. "Well, someone who was in a traffic accident here eighteen years ago."

"Eighteen years? Good luck with that."

"We went to the newspaper office and found the story and you're quoted in it. You were one of the EMTs who worked the wreck."

"I was an EMT for twelve years, so I worked a lot of wrecks."

"I think you'd remember this one, though. It was ... different." Aberdeen set the bowl of spaghetti on the table and returned to the stove to get the large pot of sauce still simmering there.

"The car went off the road and rolled," T.J. said. "Didn't nobody find the wreck for—"

He stopped when the fire chief turned to face him suddenly, his face ashen.

"Nobody found it until a squirrel hunter stumbled on the car in the woods." His voice was hollow.

"That's right," T.J. said. "The newspaper story said that the two adults, David and Susan Whitfield, were killed, but—"

"Their little girl, Caitlyn, survived." The big man's face was expressionless. He stood in the middle of the room, the spoon hanging limp in his hand, dripping spaghetti sauce on the floor.

A buzzer suddenly went off somewhere in the building. Dobbs was afraid it was a fire alarm and the man who could give them information about the child Bailey had painted, the little girl she'd connected to, would go rushing out the door to put out a fire.

But apparently, the buzzer signaled lunch rather than a fire because the firefighters who'd been out front when they arrived, plus a couple who hadn't, came through the double doors at the end of the room, laughing and talking as they came.

"I been smelling that spaghetti sauce all morning and I'm about to drown," said a sandy-haired young woman, dressed as were the others in a t-shirt and jeans, and slip-on shoes.

"You make any of that garlic bread …?"

The woman didn't finish her sentence. She and the others had noticed the fire chief's expression and stopped.

"Something wrong, Ben?" asked the woman who'd wanted garlic bread.

The fire chief looked at her as if called back from some awful dream.

"No," he said. "Nothing … I, yes, something's wrong." He turned to Dobbs and the others. "What do you want to know about this wreck for?" He sounded belligerent, but Dobbs spotted it for what it was — the backwash from painful memories he didn't want to relive. T.J. swooped in to ease the tension.

Ever-intuitive T.J.

"We're tryin' to locate the little girl, Caitlyn," he said.

"What do you want her for?" the fire chief demanded, with more emotion than was appropriate. It was clear the other men picked up on that.

"Ben, you need help with something?" one of them asked.

"We're hoping she can help us save someone's life," Dobbs said.

That part was true, in a convoluted sort of way. They were trying to save Riley Campbell. And given that they could never explain that to anybody, they had concocted a story. Dobbs was not by nature a deceitful person, and neither were T.J. and Bailey, but they had decided helping to find a kidnapped child was reason enough. As Dobbs listened to T.J. haul out the story, he marveled at how adept he was at making it seem not just realistic, but compelling. Shoot, if he'd been listening, he'd have wanted to help.

"Caitlyn's family lost track of her years ago," T.J. said. "Now, her cousin — she's nine years old — needs a kidney transplant or she'll die and she has a blood type that's real rare. Oh, it's an awful long shot, but them parents will do anything ... and the best they can determine, this Caitlyn Whitfield had the same blood type."

The fire chief bought the story, looked stricken, but said he doubted the little girl who'd been in the wreck was still alive.

Dobbs saw Bailey take the words like a blow to the belly.

"I just worked the wreck, that's all ... and I went to check on her when she was in the hospital."

"Would you tell us about it?" T.J. asked, holding up his hand before the man could protest. "I'm a grunt, too. I get it."

It wasn't until then that Dobbs noticed the USMC tattoo on Aberdeen's arm. T.J. didn't miss a thing, knew just how to play to their shared military service.

"I know what you've seen, things that's hard to talk about.

But the more we know about what happened to this little girl … any little thing, it might help us locate her."

The man let out a sigh, then started to rise.

"If I'm gonna tell this, you guys don't have to hear it."

"Sit down, Ben," said the sandy-haired woman. "Go ahead."

The fire chief shook his head.

"Not this one. This isn't a story you hear and then eat a plate of spaghetti."

He got to his feet and motioned Dobbs, T.J. and Bailey to follow. When they were seated around his desk in his small office, he told them the story.

Chapter Seventeen

NAKAMURA WAS POINTING out that the pipe-wielding Edgar Garrison's kiddie porn collection was exclusively female — "and these guys don't do crossover" — when he suddenly fell silent. Brice followed his gaze to the approaching deputy and the man's face silenced him, too.

"Sheriff, we just got a call — there's a little girl missing from the park."

It took less than five minutes, lights and siren, to get from the sheriff's office to Meadows Park. Nakamura rode with Brice in his cruiser, the black SUV with federal plates and a contingent of FBI agents following in the line of siren-wailing vehicles to the scene. The two men said little on the way, each a prisoner to the ugly but inescapable conclusion that unless these children were linked to each other in some as-yet-undetermined way, this was some sort of spree. Two children in three days. A psycho at the mercy of his own madness. Psychos on sprees grew bolder and bolder — and consequently, they made mistakes. The job of law enforcement was to spot those mistakes — fast, because the clock was ticking. Not just on these two children but on the whack-job's next victim. Psychos didn't stop until you caught them. Or killed them.

Meadows Park was a neighborhood park, four blocks long and three wide, with big leafy trees and lots of shrubs, bushes and flowers. A small-children's playground that had stationary climbing equipment a-la a McDonald's play space and soft wood shavings instead of dirt or grass on the ground beneath occupied the west end. Soccer fields and tennis courts were on the east end. Picnic tables were scattered all around, in the shade of the big trees, looked like they'd all been freshly painted — bright colors, red, orange, purple, green and blue.

A concession stand with public bathrooms was located in the center of the park and a parking lot opened off the south side. A decorative creek-stone fence a foot wide and about three feet tall ran the length of the north side. The only way to get into the park from that side was through the single opening in the fence midway. Or by climbing over it — easily doable but a monumental inconvenience, as voiced by countless protesting citizens at city council meetings over the years. To no avail.

On-street parallel parking was allowed on the narrow stretch of gravel between the fence and the street. Most people used the parking lot on the opposite side of the park instead, so there were seldom any cars there. Brice knew that keeping the narrow street mostly clear of parked cars was the reason the city council refused to make more entrances in the fence.

Three little girls had been playing under a tree in the park half an hour before. Sherri Lynn Williamson, Beth Ann Bradley and Christi Nicole Strickland. Now, Christi was missing.

A swarm of deputies, state police troopers and FBI agents questioned witnesses and took down the names and contact information for every human being who'd been in the park at the time of the kidnapping. The Cottonwood Festival next to the school had swelled that list to 150 people.

A youth league soccer game at the east end of the park had swelled this list to three hundred.

Nakamura nodded at Gascoyne and said to Brice, "Eli and I will talk to the Williamson girl. You and Hardesty talk to Beth Ann."

That was significant. Nakamura was like any good coach. Winning the game was the only thing that mattered and he relentlessly played only his best players. Apparently, Brice had finally claimed a spot in the starting lineup.

A few minutes later, a little blonde girl, her hair in a pixie cut, was describing how Christi "was there and then she wasn't."

Beth Ann Bradley wore a Wonder Woman t-shirt and sat on the bench of the picnic table with her mother draped over her like a cowl. The crowd beyond the line of black-and-yellow police tape was swelling by the second and the fright-ened/angry tone of the unintelligible grumble from them was distracting the little girl. She kept looking past Brice toward the crowd, probably hoping she'd spot Christi there.

Lying in grass that needed mowing where the girls had been playing was a small case with Barbie dolls and Barbie accessories piled in it, plus other miscellaneous Barbie equip-ment including a motorcycle and a camper.

The missing child, eleven-year-old Christi Nicole Strick-land, was in the fifth grade at Madison Elementary School, on the other side of town from Corruthers Elementary where Riley was in the first grade. Riley was small for his age, Melody McCallum had said, just seven but looked maybe five — forty, maybe forty-five pounds. At eleven, Christi was a big girl, chubby, ten to fifteen pounds overweight — almost twice his size.

"I don't know where she went," Beth Ann said and started to cry.

"You need to leave her alone now," said her mother, crushing the child to her considerable bosom. "She's told you all she knows." She started to rise. "I'm taking her home now."

"Please, sit down, Mrs. Bradley," Hardesty said. He had a booming James Earl Jones voice, but it was cranked down to soft now. Still, he was an imposing man and Brice considered that Nakamura should have teamed up with him instead of putting the two "giants" together. But that would have put Brice with Gascoyne. No, this was better.

"We don't mean to upset Beth Ann, but we have a few more questions we need to ask her," he said.

Cora Bradley turned belligerent. "I said we were done here! Beth Ann has told you everything she knows. She's upset, and she needs—"

Brice cranked up his West Virginia accent to match the level of the mother's, his voice soothing.

"Now, if it was Beth Ann who was the little girl missin', you'd want her friends to do everything they could to help police find her — why, you know you would."

Hardesty was sitting on the other side of the little girl and briefly caught Brice's eye. Just the glance told Brice the agent had picked up on the accent, and would likely let Brice do most of the talking, since his own Pittsburgh accent — though not as pronounced as Gascoyne's — was still thick enough to label him immediately as an outsider from Away From Here.

"Beth Ann, honey, would you mind sittin' over here by me so I can hear everything you say clearly?"

He patted a space on the bench beside him — beyond the reach of her strangling mother.

Pulling out of her mother's arms was like separating two pieces of Velcro.

"I know you're upset and scared, *sugar,*" he said, slathering his words in *southern.* "But I need you to focus on me, can you do that?"

The little girl nodded, seemed more relaxed sitting beside Brice, without her mother choking her.

"Now, please start at the beginnin' again and tell me everything that happened today, startin' with when you got to the park."

The little girl explained haltingly that she and Christi and Sherri Lynn Williamson — the little girl Nakamura was questioning at the other picnic table — had agreed to meet at the park to play Barbie dolls.

"Christi and Sherri Lynn live close," she said, indicating the neighborhood on the other side of the street from the park. "But Mama has to bring me."

"School let out early — of course, you know that," her mother interrupted. "And I brought her directly here, never dreamed it wouldn't be safe to drop my little girl off in a public park. What's the world coming to when you can't let your children out of your sight? And where were the police when—?"

Deputy Fletcher appeared at Brice's side like a genie out of a bottle.

"Mrs. Bradley, I'd like to talk to you, please. Won't take but a minute, but we need to know what you saw when you dropped Beth Ann off."

"I didn't see anything. I wasn't even at this end of the—"

"You might think you saw nothing at all, but sometimes the smallest detail — something you weren't even aware of seeing at the time ..." He oozed politeness as he got her to her feet and began to shoo her away from the picnic table "Step over here with me, if you would, so we can talk privately."

Translate that: Come over here and prattle in my ear so the sheriff can find out what your daughter knows.

With an almost indiscernible nod, Brice acknowledged his gratitude to Fletcher. The sheriff needed to find out everything he could while images were still fresh in the little girl's mind and before she had a chance to absorb the recollections of others and make them her own. Maybe this little girl had seen the kidnapper, could describe him. Christi Strickland's three-hour clock was ticking.

Chapter Eighteen

BRICE DRAPED a smile on his face like hanging a surgeon's mask from his ears, but it was authentic enough to fool an eleven-year-old.

"Beth Ann, is this a place you often come to play with your dolls?"

"Uh huh. On Saturdays, when the weather's nice. Today was special 'cause there was no school this afternoon so Mama stopped and got me a Happy Meal and I ate it in the car."

"Do you always play in the same spot?"

She shook her head.

"Just somewhere in the shade. There's more shade under that big tree by the concession stand." She pointed to the building in the center of the park where the restrooms were located. In the small store there, you could buy overpriced candy, soft drinks, nachos, hot dogs and ice cream. "But high school let out early, too, and there were a bunch of teenagers there and this boy and girl were making out — ugh! — so we came here."

Here was a secluded little cubby hole on the north side of the park in the shade of a juniper tree. A tangled, in-need-of-pruning lilac bush stretched out between the tree and the rock fence, dangling over it all the way to the ground on the other side. About twenty feet farther down the fence sat two sand-colored electrical boxes, both the size of washing machines. The bush, boxes and fence blocked the view of the girls on three sides.

"I was sitting over there," Beth Ann said and pointed.

"Would you show me?" Hardesty asked, and stood up.

The little girl got up and walked to a spot between the bush and the electric boxes about ten feet from the rock fence. Brice and Hardesty trailed along behind her.

"You had your back to the wall, right?" Brice asked. Hardesty was drawing a diagram on his notepad.

"Uh, huh. And Sherri Lynn was beside me."

"Her back to the street, too?"

"Mostly, but not all the way. Kinda sideways."

"Where was Christi?"

"She was sitting here."

She took a few steps into the park and turned around to face the fence and the street beyond it.

"The dolls and other stuff is just like it was before Christi left, the best you remember, right?"

The little girl crossed to the spot where she'd been sitting. On the ground there was a pink suitcase that contained a doll's wardrobe, a clear plastic pencil box with accessories — shoes, purses, hats, a tiny belt and what looked like a crumpled parasol. She pointed to the doll in a lawn chair.

"That's my Barbie. Christi was here, with her Barbie and the motorcycle. And Sherri Lynn and I had our Barbies in the camper." She gestured to a toy camper lying on its side in the grass. "Except Sherri Lynn wanted *her* Barbie to drive and it was my turn."

"To drive the Barbie camper?"

"Uh huh. I told her it was my turn, that her Barbie got to drive last time, but she said it was different now, since we had them all dressed up for the party and my Barbie's dress wouldn't fit behind the steering wheel. But it would, too. I told her it would, but she said—"

"So you and Sherri Lynn were arguing about your Barbies, is that right?" Hardesty slid the question in softly.

"She was wrong. It was my turn!"

"What was Christi doing?"

"Her Barbie was on the motorcycle and she was waiting for Sherri Lynn to let my Barbie drive so we could take them to the party."

"So Christi was just sitting there, waiting?"

"Yeah, and then Sherri Lynn grabbed the camper and said she was going to take it home, that it was hers and her Barbie should drive. And I told her fine, take it home, Christi and I would play with the motorcycle and the other Barbies. We didn't need her and her old camper anyway."

"Did Christi agree?"

"No, she wasn't sitting there anymore, but I knew she would side with me because Sherri Lynn is always pulling that, saying she'll take her Barbie stuff and go home."

"If Christi wasn't there, where was she?" Hardesty asked.

"I don't know."

"You had to see her leave. She was sitting right across from you."

"All I saw was, she got up and walked away, walked past us toward the fence, so she was behind me where I couldn't see."

"She just got up and walked away?"

"Yeah. I think … we were talking and she … she looked behind us, like there was something she was looking at and she put down the motorcycle and walked away."

"What could she have been looking at?" Hardesty said. "There's nothing here but a rock fence."

"I don't know."

"You didn't turn around to see what she was looking at?" Brice asked.

"That's when Sherri Lynn was saying my Barbie's dress

was too big. But it wasn't either too big."

"Did you hear anything? Maybe somebody was there, on the other side of the fence, and they said something?"

She shook her head. "I just remember she looked up and got up and walked past us."

"Did Christi say anything?" Hardesty asked.

"Uh uh. But I think she was looking at something, *somebody*, maybe. On the other side of the fence. She must have been and she went up to them. That was when Sherri Lynn was threatening to take her camper home and I was mad!"

"So you think it was a person standing there, someone Christi went to talk to, or maybe someone in a car on the street?"

"It was a car!" She brightened that she knew something. "I remember now. Christi got up and walked past us to the street when Sherri Lynn and I were arguing and I heard a car."

"But you didn't see the car?"

"No. I didn't even think about it until now, that there was a car, but there was because I heard the motor running."

"Did you hear the car door close when Christi got in?"

"I didn't hear a door. Just the motor."

"If Christi got into a car, you'd have heard the door closing."

"I didn't hear a car door close."

"So ... did Christi climb over the fence?"

"I guess so. She must have, but I didn't see."

Brice asked her more questions but could get no more information out of her. Hardesty was silent, adding details to the drawing he'd made in his notebook. Beth Ann had not turned to look where Christi had gone but maybe the other little girl had.

He consulted briefly with Nakamura, and then — much to the distress of Mrs. Bradley — the two sets of officers traded places. Brice and Hardesty talked to Sherri Lynn Williamson, Nakamura and Gascoyne talked to Beth Ann.

When they were finished, they compared notes.

The two girls' stories were essentially the same. Neither child heard a car door close. Sherri Lynn didn't even remember hearing a car motor on the other side of the fence. But she did remember something Beth Ann didn't notice. She remembered that when Christi looked up past them, at whatever she saw behind them, she had *smiled*, had put down the toy motorcycle, and walked right by them.

Then the officers tried to fit together the pieces of what the girls had seen so it made sense.

Two hours later, it still didn't.

"So we have a kid who walks into a rock wall and vanishes." Trimboli said. "Doesn't make a sound, doesn't say a word, just — poof!"

"Nobody saw a car pull up beside the fence here," Gascoyne said. "We've asked maybe two hundred people so far and nobody remembers a car."

"But the girls, well, one of them, says she heard a car motor." Brice said. "And she was sitting closest to the fence. The car could have pulled up and left in — what? If there was no conversation—"

"Yeah, and *why* was there no conversation?" Trimboli interjected.

"—the car could have pulled up and pulled away in ... seconds," Brice said. "Could be why nobody noticed it."

"It had to be a car, a vehicle of some kind," said Gomez. "She was there and then she wasn't; how else did she leave so fast?"

"How did that kid get into a car without the other two little girls hearing a car door open or close?" Gascoyne argued.

That was one of a handful of unanswerable questions they'd been grappling with all afternoon.

"So the kid's sitting here, facing the fence and the street, and a car pulls up next to the fence," Nakamura said, then amended when Trimboli started to argue. "Beth Ann *said* she heard a car motor."

Brice and the other agents nodded.

"She gets up, walks past her friends to the fence and ... what? *Climbs* over it, willingly, and then *climbs* in a car window?"

"She had to have climbed the fence willingly," Hardesty said.

He went to the fence, put his right foot on the edge of a rock about ten inches off the ground, and easily swung his other leg over the fence so he was seated on top of it, straddling it. Then he swung his left leg over and hopped to the ground.

"So I'm in a car and I drive up next to the fence, really close." Hardesty feigned being in a car. "The kid's on the other side of the fence. How could I possibly get her into the car against her will? Say I could instantly incapacitate her, I can't just reach out and grab her, lift her over a fence and in a window! I'm a big guy, but that little girl weighed eighty-five, ninety pounds. There's no way somebody reached out a car window, grabbed her, hauled her off the ground — ninety pounds dangling at the end of your outstretched arms — over the fence and into a car. And she didn't make a peep."

"Maybe it was a van, not a car," Trimboli offered.

"Maybe it was a motorcycle or a motor scooter," Gomez said.

"Or a yak," Gascoyne bleated.

"Even if it was a van ..." Hardesty took a couple of steps away from the fence toward the street and stretched his arms out toward it. "I couldn't reach out a van door and pick up that child, lift her over the fence, not from that angle."

"Two kidnappers, then," Gomez put out there. "A team. One's walking along the fence, spots the little girls playing, signals his partner. The partner drives up beside the fence. One or the other of them gets Christi to come within grabbing distance, the guy on the ground chloroforms her, lifts her over the fence and dumps her into the car *through an open window.* That'd work. It would at least be possible. You'd still have to have a really strong guy, but it's possible."

"So where does the second kidnapper go?" Nakamura asked. "Into the car with the little girl?"

"Not unless he climbed in the window, too — no car door closing, remember," Gascoyne said. "He just keeps walking. Walking along … grabs the kid, throws her into the car, keeps right on walking."

"So we're looking for a team of kidnappers. *Two* people — that nobody saw," Brice said. "*Two* kidnappers who snatched Riley off the playground … and nobody saw them there, either?"

"What does it tell us about the kidnapper that he was so brazen?" Trimboli mused. "Grabbing a little boy off a school playground in broad daylight, then two days later a little girl out of a park only a few feet from her friends. If either of those little girls had so much as glanced …"

"Whoever she went off with wasn't just someone she knew," Brice said. "It was someone *she was glad to see*, someone she liked and trusted. She didn't cry for help, didn't make a sound. She *wanted* to go."

Nakamura stood. "I want to know the whereabouts starting at noon today of every adult in that kid's life," he said.

Brice had his phone out, looking at the faces of the two missing children whose pictures were already in the hands of every police officer in five states. Serious Riley Campbell, grinning Christi Strickland. Nakamura looked with him.

"I have to believe there's a connection, that those kids' lives intersect somewhere," the FBI agent said. "We have to find out who was in both their worlds."

From the park, Nakamura took agents Gascoyne and Hardesty with him to talk to the Strickland family and their neighbors. Brice was dispatched back to the Campbells' to look for a connection between the two families.

As he settled himself behind the wheel, he couldn't help glancing at his watch. Riley Campbell had been missing for two days. Christi Strickland had vanished out of this crowded public park less than three hours ago.

Christi's clock had started a countdown.

Had Riley's clock already stopped?

"You could smell it from the road," said Fire Chief Ben Aberdeen. "The stink of decomp." The big man stopped, took a long, gulping drink of the glass of ice water he'd brought with him from the kitchen.

Bailey could see him mentally go there, to that day, June 25, 1997.

"A squirrel hunter found the wreck. We were called out to an injury accident, that was all. We didn't know what had happened until we got there."

He described standing at the top of the embankment, looking down at the car in a little creek at the bottom of the hillside.

"There were two dead bodies in the car and they had been there at least … for *days*. Trooper Haggarty told me later that he had to shoo away the vultures so they could see into the vehicle."

Aberdeen had asked why they'd called the ambulance, since it was obvious the victims were dead. *Long dead.* And the trooper told him that he'd gone down to the wreck, got close enough to see the bodies, started back up the hill and then spotted this little camper turned upside down, almost completely hidden in the bushes at the base of a sycamore tree.

"He went to the camper, got down where he could look in

a broken window and there was a body in it — a child. He couldn't see much — just a pink sneaker with a foot in it. But there was a big wasp nest on the ground right beside it, might have been knocked out of the tree when the camper hit it, and there were wasps swarming — he got stung twice just looking in the window and he backed out of there fast.

"He didn't believe for a minute there was any chance the kid was alive, of course — still, he called us and the rescue squad. It was obvious she hadn't died in the wreck, had lived for some time afterwards because the other two, her parents, probably … those bodies were *ripe*.

"The rescue squad pulled up right after we did. Their truck was in the shop and they were using an old fire department tanker. Hank Boward took a hose from the tanker down the hillside and trained it on that wasp nest. Washed it all the way down the hill into the creek and kept a stream of water on it while Bill Halsey and I grabbed the Jaws of Life — and two gas masks.

"The little camper was smashed, crushed like a soft drink can, couldn't imagine anybody could have survived in there. The car wasn't more than fifty feet downhill from it, but you couldn't have seen the car from the camper." He paused. "You could have smelled it, though.

"Bill used a break-and-rake and took out the little window, reached in to the shoe, and touched her leg. She was alive! Then we were all over it — Haggarty, Bill, my partner, Andy and me. Used the Jaws of Life to pry apart the camper the best we could, then the four of us — we bent the metal with our bare hands to open it up so we could get to her!

"We had to dig. There was all this stuff around her — trash, opened cans of tuna and chips and — that's what the little girl'd been living on."

When they'd cleared away enough of the mess, Aberdeen could see her face.

"Her eyes were *open*, but she was just staring."

The men maneuvered a spine board into the opening and carefully moved the little girl onto it.

"I couldn't find any apparent injuries other than a head wound — there was a big lump and bruise on her forehead."

The men carried the child on the spine board up the hill to the ambulance.

"I started an IV, checked her vitals. She was in bad shape, heartrate fast and thready, breathing shallow. We hauled her into the back and blew out of there lights-and-siren to the hospital."

He shuddered.

"I was too busy trying to get her cleaned up, checking to make sure I didn't miss any injuries, I wouldn't let myself think about what she'd ... Then they came running out with a stretcher from the emergency room and rushed her away. Haggarty, Andy and me were left standing there, just standing ..."

Another breath, then, "You get it, don't you?" He sounded belligerent, but it was just his emotion bleeding through. "That little girl was trapped in that camper with her dead parents fifty feet away — for *days*. Who knows how long. And wasp*s* ..."

He got up then and headed out of the room, walking too fast. The three sat in silence in his office until the fire chief returned. He'd gotten control of himself. His face was wet where he'd splashed water in it.

"I can't figure how hearing that helps you find Caitlyn Whitfield," he said. "But I did visit her in the hospital the next day, talked to the docs. They said I didn't miss any injuries. She didn't even have a concussion, just the bump. She had some other ... issues, though, from being out there in that environment with bugs and ... some infections, I think. They said she wasn't 'unconscious,' that she was catatonic. And I thought, 'Why wouldn't she be!'"

He stopped again.

"They'd cleaned her up, probably threw everything away but a little necklace and earrings — she had pierced ears. Little yellow flowers. And they'd taken the hair ties off her braids, washed her hair and brushed it and it was clean, all fanned out on the pillow around her face. So blonde it was almost white. She looked like ... an angel. As I was leaving her room, her grandparents came in."

"Do you remember their names?" T.J. asked and the fire chief shook his head.

"They were really torn up, said they'd lost a son so their last name was probably Whitfield."

The parents had reported the family missing. David Whitfield had told the owner of the camper he borrowed that they were going to the Smokey Mountains, so that's where authorities had searched for them.

"The next day, I went back. Caitlyn was still in pretty bad shape. You lay unmoving ... in an environment like that and ... Out in the hallway, a woman came up to me, somebody'd pointed me out, I guess, and she wanted to thank me. Said she was Caitlyn's aunt."

Did you get her name?" T.J. asked.

Bailey remembered what Katydid had said about playing in the creek behind her aunt's house.

"It was Ellen," Bailey said, and everyone turned to look at her. "A last name, though ... and where does she live — do you know?"

"Summerville, Ohio. I remember because my grandparents lived in Winterville — which is only about twenty miles from there. Summerville only had about a thousand residents when I used to visit, and that was counting the dogs and chickens. The phone book was the size of a comic book — but there were five or six pages full of Mattinglys. That was odd and I remember. So Mattingly would be a good guess." He paused. "Of course, who knows now? That was decades ago."

Chapter Nineteen

"Anybody got any ideas?" T.J. tossed the question out into the car as Bailey drove them out of Hemphill toward Kavanaugh County. No one responded.

They rode along in silence, the only sound the hum of the tires on the road.

"Brice gave me the picture of Riley and I went to that place, wherever or whatever it is, and what I found there was Caitlyn Whitfield." Bailey's voice was a little too shrill. "Why? It's not a coincidence. There has to be a reason."

"Far as I know, my mama didn't never *try* to paint one of them pictures. That was the *last thing* she wanted to do. Maybe when you try to paint somethin', *try* to make that connection, it gets all messed up and don't work right."

"And so you just paint some random scene?" Bailey said. "Okay, let's run with that. How is painting a dead child—"

"Catatonic child."

"—from a car wreck eighteen years ago *random*? Of all the possible things, events, people there would be to paint, why that? *Why her?* There's some connection to ... something. To Riley ... or the school ... or ..."

"So we're where we started — trying to find the connection," Dobbs said. He paused. "We could be in Summerville in an hour or so."

"From here to Ohio — in an hour?" Clearly, geography was not Bailey's strong suit.

"It's just on the other side of the river," Dobbs said as he fiddled with his phone, mumbling, "Whitfield ... Summerville, Ohio."

"No mountain roads," T.J. put in. "Most of Ohio's flat as a boot-stomped toad."

"There's no phone for the parents," Dobbs said. "But if they were in their fifties, say, eighteen years ago, chances are they're dead now. And we don't know for sure they even lived in the same town as the aunt."

"Might as well give 'Mattingly' a shot," T.J. suggested.

Dobbs googled Ellen Mattingly in Summerville, Ohio and found nothing. Then he called AT&T information — which operated land lines in Ohio — and got a hit.

"Would you please connect me to that number," he said, and put the phone on speaker so T.J. and Bailey could hear.

The phone rang three times before a voice answered.

"Hello."

"I'm looking for Ellen Mattingly—"

"Whatever you're selling, I don't want none!" *Click!*

"That went well," T.J. said.

Dobbs was undeterred.

"Let me see if I can grease the skids."

Five minutes and a promised $250 later, Ellen Mattingly had agreed to talk to them.

"No hundred-dollar bills," she told Dobbs. "There's too many of them that's counterfeit. I seen a notice when I was buying cat food that they wouldn't take no hundreds."

They drove across featureless Ohio countryside, a few sprinklings of houses, but mostly just green fields of corn or grain sorghum maybe, stitched at the horizon to a cloudless denim sky. T.J. could tell Bailey's car sickness had settled down soon's she got out of the mountains.

Ellen Mattingly's house was not easy to find even with a GPS. The road leading to it was unnamed, or if there had been a sign, it was gone now. And the lane leading to that road was not named either. The house was a double-wide trailer that had a permanent affixed porch and an addition of some kind of room on the far end. A ramshackle barn sat out back, but clearly this wasn't a working farm and hadn't been in decades.

The woman who came to the door when they knocked was short, almost as wide as she was tall, wearing one of those shapeless shifts the morbidly obese wore because clothing constricted.

"You the people called me, said you'd pay me two-hundred-fifty dollars if I'd tell you about Caitlyn?" she asked, without opening the storm door.

"Yes, ma'am," Dobbs said.

"Lemme see the money."

Dobbs pulled from his billfold five fifty-dollar bills he'd retrieved from an ATM machine in a convenience store on the West Virginia side of the Ohio River bridge.

"No hundreds, right?"

She opened the door wide enough to snatch the money out of his hand and counted it twice, holding each bill up to the light as she did so. Then she stepped back and said, "You can come on inside, but the place is a bit off a mess. I wasn't 'pecting no company."

A bit of a mess. Oh, my ... yes, indeedy, it was that. Ellen Mattingly was a certifiable "cat lady." T.J. saw at least a dozen of them in one glance around the dim room. And from the stink of cat pee, there were likely another dozen somewhere he couldn't see.

A hoarder, too. Newspapers, magazines, boxes and unidentifiable junk was stacked everywhere, leaving a space barely wide enough to walk through and nowhere at all to sit. But the woman didn't offer them a seat anyway so the three of them stood while she eased herself down into a recliner that had taken on her shape over the years and fit her like a comfortable slipper.

As soon as she sat down, a white cat, a tabby and what looked like a calico with only one eye immediately hopped into her lap. She petted them as she spoke.

"Why you want to know 'bout Caitlyn?" she asked. "What business you got with her after all these years?"

"What happened to her after she was released from Crenshaw County Hospital?" T.J. asked, intentionally brusque. He saw no reason to come up with a plausible excuse, given that they weren't *asking* for information. They were *buying* it. The woman eyed them, then apparently reached the same conclusion because she shrugged.

"My oldest sister Dolores was Caitlyn's grandmother — her boy David's little girl," she said. "When Caitlyn was little, she come over to my house a couple of times, played in the creek out back. Cute little thing with that blonde hair."

She paused and noticed the stern looks all around and went on with her story. "Anyway, I went with Dolores and Frank to see Caitlyn after the accident. They brought home a little sack of Caitlyn's things that'd come from the wreck, toys and things — a teddy bear, I think. And, of course, they had to claim David and Susan's bodies to bring 'em home to bury."

The woman gestured out the front door.

"You go down that road another mile and you can find the Whitfield family cemetery. It's mostly overgrown with weeds now but that's where David and Susan's buried. And David's baby brother, who died of the flu when he was two. His grave's there, too. Dolores lost both her boys. Frank had a stroke about a year after the accident, but you ask me I b'lieve he just couldn't live with what had happened to his boy. After they lost Luke so young, they doted on David. And Caitlyn was their only grandchild, of course, so it was hard for them. Dolores got cancer about five years after that and she had it awful bad. Why she—"

"Can we stick to the point here?" T.J. said. "Where did Caitlyn go after she left the hospital?"

"You don't have to get all huffy 'bout it. You said you wanted to know 'bout that little girl and I'm just telling you about her people is all." She paused. "So, after the hospital, Dolores and Frank put her in a private sanitarium — I think that's what you call it. Stonybrook Manor in Plainfield. But she wasn't there very long.

"She died." It was the first time Bailey had spoken since they arrived and it was a statement, not a question.

"Nope, they closed the place down. I only went there a couple of times, but I thought then it wasn't nowhere I'd want my kin."

She moved the calico cat to the side to make room for a scrawny black cat that was sitting at her feet and it leapt into her lap with the others.

"That place was all Dolores and Frank could afford, though. There ought to have been some insurance money from David and Susan, him being an accountant in Charleston and all, made good money so I heard. But if there was money, Dolores and Frank never seen none of it. They put Caitlyn in Stonybrook, it being cheap and close by, but Caitlyn hadn't been there oh, a month or two, wasn't that long, when somebody died, one of the patients. They had a lot of people like her there, vegetables, couldn't do nothing for themselves, but I don't think it was one of them. Anyway, his family got all up in arms about it, demanded an investigation, and then they come down there and seen all kinda violations — they had to a'been paying off the inspectors, 'cause any fool could see how filthy that place was."

T.J. thought about the pot calling the kettle black, but kept his mouth shut.

"They was roaches everywhere, and patients smelled like they'd messed themselves and was a'layin' in it. Things like that. They shut the place down on the spot and they sent all the patients somewhere else."

"Where did they send Caitlyn?"

"Like I said, Frank and Dolores didn't have much and they couldn't afford no place any better than Stonybrook, so Caitlyn was declared a ward of the state of West Virginia, her being from there and all, and they hauled her up to the state mental hospital, some woman's name, Margaret something. It's in Huntington."

"Margaret Mitchell-Bateman Hospital," Dobbs said. "I've been there."

"How long was she there?" Bailey asked.

"I don't rightly know. I never went there to see her. It was too far and what was the point? Going to visit her so you could look at her laying in the bed staring at the ceiling? She didn't know nobody, never said a word, didn't respond to nothing. I think maybe that's what killed Frank, seeing the little thing like that."

"But she was there as long as her grandparents lived?" Dobbs asked.

"Best as I recollect. They never said nothing about movin' her."

"Were you ever notified that she had died?" T.J. asked.

"No, didn't nobody tell me nothing. After her grandparents died, I'd a'been her next of kin I s'pose, wasn't nobody else, but I don't know that anybody ever knew that or wrote it down in some record or other."

She put the black cat that had jumped into her lap back down on the floor so she could pick up a fat, brown one.

"You just want some attention, too, don't you, Posie?" she crooned to the cat. "Well, you can sit right here with me."

"So you don't know how long Caitlyn was in the hospital in Huntington or what happened to her there," T.J. prodded.

"Well, I don't imagine she was there too long. They told us at Stonybrook that them people in … what did they call it … a persistent vegetative state, they don't live long, three or four years maybe, but not long. They said that after a while, their organs just start to shut down and they're gone."

Though they asked a handful more questions, Ellen Mattingly provided no more information that was valuable, and they were all grateful to leave the "cat house" as soon as they could.

Dobbs said he'd drive back to Shadow Rock and Bailey simply handed him the car keys without comment and got into the back seat. She looked exhausted. As they drove out across the flat Ohio countryside, Bailey closed her eyes, leaned her head back and rubbed her temples.

"So now we know that in the fall of 1997, a little girl named Caitlyn Whitfield was admitted to the Margaret Mitchell-Bateman Hospital in Huntington in a persistent vegetative state." She opened her eyes. "Now what? Do you think the hospital will tell us anything about her? I know her medical history would be private, but do you think they would at least tell us the dates she was there, when she died?"

Dobbs held up his hand. "I say we're done digging."

"But Dobbs, we have to find out—"

"I didn't say we should give up. I said *we* should stop digging. I decided while I was listening to that woman prattle on — I'm going to hire a private investigator. Those guys know how to get information that we'd never find out for ourselves. I'll *pay* somebody to track that child down."

Chapter Twenty

When Brice turned his cruiser onto the street where Norman and Jeanette Campbell lived, he couldn't pull up in front of their house, had to look for a place to park farther down the street. Friends and family had obviously turned out in force to be supportive.

A woman Brice had seen at the school with the Campbells the day of Riley's disappearance answered the door.

"I have some questions I'd like to ask Mr. and Mrs. Campbell," he told her.

"I'm Francine Ferrigliano," said the woman, who had a pleasant, easily forgettable face. "My husband Tony and I live next door. Norm and Jeanette are in the dining room with the other officers."

Seated around the dining room table with the Campbells were two FBI agents, Ashok Arya and Nikki Trimboli, operating sound equipment to record and trace telephone calls made to the residence.

Norm Campbell was a slender man with a neatly trimmed beard going to gray and dark-rimmed glasses. His brown hair was streaked in gray, too, but Brice didn't think he was as old as the gray would make it seem. If he was, then he and his wife had had their first child late in life.

Jeanette was what appeared to be a natural redhead. Brice could usually pick out the ones whose red came from a box, could tell by their complexion. He hadn't been the only redhead in his family and Jeanette reminded him a little of his Aunt Myra, whose hair had been described to him as a child as "strawberry blonde." Which made no sense, since there was nothing about the color of her hair that looked like strawberries.

Jeanette's features were attractive and perhaps under normal circumstances he would have thought she was pretty. Now, the lines around her mouth had deepened, and dark circles formed half-moon crescents under her eyes.

Francine sat down at the table on the other side of Jeanette.

"I am sure you've heard by now," Brice told them without preamble. "A little girl is missing; she disappeared from Meadows Park this afternoon."

"We heard," said Francine and put her arm around Jeanette Campbell's shoulders. "What does that mean?"

Jeanette put her head in her hands and whispered, "It's not her, then."

Brice and the two FBI agents were instantly alert.

"Not *who*?" Brice asked.

She shot a look at her husband Brice didn't like at all. It was an oops-we-got-caught-you-wanna-tell-him-or-should-I look.

"Not …" Jeanette Campbell began, then fell silent.

"Mrs. Campbell, if you know something about this case that you're not telling us, you need to get real," Agent Trimboli said. She had a hard edge, came off hostile. "As in *right now*!" Needlessly confrontative wasn't the right tone here.

Jeanette looked at her husband, and then put her head in

her hands and began to cry, choking out words through her tears.

"Riley's ... Riley's ... adopted."

The neighbors looked as surprised as did Brice and the two FBI agents.

"Adopted?" Arya and Trimboli spoke in unison.

"What?" The word burst out of Brice's throat and then he grabbed hold of himself. When he spoke again, his voice was so cold and sharp you could have used it to filet a fish. "Why didn't you tell us that in the beginning?"

The husband put his hands out in a placating gesture. His wife continued to cry on her neighbor's shoulder.

"Nobody knew. Nobody." He said the words softly, looking around, not wanting anyone beyond the room to hear. Like he still wanted to keep the whole thing a secret! "Not even my parents." He paused. "Especially not my parents."

"Tell us *everything*, Mr. Campbell," Agent Trimboli said. "All of it. Now is no time to be concerned about keeping family secrets."

Though he said, "Alright, alright," Norm Campbell still looked around and spoke softly.

"My parents ... the Campbell family name ... it really matters to them, tracing their ancestry back to the 1600s. They were living in London when we told them Jeanette was pregnant. We'd tried before and they were so anxious to have a grandchild."

He stopped, and his wife continued, her voice tear-clotted.

"When I miscarried — for the third time — we were devastated. It was the first time we ever considered adoption, but we wanted to break that to them in person. To explain it."

"And then it all happened so fast," Norm Campbell said. "We'd hired the best private adoption attorney in Savannah and he said he had a girl who wanted to give her baby away ... and she was due about the same time Jeanette had been due. So we ..."

Decided to lie to and deceive everyone in your life, Brice wanted to say, but didn't.

"It all worked out and there was no reason my parents had to know. Certainly, we love Riley as much as we do his little sister, Holly, who is our own biological child. But my mother and father — particularly, my father — they never would have."

"I want every speck of information you have about that adoption," Agent Trimboli said. Brice saw Agent Arya on his cellphone and knew he was relaying this bit of information to Nakamura. "The name of the attorney, the adoption papers. What do you know about the mother?"

"Nothing. The attorney showed us a picture, but he wouldn't let us keep it. She was a beautiful young girl. He said she was in college and having a baby would ruin her career plans, so ..."

"What did it cost?" Trimboli asked.

"The adoption?"

"All of it," Arya said, putting his phone back in his pocket. "What did you pay this man?"

"Fifty thousand dollars."

Francine Ferrigliano gasped audibly.

"Mr. Campbell," Brice's words were measured, "did you ever stop to consider that this attorney might not have been telling you the whole story? *A college student? Seriously?*"

"She wasn't some druggie, if that's what you're implying." Norm Campbell was indignant. "Riley was in perfect health. We had him examined by our own pediatrician and he said the baby was ... flawless. Absolutely perfect."

"Have you ever heard of a black market for babies?" Trimboli said, her voice as icy as an Arctic winter.

The man's face turned white but he said nothing.

"There is such a thing, you know, babies for sale," Brice said. "Do you honestly think the birth mother's medical bills and your attorney fees totaled fifty thousand dollars?"

Norm Campbell's face grew tight.

"We would have paid twice that, three times that ... for our son. *He is our son.* Legally adopted. *Ours.*"

"And if you'd told us the truth in the beginning, we might have been looking for him in other places," Arya said.

"There's no way ... the mother doesn't know who we are. She couldn't possibly trace us, find us. The attorney said—"

"Like I said, Mr. Campbell, we need *every speck* of information you have about the attorney and the adoption," Trimboli said.

"The file is downstairs in my office, in the safe." He merely looked at her, almost defiant. The look she gave in return sent him scurrying out of the room.

Jeanette Campbell's teary voice filled the silence that followed.

"You think it's the same person, don't you? The same person who took my Riley took that little girl." She paused, drew a shaky breath. "What does that *mean*?"

"We don't know that, Mrs. Campbell, but it is a reasonable assumption. At least it was until ..." Brice didn't finish the sentence, just looked toward the door where Norm Campbell had exited.

"If someone, some ... if a person takes a child and then two days later takes another one, what does that mean for the *first child*? Why would they take two, unless the first ...?"

Jeanette put her head in her hands and this time began to sob.

"Who was the child from the park?" asked Francine Ferrigliano.

"Her name is Christi Strickland," Brice said. "She's eleven years old, in the fifth grade at Madison Elementary School. Do any of you know her?"

Francine Ferrigliano shook her head; Jeanette Campbell continued to cry. Norm Campbell came back into the room and handed a file to Agent Arya, who opened it immediately, sat down with it and began flipping through the papers, making notes on his laptop.

"We were asking your wife if you know the second child who was taken — Christi Strickland?" Brice said.

"No, I don't think … I don't recognize the name."

"She's not someone Riley played with, or maybe you know the parents?" Trimboli said. "Perhaps you were together with the parents somewhere and the children would have met."

Brice pulled up the little girl's picture on his phone and handed it to Norm Campbell. He passed it to his wife to look. Both of them shook their heads.

A large man came into the room then. He was older, his gray hair cut military short, his eyes deep set and intense above a nose that had clearly been broken multiple times.

"This is my husband, Tony," Francine said. To him, she said, "They say another child is missing, a little girl named Christi Strickland."

"I was asking the Campbells if they knew the little girl," Brice said and handed the picture to Tony. "Do you?"

"No, I'm afraid I …" He stopped. "Wait a minute. Isn't there a family at church named Strickland?"

"I don't remember anybody—" Francine began.

"Yes, now that you — I think the name was Strickland," Norm said, recognition lighting his face. "I met him when I was working the welcome center. They were attending for the first time. Let me think … yes Russell and Claire … no, Claudette Strickland. And I think they had a little girl, but I'm not sure."

"What church is that?" Brice asked.

"We go to Covenant Community Church on Haverton Drive," Norm said. "It's a big church. We have a service on Saturday night and two on Sunday and with that many people, you just don't know everybody."

Brice messaged the information about the church to Naka-mura, who at that moment was talking to the Stricklands, then he and the two agents continued with more questions, picking and prodding, looking for any time the Campbells might have crossed paths with the Stricklands or their children might have met. Karate lessons, maybe. Swimming lessons. Sports — baseball, tee ball, soccer, gymnastics?

Were the fathers on the same bowling league? The mothers in the same book club? Did they meet at the country club or maybe at a social event, a party at the home of some mutual acquaintance? Russell Strickland was a bricklayer — had he maybe worked on a project, built a patio for them or for a neighbor, worked on a retaining wall? Claudette Strickland worked at the Kavanaugh County Savings and Loan. Did they maybe meet there?

At the end of all the questions, the only possible link Brice could find was that both couples attended the same church, though they clearly weren't friends there.

Finally, Brice flipped his notepad closed.

"Thank you for your time—"

"Wait — what can you tell us about Riley?" Norm Campbell demanded. "We ask and ask, but nobody knows anything. They just tell us they're investigating or they're doing everything they can, or ... or ..."

"My little boy is *gone!*" Jeanette Campbell cried. "His little sister wanders around the house looking for him, wondering what happened to him. Please, you have to find him, you have to—"

She broke down then, wrenching sobs shaking her whole body. As her husband and Francine tried to comfort her, Brice glanced out through the bay windows and saw a lone little girl in the back yard, about five, swinging slowly back and forth in the swing.

He caught Trimboli's eye and motioned with his chin toward the child. The agent got it and nodded. She'd keep the parents occupied to give Brice a chance to talk to the little girl.

Brice went out into the back yard, closing the door quietly

behind him, and approached the little girl.

"Hi Holly, I'm Sheriff McGreggor."

The little girl had red "strawberry blonde" hair almost the same color as her mother's. Riley's hair had been deeper, more wine-colored, but then he wasn't Jeanette Campbell's biological son, either. With the red hair, Brice was sure nobody'd ever questioned his heritage.

She stopped swinging and looked up at him with huge gray eyes.

"Are you helping them find Riley?"

"I'm trying."

"Find him. I'm scared of the dark. Sometimes at night, I go get in bed with Riley, but he's not there and I'm all by myself."

Brice settled on one knee in front of the child so he wasn't so imposing a figure.

"We're doing everything we can to find him. Is there anything you know about him that might tell us where he is?"

"What kind of thing?"

"Oh, I don't know … some … secret maybe he told you, about somewhere he went or someone he knew."

The little girl froze, instantly closed up. He could almost hear the doors banging shut inside her.

"I don't know any secrets. Secrets are for grownups and little kids don't get to keep secrets. Mommy said."

"But you and Riley had secrets, didn't you?"

"Secrets are for grownups. I don't know any secrets."

She hopped down off the swing and ran toward the house. Brice watched her cross the yard and go in the back door.

That child knew something she wasn't telling, something Riley had confided to her, some secret they shared. It probably had absolutely nothing to do with the boy's disappearance, still … Brice didn't want to push, though. That would drive the little girl further away. He'd let it go for now, come back to it later.

Chapter Twenty-One

WHEN BRICE RETURNED to the courthouse, he found Nakamura in the conference room command center where he and agents Gomez and Hardesty were peering into a large computer monitor. Deputy Tackett had obviously sweet-talked the librarian into letting him borrow it. Nakamura caught Brice's eye, glanced toward the monitor and actually smiled. That was probably as close as Brice would ever get to earning the man's approval.

The agents were looking at a view from a security camera. Only a portion of the street was visible and it was possible to tell only the color, and in some cases the make or model of the cars driving past.

"This is the camera from the ATM at West Side Bank," Agent Gomez said.

"That's four, no, five blocks from the park," Brice said.

"It's the closest camera, though, on Hickman Street and on the same side of the street as the park. If a car picked Christi up there, it would have been driving north on Hickman."

"And could have turned off at three other streets before it got to the bank," Brice pointed out.

"Your deputies said there are no traffic camera surveillance cameras anywhere other than in downtown," Nakamura said and Brice nodded.

"There are several hundred of them there, on a grid at every other intersection, going from Second through Eleventh Streets east to west and starting at Bartlesville Lane and going ten blocks north of Phelps Street. There's a camera on Parker's Jewelry Store on Marrow Street, but that's five blocks south of the park, and several office buildings have cameras, but they don't show much beyond the entrances and exits. And, of course, the old homes in the Historic District are broke out with security cameras, but that's on the other side of town from the park."

"Starting fifteen minutes before and for an hour after the little girl went missing, more than a hundred cars went by the ATM camera at this bank," Gomez said. "We've compiled a list of colors, makes, models — sixty-one white, nineteen silver or gray, twenty-two black or dark blue, Hondas, Nissans, Fords, Toyotas, four pickup trucks, a UPS truck, a bread truck, a plumbing company service van and four motorcycles."

"That narrows it down," Brice said.

Nakamura sat back and rubbed his eyes.

"Anything promising from the Stricklands?" Brice asked.

"Nothing that leapt out. They don't know the Campbell family. I sent Gascoyne to that church both families attend. He said children's classes there are divided according to sex — little boys in one room, girls in another. And by age. Since the Strickland girl was eleven and Riley was seven, there's no way they would have been in the same classes."

"I had deputies check with the neighbors up and down the Campbells' street, trying to find anyone who knew the Stricklands," Brice said. "Maybe had them over for a cookout or something. Other than the Ferriglianos from next door, so far we have found no one in the neighborhood who knew the Stricklands."

"Still working on the Stricklands' neighbors," Nakamura said. "But I'm not hopeful. A working-class neighborhood like that, not the kind of place where people would socialize with a family like the Campbells."

"Anything on Riley Campbell's adoption?"

Nakamura shook his head. "So your son's kidnapped and you don't think it might be a good idea to tell the FBI that he's adopted, that there's maybe a mother, a father … somebody out there who'd be interested in him."

Brice rolled his eyes in agreement.

"We found the attorney and at first blush he appears to be on the up and up — a greedy bloodsucker, but not shady. He's giving us the runaround about producing records on the mother in the adoption. That might have been a promising lead, except …"

Nakamura sat down on the edge of the table and looked up at Brice.

"Two children."

He didn't have to say more. Mrs. Campbell had guessed. Brice *knew.* The second kidnapping changed everything. Clearly, they weren't dealing with some now-adult teenage girl who'd been pressured into giving up her child for adoption.

Why would a kidnapper take a second child unless he was "finished" with the first one?

What did that mean to the little boy with red hair and a serious face who had walked out onto a school playground two days ago and vanished?

THERE WAS a knock at Bailey's door, firm and authoritative. Brice.

She had been able to distinguish Bethany's cries from the cries of other babies in the hospital nursery, too. Why that popped into her head at that moment, she couldn't have said.

"You heard?"

"I heard." The Amber Alert app had gone off on T.J.'s phone as they drove back to Shadow Rock from Ohio.

Brice sat down on the couch, collapsed on it, actually.

"Coffee?"

"If I drink one more cup of coffee …"

"Soft drink then, tea? Glass of water?"

"Water, yeah, that'd be good."

When she returned with the water and he took it, she saw that the back of his right hand was an ugly blue-black, and swollen like he'd stuffed cotton beneath the skin from his knuckles to his wrist.

"What on earth happened to your—?"

He followed her gaze. "Pipe," was all he said, as if that were an explanation. She opened her mouth to ask what he meant, then closed it. He wasn't even aware of the injury, merely sat clinking the ice against the edges of the water glass without taking a drink.

She let the silence linger for a little longer before she spoke.

"Do you have something of the little girl's?"

His thousand-yard star yanked instantly to her face.

"Oh, no, no, no, we're not going there. *You're* not going there. That's not why I came by. I just … needed a break."

He cast a glance toward the hallway that led to her studio.

"Besides, *trying* to paint a portrait wasn't exactly a spectacular success last time."

They both fell silent. The only sound was the clinking of ice cubes in Brice's glass.

"What did you find out about the little girl you painted?"

"Nothing that would help you find Riley."

And again, silence.

Then a thought occurred to her.

"Okay, so the painting part isn't working out very well right now, but I made a connection — a *psychic connection* —

when I was in Riley's classroom, which is where he'd been minutes before he disappeared ..."

She let the statement dangle.

"And ...?"

"Maybe if I was where Christi Strickland had been minutes before she disappeared, I'd connect to ... *something*."

"To what?"

"I don't know. Barney the purple dinosaur, maybe." She'd made a remark about Barney when she'd awakened in the hospital with a bullet stuck in her brain — and nobody'd appreciated it then, either. "I probably won't connect to anything at all. Or to something as random and unhelpful as a little girl in a wrecked camper. But ... there's always a *chance* ..."

Brice said nothing.

"It's not like you're covered up with more reliable leads, you know."

He wouldn't have been sitting helpless in her living room if there were a single, tiny stone anywhere in Kavanaugh County he hadn't already looked under.

As they drove to the park on the other side of town, Bailey filled him in on what she, T.J. and Dobbs had found out about the little girl she had painted — Caitlyn Whitfield.

"If you try to trace her through the state hospital, they'd be violating HIPAA laws to give out any medical information."

"We're not trying to trace her anywhere. Dobbs hired a professional investigator." Minutes after she'd dropped him off, Dobbs had called to tell her he'd found someone. She couldn't remember the name — something Polish, Slavic. "Every time he comes up with a bit of new information, he's going to let us know and then he'll file a full written report when he's finished."

"I'd be interested in seeing that report."

"I'll tell Dobbs to get the guy to send you a copy."

Brice parked the cruiser beneath a streetlight next to an opening in a decorative rock-wall fence that appeared to stretch down that whole side of the park. She saw a closed concession stand with multicolored lights outlining its roof — surely not last Christmas's decorations — and picnic tables painted various crayon colors scattered around beneath trees. They walked along the rock wall as Brice told her that the forensics team that investigated the area found nothing. The neighborhood surveillance cameras were equally unhelpful. The little girl had vanished. Poof. Just like Riley Campbell. No footprints. No dropped cigarette butt. No microscopic fiber. No trace of anything. Nothing.

Brice indicated an area next to the rock wall, enclosed by a lilac bush on one side and some big metal boxes on the other, and told Bailey how the two little girls had been arguing over the Barbie camper when Christi got up and walked away — toward the rock wall next to the street.

He handed her his phone with Christi's picture, then stepped away and waited for Bailey to "work her magic."

Right. Copy that.

Bailey didn't know what to do. It was like … like trying to sneeze. Like deciding, okay, now I'm going to sneeze and then willing all your automatic reflexes to get with the program and produce a sneeze. Nothing. She didn't even know how to try to connect to the little girl. She concentrated, looked hard at the picture of the chubby child on Brice's phone. Stood waiting for lightning to strike, to be catapulted into another reality where she was sure bad things, really bad things were happening.

Nothing. She closed her eyes. Concentrated harder.

She'd known in her heart it was likely to be futile, but was both disappointed and relieved when her suspicions were confirmed. She didn't have that kind of control over whatever it was she could do. She couldn't will herself to paint a picture or to connect to someone she had painted. It happened —

without her consent and outside her control. If she connected to Christi Strickland, it would just happen to her, not because of something she did. What little she'd learned about her strange "gift" was that connection had something to do with what the other person had touched. Like Macy Cosgrove and the Adirondack chair.

But with Riley, she had sat in his desk, which he clearly had touched, but instead of connecting to him, she connected to Caitlyn Whitfield the moment she touched … what? Right, what? What had been the connection? The birthday present, maybe. But what had that been? And how could she find out, given that Caitlyn was dead — they hadn't yet tracked down when and where, but the lifespan of a catatonic person was almost always a one-digit number. And if she were alive, Bailey would know it. No … actually, she would only feel the connection break when the little girl died. But she'd never connected to Caitlyn and surely the child had died long before Bailey had put Oscar in her skull.

"I'm sorry, Brice. I tried, but …"

"It was a long shot, I know."

She knew he hadn't really expected it to work any more than she had. Still … She stepped to the wall. The little girl must have climbed over it. Why? She put both hands on the top of the wall to lean out over it and—

THE WORLD VANISHED. Only it didn't *vanish*. Bailey wasn't suddenly thrust into another reality entirely, where she might be trapped in a wrecked car or drowning in a flood. She was still here, in this world, standing with Brice in the park. But everything about her surroundings was different and foreign.

All color had drained out of the world — the twinkling of the lights around the concession stand, the picnic tables — all shades of black, white and gray.

And she seemed to be looking at the world through a

strange lens, a warping lens that elongated the images. Not just one lens, several lenses. It was like a weird distortion of a Skype call where you can see the person you're talking to and smaller images of other people also on the call.

Bells!

Ringing so loud she couldn't catch her breath. She was so shocked, she wanted to cover her ears with her hands. But the sound was *inside her head*. Like the tinkling jingle of tiny bells multiplied a thousand times over, so loud she could feel the vibration in her teeth, her bones, her—

She was suddenly overcome with the overwhelming but *glorious* aroma of *roses*.

As if she had buried her whole face in a bouquet. As if her nostrils were full of rose petals. The fragrance was sickeningly sweet, cloying, left no unscented air in the world, engulfed her in an aromatic miasma that seemed to penetrate her body through more than just her nose. It seeped into her skin, oozed through her pores.

The smell was almost color it was so strong. The bells were deafening. The ground moved, shook beneath her. She was Jack, running away from the beanstalk with the giant lumbering along behind, jarring the world with every step.

Fee, Fi, Fo, Fum.

Everything around her shook.

She couldn't breathe, felt dizzy, stepped drunkenly back from the wall and—

The world instantly righted itself.

Color returned.

The bells fell silent.

The only smell was … Brice's aftershave. He stood beside her now, had taken her arm.

"You looked like you were about to faint."

She wanted to voice the scream that had been crawling up

the back of her throat. But her mouth was dry and no words formed.

"What did you see?"

"I have absolutely no idea."

She tried to describe the sensation of foreignness, the sounds and smells, but nothing she said came anywhere near the reality of it.

"I didn't connect to Christi. Unless Christi was on LSD. I connected to ... what? Maybe I'm the one having a psychotic episode."

She'd been joking, but hearing the words said aloud granted them substance. Maybe she *was* losing it. She didn't often think about Oscar but she thought about him now. The bullet snuggled up somewhere in/near her frontal lobe. Was Oscar messing with her? The doctors had told her that he could cause all manner of damage, anything from paralysis to death. Distorted reality, deformed sensory perceptions — and a whole bunch of other really scary stuff could be lurking in the haunted chasm between paralysis and death. It seemed a more reasonable explanation than suspecting an eleven-year-old was taking hallucinogenic drugs.

Chapter Twenty-Two

SHE WAITED until the digital readout on the nightstand clock clicked over from 4:59 a.m. to 5:00 a.m. before she actually got out of bed. Maybe she had slept. She'd tried. Took a hot bath. Drank warm milk — yech! Turned off her phone to silence the telemarking calls.

Then she lay in the dark watching the numbers change on the clock one after another the whole night. Seemed like it, anyway.

As she sat on the edge of the bed, feeling around with her toes on the dark floor for her slippers, Bailey wanted only one thing … no, wrong word, not *wanted*, never wanted, but *needed*. She needed to run.

She dressed quickly and headed out the door into the still darkness, the rhythm of her New Balance shoes slapping the sidewalk, soothing, predictable. Normal.

Darkness still puddled in the valley between the mountains, even though it was sunrise out there on the flatlands, the dawn sky shifting through ever brighter shades of gold, crimson and azure — *color* — not the hideous black-and-white world she'd glimpsed yesterday in the park. Banishing the images as soon as they formed, refusing to allow her mind to haul out the sound of bells or the smell of roses, she kept going, moving faster, increasing the speed of the splat, splat, splat of her shoes.

She had played sports in school, but there was always a game involved, a ball, a communal activity. Running had never appealed to her until …

Yeah, her life was divided into two parts and in Part One, she had been a team player. In Part Two, she had gone solo. It had been self-preservation, of course. In Albuquerque almost two years ago, sitting in an anonymous house in an anonymous neighborhood, no friends, no one to talk to, nothing to … and one day, she had just walked out the door. She didn't have anywhere in mind to go, she just had to move, like she was running away from her grief and fear.

She had walked for hours that day. In the wrong kind of shoes. She hadn't cared. She remembered how foreign that walk had been, how otherworldly — in the desert heat when she was accustomed to snow crunching under her feet this time of year, passing cactus and yucca plants as gardens, looking up at Sandía Peak, the mountain rearing up out of the desert floor, stark and rocky.

By the time she got back home, her feet, in Crocs no less, were blistered. But she was tired and she actually slept that night. She got Band-Aids, covered over all her blisters, put on used sneakers and walked the next day. And the next. She bought running shoes, covered her still-healing feet with more Band-Aids and began to jog. She liked the sense of *fleeing* that running gave her, like she was moving away from something, leaving something behind. She liked that it took effort, actually enjoyed the stitch in her side because that was a physical pain and she used it to mask the emotional pain that was cutting her in two.

The more she jogged, the farther she had to go to accomplish her pain goal. And then she finally ran far enough one day to tap into what she'd heard about but never experienced.

A runner's high. The sense of wellbeing and euphoria were not complete for her, of course, but tempered. But it was the first time she had felt anything approaching good in the months since she'd been violently yanked out of her life, away from everything and everyone she knew or cared about, and secreted away in the night.

So Bailey had continued to run. She wasn't training for anything, but she discovered a competitive spirit in herself she hadn't experienced since she played team sports in school. She wanted to go farther than she had gone the day before, run faster.

She did other physical things in the ensuing months she never would have believed she'd do. She'd taken up yoga. It had helped calm and center her. She'd even taken two classes in kickboxing, for crying out loud, only because she ran past the same storefront gym every day and watched the participants through the glass. She decided she might be able to put a skill like that to good use someday, given that there were dangerous men who would kill her if they knew she was alive. She'd been good at kickboxing. Surprisingly good.

But none of the other activities gave her the satisfaction, the sense of wellbeing that running did. It became as much a part of her daily routine as brushing her teeth. She particularly enjoyed it on the days Sparky visited. The little dog didn't run, he *pranced* along beside her.

She rounded the corner of her block and broke into the all-out sprint she always tacked onto the end of a run, and spotted Dobbs and T.J. sitting on her porch in the growing dawn light.

Sparky dashed out to meet her, prancing/dancing along beside her as she ran up the sidewalk.

"What are you doing up so early?" Bailey asked Dobbs between gasps. "Mattress catch on fire?"

T.J. teased him unmercifully for "lying a'bed" in the morning. T.J.'s ear was always tuned to an imagined reveille.

"Why are you sitting out here? You know where I keep the key."

"So's every burglar in the tri-state area. Under the mat? Seriously?"

"I left you a message last night," Dobbs said. She hadn't yet turned on her phone. "The private investigator I hired was able to access the records at the Bateman hospital, some of them."

"Legally?"

"I don't know. I didn't ask."

"Plausible deniability," T.J. put in.

"Starting at Crenshaw County Hospital, he traced Caitlyn to Stonybrook Manor, where she stayed less than two months before the place was closed down by the state. His report will detail the whole story, but he's giving us everything new he finds out immediately. He found the admission records for Caitlyn Whitfield, on November 21, 1997 at the Margaret Mitchell-Bateman Hospital."

He stopped.

"Now for the bad news. It seems there was a flood in the basement of the hospital in April of 2001, a pipe burst in the basement — it'll all be in his report — and lots of old records were destroyed."

"Cut to the chase," T.J. said.

"Zankoski was able to find Caitlyn's admission record but no record of her discharge. She is listed on patient records until 1999. Whatever happened to her — discharge or death — happened between then and when there are records that survived the flood."

"So she was there until 1999, at least. And she wasn't there after 2001."

"Correct."

"Swell. So we don't know—"

"There's more. He was also able to access hospital employment records for the time between 1999 and 2001, by department. So he has a list of the employees who'd have been working in the chronic care ward when she was there."

"That it?"

"Three of the people on that list are *still* working there — a nurse, a doctor and an orderly."

Bailey's breathing had returned to normal from her run, but now she couldn't seem to catch her breath.

"And you two are here while the chickens are still in their pajamas because you think we ought to go talk to those people, right?" Their communal nod couldn't have been more perfectly choreographed if they'd been practicing it for years. Which they had. "In Huntington?"

"It ain't like that's on the other side of the moon."

Dobbs looked her up and down. "You're not one of those women who take a couple of hours to get ready, are you?"

Ten minutes later, Dobbs pulled his Jeep out of her driveway.

It was obvious to T.J. that the investigator Dobbs hired had hacked into the records of the Margaret Mitchell-Bateman Hospital, but that was in the category of things you was better off not knowing. Zankoski'd found out that Dr. Leonard Nisole was the physician of record for chronic care patients at the hospital when Caitlyn had been there. His offices were in a medical office park, not in the hospital. He was semi-retired now. If they wanted to talk to him, they'd need to make an appointment with him.

They'd save that as a Hail Mary if they weren't able to locate the other two leads. Lamar Howard had been an orderly twenty years ago at the hospital and he was still an orderly now. According to timecard records — that the investigator would only have been able to see if he hacked into the computer system — Howard would be at work at the hospital today.

Nurse Naomi Mason had been a licensed practical nurse twenty years ago. Now she was a registered nurse, the charge nurse on the third-floor chronic care wing. She was scheduled to work today on the 7 a.m. to 3 p.m. shift.

Bailey, Dobbs and T.J. were sitting in the hospital parking lot in Dobbs's Jeep at seven-thirty.

"I figure the best approach is the least intrusive," Dobbs said. "We go to the information desk and ask to see Lamar Howard. See what happens."

"How about only one of us goes?" T.J. said. "Let's not put all our eggs in one basket if it doesn't work."

T.J. went to the information desk in the lobby of the hospital, introduced himself and said he was looking for Lamar Howard.

Easy peasy. The woman working the desk, a nice, plump woman with white hair who reminded T.J. of Tweety Bird's grandmother, looked at a computer screen and said, "Lamar is working today on Two West. The elevators are over there."

Bailey followed T.J.'s example. As he crossed to the elevators, she went to the little old lady in the information booth. T.J.'d told her to say as little as possible, but she musta cooked up a story in her head because when she asked to see Naomi Mason, she kept right on talking.

"She's my aunt. She left her cellphone at my house yesterday and I'm sure she's frantic for it." She held up a cellphone as proof. "I was in this part of town so I thought I'd drop it by."

T.J. rolled his eyes. When you was lying, the less you said the better off you was.

"You can leave the phone here with me, dearie," the woman said cheerily. "I'll see she gets it."

T.J. was amazed Bailey didn't stumble, but she went right on like a pro.

"Thanks so much, but I need to find out if she's going to be at Joey's birthday party on Saturday. I won't take but a minute of her time."

"She's the charge nurse, so I'm sure she's busy."

"Just a minute, please."

"Alright, she's working on Three North." Bailey walked to where T.J. and Dobbs were waiting for the elevator, and suddenly froze. She looked around, fearfully.

"What's got you spooked?" T.J. asked.

"Don't you hear it?"

"Hear what?" Dobbs asked.

"You really don't hear it?"

"I can't say with any degree of certainty that I don't since you ain't told me what it is I'm supposed to be hearing."

"That scraping sound." She shook her head as if to clear it. "Scratchy. You don't hear it?"

"I don't hear nothing scraping."

Dobbs shrugged, too.

Then Bailey's face relaxed.

"It's gone now. It was grating, worse than fingernails on a blackboard."

"Is this anything like when you heard music when you was connected to Macy Cosgrove?"

"Maybe. I don't … but it can't be. I'm not connected to anyone, remember. The little girl in that picture is dead. So where could the sounds be coming from?"

The elevator door opened. Dobbs waited in the lobby while T.J. and Bailey got on. T.J. got off on the second floor and left Bailey to ride up to the third.

When T.J. asked a nurse's aide to point out Lamar Howard, she indicated a man pushing a linen cart down the hallway toward the linen closet. T.J. approached him.

"Are you Lamar Howard?"

"Yeah, what you want?"

"Like to talk to you for a minute, if you don't mind."

"And what if I do mind? I'm busy." The man turned away from T.J. and continued down the hallway. T.J. took two steps and caught up with him.

"I just need to ask you a couple of questions."

"What about?"

T.J. took a deep breath. "I'm looking for a little girl who was a patient in this hospital in 19—"

"You can stop right there. I ain't 'lowed to talk about patients."

He turned away again.

"I don't want medical information. I just want—"

The man turned on him then.

"You tryna get me fired or somethin'? I done told you. I don't talk 'bout patients. You wanna know 'bout patients, go ask the nurses or the doctors. Leave me be."

T.J. watched the man walk away, thought about giving it one more shot and then decided not to. This man wasn't the kind who noticed things. He was a keep-his-head-down-and-do-his-job kinda guy. He wouldn't likely remember a patient here last week, let alone twenty years ago.

T.J. got back into the elevator and rode it down to the lobby to wait with Dobbs for Bailey to return from her meeting with the nurse. He hoped Bailey'd had better luck than he'd had.

Chapter Twenty-Three

NAOMI MASON WAS A TALL WOMAN, big boned, but not heavy. She had curly brown hair with gray at the temples, a hawkish face, with riveting brown eyes and a beak nose. Her hands looked more like the hands of a lumberjack than a woman who put in IV needles and operated life-and-death equipment. She was seated behind the nurse's station counter working on patient charts when Bailey approached her.

"Excuse me. You're Naomi Mason, aren't you?"

"Yes, how can I help you?"

"I just want to ask you a couple of questions, if you don't mind."

"Questions about what?"

"I'm looking for a girl who was a patient here in 1999——"

"If you're looking for patient information, you need to go down to medical records. That's on the first floor."

"I don't want medical information. I'm just trying to find a girl who was transferred here from——"

"I am not allowed to give out patient information. You'll have to——"

"Her name was Caitlyn Whitfield and she was just a little girl." Bailey hadn't intended the plea to come out so plaintive, but her emotions had been rubbed raw by the scraping, scratchy sound. The sound she heard but T.J. and Dobbs did not.

As soon as Bailey said the girl's name, Naomi's eyes opened wide.

"Are you a relative of—?"

"No," Bailey said, but hurried on. "I don't want medical information about her. I'm just trying to find out what happened to her. I know she was in a car wreck in 1997, her parents were killed and she was in a catatonic state … and then she was sent here and the records were destroyed and I—"

Naomi held up her hand and turned to the other nurse seated at the counter beside her.

"Will you watch the desk for a few minutes? I'm going on my fifteen-minute break a little early."

When the other nurse nodded, Naomi led Bailey to a door marked "Nurse's Lounge." The small room that smelled of old coffee was empty.

"Have a seat," she said and crossed to where the coffeemaker sat on a counter beside an assortment of coffee mugs, rinsed out and sitting upside down on a towel. The nurse picked up one that had a picture with the caption "Mount Rushmore from the Canada side," and showed the backsides of four men, bent over so their heads would show on the other side of the mountain. "Would you like a cup of coffee?"

"No, I'm good."

Suddenly, Bailey heard an odd hissing sound, not so much like steam escaping from a teapot but more like a snake. She looked around, suddenly apprehensive. The sound grew louder and louder until Bailey wanted to put her hands over her ears to make it stop. Then it was gone. Hissing and then no hissing. There and gone. Bailey was glad the nurse hadn't seen her reaction to … Yeah, that's right — to *what?*

The nurse sat down across a small table from Bailey, picked up one of the sweetener packets out of a bowl, tore it open and began to empty the contents into her cup.

"I remember Caitlyn Whitfield, alright. I'll never forget her. Why are you looking for information about her after all these years?"

"It's a really long story and I don't mind telling it to you, but you don't have much time and I really need to hear what you have to say."

The nurse picked up a swizzle stick and stirred the sweetener into the coffee, took a sip and grimaced.

"I was an LPN, just got my cap, and this was my first job. I hadn't been here but a couple of weeks when they brought in this little girl, a transfer from … I can't remember—"

"Stonybrook Manor."

"Yes, Stonybrook. She was catatonic. Totally non-responsive. Her eyes were open, she blinked, but when you looked into those eyes there was nobody home. She wasn't on a feeding tube like so many of the PVS — permanent vegetative state — patients. Every morning, one of the aides would go in, crank up her bed and feed her. You put a spoon to her lips and she would open her mouth, take the bite and swallow it. Had to be something like applesauce or mashed potatoes, something she didn't have to chew or she'd get choked. When you put a straw to her mouth, she would drink. She wore a diaper, was incontinent, so the aides had to change her."

The nurse said physical therapists worked with the child every day so her muscles wouldn't atrophy from disuse and twist her limbs.

"She could sit up in a wheelchair, and we'd roll her out onto the balcony when the weather was nice. I liked to think she enjoyed the warmth of the sun on her face. She had way, way better muscle tone than the others in the unit and I don't know why that was. I thought at the time it was about awareness, that she responded to her environment — tensed and relaxed her muscles — even though she wouldn't mentally engage. But I was just guessing."

The nurse stopped.

"I was brand new, green as a gourd, and I … I — you had to see her, maybe, to understand. She was a precious little girl, long blonde hair, big blue eyes, and so fragile, like a china doll that would break."

"Did you know what had happened to her?"

"I found out. Asked around. I was horrified."

"Who wouldn't be?"

"And every day I'd come in and there she was. Just like I left her the day before. So I decided that since she functioned on some levels, she wasn't just lying there, but would eat and drink … I decided I'd try to get through to her. The other nurses made fun of me for trying."

She smiled self-consciously.

"I understand their skepticism now, but at the time it just made me that much more determined to reach her. So for part of my shift every day, I would go into her room and talk to her. I brought story books — I was living at home and had a little sister a year or two younger than she was.

She looked into Bailey's eyes. "That was part of it, of course, that she reminded me of Kelly. So I borrowed some of Kelly's books, and I read to her. It just became part of my routine, what I did every day. Day after day. Week after week. There was no response, no change. I'm not sure I even continued to believe she ever would respond to me, but it was just what I did every day."

She smiled again.

"I was a total newbie, fresh out of nursing school, and I was always coming up with ways to engage the patients. Most of the ones on the chronic care wing were in worse shape than Caitlyn, totally non-functioning. Over time, I watched them wither and die. Organ shutdown."

Bailey began trying to steel herself for the rest of the story.

"So ... I was an elf at Christmas, came in all dressed up with big green elf ears and curled-toe shoes, bearing presents in a big sack. The first Christmas she was here, I got her this little soft — you remember Lamb Chop, the hand puppet that Sherri somebody used to use on some show I don't remember?"

"I know the one you mean."

"Well, I got Caitlyn a Lamb Chop and stuck it in bed beside her. She never touched it. I dressed up as the Easter Bunny at Easter, had this costume with white ears and a fluffy tail, and I'd go around the ward hiding Easter eggs and then help the ones who were able find them. I dressed up for every holiday."

She paused.

"Caitlyn was brought in the first of November in 1997. She'd been here almost a year on Halloween, 1998. I did what I always did. I dressed up in a costume. I was a witch, painted my face green, black dress and broom, I had a witch's hat with a hairy black spider dangling down from the brim of it and I had a sack of candy I handed out."

"So I did my Halloween schtick, handed out the goodies. And then later that shift, I came in to read to Caitlyn, like I did every day. I stood by her bed with a book. I still remember it was *Where the Wild Things Are*. And I read dramatically, making voices, kind of stomping around for the monsters, stuff like that." The nurse stopped. "When I finished, I tucked the book under my arm, looked at Caitlyn and ..."

Suddenly, the nurse's eyes filled with tears and a single fat one slid down her cheek, leaving a shiny trail behind that glistened in the overhead florescent light.

"I mean, I didn't intend to get so attached. I hadn't even realized how attached I was until that moment. I definitely went to school on that little girl, took a cram course in professional distance, caring but not ... caring, if you know what I mean. I never realized how hard it would hit me when ..."

And in that moment, Bailey knew. Caitlyn Whitfield had died. Of course, Bailey'd known all along what'd happened to the little girl, had been surprised they'd been able to track her so far, that her little heart had kept beating all those years while she lived inside herself, deep in the dark there with all the breaker switches thrown.

The two spoke softly at the same time.

"She died," Bailey said.

"She woke up," the nurse said.

There was a heartbeat pause.

"What did you say?" Bailey must have misunderstood.

"Caitlyn's eyes were moving. I just stared, dumfounded. Her eyes were focused, *looking up at me.* I moved and her eyes followed me, moved with me. She didn't look me in the eye, or anything like that, but she was aware, she followed my movements."

"You mean, *she woke up*? She saw you?"

"Yes! I got down close to her face — and she still wasn't looking me in the eye, but she was looking — *seeing,* or at least I thought she was. Looking at my hat, and the spider, watching it sway when I moved. My hooked nose with the wart on it. My green face. Taking it all in.

"I grabbed the call button and summoned the charge nurse. And pretty soon the whole shift was by her bed. She watched me, her eyes followed me, ignored the others. They called the doctor and when he finally came in, we all backed away. He examined her, used a pin light, and her eyes followed the light."

She reached up and wiped away the tear that'd slid down her cheek.

"That little girl came back!"

Bailey didn't know what to say. She was dumfounded.

"So what … happened to her?"

"She grew more and more aware. It was slow going, but she responded to sounds, to words. Eventually, she looked me in the eye, looked everyone in the eye. About a month later, the doctor asked her if she wanted ice cream and she nodded her head yes. After that, she spoke, a word or two. It was a gradual process, but it was an amazing thing to watch that little girl come back to life."

"What … what happened to her? Did she know who she was, what had happened to her?"

"She had no memory of anything for a long time, but eventually she got to the point that she could remember her parents, things she'd done with them, finally down to the wreck. She remembered it was the end of summer and they were going camping. The memories ended right there. The next thing she knew, she woke up here. She had no memory of anything that happened in between and Dr. Nisole said he was sure she never would. That kind of specific amnesia is not uncommon for trauma patients. Her memories had just been wiped away because her mind couldn't deal with them."

Bailey was still reeling, trying to take in the reality that the little girl whose portrait sat on an easel in her studio had survived.

"Before long, she was laughing, really enjoying the books I read to her."

"What … what was she like?"

"She was precious! Sweet, loving. She found something nice to say to everybody, couldn't do enough for you. I *really* missed her when they transferred her to the rehab facility."

"What rehab facility?"

"Frazier Rehab in Charleston. I went there to visit her once, but she wasn't there long. She didn't have any family that they could find."

Well, she had a great aunt, Bailey thought, but it was a good thing they didn't put the child in her care.

"So the Department of Human Resources checked her out of the rehab facility sometime in early 2000 and put her in a foster home."

A foster home.

The words banged around inside Bailey's head, colliding with the walls of her mind, making awful thudding sounds as she rode down in the elevator to the first floor. Foster care. She knew what *that* meant — *could mean.* Not always, not every time. Still, a small child at the mercy of adults who … Bailey shook the thoughts away as the elevator doors opened and T.J. and Dobbs looked at her expectantly. And she let it go. After all, she had an amazing story to tell. They listened, spellbound.

"That little girl got well," Dobbs said, shaking his head in wonder. "She grew up."

"I hope so," Bailey said. "Which means she's out there somewhere, alive, living her life. And if we find her—"

"*When* we find her," Dobbs corrected her. He pulled his phone out of his pocket and called the investigator, told him the story as they left the building, sent him digging for the foster home where Caitlyn had been placed.

"Pro'lly won't take him long to find it," T.J. said as they walked out across the parking lot, "if he lets his fingers do the walking."

Dobbs feigned innocence. "Not all hackers use axes," he said.

Bailey stopped in her tracks and the others continued on a couple of steps before they noticed and turned back to her quizzically.

A new, horrible thought had struck her.

"Caitlyn was, what, almost nine years old when she left this hospital. Still just a little girl."

"Uh huh. Where you goin' with this?" T.J. asked.

"What if … what if she's *not* alive, not 'living the good life' out there somewhere?" She paused and gathered herself. "I am not connected to her the way I was to Macy Cosgrove. Macy was alive and I would get piped in and out of her life — remember?"

"You talkin' about when you seen out her eyes?"

"No, not when I touched something she'd touched and BOOM, I could see what she was looking at, or would be looking at — that what-hasn't-happened-yet thing. I'm talking about waking up to the smell of bacon frying, or hearing a song on the radio, only the radio was turned off."

"Like my Mama done when she'd get that look on her face like she was hearing somethin' I wasn't. But that ain't happenin' with Caitlyn."

"I've said it all along, I'm on the phone, but nobody's on the other end of the line."

Bailey took in a breath and let it out slowly.

"Caitlyn Whitfield does not exist — she *couldn't* be alive or I'd be connected to her. And if she's dead ..." The thought formed in her head whole, hot and stinking and oh-so-very plausible. "Maybe Caitlyn isn't connected to Riley Campbell at all. Maybe Caitlyn is linked to whoever *took* Riley. Maybe Caitlyn Whitfield's connection to Riley Campbell is that the same person kidnapped them both."

Saying the words out loud, voicing the thought as she thought it, knocked the breath out of her. Hearing it knocked the breath out of the other two.

All three fell silent.

"And if the kidnapper killed Caitlyn ...?" Dobbs didn't have to finish his thought. Bailey did it for him.

"He's going to kill Riley, too."

"It's likely he already has." T.J. held up his hand before Bailey could protest. "It's an awful thought, I know, but reality's reality. After twenty-four hours ..."

She could see him watching her face, knew he was trying to find a way to say what he knew to be truth in the least painful way possible. But there was no "least painful way."

"Bailey, girl, a kidnapper don't kidnap a second child 'less he's finished with the first one."

She felt like he had slapped her.

"And him takin' that little girl so soon after he took Riley tells me he's gonna keep snatchin' kids until somebody stops him."

"A serial kidnapper?" Dobbs asked.

"No ... a serial *killer*."

Chapter Twenty-Four

Brice had gone home shortly before dawn on Saturday morning, slept fitfully for a couple of hours, then showered, changed and arrived at the station about the same time Bailey, Dobbs and T.J. arrived in Huntington.

He found Nakamura conferring with one of the agents who'd been checking out traffic cameras in the intersections around the park where the second child had disappeared. He'd crosschecked the cars that passed by the ATM with the huge list of car license plates, makes and models of those that'd been parked at the school the day Riley was taken. They'd come up with more than eighty-one possible matches … and that only mattered if the car that picked up Christi hadn't turned off at any one of three side streets before it got to the bank.

Nakamura looked up questioningly when he approached. Brice was certain Nakamura'd only caught a couple of hours of sleep here and there since he'd arrived from Pittsburgh Wednesday afternoon, but his face showed none of the fatigue he surely felt. It had to be that since his emotionless countenance never wavered it didn't show wear and tear like other people's did.

"Got something?" he asked.

"Maybe. Long shot."

"I don't have any short ones. What is it?"

"Riley's little sister, Holly, knows something."

"What is she, five? You talked to her? What'd she say?"

"It's not what she said, it's what she wouldn't say. She's hiding something, a secret she and Riley had that they didn't tell their parents. Might have nothing at all to do with the boy's disappearance, but I want to talk to her again — with more time and her parents not around."

"I can arrange that."

At the Campbell house, Nakamura gathered the parents to go over, yet again, their understanding of the events surrounding the adoption of Riley seven years ago.

"If you don't mind, Sheriff McGreggor would like to wander around Riley's room, see if we missed something."

"What could there possibly be in Riley's room that would tell you who took him?" Mrs. Campbell had become querulous.

"That's not your concern, Mrs. Campbell. You need to concentrate on telling me about your son's secret adoption." Nakamura's voice was as cold as a nuclear winter.

That shut them up and Brice climbed the winding staircase to the second floor where the little boy's bedroom was the first one on the left. It was as *little boy* as money could buy. A fireman motif. Pictures of firehouses and fire hydrants and fire hats on the wall. The bed was actually a fire truck, with a light on the top of the headboard that — he assumed — flashed red and blue when you flipped a switch. It was a bed — surely it didn't have a siren!

There was a huge stuffed Dalmatian, probably as big as the child himself, at the foot of the fire truck bed, and a wallpaper chair rail showing ladder trucks and pumper trucks putting out blazes.

Brice intended to casually wander into Holly's room —

he'd heard her in there singing an off-key nursery rhyme song when he climbed the stairs — but she saved him the trouble by coming into Riley's room behind him, holding a baby doll in her arms, gently cradling it.

The only place to sit was on the fire truck bed and Brice feared he'd crush it. Still, he was way too big to talk to such a small child standing, so he sat down on the floor, folded himself up and leaned against the wall, his legs crossed Indian style in front of him.

"I saw your room when I came upstairs. You're a little princess."

She smiled, but not a bubbly smile. "Riley doesn't want to be a fireman when he grows up. Mama saw the fire truck bed and bought it for him and didn't ask if he liked it."

"Did she ask if you liked the fairy princess bed?"

She nodded. "I want to be a princess with a magic wand and make apples into puppies."

He laughed at that.

"Riley wants to be a pirate when he grows up."

Brice saw his opening and dived at it.

"Pirates bury treasure and don't tell anybody where. It's a secret. Does Riley have secrets he doesn't tell anybody?"

"Uh huh."

"What about?"

"Like a pirate, but the treasure's not buried."

Brice's heart kicked into a gallop.

"He has a treasure?"

"It's a secret."

"You can tell me."

"No, Riley made me pinky swear I wouldn't tell."

"But pinky swears don't count for policemen." Brice pointed to the badge on his shirt.

"They don't?"

"Nope. There's a special kind of policeman promise. You put your hand on the badge." He took her little hand and put it on his badge. "And you promise on the badge. That counts for policemen."

"Riley doesn't have a badge."

"So you didn't promise not to tell on a badge?"

She shook her head.

"Well, then it doesn't count for me because I'm a policeman. You can tell me and it's not breaking your pinky-swear promise."

The logic was convoluted, but she was, after all, only five years old.

"Oh."

"So Riley has a buried treasure?"

"Not buried."

"Okay, just a treasure. Where did he keep it?"

"In Biscuit."

"Biscuit?"

She reached out to the gigantic stuffed Dalmatian.

"It's in there."

"Can you show me?"

He helped the little girl turn the dog over. On the bottom, there was a small place where the seam had come undone.

"My hand's too big. Would you reach in there and get it for me?"

Holly stuck her hand into the stuffing of the dog, buried her arm almost up to her shoulder, then pulled out a small pouch. On the outside were the words SCRABBLE, so it evidently had once held the letters for a game.

He slipped the bag into an evidence envelope, careful not to touch it. As he got to his feet, he asked Holly to go play in her own room for a little while. Then he went back downstairs.

"You're going to want to get the forensics team on Riley's room," he told Nakamura, holding up the envelope. "This was Riley's hidden treasure."

Ignoring the parents' questions, Nakamura sent Gascoyne up to Riley's room to secure it until forensics could go over it.

Then Brice carried the evidence envelope to the Campbells' kitchen table.

"I'm going to empty this here so maybe you can help me determine where he got whatever's in here," Nakamura said. "But don't touch anything. Is that clear?"

The boy's shocked parents nodded.

Nakamura spread out a clean dish towel on the table, then took the envelope from Brice and dumped out the SCRABBLE pouch. Pulling open the drawstrings on the pouch, he poured out the contents.

Lying on the towel was a Boy Scout knife, new, looked like it had never been used. A pin, the kind that stuck through fabric into a separate catch on the back. It was round, the size of a quarter, gold-colored. Emblazoned on it was a music note and on top of the note was a cross. There were three action figure dolls — Batman, Superman and Spiderman. Three silver dollars. A shark tooth on a leather thong. The final item was a globe with the skyline of Chicago inside, that you shook up so it would snow.

"Where on earth did Riley …?" Mrs. Campbell began but didn't finish.

"Did you give the boy any of these items?" Nakamura asked.

"No," both parents said in unison.

"Do you know where he got them?"

"I have no idea. I didn't even know …" She turned. "I'll ask Holly—"

Brice stopped her before she had a chance to call her daughter and told both the parents, "I need for both of you to step outside while I talk to Holly."

"Why would we do that?" her mother said, frightened. "She's only five years old. You can't—"

"She promised Riley, a pinky-swear promise, that she

wouldn't tell anybody about this 'treasure.' I have her convinced pinky swears don't count for police officers, but she won't talk if anyone else is around. Just for a few minutes."

The parents left grudgingly and Brice went upstairs and brought Holly down from her room. She saw Riley's treasure on the table and cried, "You *told*!"

Nakamura reached into his pocket and pulled out his FBI badge.

"I'm a police officer, too," he said. "See. You didn't break your promise telling me."

She seemed only half-convinced.

"I need to ask you about these things, Holly. Do you know where Riley got them?" Nakamura continued.

She shook her head.

"He didn't tell you who gave them to him?"

She shook her head. "He said it was a secret." She put her finger to her lips and made a "shhhhh" sound.

"If it was a secret, why did he tell you?"

"He didn't. I found him putting the sack in Biscuit and he made me promise I wouldn't tell anybody about it."

"You never asked him where he got these things?"

She shook her head.

"Weren't you curious?"

She nodded.

"I know about that one," she said, and pointed to the pin with the music note and the cross. "That's the last one he got. It's from church, for singing."

"When did he get it?"

"The day before he … left."

Chapter Twenty-Five

T.J., Bailey and Dobbs stopped at an IHOP on their way out of Huntington.

Nobody had much appetite, though. Bailey pushed chunks of a make-your-own omelette around on her plate. Even Dobbs didn't gobble down his sticky pile of strawberry-banana pancakes. T.J. ate, of course. If they's food in front of you and it's edible, you eat it. He'd learned that lesson as a child growing up in a home where wasn't nothing predictable, including where the next meal might be coming from. You got yours, or you went hungry. It was a lesson served him well later in life, in the military, eating food you didn't know the name of and it was a good thing you didn't.

Dobbs's phone rang as they waited for the cashier to ring up their bill. He handed the woman behind the counter a credit card that was likely of the "no limit" variety as he spoke to the caller, the look on his face downshifting from surprise through wonderment to something T.J. would have translated: I don't want to know how he did that. He ended the call and smiled so broad his eyes almost disappeared above his round cheeks.

"He found them," Dobbs said. "Caitlyn's foster parents.

Wendell and Juanita Bartley. They're right here in Huntington, in the Hollyhock Apartments on Stone Branch Road."

The three of them stood stock still for something like a single beat, unspoken agreement passing among them. Then they went out to Dobbs's Jeep in the parking lot as Bailey entered Hollyhock Apartments into the maps app on her phone.

The neighborhood was "in decline," might have been nice once but now it was worn out, houses and people. The grass between the buildings needed mowing, and was full of dandelions and sticker weeds. There was trails worn down to dirt through the yards where people had cut across to a doorway from the sidewalk so many times the grass was completely gone.

There were four buildings, all a rusty red brick, with the look of prison dormitories. The buildings' doors faced out, like a motel where all the doorways faced the cars parked out front. But the steps up to the second-floor apartments were reached from the inside courtyard, where each of the apartments had a separate mini-deck. The decks were jammed with barbecue grills and children's riding toys. There was a bicycle parked in the stairwell of cracked concrete steps and the common area in the courtyard had no grass at all, just dirt.

They decided to let Dobbs do the talking, since he could sound like the Senior Senator from Somewhere when he wanted to. Bailey and T.J. would stand back a ways, so as not to intimidate, 'cause three people showin' up at your door was not likely to induce cooperation unless it was finessed just right. Dobbs was a master at it.

He knocked confidently — but not belligerently. A woman came to the door before he had a chance to knock again. She was skinny and pale, no, more sallow than pale with a yellow cast to her skin. She was wearing one of those close-fitting hats that always reminded T.J. of the top part of the ski masks so favored by bank robbers. It was clear there was no hair beneath the hat, that hiding the bald head was the purpose of it.

"Excuse me, but are you Juanita Bartley?" Dobbs asked.

"I am. What can I do for you?"

Dobbs launched into his spiel.

"We're trying to locate a child that records indicate was in your care in 2000."

"We had a lotta foster kids over the years, don't rightly remember all of them."

"This was a little girl who'd have come here from the Frazier Rehab Center in Charleston. Her name was Caitlyn Whitfield. Do you remember her?"

The woman looked momentarily shocked, then smiled.

"*Remember* Caitlyn?" she said wistfully. "No way we coulda forgot about Caitlyn."

"What can you tell us about her?"

"What do you want to know?"

Bailey blurted out, "Everything!" Then she softened it with a "please" that woulda broke your heart.

"Well, then you best come in and have a seat, 'cause there's a lot to tell."

They filed into the small, dim living room that smelled unpleasantly of disinfectant and illness. There were pictures of sailing ships on the walls, all different kinds. One of the lamps had a shade decorated with dolphins, but there was only one bulb burning and it made the dolphins look faded out, tired. Like the room. And the people. And the neighborhood.

The woman went to the hallway and called out, "Wendell, come on in here. There's folks here wants to talk about Caitlyn."

She looked momentarily flustered, as if suddenly remembering her manners, and offered to get them coffee, ice tea or a soft drink. She seemed relieved when Dobbs said they'd just left IHOP, but insisted they all have a seat.

A wizened man with a shock of thick hair the color of a gun barrel wheeled slowly into the room in a wheelchair. Dobbs introduced the others and repeated for Mr. Bartley their request to hear "everything you can tell us" about Caitlyn Whitfield. They had a reasonable story cooked up for why they wanted to know, but the Bartleys never even asked.

"We took care of ... shoot, more'n two hundred children, I guess, in the twenty-three years we worked for the Department of Child Protective Services." Wendell's speech was slow, not slurred. You could see him concentrate to form the words. "Then I got MS and we couldn't do it no more."

"We got into it with such starry-eyed enthusiasm," Juanita said, her smile full of broken dreams and unfulfilled expectations. "We couldn't have any children of our own, so we thought about adoption. But then we thought about all the children there were out there who needed love and a family just for a time."

"We wanted to save 'em all." He gave his wife a sad look. "Not sure we ever saved any of 'em."

"That Caitlyn, though, she was something special."

The man nodded, but said nothing.

"She had been catatonic, in an awful wreck and didn't wake up for more than a year so all her muscles had atrophied. She done exercises and such at the rehab. And they done a bunch of dental work on her, too. Caps in the front. Her teeth — you don't use 'em — they were a mess."

"When we got her, she was still weak," Wendell said. "She could do for herself, but she wore out easy."

"And she was skinny, of course, needed to get some meat on her bones, but I plumped her right up."

The woman smiled.

"You got to understand, the kids we took in had had rough lives and for lots of them we weren't their first placement. Or even the second or third. They'd been taken out of their homes because of some situation that was not healthy.

Domestic violence. Drug abuse. Alcoholism. Or they was just neglected."

"Lot of them got here with a chip on their shoulders the size of Mount Rushmore," Wendell said.

"You could take the hostility. Understand it. Even expect it. But it wore on you. Kids always acting out, always fighting, bickering, being selfish and belligerent. We got that, but still … it grated on you."

"Not Caitlyn, though."

The two exchanged a smile and then Juanita said, "Caitlyn was an angel."

In a wistful tone tinged with a sadness T.J. couldn't miss, the woman described Caitlyn — "beautiful, with white-blonde hair, wispy-like and blue eyes clear as a summer sky." A child who "wasn't mad at the world like the rest of them was."

"She wasn't unhappy, or feeling abused and neglected," Wendell said. "That little girl was grateful to be alive and … I swear, she reminded me of those old—"

Juanita took up the story from him, "—Shirley Temple movies. They was all about a sugary-sweet little girl who changes everybody. You don't think a thing like that can happen—"

"But it can."

"The mean kids, the angry ones, older girls and boys. Didn't matter who you was, you just couldn't be mean and angry at Caitlyn. All she did was smile and laugh and ask could she help you or she'd do something nice for you and not even tell you. The other kids changed soon as she got here. The boys was still boys, of course, acting out with each other, but after Caitlyn moved in, they left her and the other girls alone, never so much as teased them. All the kids loved her and she was strictly hands-off. You didn't mess with Caitlyn or you'd have to answer to every other kid in the house."

"She was here for almost nine years and that was the best years of our foster care." Wendell appeared to be tiring from the effort to speak. T.J. watched Juanita step in to carry the story forward.

"As she got older, she was like a mama to the little kids, got up in the middle of the night when one had a nightmare, cleaned up vomit without complaint when they were sick." Juanita held up her hands as if she could hear the comments coming. "Oh, we got it, we understood she was *too* perfect, that it wasn't healthy her being like that. We figured musta been somethin' happened to her that she was reacting to and we told the social workers, said she needed counseling."

She drew a breath and Wendell put in, his voice thin and trembly.

"They was too busy with the bad ones, told us to be grateful she wasn't no trouble."

"Her caseworker was a good woman." Juanita was defensive. "She tried. She was just covered up with kids is all. She did say, though, that the psychologists who had worked with Caitlyn when she was in the rehab facility said it was like she had reinvented herself when she woke up from that coma or catatonic state or whatever it was. She had no memory, or said she didn't and I never saw any indication that she did, of what had happened to her before. No memory of the accident where her parents were killed. Nothing. It was like she began life at nine years old and I figure she just musta decided she was gonna have a happy life." She turned to her husband. "I never seen that child angry. Did you, Wendell?"

The old man shook his head.

"I never saw her cry, neither," Juanita said. "She was smart, got good grades in school. We did all we knew to do about the too-perfect part. Gave her permission to be real. But after all those years, we just decided …"

"We decided she was just what she appeared to be — the perfect little girl."

Chapter Twenty-Six

BEFORE NAKAMURA PICKED up the items off the kitchen table with gloved fingers and placed them back into the pouch, he took a picture of each with his phone, a close-up front and back. Then he gave Gascoyne the bag to hold for the forensics team.

"I'm betting we'll get prints," Gascoyne said.

"They'll help us nail him, but I doubt they'll do any good finding him," Nakamura said. "This feels home grown."

Brice agreed. He'd be surprised if they found a match for whatever prints were on the items in the Scrabble pouch. He didn't believe the kidnapper was in the system.

"No more chasing down strangers," Nakamura said as they stepped out onto the Campbells' porch. "This little treasure chest — that's the work of a pedophile, giving gifts to the child in exchange for silence. A pedophile who had close access to the boy."

"Lots of candidates — neighbors, teachers, older friends, relatives ..."

"We know where that pin came from. The little girl said it was for singing at church. Let's start with the director of the choir at Covenant Community Church."

They got into the car and Brice pulled away from the curb.

"Sexual predator kidnappers tend to stick with one sex," Nakamura continued, musing.

"Could be it's someone who works at the church — the choir director, most likely — and his connection to Christi Strickland was to silence her. Maybe she heard or saw something going on between him and Riley. They would all have been together during the children's choir rehearsals."

"Might be."

The pastor of the church looked like Friar Tuck, round and affable. Even when he was being serious about the disappearance of a child, his eyes had an inextinguishable merry twinkle.

Oh, yes, he said, the pin pictured on Nakamura's phone was one of those the choir director, Dominic Ingerson, gave to the children who participated in the festival performances the choirs gave twice a year, spring and fall. There was a festival coming up, he said, and the choirs had been rehearsing a couple of times a week for it.

"But now, you know, with everything that's happened …" The pastor stopped. "Two children from our church family. *Two.* How …?" He let it go. "I'm seriously considering cancelling the festival performance altogether."

"Were Riley Campbell and Christi Strickland both in the choir?" Brice asked.

"Riley was, but I'm not sure about Christi. You'll have to ask Mr. Ingerson about that, and unfortunately he is not at work and won't be back for a week."

Nakamura shot Brice a look. "When did he leave?"

"Yesterday. He was terribly upset over what had happened to those children." The cheery man leaned close. "He is … how can I put this? A *fragile* soul and the strain of all this … Riley was bad enough, but when he heard about Christi, he just wasn't up to it."

"When was the last time you saw him?" Brice asked.

"He came into my office yesterday morning and said he'd be taking a leave of absence. I told him I didn't think now was a good time to be away from his office but there was no changing his mind. He has worked here seven years and never taken a leave, so he was due one. And it was clear he *did* need to get away."

Brice and the FBI agent took Ingerson's address from the pastor and pulled up in front of his house fifteen minutes later. It was on a tree-lined street that looked like the neighborhood where Wally and Beaver Cleaver grew up.

"This whole place is like a town off a Christmas card," said Nakamura. "Don't you have any slums?"

"Actually no. There are some modest homes in Shadow Rock, but mostly those are on the outskirts. The rich and famous who built this place made sure to keep the riff-raff at a safe distance."

Nakamura rang the bell, a pretty ding-dong chime, and the woman who opened the door was almost as tall as Brice, towering over the FBI agent. She was a scarecrow of a woman, with pipe-cleaner arms and a scrawny neck on which rested a big head with a weathered face that was severe — with lines moulded around her mouth by perpetual frowns, not smiles. Her hair was the color of a ten-penny nail, stylishly cut. She was wearing an apron — who wore aprons anymore? — and was wiping her hands on it when she opened the door. She took note of Brice's uniform and he thought he could see doors slamming shut behind her eyes.

Nakamura did the talking. Holding out his FBI badge, he said, "My name is Haruto Nakamura, this is Kavanaugh County Sheriff Brice McGreggor. Are you Mrs. Ingerson?"

"Yes, what can I do for you?"

"We would like to talk to Dominic Ingerson, your son. Is he home?"

"No, he's not here."

"Can you tell us where we can find him?"

"You can't disturb him now. He took a leave of absence to rest to get his strength back. He doesn't need company."

"Ma'am, we're not company. We want to talk to him about the case of a missing child."

"*Oh, absolutely not.* Why do you think he went on the leave of absence?"

"Mrs. Ingerson, we need to know the whereabouts of your son. *Now.*"

Brice continued a beat later, "If you refuse to tell us, I will charge you with hindering law enforcement."

At this point, they did not have probable cause to believe her son had committed a crime, and therefore her refusal to give up his whereabouts was not illegal, did not make her an "accessory" to anything. At least, not according to state or federal statutes. But local ordinances did apply here, and Brice had long ago pushed through the town council a rather all-inclusive ordinance that forbade any resident of the county to "hinder law enforcement." He'd never charged anyone with that particular misdemeanor and suspected the county attorney would decline to prosecute if he did. But it had often proved useful as a bluff.

Of course, Dominic Ingerson's mother didn't know any of that.

"Oh, don't be ridiculous. I'm not hindering anything. You have to leave Dominic alone."

The stern tone in Nakamura's voice was sharp enough to filet a fish.

"I won't say this again. Tell us where to find your son … or the sheriff will place you under arrest."

"You can't … I mean, that's absurd. You don't understand." She had been standing bold in the doorway, as if to bar their entrance, but she moved back now. "Come in, then, so I can make it clear why you absolutely cannot bother poor Dominic right now."

The two officers stepped into the foyer and she gestured toward a doorway into a small parlor.

"Have a seat."

"We'll stand," Nakamura said.

She was offended and made sure the two officers knew it.

"Very well, then." She took a breath, then continued in a strained, patient tone. "Dominic can *not* be disturbed because—"

"I don't care why your son wants to be left alone. We have to talk to him and you're going to tell us where he is."

The woman began to pace back and forth in front of them, literally wringing her hands.

"You don't understand Dominic. He's … his psyche is delicate, fragile. That's what ended his singing career. He has a trained operatic voice, you *do* know that, don't you? Surely they told you that at the church."

"I'm not interested in your son's training—"

But she was on a roll and there was no stopping her.

"He's not just some 'church choir director.'" The words dripped with disdain. "He was trained at Juilliard in New York. I moved there from Cleveland to make a home for him while he studied. Oh, he showed such promise. All his professors said so. I have voice recordings of him singing Habanera from Carmen. It is truly breathtaking, really it is."

She turned and Brice realized she intended to go get the recordings to play for them. Nakamura stopped her with a question.

"Fragile? What do you mean he is *fragile*?"

She turned back to them.

"He couldn't take the pressure of performance. It just wasn't in his gentle nature. I had hoped he would overcome the stage fright with age, that he'd be less nervous as he got used to it. At five years old his talent was so obvious I realized I had to prepare him for a future of fame, so I got him up to sing before every group I could think of. A five-year-old was frightened, of course, but I wouldn't let him give in to it. No sir, I *forced* him out there because I knew he would thank me for it one day ... but ..."

"But?"

"His stage fright got worse instead of better as he got older. At Juilliard, he would get nauseous before a recital and ... well, he had intestinal issues as well. His hands would shake and ... Once he started singing he was fine; he would get lost in the music and his voice would positively soar. But it got to the point that he was too upset to perform. And then ... it was his final recital after his sophomore year. He was singing a very intricate piece — so difficult and he did it flawlessly, absolutely flawlessly, in rehearsal. He never performed anywhere without me by his side, of course, and the afternoon of the recital I left his dressing room for only a moment to get a soft drink and when I got back ... he was gone. Just *gone*. We finally we located him in a broom closet, sitting in a corner, sobbing. He had ... a complete mental collapse, had to be hospitalized."

"So he was institutionalized in a psychiatric hospital?" Nakamura confirmed.

"Oh, the professionals never did know what to do with him. It was an absolutely horrible time, the poor boy. In and out of one place after another. Do you know they actually diagnosed him with DID? Do you know what that is?"

Brice knew what it was, knew much more than he wanted to know about all manner of mental illnesses, in fact. He was especially familiar with Dissociative Identity Disorder, commonly called split personality, because he and T.J. had had a conversation about it only a week ago. The whole crew had been at Bailey's grilling hot dogs and hamburgers when she dropped a dog on the ground and the real dog snatched it up and ran off with it. When T.J. started scolding Sparky, Bailey'd defended him, saying the hot dog thief wasn't the real Sparky, that he had an alter ego, and that had launched T.J. into the tale of an arrest he'd made once, a guy named Pepe he'd hauled off to jail for domestic violence who'd claimed "Malcolm had done it," Malcolm being his alter ego.

"It was almost believable because this guy was barely five feet tall, a hundred pounds with concrete blocks in his pockets, and the girlfriend he'd beat the crap out of was over six feet, easy two-hundred-fifty pounds."

T.J. had done some snooping, discovered the foremost expert in DID was right there in New York City, and went to talk to him.

"His name was Dr. Milton Brazinski, and it was hard to buy what the shrink was selling, that some people suffering from DID — depending on the severity of the childhood trauma that caused it — had the ability to change their own body chemistry with their minds. He said they 'become who they believe themselves to be.' He even described the case of a man who was a diabetic with multiple personalities — one of which was not diabetic. When the man assumed that personality, he required no insulin — his body produced it normally."

T.J. had cocked his head to the side then and said, "All I know is that according to Pepe, Malcolm was a professional wrestler. And according to the woman he beat up, Pepe had pinned her down on the floor and broke her arm."

Brice was wondering what other personalities Dominic Ingerson might have had who'd have been willing to kidnap two children. But his mother made it clear there was only one Dominic.

"Can you imagine that — *my Dominic*, crazy? The very idea was insane. He was just terribly upset, that's all, was too fragile to withstand the pressure of his great talent. I tried to tell them that, but that doctor was determined Dominic was more than one person."

"So you're telling me your son has a history of mental

illness? How did he get a job with a church working with kids—?"

"They did a criminal background check," she said, offended. "He is not a *criminal*, has never been arrested for anything, and after that horrible year when they had him misdiagnosed, now he is fine. Dominic has bipolar disorder, that's all. And with the proper medication, he can function normally in all situations. He takes his meds. Every day. *I make sure of that.* He is perfectly fine."

"Where is he now?"

"Weren't you listening to a word I said? He needs his rest. He was so upset over that little boy. The child was in Dominic's children's choir, you know. Poor Dom … he wasn't eating, wasn't sleeping. I told him, I said 'Dominic, dear, you need to get away. You need to rest and relax, center yourself.' I finally had to lay down the law, told him he *had* to take a leave of absence, that I wouldn't stand for anything less. Now do you see? You understand now, don't you, why you absolutely can *not* disturb him?"

"Ma'am, I am going to ask you one final time. Where is your son? If you refuse to answer, you will be arrested and charged with—"

"I am a mother guarding my son's mental health. I have a right to protect my child."

The FBI agent had had enough. He nodded at Brice, who removed handcuffs from his belt as he stepped forward

"Mrs. Ingerson, I am placing you under arrest for—"

"You can't do this!"

"Watch me. Put your hands behind your back."

She was horrified.

"Oh alright. Alright. I'll tell you. But this is police harassment, it's police brutality. You will hear from my attorney. You can't just barge in on him. You must speak softly and be gentle. He's doing his exercises, yoga, he is in a dark environment, without stimulation. You mustn't frighten him!"

"Where is he?" Nakamura ground the words out through clenched teeth.

"He is in the Nautilus Hotel on the other side of the lake. Room 435."

"Listen to what I'm telling you, Mrs. Ingerson," Brice warned, loading his voice with threat. "You are not to call him and tell him we are coming. Do you understand? If you do, you will be charged—"

"Oh, I can't call him." She picked up a cellphone off the coffee table. "I took it away from him. He was too caught up in it, checking it all the time, getting texts from people I didn't even know. It was unsettling him, upsetting his equilibrium. I had to put a stop to it."

Out of curiosity, Brice asked. "How old is Dominic?"

"He is forty-three, will be on Christmas Day, the only Christmas present his worthless father ever gave me."

Chapter Twenty-Seven

Sadness passed between Juanita and Wendell Bartley as palpable as a cold breeze.

"Part of what happened was our fault," Wendell said. "We got to depending on Caitlyn and we shouldn't have done that. If we'd gotten out of the foster care system when we should have … but with Caitlyn around, to help and to just … just *be*, we stayed with it."

"You can only do something like that for a time, then it wears you down. It's like you're a pencil eraser and the rubbing back and forth is all the frustration, all the difficulties. But Caitlyn changed everything. We tried to adopt her." Juanita paused and when she began again her voice was tear-clotted. "We did love that little girl somethin' fierce. We wanted her to be our little girl for always. And maybe we could have, but some of her medical records had gotten destroyed in a flood, and they wasn't sure whether or not she had family somewhere. They looked, but they wasn't in no hurry. And we wasn't neither. She was a teenager by then. Time just got away from us."

"In the foster care system, you rotate out at age eighteen," Wendell said. "When you're a legal adult, you're on your own.

But we didn't intend that for Caitlyn. Soon's she started high school, we started talking about her future. Got serious about it when she was a senior. She wanted to be a scientist, loved to study, a biologist. Or maybe a fashion designer. Those wouldn't seem to go together, but with Caitlyn, you could believe it as possible. She'd been accepted, already enrolled in a community college and she was going to stay with us. She could have moved into a dormitory with other girls, but she wasn't interested, said she wanted to stay 'home' with her 'family.'"

"We had a party for her eighteenth birthday a week before classes started," Wendell said laboriously, then ran out of gas and Juanita continued.

"At that time, we had three junior high boys and a five-year-old girl named Missy — who'd been taken away from her parents because they was abusing her. She was shy, quiet, withdrawn, scared of her own shadow. The boys were … oh, they were just boys. Acted like boys, a little too rough and rowdy, but not as bad as lots of others we had. They went to a flea market the weekend before the party, and they came back with a sack full of stuff they wouldn't let us see. Secret stuff."

She smiled.

"Of course, as soon as they went to school, we searched their rooms, making sure they hadn't got something they shouldn't have. And it was basic junior-high-boy stuff. A whoopee cushion, fake vomit, a couple of plastic turds, a big black rubber spider, a dead rat, and a rubber snake. Because they were so secretive about it, we knew they were planning to haul those out at the party. We told Caitlyn they were going to play tricks on her and she just laughed and said she'd enjoy it."

"They did, too. At the party, there was a plastic turd in the water pitcher."

"Wendell sat down on a whoopee cushion. Clayton threw down plastic vomit in his plate. Stuff like that. It was all harmless fun. Neither one of us was in the room when it happened so … we suddenly heard screaming and we ran into the family room. Missy was totally hysterical. She'd been sitting in Caitlyn's lap and the boys gave her a box, said the present was for her, and when she opened it, the rubber rat, the snake and the spider were in it. That child totally lost it, shrieked, knocked the box away, ran to a corner and put her hands over her face and screamed and screamed. Caitlyn tried to calm her, but she couldn't do a thing with the child. We couldn't either. I never seen a child as freaked out as she was."

"Being abused like she was, she musta had some kind of bad experience, you know, maybe with a rat or something."

"Nothing we done would soothe her. The boys apologized, tried to show her that stuff was just toys, wasn't real. The snake was one of those wooden, jointed ones and Kyle took it apart to show her the pieces, Tyrone pulled the legs off the spider, showed her they was just rubber. They both jumped up and down on the fake rat. They really did feel bad but didn't nothin' they tried work. That child was so hysterical, we finally had to call an ambulance and take her to the emergency room so they could give her something to calm her down."

"That was the end of the party. Juanita didn't get home with Missy until two or three o'clock in the morning. Caitlyn had cleaned up the mess, done the dishes, waited up and she sat by Missy's bed holding her hand while we went to bed." The couple stopped and looked at each other. When Wendell continued, his thin voice was soft. "The next day, Caitlyn was gone."

"Gone?" Dobbs said.

Wendell nodded sadly. "Without a trace."

Juanita was holding back tears.

"She was kidnapped! I know she was, but the police never believed that."

"Kidnapped," Bailey parroted the word, no emotion at all in it.

"Now, Juanita—"

"Wendell never believed it either, said she just left. But I know somebody took her."

Juanita finally let go, put her head in her hands and began to cry, not great gulping sobs which was what T.J. figured she felt like doin', just cried softly 'cause that's all she had the strength for.

"She didn't say goodbye," Wendell said, "didn't leave a note. Her bed was made and her clothes were still in her closet, so Juanita thought—"

"I *knew* she …" Juanita wiped tears off her cheeks as she spoke. "Caitlyn went out with Bradley almost every night — just a rescue mutt but she did love that dog. We had a doggie door so nobody *had* to take him out, but almost every night before she went to bed, she'd go out in the back yard with him to do his business. And every now and then, she'd go down to the convenience store on the corner and get a bag of M&Ms. She loved M&Ms, but if you had candy, you had to share with all the kids so you never got more than a piece or two. So when they were all in bed, sometimes she'd get a bag she could have all to herself."

Juanita took a deep, shaky breath.

"She kissed me goodnight before I went to bed — I was exhausted. She thanked me for the birthday cake. We never saw her again."

"Her purse was gone, but not her cellphone. She'd always had after-school jobs, always worked, for years, saving her money for college. Flipping burgers, babysitting — making lattes at Starbucks was the last one. We never seen how much she'd saved. And we didn't find no money in her room, so—"

"She decided to get M&Ms — that's all!" Juanita said. "So she took her purse. Maybe she kept all her money in her purse; it was one of those big ones, size of a diaper bag, and with so many kids around, things had a way of disappearing. She went out with Bradley into the back yard, and then started to the convenience store, but somebody …" She looked deep into Bailey's eyes. "She wouldn't have run off without a word. Caitlyn wouldn't have done a thing like that."

"At first we thought she took Tyrone's bike, cause he said it was missing. But he found it a few days later, left it at a friend's house down the street."

"You called the police?" T.J. asked, and the couple nodded. "What'd they say?"

"Since she wasn't underage, she wasn't a runaway. And since she took her purse and her savings, no sign of a struggle … they asked questions, talked to the neighbors. The man at the convenience store said he might have seen her walk by, he wasn't sure, but she didn't go in. The police said there was no evidence of a kidnapping. She was an adult, had a right to leave if she wanted to, go anywhere she chose."

T.J. caught the time-dulled edge of anger and outrage in Juanita's voice when she spoke again.

"The real reason they didn't dig into it was because of us taking Missy to the emergency room. We explained what happened, but they … they thought since this was a *foster home*, Caitlyn had run away from us, left soon as she could, the very day she turned eighteen. But it wasn't like that. She loved us."

After they'd found out everything they could from the Bartleys, the three of them walked to the car in silence. Bailey stopped and didn't get in, turned and said the one word, "kidnapped," but it was colored in so many layers of emotion T.J. couldn't have said what she was thinking about it. He hooked his fingers in his red suspenders as they stood there.

"I feel no connection to Caitlyn Whitfield, so that means she's dead. And there's no link of any kind between her and Riley Campbell … unless they were both kidnapped and *murdered* by the same person."

"That bucket's got lots of leaks," T.J. said. "Serial killers stick to a pattern, select their victims for a reason. We're saying he killed a grownup — Caitlyn wasn't no child — seven years ago here in Huntington, got rid of the body so nobody ever found a trace of it. Then takes a little boy and two days later a little girl in Shadow Rock?"

"I have to find a way to connect to Caitlyn again," Bailey said.

She turned and looked deep into T.J.'s eyes. "Your mama painted pictures of people when … bad things were happening to them. They were dead or dying. If I could connect to Caitlyn when … when she was being murdered, surely I would see something, some detail … even if it's just colors reflected in a toaster … *something* that would help identify the kidnapper."

"You want to crawl inside the head of a woman's being murdered, do you?"

"Of course I don't *want* to."

"How you plannin' on doing that, connecting again?"

Dobbs interrupted in his made-for-radio voice.

"I'll call Zankoski, fill him in on what the Bartleys told us and get him to keep checking. He got us this far. Before we leap on our horses and ride madly off in all directions, let's see what else he can find out."

Chapter Twenty-Eight

BECAUSE IT WAS FASTER than driving around the lake, Brice called for a West Virginia Water Patrol boat to take him, Nakamura and Agent Hardesty across to the Nautilus Casino and hotel complex on the other side of Whispering Mountain Lake. He'd arranged for two West Virginia State Police troopers to provide backup on the other side. Though it was noon, the day was not yet hot, the glassy smooth water mirroring the multi-hued green of the mountains, the azure sky and a dusting of cottony white clouds in postcard perfection. Even Nakamura noticed.

"No wonder the tourists come here," he said.

"Andrew Carnegie turned it into a resort for the uber rich. There's a similar place off the coast of Georgia called Jekyll Island. It was the playground of the rich and famous, too, until World War II when it was too dangerous to have that many movers and shakers dangling out there off the coast in range of German U-boats."

As they approached the casino, Brice provided Nakamura and Hardesty the CliffsNotes on the facility, a running commentary that kept his tired mind occupied and helped him fight the compulsion to check his watch. And it had become a compulsion, like he could somehow look at it and freeze the digital display, stop the numbers from relentlessly counting down, shrinking with each click the odds of finding two missing children. Riley Campbell had vanished off a school playground almost *three days ago.* Christi Strickland had climbed over a rock wall at a crowded park and disappeared — *poof!* — going on twenty-four hours ago.

Brice was sure the unemotional Nakamura was doing the math in his own head. The verdicts those numbers pronounced were inescapable: Riley Campbell was dead — why else had the kidnapper snatched a second child? And Christi Strickland — if she wasn't dead yet, she soon would be.

The craft skirted the floating casino with its luxury hotel stacked up on the floors above and continued to the dock that extended from the shoreline beyond. Brice and the two FBI agents disembarked there. Though you probably couldn't rent a broom closet in the Nautilus Hotel for less than a thousand dollars a night, a more reasonably priced hotel was located across the road, Ohio Route 7, and it was there that the church choir director had holed up to take his sabbatical. After stationing a perimeter of West Virginia State Police troopers around the building, and Hardesty at the end of the hallway, Nakamura and Brice approached Room 435 warily, Nakamura on one side of the door, Brice on the other, weapons drawn. Then the FBI agent reached out and knocked.

"Dominic Ingerson, this is FBI Special Agent Haruto Nakamura. Open the door."

There was no response.

"Mr. Ingerson, we know you're in there. Open the door or we will break it down."

They heard movement from inside and the door opened the length of the guard chain. Nakamura held his badge in front of the crack but stayed beyond the door.

"Open the door, then step back away from it and clasp your hands behind your head."

"Alright, alright. Let me get it unhooked."

Ingerson fumbled with the chain, then opened the door and stood in front of it, a portly man in a burgundy bathrobe. He had white ultra-sunscreen on his forehead and nose. The room was dark, with only shadows beyond the light of the hallway.

"Put your hands up, lace your fingers together behind your head," Nakamura said, remaining flat against the hallway wall beside the door.

Instead of doing as he was directed, Ingerson turned away from the door and flounced down on the side of the bed, his voice like a petulant child.

"I'm not going to be treated like some criminal. You shouldn't be here. You're upsetting me!"

Nakamura nodded and Brice crouched low and swung into the room with his gun drawn. Ingerson saw it and leapt back as if he'd seen a snake.

"Don't … don't point that *thing* at me… What if it goes off? Stop it!" He sat cowering in the middle of the bed while Brice holstered his weapon and Nakamura came into the room and did the same.

"Are you Dominic Ingerson?" Nakamura said.

"Of course, I am, you know I am. Why would you point a gun at me? This kind of stress — it's too hard on me."

Then he reached down and began taking his own pulse as he spoke.

"Mama said you were coming here but I told her that was ridiculous, why would you need to talk to me? I don't know anything."

Brice shot Nakamura a look that said he would *cheerfully* charge this man's mother with hindering law enforcement.

Ingerson stopped taking his pulse and announced

triumphantly, "See! See what you've done? God only knows what my blood pressure is. You need to leave right now."

Dominic was a round man with chubby cheeks, thinning hair and a paunch that protruded so profoundly he looked pregnant. The unfortunate man-breasts resting above it added to the illusion. The silk pajamas beneath the robe were unbuttoned several buttons to reveal a bony, white chest and several layers of bling.

"Mama said she told you I came here to rest, to get some distance between me and all the awful that is happening. I need quiet, dark, not the Gestapo barging in here in jack boots."

He sounded like he was about to cry, his hands fluttering around in the air as he spoke, as if they were twin birds over which he had no control.

"Mr. Ingerson, we want to talk to you about Riley Campbell," Nakamura said.

"Of course you do. That's what Mama said. And it is so awful, so horribly awful. A missing child, no, *two* missing children. That Christi Strickland, poor little thing."

"So you know both Riley Campbell and Christi Strickland?"

He looked up and gave them a baleful look.

"Don't be obtuse, of course I do. They both were in my children's choir. Christi, poor little thing, couldn't carry a tune in a guitar case, but Riley was … well, he had promise."

"So you took a special interest in Riley Campbell, is that what you're telling us?"

"Oh, gracious no. If you mean something like private coaching. I only have limited time. I can't get too tired, can't wear myself out, so I keep to a rigid regimen of how many after-work hours I will spend. Never more. And that time was, of course, spent with the soloists."

"So you're saying you never gave Riley special attention, didn't meet with him privately, spend time—?"

"Oh, no. Not Riley. Now Roger Cromwell, there's a *voice*! A tenor, perfect pitch. After rehearsal almost every day I spent a half hour coaching him."

"So you never gave Riley any gifts?"

"Why would I give him gifts?"

"And you're saying Christi Strickland didn't witness you spending time with Riley, maybe saw something she wasn't supposed to see?"

"Whatever in the world are you talking about?"

"You didn't give Riley action figure dolls, or silver dollars, maybe, because he was ... special?"

"Why would I do that? He wasn't special. I mean, he had a good voice, but—"

"Don't lie to us, Mr. Ingerson. We have forensics going over those objects right now and we can lift your fingerprints off them. It will go easier on you if you tell us the truth now."

"I don't have any idea what you're talking about. I never gave Riley a silver dollar. For what?"

"How about this?" Nakamura held out his cellphone with the picture he'd taken of the pin with the music note and a cross on top of it. "If you didn't give it to him, where did he get it?"

Brice spoke for the first time, firing the question like a bullet. "The minister said you gave out pins like this every year to different students — are you saying the minister was lying?"

"No. I mean, yes. Oh, this is so upsetting!" His voice broke. "I'm not calling anyone a liar!" He sobbed, sucked in a few sniveling breaths, then got control. "I *do* give out pins every year after the fall and spring performances. But we're still rehearsing for the fall performance and I haven't even selected for certain who will get this year's awards."

He took a deep breath, let it out slowly.

"There are two awards, one for the older choir and one for the younger choir. Actually, I do know that the one for the younger choir will go to Roger Cromwell. That boy is only eight, but with his perfect pitch—"

"You didn't give this pin" — Nakamura wagged his phone in front of the man's face — "to Riley Campbell?"

"Are you not listening to a word I say?" He put his hand on his breast in a dramatic gesture. "You're distressing me, can't you tell that? My heart, it's like a jackhammer in my chest. It is hard enough to engage in this discussion at all. Talking to the *police* about such a horrible subject, but if you don't even listen and I have to repeat myself."

"Go ahead, humor us. Repeat yourself. You're saying you didn't give this pin to Riley Campbell, is that right?" Nakamura continued to hold the phone in front of Ingerson's face.

"Of course I didn't. I haven't given out the pins yet. I don't give them out until *after* the performance — are you listening to me? We're still just rehearsing. And even if I had given them out, I wouldn't have given one to Riley. I already told you, his voice is average at best. Pedestrian. He can hold a tune, but he has—"

"If you didn't give him this pin, where did he get it?"

"How would I know?" Ingerson's face had been getting redder and redder, glowing beneath the white sunblock. "Do I look like a psychic to you?" He snatched the phone out of Nakamura's hand and placed it dramatically against his forehead. "Like I can concentrate and divine somehow where the boy got it?" He moved it off his forehead and held it in front of his face. "Like I could just look at it and …" He moved it farther from his eyes, like someone farsighted, then handed it back to Nakamura with a dismissing sound.

"That's not even a Junior Choir pin! It's a Senior Choir pin, and not even the same design as this year's. I design them myself. I'm very artistic — with a pen and paper, oils and pastels, of course, not with one of those computer design programs." He grunted in disdain. "I redesign the pins every year. You can see the design of this year's pins if you like. It's in my file cabinet at the church, but the pins I ordered haven't come in yet."

"You say this is an old design, an old pin?"

"Oh, indeed yes. At least a year, maybe more than that."

"I'll need a list of every child you've given one of these pins."

"Oh heavens, there are quite a few of them. Last year the pin went to Arnold Westerman. The year before, 2013's pins went to Michael Hardesty and Zach Kirkland — they were both equally talented. I gave a pin in 2012 because, well, it was a tradition and I couldn't break the tradition, but ..." He leaned closer and spoke conspiratorially. "Between you and me, there was not a single child worthy of the award in the whole choir that year. Not a single child. Then in 2011 ... so sad." He paused, shook his head. "You should have heard that boy sing *before* his voice changed. At twelve, he had the voice of an angel. But when he turned thirteen ... puberty hit him hard. He didn't even belong in the choir, couldn't carry a tune, just sort of bleated like a goat."

"What boy? Who?"

"Why Lucas Ferrigliano, of course."

Chapter Twenty-Nine

As THEY RE-CROSSED the lake in the water patrol boat to the dock on the Shadow Rock side, Nakamura sat on a bench in the stern, staring out at the wake churned up by the big engines. He'd called Trimboli, one of the agents at the Campbells' house, and dispatched her to the Ferriglianos next door to detain the boy for questioning.

Brice stood near the bow, chatting with the water patrol officer to keep his mind off his growing list of misgivings about their only current lead. Lucas Ferrigliano didn't tick all the boxes. Since sexual predators tended to stick with one sex or the other, what connection did the sixteen-year-old boy have to Christi Strickland? The maybe-Christi-saw-something connection they'd theorized about the choir director didn't fit the teenager, who lived next door to the first kidnap victim. And why would Christi have smiled when she saw the Ferrigliano kid at the park? Why would she have willingly gotten into a car with him when she barely knew him if she knew him at all? If the boy was the kidnapper, there had to be information they didn't have to tie all the loose ends together.

While they were talking, Nakamura's cellphone rang. His face showed no emotion whatsoever, but some other unidentified body language was shouting that something was very, very wrong.

Brice made his way to the back of the boat as Nakamura clicked off the call.

"There's another child missing," the FBI agent said, his voice as controlled and emotionless as if he were reading the fine print on a credit card application. Brice, on the other hand, took the news like a kick to the belly. He couldn't even speak for a moment, and when he did, he didn't seem to have quite enough air to support his words.

"Who? Where?"

Then his own cellphone rang. Caller ID showed it was Fletch. He didn't answer.

"A little girl, Marley Nicole Ewing," Nakamura said. "She was taken from a department store at Oak Ridge Mall. She's three years old." He took a breath before he said the rest. "And she's deaf."

"Three children in four days."

"Something set him off." There was a heartbeat pause before Nakamura continued. "A serial killer on a spree won't stop until we catch him."

"You think it's a killer, then, not just a kidnapper who—?"

"How's a kidnapper going to corral *three* children?" Nakamura's words were clipped, probably as close as he came to snapping. "And why would he try?"

The mic on Brice's shoulder radio spoke into his ear. "Unit One, this is dispatch." His phone rang a second time.

"I'm calling for reinforcements," Nakamura told Brice as the boat ignored the no-wake zone and only throttled down as it neared the dock. "I'll have four more agents on the ground here before nightfall."

As he and Nakamura raced to his cruiser, Brice told the dispatcher they were on the way to the mall, to have Fletch meet them there.

It wasn't a big mall, fewer than two dozen stores, a Planet

Fitness gym and a small Cinema City movie complex with eight screens. Shaped like a wagon wheel with a food court and fountain in the center, four hallways branched out from it with stores on both sides of the hallways. There were large public entrance/exits at the ends of all four halls, and a separate entrance directly into the food court between the East and South Halls. There were also rear delivery entrances to most of the stores. The child had been snatched from a department store called Your Style Your Way, which was the center store of three on the right side of the North Hall. Next to it was a Stride Rite shoe store and on the end on the other side was a pizza parlor called Andolino's Pies. Facing those stores across the hall were only two businesses, a jewelry store called Love Stones and a large chain bookstore, Billions a'Books.

Combined law enforcement — Brice's deputies, city and state police — had locked down the whole mall. No one in or out either of the four hallways, the food court entrance or the back doors of the stores. All the exits from the parking lot had been blocked by police vehicles. As he passed through one of the roadblocks, he saw West Virginia State Police Trooper Corbin Hollister gesture for the driver of a minivan attempting to exit the parking lot to roll down his window. The last time he'd seen Trooper Hollister was on the Fourth of July, just minutes before Fletch had been shot by a crazed meth-head who planned to blow up a dam.

"I am respectfully asking you to step out of your vehicle and give me your permission to search it," the trooper said. "You have the right to refuse. If you choose to exercise that right, you'll have to return to the parking lot while we secure a search warrant."

With hours of waiting as the alternative, the driver couldn't get out of his vehicle fast enough.

Brice understood with a sick feeling in the pit of his stomach that the effort was almost assuredly too late, that whoever had taken the child had spirited her away before the police arrived.

Fletcher met them as they entered Your Style Your Way. Like a Sears store or JCPenney, it featured clothing for men, women and children. Shoes, too, on the back wall. The men's and boy's departments were mostly on the left side of the store, the women's on the right. But children's clothing was intermingled with both and there were men's and women's accessories — scarves, gloves and hats — on racks in the front of the store, as well as a jewelry counter that featured both women's jewelry and men's watches.

"Mrs. Ewing, first name Candice, lives in Fairmont, was over there," Fletch said, pointing to a section of merchandise cordoned off with yellow-and-black police tape. "Behind that rack."

Fletcher lifted the tape for Nakamura and Brice to cross under it as he continued. "She had the little girl, Marley, three years old, in a basket." The clothes in that section of the store were dresses, most of them evening gowns hanging on racks that were probably nine or ten feet tall. The sports clothes, pants and shirts and shorts were farther down."

"You could start a bonfire and roast marshmallows back there and nobody'd see you," Brice said, nodding at the clothes racks.

"The mother said she just went around a single rack of long dresses, pulling them out and looking and letting them drop back. The little girl was in the cart where the mother started. She said she wasn't even gone a minute, but ..."

"But?" Nakamura asked.

"I'm betting it was longer than that. Women get interested in clothes, they hold them up to themselves, imagine how they'll look with this pair of shoes or that handbag. They lose track of time."

Brice looked at Fletcher with a new respect.

"When she got back around and saw that the little girl

wasn't in the cart, she thought the child had climbed out, and even thinking that she was frantic. The little girl is deaf, couldn't hear her mother call her. Mrs. Ewing immediately called out, 'I've lost my little girl. She can't hear. Please help me find her!' And all the women in that section, store employees, everybody who heard her, started searching. They probably looked for five, maybe ten minutes before they dialed 911."

And after that it was another four or five minutes before the first units arrived, three or four more minutes before they locked down the parking lot. The kidnapper had ten, maybe fifteen minutes to get away.

Nakamura pointed up to the dark circles on the ceiling.

"Security camera footage?"

Fletcher shook his head. "Those are just for show, to curb shoplifting. There aren't any cameras in them. But there are cameras at all the entrances to the four halls of the mall and to the food court. There are also security cameras mounted on the back sides of all the buildings, on the end, that cover the loading docks and back entrances. I have the mall manager cuing that up for you in his office."

"The people who were in the store—" Nakamura began.

"Kept them all here," Fletcher said, pointing out a group of people standing with a police officer on the other side of the store's glass front doors. "The thing is, Mrs. Ewing said she would have sworn she was the only person looking at clothes. She didn't see anybody else. And in the women's section, you'd think if the kidnapper is a man, she'd have noticed him."

Brice looked around.

"A man would stick out like a bump on a pickle in a place like Victoria's Secret, but a father could have been going through this area on his way to look at children's shoes." Brice turned back toward the front entrance to the store. "To get to the men's department from the entrance, the most direct route is right through here."

"Nobody else in the store noticed Mrs. Ewing or who might have been standing near her. The woman who runs the jewelry kiosk said there were several men and boys in the store at the time. She was helping one pick out a watch when the mother started screaming."

A youngish man wearing a stylish men's-store suit, a baby blue shirt and pink tie approached them.

"I'm Donald Bridger, the mall manager," he said to Brice. Brice directed his attention to the diminutive FBI agent and pointed out he was in charge of the investigation. But the man still addressed Brice when he spoke. "We have the security video cued up for you to watch. If you will follow me, please."

As they walked out of the store, Brice examined the stores to the left and right. The front of the shoe store was solid glass. The shelves were low, the view unimpeded. Only the clearance sale shoes in the back of the store were on racks tall enough to hide anything from view, and they were placed at right angles to the door so you could see down them all the way to the end.

On the left, the double doors into the pizza parlor were glass, but there were no windows that looked from the restaurant into the mall. Instead of following Fletcher, Nakamura and the mall manager, Brice walked toward the big mall doors, stepped back out onto the portico in front of them, looking at the pizza parlor to his right. The business didn't have an outside entrance. But there was a drive-through window that opened on that part of the building in the back, and a lane of traffic peeled off in that direction from the street in front of the mall. No cars were going through there now, but a car right in front of the mall entrance would appear to be waiting in line to pick up a pizza.

Brice turned and went back into the building, examining the jewelry store and the bookstore. Both had all-glass fronts. The jewelry store was wide open, with glass cases and nothing tall enough to hide behind. The bookstore was the opposite.

Though the front was glass, the bookshelves lining the store were in no particular configuration. Some sat at right angles to the front windows. Some didn't. It was an intentionally cozy rabbit warren in there, plenty of cubby holes where sight lines were blocked all around.

He caught up to Fletcher and Nakamura at the end of a hallway in front of a door marked "Security." A gray-uniformed mall security officer sat at a desk in the small room beyond in front of a big monitor on which were displayed the views from every camera in the building, on both ends of each side of the main hallways.

Some of the screens were blank.

"What's up with that?" Brice asked.

"Those cameras are … non-functional," the security officer said.

Each view was identified with lettering on the bottom of the image. Only one of the North Hallway cameras was working — the one on the Your Style Your Way side of the hall. It faced the jewelry store and the bookstore, displayed an area in front of them all the way to the middle of the main hallway. But the fronts of the department store, the shoe store and the pizza parlor were not visible.

"The jewelry store and Billions a'Books have their own security camera systems," the mall manager said. "They might have caught something on those that wouldn't show up on the mall hallway cameras."

Brice turned to Fletcher and told him quietly to get the managers of both businesses to cue up what their cameras had recorded, that he'd be by in a little while to take a look at it.

All the video would be studied thoroughly, frame by frame, by FBI forensics experts, but Brice and Nakamura wanted to get a look now to see what they could turn up. Together they studied the big multi-framed screen, scrutinizing the videos from fifteen minutes before the child was reported missing until fifteen minutes after. The security guard fast-forwarded the images to 1.5 speed but stopped them as directed.

Brice concentrated on the half image of the North Hallway, watched the people crossing the centerline of the hallway from the stores on the other side. He was, of course, looking for anybody with a small child in their arms or walking by their sides, but also for anything big enough to put a child into. After more than a half hour of study, and running the tapes back to play again in several places, the smoking gun they were looking for wasn't there. Four people were accompanied by small children. In three of the cases, there was more than one child with one or more adults. In the fourth case, the man and little girl were black.

Three strollers exited the building by the North Entrance doors, two pushed by women, one by a man. It was impossible to see the children in the strollers, though one was the kind into which an infant car seat fit — too small for a three-year-old. The others, though — they needed to find those.

A woman wearing a baseball cap with a ponytail sticking out the back and a baggy sweatshirt over black exercise tights crossed the hallway from the department store side and exited the far-left outside door. She was carrying a Planet Fitness gym bag — *conceivably* big enough to hold a three-year-old, he supposed, if you folded one up and stuffed it in. But the woman was small, and it was clear by the way she casually tossed the bag up onto her shoulder as she pushed open the door that the bag was empty, maybe a pair of socks and some gym shoes.

A UPS driver hauled out a box big enough to hold a child. From what it was possible to see of him loading the box into the truck, its contents were heavy. Then he returned to the mall and exited again a short time later with an even bigger, even heavier box.

An old nun, the kind you didn't see very often, in a long

black habit and black headpiece, hobbled with her cane toward the outside entrance beside the pizza parlor.

Brice asked to see the views from the two outside video cameras that covered the back side of the department store, shoe store and pizza parlor. No one came in or went out the back entrances during the time frame. A garbage truck emptied the four dumpsters in the alleyway, two behind the department store, two on the other side. A stream of cars, fairly steady, passed through the drive-in window of the pizza parlor.

Nakamura took a call, then turned to Brice.

"Trimboli says Lucas Ferrigliano hasn't come home from work yet, is out on deliveries. The parents tried calling but didn't reach him. The little Campbell girl, you got her to open up. Go take a crack at the boy."

As Brice hurried to his cruiser, he acknowledged to himself what he hadn't admitted to the others. He couldn't put his finger on what it was — couldn't identify the niggling itch in his mind, but *something* about the images from the security cameras set off an alarm, something that was right there but he wasn't seeing it. What it was eluded him, fluttered like a moth around a back porch light. He couldn't shake the feeling, though. He had *missed* something.

Chapter Thirty

As THEY DROVE BACK to Shadow Rock from Huntington, T.J. and Dobbs discussed different possible scenarios and each one of them seemed worse to Bailey than the last.

T.J. pointed out that since Caitlyn was an adult, and since the Bartleys were not legally related to her, the police could have found out all manner of things about Caitlyn that the couple was never told.

"Might be her body turned up somewhere three, four years after she went missin'," T.J. said. "Caitlyn was a ward of the state of West Virginia and her records was on file — all that dental work, police coulda identified a Jane Doe with that."

"So it's possible there was a murder investigation *somewhere*, which means maybe the police found clues, evidence, something that'd help Brice."

"It's a whole lot more likely that if she was kidnapped — and it is *if*, we just speculatin' here — but if she was snatched by the same person as took Riley Campbell and Christi Strickland, that means he got away with it. Probably 'cause nobody ever found her body."

"Or if they did, the police investigation didn't turn up anything," Dobbs said as he pulled up to the Watford House.

T.J. had left his car in the driveway and he went through the gate to get Sparky. He'd left the dog there instead of at home because Sparky liked playing in Bailey's fenced-in back yard. She was making coffee when he came into the kitchen through the back screen door.

"I'm going to get Sparks a ball," she said, turning to him, "so he can—"

The look on T.J.'s face stole her breath.

"What?"

He held out his phone. "I just seen it … there's another child missin'."

The coffee mug fell out of her suddenly numb fingers. It was plastic, so it only bounced on the hardwood kitchen floor. She didn't even bother to pick it up.

"Who? Where?"

"A little girl, name of Marley Ewing. She was took out of a shopping cart in Your Style Your Way while her mama was on the other side of a rack of clothes and couldn't see."

Bailey sank down into a kitchen chair.

"She's three years old. And she's deaf."

"Three!"

Bailey wanted to cry. She wanted to scream and curse and throw something and— She did none of those things, and even if she had they wouldn't have relieved the agony in her belly. Marley Ewing was Bethany's age! Someone … someone who'd already kidnapped two other children — and likely *killed* them — had snatched her right out from under her mother's nose.

It could have been Bethany!

María could have left Bethany like that — of course, she could have! Her sister loved to shop. She'd get so engrossed in what she was looking at, not paying attention, and somebody could come along and take her, take Bethany.

"I ain't gone ask if you're alright cause it's clear you ain't. Can I get you some—?"

Bailey got unsteadily to her feet and brushed wordlessly past him toward the hall, went into the bathroom and closed the door firmly behind her, leaned against it. Then slid down it until her butt hit the floor, wrapped her arms around her knees and rested her forehead against them. She sat like that, not thinking anything and thinking everything, her emotions so tangled up she couldn't even cry, her mind spin—

Stop it right now!

She was *not* going to go there. She was better than this. She was *stronger* than this. Bethany was *just fine*. Another mother's child had been ripped away from her and Bailey was sorry, so very sorry. But it wasn't Bethany and Bailey was not entitled to throw a self-indulgent self-pity party just because the child was Bethany's age.

Get. A. Grip.

She clenched her jaw and got to her feet. Avoiding looking at her reflection in the mirror, she ran cold water into the sink and splashed it on her face. Then she looked up and her eye fell on the tiny scar on her temple that you could only see if you were looking for it, the scar she'd put there when she shot herself in the head ... so she wouldn't have to endure being separated from Bethany on her third birthday.

"Hello, Oscar," she said to the bullet in her brain Brice had named the day they'd ridden out across Whispering Mountain Lake together on jet skis. "I was a pathetic idiot to put you there. A weak, whiny wimp." There were way, *way* worse things in life than being separated from your child. Riley Campbell's mother, Christi Strickland's mother and now Marley Ewing's mother could all testify to that.

She took the hand towel and scrubbed her face with it, then went back into the kitchen, where T.J. was sitting with Sparky at his feet. He'd finished making coffee, she could smell it. She went to the coffeemaker, poured the rich brown liquid into the mug T.J.'d picked up off the floor and took a small sip.

"You gone be alright now." It wasn't a question, but it *was* unnerving the way that man could read her like a cheap novel.

"I have to do something." Her back was still turned to him.

"And that somethin' would be …?"

"You know as well as I do what — I have to connect to Caitlyn—" She stopped, froze.

"What?"

"The portrait. Maybe I can … oh, I don't know … paint more of it, connect that way."

"Dobbs stopped you before you was done when you was paintin' Macy Cosgrove, 'fore you painted her face, and you connected when you went back and finished it. But you finished this one all the way to the end, didn't leave a speck of bare canvas."

She took a big gulp of coffee, set the mug down and turned to face him.

"Let's go see."

"You sure this is a good idea?"

"Oh, I'm sure it's a terrible idea."

T.J. followed her down the hallway to the studio. The portrait of the catatonic little girl lying on the ceiling of an overturned camper was hard to look at. Bailey only let her eyes skim over it before she went to the shelves by the window and began to prepare a pallet.

T.J. said nothing, just stood in the doorway watching.

She moved quickly and efficiently, hurrying to do the thing before her courage abandoned her. She was, after all, attempting to *live through Caitlyn Whitfield's murder* with her.

She set the pallet on its stand beside her easel and picked up a brush, dipped it into a gob of white paint and held it out in front of the picture. She took a breath, then resolutely touched the brush to the canvas.

BAM. She was gone.

. . .

THE WORLD DOESN'T LOOK RIGHT, ONLY she isn't outside this time, like the last time she saw the world distorted this way, yesterday in the park.

As before, what is in front of her is oversized, out of proportion. She can make no sense of what she sees because somehow she is able to see to the right, the left, above and below, too.

There is no color. The world is striated. Not one world, multiple views of the world and it looks like it has been cut apart, torn apart and the frayed edges don't quite meet.

She feels a weight, like she's carrying something but it's not heavy. The thing she is carrying … it's white, shiny.

All she can see is multiple views of a colorless world with dim sparkles of light.

Hissing. She hears that strange hissing sound she had heard the other day. This hissing doesn't sound like steam from a pot, or even a snake. The hissing is almost a rasping sound.

AND THEN IT WAS OVER. The world of the studio began to reform around her and she felt her hands relax and heard a clatter as the paintbrush she'd been using fell to the floor.

"You back now, sugar," T.J. said from behind her and only then did she feel his steadying hands on her upper arms. "You need to sit."

But she didn't want to move, stood searching the canvas, examining the portrait. Looking for—

"It's the same," she bleated, bewildered. "I know I painted *something*."

She looked down at the paintbrush that lay at the floor at her feet, smearing white paint on the hardwood. Given that she dropped paint-loaded brushes on a fairly regular basis now, she really ought to put a drop cloth under her easel.

She noted then that it was a single paintbrush. She'd only used one.

"Nothing's changed."

"Yeah, it is. Look there. That's what you was working on."

A small space in the upper right corner of the portrait was shiny with wet paint. It was a portion of a broken window, out of which you could see the woods beyond. And you still could see the woods, just not quite as clearly. Obscuring the view was an overlay of white spots, no, silver spots. Twinkling.

The spots hung suspended in the air on this side of the broken pane of glass. They sparkled, not just because the paint was wet. They'd been artfully crafted to look like shimmering dots, twinkling like Christmas lights and Bailey had no idea what they were.

"It's dew." T.J.'s voice was soft beside her. "I get up every morning early, *before sunrise.*" Clearly, he wore that as a badge of honor. "And that's when they's dew, sparklin' like diamonds on everything, little blades of grass, each with a single drip of water on them, all shiny."

"Dew doesn't hang suspended in the air."

"No, but I s'pect they's a screen over that window up there. I doubt that even Sophia Watford in the flesh coulda painted the tiny squares of a mesh screen in" — he looked at his watch — "maybe a minute and a half."

That felt right. She hadn't been in the "alternate reality" long at all, not nearly as long as when she was watching Macy Cosgrove feed carrots to her baby brother. But unlike what she'd seen then, this little foray into the Twilight Zone had provided no clues at all — certainly nothing as illustrative as the reflective side of a shiny toaster in the background.

"Well *this* was a colossal waste of time." She started to reach down and pick up the brush off the floor, but T.J. wouldn't let her.

"I said, *you need to sit.*" Gently but firmly, T.J. guided her to the overstuffed chair in front of the shelves by the door and she collapsed into it.

"Where'd you go? What'd you see?"

"I don't know and I don't know. It was more … more a hallucination than a vision."

She told T.J. what she'd seen, how it was vastly distorted reality.

"It was like I was connecting to someone who was taking drugs, or dreaming some horrible black-and-white nightmare. What's happening to me?"

"I don't know, but I got a pretty good guess. Seth Cosgrove's daughter was a normal, happy little girl." He gestured to the portrait with still-wet paint. "Caitlyn Whitfield ain't. She's *insane*, and when you connect to a mind that's all tore up like hers, ain't no telling what kind of random images, nightmares, garbled memories you gonna stumble over."

Bailey thought about how she'd felt when she first awoke with Oscar in her skull, like someone had taken her box of crayons and turned them upside down on the floor. All the crayons were still there, but it took her a while to find everything, and to put the crayons back into the box in the right spots. Caitlyn's crayons had been dropped into a blender.

"Let's go finish that cup of coffee."

She'd left her cellphone on the kitchen counter and it rang as she walked back into the room. Caller ID identified Dobbs.

"Houston, we have liftoff," he said.

"What?"

"Just got a text from Zankoski. He found out what happened to Caitlyn Whitfield."

Chapter Thirty-One

BRICE PULLED up in front of the Ferrigliano house and Agent Trimboli, who'd been assigned to detain the boy for questioning, walked out to meet him as he came up the sidewalk.

"He's not home yet," she said, her voice as tired as the circles under her eyes indicated she was. Fatigue had dulled the sharp edges of her personality, sapped the energy it took to emasculate anyone near her unfortunate enough to possess a Y chromosome. "The parents went next door to the Campbells'."

As he stepped up onto the Campbells' porch, he could hear the sound of raised voices inside. He didn't bother to knock. Ashok Arya, seated at the dining room table with headphones tethering him to the recording equipment on the Campbells' phone line, nodded toward the kitchen where an argument was raging.

"Natives are getting restless," he said.

Brice stepped into the kitchen doorway and stopped there.

"I want to know what your Lucas was doing with my baby," cried Jeanette Campbell, her voice high and reedy-shrill.

"Now, Jeanette, you're jumping to—" Norm Campbell was obviously trying, and clearly failing, to be the voice of reason. Tony Ferrigliano was obviously trying, and apparently succeeding, to stay out of the fray. It was the women who were going after each other.

"Why would you accuse Lucas of something so ... *horrible*?" said Francine Ferrigliano. "You've known him his whole life."

"And he's known Riley his whole life, too," Jeanette Campbell said. "So what does he know that he's not telling?"

"He doesn't know anything."

"He knows something, or the FBI wouldn't want to talk to him."

"That's right — *Talk. To. Him.* That doesn't make him a suspect. You're blowing this all out of—"

Then Francine spotted Brice.

"You tell her, Sheriff. Tell her my son didn't—"

"Do you think Lucas had something to do with Riley's disappearance?" Jeanette Campbell was hanging onto control by a thread. "Do you?"

"Everybody needs to calm down," Brice said.

"My little boy is missing. He's *gone.* And if Lucas knows what hap—"

"He doesn't know anything about Riley's kidnap—"

"Then why does the FBI—?"

"I said, *calm down!*" Brice's voice was sharp enough to cause internal bleeding. "We want to talk to Lucas because he might have information we need." He held up his hands as all four of the parents chimed in at once, the Campbells with accusations, the Ferriglianos with denials. "We have some things we want to discuss with him." He turned to Francine. "I thought you said he'd be home by now."

"He'll be here any minute. He usually gets off at noon but he went out on a final delivery." She stepped up to Brice and looked pleadingly into his face. "Tell us what's going on,

Sheriff McGreggor. Please. Why do you want to talk to Lucas about Riley? What could he *possibly* know that would be helpful?"

"We won't know that until we talk to him."

All four of the parents exploded with questions, accusations and denials at once. It was time to separate them before they came to blows.

"Would you please come with me?" he said to the Ferriglianos. "I'd like to speak to you privately."

"What do you want to ask them that you can't say in front of us?" Jeanette demanded. She turned to Francine, glaring. "We were best friends, had no secrets from each other, lived in each other's pockets. And all that time Lucas was ... was ..."

"Was doing absolutely nothing!" Tony Ferrigliano finally leapt off the fence, roaring into Papa Bear mode. "My boy is not a ... he could *not* have hurt Riley. Don't you dare suggest—"

"*I'm* not suggesting. The FBI is suggesting—"

"That's enough!" Brice's voice reverberated like a Howitzer. In the stunned silence that followed, he took Francine's elbow and shoved her toward the door, cocked his chin in that direction and told Tony, "*Now!*"

The Campbells fell silent and the Ferriglianos preceded Brice out the door and across the yard to their home. Agent Trimboli stood in the doorway of the living room. It was fashionably rustic — a high-beamed ceiling with hunting and fishing trophies on the walls, each with a plaque providing the weight/length of the fish, or the distance from which the buck, elk, caribou or — that was a buffalo! — had been shot, and who'd pulled the trigger.

Brice studied the trophies for a moment, ignoring the parents as they bombarded him with questions. Then he turned to them. Stood silent until their babble ran out of steam.

"Sit down and listen to me," he told them.

They sat.

"Nobody's accusing your son of wrongdoing. Nobody's saying he had something to do with the disappearance of Riley Campbell."

"Tell that to Jeanette Campbell," Francine muttered.

"I would like your permission to search Lucas's room."

Tony went off like a bottle rocket.

"You just said you didn't think he'd done anything wrong, so why do you want to search his room?"

"It's my job to turn over every stone, look under every rock. You have the right to refuse to allow me to search the property, in which case I will secure the area, no one in or out, and I'll get a court-ordered search warrant. That will eat up time I could spend looking for three missing kids, but it won't change the outcome."

"Oh, go ahead," Tony said. "He didn't do anything, so what could he possibly have to hide?"

Brice turned to go upstairs and both parents started to accompany him.

"You two stay down here with me," said Agent Trimboli, with no less steel in her voice than there'd been in Brice's.

Francine started to protest but Tony touched her arm and shook his head. Then they both sat down heavily on the couch.

"It's the first room on the right," Francine said.

Brice stepped into Lucas's room and the sweat-sock, tennis-shoe, pile-of-dirty-laundry stink, the universal aroma of teenage-boy-dom, assaulted his senses. Clearly, the boy had gone "nose blind."

West Virginia University pennants competed for wall space with posters of a sensuously thin blonde movie star. Brice supposed she was a movie star, but maybe she was a rock singer. She looked vaguely familiar but he couldn't place her face. He searched the contents of the drawers in the bedside nightstands and the dresser. No drugs, nothing out of the ordinary. Boy stuff.

Under the mattress on the unmade bed he found a "true crime" magazine missing a cover that contained staged shots of women being tortured, lots of blood and gore, out there on the edge of appropriate for a teenage boy. Obviously, Lucas knew his parents would not approve.

The laptop on the desk was turned off. He examined the contents of the desk drawers and turned up nothing. The clothes in the closet were fashionably "shabby chic," ragged shirts and jeans with holes in the knees along with stinky sneakers and a pair of muddy boots. Feeling around on the top shelf, he found sweaters, out-of-season hoodies and … his fingers brushed something in the back corner.

Tall as he was, he didn't need to climb on a chair to move the clothing that obscured what he'd touched — a shoebox. Not one that'd held the teenager's own size-eleven shoes. This was much smaller, must have been his little sister's. Brice took out gloves and put them on before lifting the box off the shelf and setting it on the desk. Inside were several pieces of jewelry — shiny bling, gold chains and two rings. Brice was no expert, but he thought they were just knockoffs. If they were authentic, though, real gold and the ring stones not zirconium, the boy had some source of income in addition to working as a delivery driver. In the bottom of the box were photographs.

Pictures of Riley Campbell.

Brice picked them up and examined them, one by one. The first was a school picture, this year's. Beneath it was the kindergarten picture, where his front teeth were obviously missing. Other pictures were snapshots, many of them with other members of both families. Campfire pictures. Lake pictures. Picnic pictures. Holiday pictures. But all of them were centered on Riley. Riley roasting a marshmallow on a blazing campfire. Riley sitting on the shore studying the cork floating on the water at the end of his fishing line. Riley mugging for the camera in his Halloween costume. The Spiderman costume all built out, stuffed so it looked like the wearer was as buff as Ben Affleck, put Brice in mind of the superhero dolls he had found in Riley Campbell's secret treasure.

None of the pictures were in any way lurid or inappropriate. Oh, there were shots of the boy in swimming trunks, one of him coming out of the water with a towel wrapped around his waist, as if something had happened to his trunks in the lake. The photos showed nothing of a prurient nature. But the sheer number of them made a statement, said … something, but Brice didn't know what.

What he did know was that Nakamura would want to have a long talk about them with Lucas Ferrigliano.

Leaving the box of photos on the boy's desk, Brice closed the bedroom door behind him and went back downstairs where the parents were waiting in the living room. They both jumped to their feet when he entered.

"Did you find … well, anything?" Tony wanted to know.

Brice sidestepped the question.

"I thought you said Lucas would be home any time now. That was fifteen minutes ago."

"You said the same thing half an hour before that," Trimboli said. "Where is he?"

"I left him a message that you wanted to talk to him," Francine said.

"So his phone's off?" Brice asked.

"No … that's the thing." She cast a look at her husband. "It's not off. It rings. He's just not picking up."

"The store manager said he was out on a delivery and—" Tony began.

"No, I didn't talk to the manager," Francine corrected. "He … doesn't like Lucas, threatened to fire him if he took his dog on deliveries again and since she's not here, Lucas must've—"

"Who *did* you talk to?" Brice demanded.

"That little girl who works the drive-in window."

"The drive-in window where? Where does Lucas work?"

"Andolino's Pies, the pizza place in the mall."

Chapter Thirty-Two

"T.J.'s still here," Bailey told Dobbs. "He'll want to hear. Putting you on speaker."

Dobbs's deep baritone boomed in mid-sentence out of the little device on the kitchen counter.

"— a written report along with his bill, which he let me know would be enough to put his kids through Harvard."

"Okay, Dobbs, we're both here," Bailey said.

"Like I said, this is just a synopsis. Zankoski has all the details and said he'll email it to me in a little while. But I knew you'd want to know."

"Stop fiddle-fartin' around and tell us."

Bailey stood with her arms crossed, felt her fingernails digging into her upper arms as she tensed for the blow.

"Caitlyn Whitfield wasn't kidnapped and murdered by the same person who kidnapped Riley and Christi."

Bailey stopped breathing, couldn't speak, but T.J. voiced her thought.

"And you know that how?"

"She wasn't kidnapped by anybody. Or murdered by anybody. Caitlyn Whitfield is alive."

"Alive?" The word burst with a breath out of Bailey's

mouth. Then she started sputtering. "But how did she ... where did she ... why—?"

"Do you want to ask questions or do you want me to tell you what I know? You get to pick one."

"Okay, tell us," T.J. grumbled.

"He found Caitlyn in Kentucky. Remember the Bartleys saying she'd worked at a Starbucks? Well, she got a job at one in Louisville about a week after she vanished from Huntington."

Alive! Alive! Alive! was reverberating in Bailey's head like she'd climbed inside a kettle drum. But if Caitlyn was alive, why didn't Bailey feel any connection to her?

Dobbs was saying something, and she had to ask him to repeat it.

"I said, she met a young man there, whirlwind romance and they got married."

"*Married?* But she was only eighteen."

"Save the commentary," T.J. warned. "He'll drag this out all night if you don't shut up and listen."

"Lip zipped."

"So the man she married came from money, as in Kentucky-horse-farm money, which is *oooold* money."

Bailey knew what came next — his family was *not* happy about their son marrying somebody who was not of equal old-money stature. Been there, done that, bought the t-shirt, wore it out, cut it up and used it for a dust cloth. She wondered if they'd managed to convey to Caitlyn their disdain and disapproval, as Aaron's family had conveyed it to her, without ever saying a word of it out loud.

"... on a honeymoon to the Caribbean, occupied the honeymoon suites in the most expensive resorts in Antigua, St. Martin, Grand Cayman. They were booked for two weeks of wedded bliss. But it ended after eleven days when her brand new husband died."

"Died?" T.J. was incredulous.

"Was *killed,* actually."

Bailey sucked in a gasp of horror.

"Zankoski said there'd be more details in the final report, but in brief it seems the two of them were out alone and got mugged — attacked by a gang, most likely. Caitlyn was just knocked unconscious, but they beat her husband to death and Zankoski said that in the crime-scene pictures he saw the guy was totally unrecognizable. Not just you couldn't tell who he was. You couldn't tell *what* he was. He was so torn up the body didn't even look human."

Bailey was so horrified she couldn't speak. First a poor little girl survives the wreck that killed her parents ... and the nightmare after. Goes zombie for almost two years, and when she finally finds happiness ... a *life!* ... her husband gets murdered.

"After that it got a little tricky. She had money — lots of it, apparently — from her husband's estate and from his insurance policies. She used it to pull another vanishing act, only this time she had the funding to do it right. She changed her name, got a whole new identity and sprang back to life again in Pittsburgh, where she enrolled as a freshman at Pitt, graduated in three years and immediately got a job. She worked at the first job for three years, and has been working where she is currently employed for the past two years."

"I don't know if this sounds like a fairytale or a horror story," Bailey said, her voice airless. "I'm still trying to figure out ... if she's alive, then why is there no connection?"

"Sweetheart, you ain't heard nothing yet."

"You sayin' there's more weird? Now, *that's* scary."

"Are you two sitting down?"

"What? I'm gonna be so shocked I pass out dead on the floor?"

"You never know. Okay ... Caitlyn Whitfield married Darren Foster, III, of the Lexington, Kentucky, King Farm

Fosters. So she became Caitlyn Foster. After his death, she changed her name to … Melody McCallum."

Bailey lost her breath, literally couldn't seem to draw any air into her lungs. If she hadn't been sitting down, she might actually have collapsed in the floor from shock.

Melody McCallum!

She realized Dobbs was still talking and forced herself to attend to what he was saying.

"… majored in education and minored entomology at Pitt. When she graduated, she took a job teaching second grade at Madison Elementary School here in our very own Shadow Rock, West Virginia, and then became a first-grade teacher at Corruthers Elementary. When she moved here, she had a holding company purchase The Cedars."

"The Cedars!" T.J. cried. "As in *the* The Cedars?"

"The same. It was a rooming house at the time and she just moved in — people thought she was a boarder — and one by one the other roomers moved out until the house was hers. I guess she didn't want to flaunt the fact that a first-grade teacher owned one of the most famous homes in Kavanaugh County."

"She lives in The Cedars … *owns* The Cedars …" T.J. was obviously scrambling to make it all fit into his head, too.

As puzzle pieces began to fall into place for Bailey she realized what a fool's errand she'd been on, they'd all been on, from the very beginning.

"Painting the little girl in the car didn't have a thing to do with Riley Campbell," she said, the full impact of that taking her breath away. "All this chasing around, searching, trying to find … I painted Caitlyn Whitfield because 'Melody McCallum' gave Riley's picture to Brice. He told me so when he handed it to me."

"Well …" T.J. stopped. Then he continued. "There wasn't no way to know whether or not you could paint somebody — Riley Campbell — just 'cause you'd decided that's what you was going to do. I guess the answer is no, you can't. You painted that little girl 'cause of the … whatever it is, the energy, the vibe, whatever … was left on the boy's picture by the teacher who'd given it to Brice."

Bailey sat where she was, letting the information sink in slowly, trying to assimilate it.

"I don't have the whole, detailed report yet. Soon's I get it, I'll bring it over."

Bailey punched the off button on the phone and looked at T.J. She repeated it again, out loud, trying to make it real.

"We never were helping to find that little boy."

"We was lost ducks in high weeds, honking out one explanation or another but we didn't have no real idea where the pond was. Still, don't be so hard on yourself. There wasn't no way to find out the little girl didn't have nothing to do with Riley except to chase it down and find it out."

"And now we know."

Some of the pieces didn't fit, though.

"If that little girl in there," she gestured toward the studio, "is Melody McCallum, why haven't I been connecting to her? Melody … *Caitlyn* was right here, probably not ten miles away, but I never once sensed her the way I did Macy Cosgrove. Why not?"

"I can't answer that question. But I 'spect it's what I was sayin' before. That little girl … Caitlyn, or Melody … she wasn't draggin' a full string of fish. Connecting to her mind was like sticking a finger in a light socket."

"Maybe. Still …"

"You'd best be careful."

"Huh?"

"I bet you ain't even *got* a fire extinguisher."

"What are you talking about?"

"All them thoughts spinning 'round in your head like that — friction's likely to catch your hair on fire."

Bailey couldn't even manage a grin.

"I ain't the one's got the 'sight' — you do. But a body don't have to be psychic to know what's on your mind."

"And that is …?"

"You want to go talk to Melody McCallum."

Actually, she hadn't gotten that far yet. The hurricane that'd just blown through her mind, rattling all the doors and windows in her soul, had left her disoriented, with only one clear thought: it'd all been for nothing.

But T.J. was right. She had to talk to Melody McCallum. She'd never be able to make sense of all this until she did.

T.J. set down his coffee cup and got to his feet. "Let's do this."

"Go see Melody? *Now?* Why now?"

"Why not now? Needs to be sometime today 'cause you ain't gonna sleep a wink tonight until you talk to that woman."

"Just show up on her doorstep? *Hi, you don't know me, but I painted a portrait of you and then tracked you down. So naturally I came right over.* Shouldn't we … call first?"

"You got her phone number?"

She shook her head.

"I ain't bothering Brice to get it." He turned toward the back door and motioned for Sparky to follow. "Go chase some more butterflies. We'll be home directly."

Sparky didn't move. He sat looking at T.J.

T.J. had already pushed open the screen door before he realized Sparky hadn't moved.

"Sparky?"

Arf!

A solitary bark. T.J.'d told Bailey the sound was like "aloha" — had lots of meanings. It could mean *help me, my ball's under the chair.* Or *pet me immediately.* Or *it's cold, can I get in the bed with you?*

Or … *something's wrong, but I don't know what.*

"Sparky, come!"

Instead of bounding to T.J.'s side, the dog lowered his

head and walked slowly across the kitchen floor and out the back door.

Bailey looked at T.J.

"What was *that* about?"

"It's supposed to rain later today. Guess he knows a storm's comin'."

Bailey could tell T.J. didn't really think that's what was bothering the dog.

Chapter Thirty-Three

BAILEY HAD HEARD about but had never actually seen the historic old homes in Shadow Rock, had been promising herself she'd spend two or three days just being a tourist to get the lay of the land in the fairytale town filled with "lake cottages" built by the Carnegies, the Rockefellers, the Fords and the uber rich Whoever-Elses they hung out with. A handful of the cottages were still privately owned, a few had been transformed into hotels or rooming houses, but most were museums, still filled with all the finery they'd had back in the day, with guided tours to show how the other half had lived. It was the tourist-trade draw of those mansions, along with the pristine, crystal-clear lake that had brought the rich icons to build in Kavanaugh County in the first place, that kept the lights on for a good-sized hunk of the town's residents.

The huge house where Bailey lived, the Watford House, was a historic home with an impressive history, but it was a servant's shack compared to the lake cottages. The grandeur of The Cedars was on par with all the others, though it had been transformed into a high-end rooming house half a century ago. T.J. and Dobbs, and probably most of the other residents of Shadow Rock, assumed it still was. Until the private investigator dug out the information, they didn't know that Melody McCallum wasn't a boarder. She owned the place, courtesy of the fortune she had inherited from the husband she'd been married to for less than a month before he was killed. She must have paid a king's ransom for The Cedars, and then kept the sale private because ... yeah, because ...? The most reasonable explanation was that she didn't want to flaunt her wealth, didn't want the whole world to know that a first-grade teacher owned one of the most historic mansions in the whole county. But somehow that didn't ring true, felt a little hollow, didn't quite fit.

This Melody McCallum was a strange duck.

Like the other mansions scattered across the town, The Cedars was not visible from the street. All the old homes rested on acreage surrounded by big trees, fences and tall impenetrable hedges, protective landscaping which prevented gawkers. Bailey didn't know if the original owners had made the barriers for themselves or the town had erected them later when the place was populated with normal people. After all, the Rockefellers could likely be trusted not to break into the Carnegies' to steal a silver tea service, a Faberge egg or a Ming vase.

There was an ornate gate at the entrance of the winding driveway that led to The Cedars and a guardhouse done in the same architecture as the house beyond. No one occupied the guard house now and the gate stood open.

The winding driveway brought the house into view after several twists and turns. The Cedars might not be the biggest or the fanciest home in Shadow Rock, but it was definitely one of the most unique and Bailey couldn't help gasping at the sight of it, painted against the forbidding sky of a coming storm.

T.J. looked across at her and grinned.

The house had three floors with a wide veranda stretching,

as far as Bailey could see, all the way around the ground floor. A portico roof offered a place out of the elements to disembark from your chauffeured limousine at the front door. At one end of the ground floor was a glassed-in circular room — a "conservatory" with a wide garden stretching out from it that featured flowers in every imaginable shape and color. But the house's most interesting feature was on the opposite end from the conservatory. Fully half the house on that end rose up in a turret, a circular structure like a castle. The turret stretched up above the roof of the third floor with a balcony all the way around it and tall windows, featuring a pointed roof that made it appear a lighthouse had been ripped off some rocky seashore in New England and attached to that end of the house.

"I was in this place once years ago but I don't 'magine it's changed much since then. The historical society Nazis in Shadow Rock won't let a little kid build a street-side lemonade stand without their approval. And a permit from the zoning board. And an in-depth study by the Environmental Protection Agency to make sure their presence won't cause an uptick in migraines in indigenous June bugs."

T.J. pointed to the turret/lighthouse as they drew nearer the house along the driveway lined with flower beds and tall poplar trees.

"That right there is amazin' on the inside. The whole second floor is a single gigantic ballroom, and the turret forms one end of it, up through the third floor all the way to a ceiling that's the floor of that pointed cap thing on the top. The chandelier hanging down from that ceiling is ... *amazing.* You'd have to ask the Historical Society Nazis to get the specifics. All I know is that it's the biggest chandelier I ever seen — has thousands and thousands of pieces of multicolored cut glass, dangling in seven graduated circles. Turn off all the lights 'cept that chandelier — more'n five hundred light bulbs, red ones, blue ones, green, all different colors shining through that cut glass casts sparkles like hundreds of thousands of little colored flames on everything, a kaleidoscope of color on the walls and floor — it's stunnin'."

"Did you ever go to a ball there?"

T.J. gave her a baleful look.

"Right, like they'd invite the hired help to the party. But my mama and some of her friends cleaned the place and I seen it once as a kid, and later I come back as an adult. The walls of the ballroom have box seating like in a nineteenth-century opera house so the whole floor is open for dancing. Guests go up into them boxes, sit around tables under crisp white awnings, sippin' wine and eatin' … whatever uber rich folks ate for snacks a hundred years ago, probably wasn't Cheetos. And while you's munching your not-Cheetos, you can watch the dancers down below. Them balcony boxes is staggered at different heights, might be two dozen of 'em, all with ornate spindle railings. Each one of 'em must be big enough to seat twenty, thirty people."

"How do you get to the box-seat balconies?"

"You gotta climb up circular staircases that wind up from the floor — enclosed, so on the dance floor level, there's all these ornate archways along the wall that led to the staircases. After I seen the movie, I realized them archways looked like Hobbit-hole doors. And the balconies are connected to each other by suspended walkways like beds on a string, so you can climb around from one to the next …" He stopped. "'less you's afraid of heights, of course. There's people — present company excluded, of course — who'd rather lick a truck stop toilet than clamber 'round on them balconies like a monkey — dangling twenty, thirty, fifty feet off the floor."

"You're afraid of heights?"

"I never said that!"

"But you climbed up that tree in Turkey Neck Hollow when the explosion—"

"I coulda climbed the back side of the Hoover Dam that day."

They rounded the last curve and pulled up in front of the house and T.J. finished his description.

"On the back wall of the ballroom — if a round room's got a *back* wall — is a winding staircase with switchbacks that crisscrosses it and opens up into that turret thing on the top. There's also a glassed-in elevator for those who want the view of the whole ballroom without the climb. At the top, there's steps on the outside of the turret that go down through the ceiling of the veranda into the back yard. And the whole back yard, shoot, must be big as a football field, is a hedge maze. I thought it was cool 'til I seen *The Shining.* You couldn't drag me in there now with a team of Clydesdales and the Budweiser beer wagon. Ever time I turned a corner I'd be s'pecting to meet Jack Nicholson with an ax."

Chapter Thirty-Four

Dobbs had just opened the email from the private investigator when his phone rang. He was surprised to see the caller was Zankoski.

"You get the report I sent?"

"Like two seconds ago. I haven't had time to read it."

"I put *everything* I turned up in the report. It's all there, even the parts that don't make sense. That's why I need to … explain …"

"Okay."

There was silence on the other end of the line.

"I'm listening."

"You know I'm a retired police officer, right? I told you that part."

"You did. And you came highly recommended by the police officers you listed as references."

"You called the references? I didn't think anybody actually did that."

"The lieutenant on the Milwaukee Metro Police Department said he'd hire you back in a heartbeat, but he figured you were making so much money as a private investigator he couldn't get into a bidding war. You haven't billed me yet, so I'm hoping he was wrong about that part."

"He wasn't."

"I can always refinance my house."

"I'm calling you because … I went a little above and beyond on this case."

"Angling for a bonus?"

"No, just explaining that there's information in the report you didn't ask me to gather. I did it on my own."

"Because …?"

"Have you ever heard of a police officer's gut? You know what it means?"

"Intuition."

"Yeah, but more than that. When you've been a cop for fifteen, twenty … in my case twenty-five years, sometimes you get a feeling about things. Maybe more like a sixth sense than intuition. You see patterns maybe other people wouldn't see."

"And your police officer's gut kicked in here."

"When it's really strong, it's an itch that gets worse and worse. The only way to scratch it is to find out if you're right, or if it's just a swing-and-a-miss this time."

"What's to be suspicious about looking for a little girl who was in a wreck and who, according to your text, grew up to be a first-grade teacher?"

"Like I said, patterns. It's in the details of the report I sent to you. Might mean something, probably means nothing at all. Safe money's on nothing at all, but you get to decide what to do with it. Open the report to page two where the trail starts at Crenshaw County Hospital and let me walk you through it."

"Okay."

"Caitlyn Whitfield was taken there by ambulance from the site of the wreck that killed her parents. Catatonic, totally unresponsive. After that, she was transferred to Stonybrook Manor — primarily a mental hospital but with a few cases like her, the medical term is 'persistent vegetative state.' You see that part?"

Dobbs scanned down through the report.

"Yes, I'm on it."

"About two months later, the girl was transferred out to the state hospital because Stonybrook was closed. It was closed because the family of a patient who died there raised such a stink about his death that the state inspectors descended on the place like flies on roadkill, found all kinds of violations of sanitation and other regulations, and shut the place down."

"That's about what her aunt told us."

"I could have blown by that, but I picked at the scab. Didn't take much digging. The place was shut down because of an *unsolved murder*. This is where it starts getting weird. A mental patient named Sherman Potter had been committed by the court, ordered him to remain until his eighteenth birthday. He displayed all manner of disturbing behavior as a boy and a teenager, a fetish for women's shoes, several episodes of flashing young girls and peeking in windows. What got him locked up was when he got caught at the high school in a closet where he had drilled a hole in the wall into the girl's locker room shower.

"He was a big kid, six-two, fat — maybe two hundred seventy-five pounds, seventeen years old and set to be released in less than a month. They found his body lying on the floor of a room in a ward at the opposite end of the hospital from his room. Parents pitched a fit, inspectors showed up, bada boom, bada bing, the place is closed. They never did find a single clue in the murder case."

"And this has what to do with Caitlyn Whitfield?"

"The room where Sherman Potter's body was discovered was Caitlyn Whitfield's. The staff theorized he'd sneaked out of his ward and wandered the halls, found a pretty little girl who was incapacitated — maybe decided to try out some of his sick fantasies in the real world. Nobody knows. Potter's not around to explain what he was doing there or finger who killed him."

"You said he weighed two hundred seventy-five pounds, right?"

"And whoever did it killed him by crushing his neck, trachea was ruptured ... more like pulverized."

"Okay, go on."

"So Caitlyn was transferred to the Mildred Mitchell-Bateman Hospital, where she was in the persistent vegetative state ward for more than a year. And during that time, a couple of odd things happened. No connection to her, of course, she was just lying there staring at the ceiling, hadn't responded to any outside stimuli since they pulled her out of that wrecked camper.

"One incident involved an orderly who'd been accused of abusing Alzheimer's patients, apparently had an ax to grind against old people. He was never caught dead to rights doing anything. But way more often than chance could explain, patients left in his care developed hearing problems — punctured eardrums, unexplained bruises, even cigarettes burns. He was found dead on the hospital portico after a three-story swan dive out a patient's window. There were two patients in the room at the time he went air sailing — an eighty-seven-year-old woman who had blood dripping out her ear ... and Caitlyn Whitfield."

"So somebody in that room — what? Pushed him?"

"Must have — he went *through* the screen."

"I thought you said neither of the people in the room was physically able to do a thing like that."

Zankoski paused. "I did." He took a breath and added, "The guy had ... *injuries* you don't get from falling out a window, too. It's in the report."

He didn't elaborate and Dobbs didn't ask.

"Another incident involved a fire. Some whack-job lit up a couch cushion in the craft room and that whole ward of the hospital had to be evacuated because of the smoke. When they went to get Caitlyn, she wasn't in her room, and they went nuts looking for her, finally found her in the basement laundry room lying on her back on the concrete floor. They never found anybody who'd admit to moving her, but *somebody* did. By that time, her muscles had atrophied. She had physical therapy every day so she wasn't all twisted up, but it took months of rehab after she 'woke up' for her to get full use of her body again. Before that she couldn't even have sat up in bed on her own, let alone climbed out of it and — what? Crawled down three flights of stairs by herself?"

"And you're sure—?"

"I'm telling you what was in her file."

Which meant Zankoski had *seen* Caitlyn's medical records. But Dobbs didn't go there. He reached into his pocket without thinking about it and drew out his watch, flicked open the catch, didn't bother to look at the watch face because it didn't keep time.

"Foster care … it's usually survival of the fittest in those places. Kids who just met expected to relate to each other like siblings when their home lives didn't likely model warm fuzzy behavior. The house parents, the Bartleys — I talked to them on the phone after you left."

Dobbs didn't question that, but Zankoski explained anyway.

"Their names and address — that's all you requested but I talked to them anyway. Just … scratching that itch. They said that after Caitlyn got there, the boys treated the girls … with *respect*, said it was because all the kids loved her."

"That's what they told us."

"That's not the story I got when I talked to one of the kids. Just got off the phone with a young man named Tyrone Jefferson who told me he and the other boys were scared spitless, terrified all the time *for years*. Nobody believed them when they told, but if they so much as looked cross-eyed at one of the girls, they heard hissing and grating sounds in the middle of the night, found their toys destroyed — a metal dump truck so crushed you couldn't tell what it was, shoelaces tied together and the shoes left dangling from the highest limb of a *tree nobody could have climbed.*"

"And he thought *Caitlyn*—?"

"No, but it never happened again after she left. There was a party that night, and he and some other boys played a joke on a little girl named Missy, really frightened her and they felt bad about it."

Dobbs remembered — the Bartleys said the boys had tried to calm her, tore the snake and spider apart to show her they weren't real.

"The next morning, Tyrone's bike was missing and for a day or two, they thought maybe Caitlyn had ridden away on it. Then he found it — mangled, twisted up like a pretzel on the roof of a friend's garage."

"And Caitlyn had vanished."

"She was *gone*, but it wasn't a Houdini vanishing act or anything like that. If the police had tried, they could have found her easily enough. She walked from the Bartleys to a bus station and bought a ticket to Louisville, Kentucky."

"The Bartleys told us the police weren't trying very hard."

"Why would they? No sign of a struggle, a legal adult who wasn't required to get anybody's permission."

"Then she got married, right?"

"Wasn't married long, though. She and her husband were in St. Martin on their honeymoon and were attacked. She was found lying on the beach unconscious, her only injury a colossal shiner. But her husband had been dragged off into the bushes and beaten so savagely the police would have had to use dental records to identify the body if he hadn't been carrying a wallet — get that part, *a wallet.* The man had credit cards and several hundred dollars in cash — a Rolex watch, too. Nothing stolen."

He paused.

"Like I said, I saw the crime scene photos. Never seen a worse beating in twenty-five years as a police officer."

"And you think all this means …?"

"I have absolutely no idea what it means!"

Dobbs was surprised by the intensity of the outburst.

"I'm just saying that the alarm in my cop's gut has been going off ever since I started this case. There are too many unexplained … I mean, I checked everything I know to check and all I can prove to be fact is that ever since that wreck, bad things have been happening *around* Caitlyn Whitfield but not *to* her. It's like somebody's … is it possible there was somebody in her life I didn't find, somebody who … I don't know, kept showing up … to *rescue* her?"

Chapter Thirty-Five

T.J. HADN'T NEVER MET Melody McCallum, had listened to others talk about her and had an image of her in his head. But he found it hard to think about her because whenever he did, his thoughts was overlaid by the image of Bailey's portrait of that poor little blonde girl trapped in the wrecked camper, and his mind'd shy away from that like a long-tailed cat from a rocking chair.

He had suggested to Bailey on the way to The Cedars that she might want to make up some reason why they was droppin' by, but Bailey just planned to wing it. Most times in his experience, if you decided to wing it, you ended up falling out of the sky and face-plantin' in a parking lot.

They parked T.J.'s old Ford pickup out front, and he thought he seen the heavy drapes on one of the front windows move as they was walking up the steps. The big, ornate front door looked like it had come out of some medieval castle, built with old, hoary wood and cross beams and metal straps. It was set in an arch of stonework so the door itself must have been twelve feet tall. He figured the ceilings inside were at least that, probably taller. Most of these old houses had high ceilings — built before the advent of air conditioning like they was.

A perfectly manicured flower garden snuggled up against the house on both sides of the porch. The rose bushes next to the walkway had huge, blood-red blossoms. A wind had come up ahead of the storm and the laden stems slow-danced back and forth. Bailey paused to smell them, stood for a moment, then squared her shoulders, climbed the steps, crossed the porch and rang the bell. They heard no sound so maybe it didn't work, but more likely the door was so thick you couldn't hear nothin' on the other side of it.

But wasn't two seconds later that the huge door began to flow so smoothly inward that it had to have been like power steerin' in a car, specifically designed to move effortlessly. The security system tone that sounded when the door opened tinkled like wind chimes.

Standing inside was a small, almost fragile woman with the delicately beautiful features of a cherub.

He'd been expecting her to have the almost-white blonde hair of the little girl in the portrait. But this woman's hair was the color of liquid caramel. Lots of kids' hair changed, got darker as they got older, but he figured this color was somethin' she'd picked. Her hair had red highlights, too, that she'd probably paid some hairdresser more'n his monthly pension to put there. It was thick and shiny, pulled into a curly ponytail.

Her complexion was pale, though, like that of a blonde.

All the descriptions of Melody McCallum had failed to paint the picture of gentleness she radiated, like warmth from a wood stove. He could easily see her cast as Glenda the Good Witch in the Wizard of Oz.

"Yes?" she said, her voice soft. No, it was more than soft. It was ... soothing. She had been so totally typecast as a first-grade teacher she would have been a caricature if it hadn't been genuine.

"Miss McCallum, you don't know me. My name's Bailey Donahue."

Her face lit up like a candle flickering inside amber glass.

"Bailey Donahue! Brice's friend."

She reached out and took Bailey's hand in both of hers and squeezed.

"I'm so glad to meet you." Then she looked instantly self-conscious. "I was working out," she said, glancing at her long-sleeved black turtleneck and black tights. "I wasn't expecting company."

"I'm T.J. Hamilton and I'm Brice's friend, too."

He said it as if being a friend of the sheriff was some kind of magic word, and apparently it was because Melody took his hand without letting go of Bailey's and began to gently tug both of them into the house.

"Come in, come in. It's such a pleasure, really."

As he stepped across the threshold, T.J. felt … *something.* Not a premonition, but the hairs on the back of his neck stood up. He looked around, saw nothing out of the ordinary, nothing that would cause … it was *nothing,* and he shook off the feeling.

The foyer of the big house was stunning. T.J. remembered the second-floor ballroom but had forgotten how unique and lovely the rest of the house had been as well. The foyer rose up to a ceiling not twelve but at least sixteen feet tall, with a chandelier dangling there that appeared to be a smaller version of the one on the second floor. Instead of multi-colored lights, the bulbs in this smaller chandelier were all clear, though the crystals dangling beside them fractured the light into rainbows that danced on every surface they touched. But … there was an odd smell.

At first, he thought he was imaginin' it, but the longer he stood there the more certain he was that the smell was real. He had no idea what it was. An earthy smell, though, like the dark ground where he used to dig earthworms to go fishin'. Fishing, that was it. It smelled like something having to do with fishin'. Somethin' about the smell put him in mind of baitin' his hook and tossin' it into the creek. He shot a glance at Bailey and wrinkled his nose. She wrinkled her nose, too, and looked confused. A multimillion-dollar house, furnishings that were one-of-a-kind antiques of incalculable value, beautiful flooring and drapes and rugs … what was there about that to smell bad?

And if you could afford all that — and obviously Melody McCallum could — why would you pay no attention to something as off-putting as a bad odor? Then it occurred to him that maybe *Caitlyn Whitfield* had never flipped the switch to restore her sense of smell.

"Come in and sit down, both of you," she said, gesturing into the parlor from the doorway. The room reminded T.J. of the rooms in Windsor Castle, absent the huge portraits of British royalty. Plush wallpaper, velvet curtains, furniture he would bet a year's pension had been made specifically to fit in this room — overstuffed lounge chairs, wingbacks, velvet sofas and settees. A huge china cabinet rested against the wall by the door. The other walls were lined with bookcases filled with ancient books, or displaying porcelain figurines or … was that a Faberge egg?

Bailey suddenly stopped stock still.

"That necklace." She pointed to the locket that hung on a thin gold chain around Melody's neck. "I saw … wasn't that on Riley Campbell's desk the day I went to your classroom?"

Melody reached up perfectly manicured fingers and touched the locket. "You're very observant."

There was a blankness to that statement that clanged, like it'd been spoken by an automated attendant. Bailey didn't react, apparently didn't notice.

"Until I saw it, I'd forgotten there had been a locket on the desk. But I remember it now."

"I used the locket to demonstrate to the children what I meant when I asked them to bring to school something that was special to them. I told them how important this was to me, then I took it off and put it on Riley's desk. I said that now when I looked at his desk, I would see something there I loved."

"Where did you get it?" Bailey asked.

Melody rolled the locket around in her fingers as she spoke. "It's all I have from when I was a little girl."

Bailey shot T.J. a look.

"It was a birthday present, wasn't it?" he asked and Melody looked surprised.

"Maybe. I don't know. I was wearing it when I … I've just always had it. I never take it off. And that's why I … I felt lost without it, so after that first day, I took the locket back and the children never noticed it was missing."

She must have touched some tiny catch because the locket sprang open, revealing a picture in each half.

"These are my parents." Her voice was barely audible. "The only pictures I have of them."

She held the locket out and Bailey leaned closer, took the locket in her hand—

And froze.

T.J. had seen that look before. Bailey Donahue had left the building.

~

THE STENCH!

It's breathtaking, so foul it is not just a smell but a taste. It is so gross the little girl tries to breathe through her nose so she can't taste it, but when she does that, the stink is worse. It smells so bad it makes her nauseous, but she has already thrown up over and over and there's nothing left to vomit.

It is not morning yet, but the black outside is fading and the sun will come up soon. When it does, the wasps and flies and bees will come.

She has to keep the wasps away. They hurt!

She's so tired, unable to sleep in the wet darkness. She knows the warmth from the sun will make her sleepy but if she sleeps, they will sting her. She's so tired of fighting them off, shooing them away, swatting at them. She can hear the hum of the swarm.

She wonders if a wasp sting could kill you. Not one, but a whole bunch of them. How many would it take? More than seven, she already has that many stings. How many more? Twenty maybe? She couldn't stand to be stung twenty more times!

She has trouble remembering the time when she was riding in the camper that was her castle she hadn't named yet, and her parents were singing along with a song on the radio. It is as if that time never happened, as if she has been all her life in this stinky place, that's wet now and cold and where wasps sting her.

As the light grows outside, she is able to make out … something that sparkles. In the place where the window was broken out, there is something shiny. Sparkly things, like tiny drips of water, hang there in the air. Gradually, the growing light reveals the rest — the twinkling things are dew drops on a spider web! The web stretches all the way across the hole in the window. It is beautiful, glowing red in the first shaft of sunshine through the trees. She stares at it, the only lovely thing she has seen since—

All at once, the sparkles begin to dance. It's the web, vibrating. She sees then that a fly has been caught in it, up near the corner, wiggling, trying to get free.

Suddenly, a black, hairy spider runs out across the web, grabs the fly with its front legs and the fly stops wiggling. The spider carries the fly away, crawls back with the fly into the shadows at the top of the web where she can't see.

She continues to stare at the web, glowing in the morning light that's growing brighter outside in the shadows of the forest floor. Then a wasp hits the web. It gets stuck there, just like the fly. It wiggles to free itself but it is caught tight. The significance of that grows in Katydid's tired mind slowly. That wasp would have come in and tried to sting her but it couldn't get in! The spider web stopped it. And soon the spider comes and rips the wasp apart.

All day long she watches the web. Wasps, bees and fat green flies get caught there. Whenever something hits the web, the spider races across and kills it, bites it, she supposes, to make it die. The spider isn't very big. She watches it rip apart the dead wasps, but it carries away the smaller bugs — little wasps and bees and flies.

She can't see up into the shadows at the top of the web, but then she notices a piece of broken mirror on the ground outside. In its reflection, she can see where the spider lives and it is full of little white sacks. She watches the spider carry away a bee into the shadows, watches it wrap the bee in shiny white stuff, like the spiderweb is made of, and hang it up with the other white sacks.

The spider is scary. It's ugly and creepy and has a monster face. But she remembers that Mommy said spiders were good bugs. It's hard to remember things, hard to think, but she remembers that, how Mommy said just because a thing was ugly didn't make it bad. She told Katydid that some pretty things are bad, like pink jellyfish that float in the ocean and have dangly things that look like Christmas tree garlands but if you touch them you die.

So the spider isn't her enemy. He's her friend. He protects her!

Tears well in her eyes and spill down her cheeks. Mommy always said that if she was afraid, she should ask for help from God. She had tried doing that a couple of times before she did the bad thing — whatever it was — and her parents left her here. But it hadn't worked. She had asked God to help her find Mommy when she got separated from her in the grocery store, and to rescue her when she climbed too high up into the tree. But God hadn't done anything either time, so she had stopped talking to him.

She had asked God to bring Mommy and Daddy back, but he didn't. She'd asked God to make the stink go away, but he didn't do that either. Last night she'd tried again, though. Shivering in the dark, she'd begged God not to let the wasps sting her.

And this morning, the spiderweb had appeared. It stopped the wasps and the spider came and killed them! Did God send the spider to help her? Did he answer her prayer this time?

He must have. God had summoned the spider!

She cries and thanks God for sending the spider to protect her. She names the spider Shannuck. She doesn't know where the name came from. It just dropped into her head and so it must have come from God.

Chapter Thirty-Six

BAILEY STOOD as frozen as an ice sculpture, holding the locket at the end of Melody's necklace. T.J. put his hands on her shoulders because he knew she'd be kinda woozy when she come back.

"What's wrong with her?"

T.J. didn't know what to tell Melody, but it was clear that Bailey had connected through the locket, as she had when the locket was on Riley Campbell's desk. And if she was connected to that little girl in the camper, what she was experiencing right now likely wasn't no walk in the park among the petunias.

"Oh, she's fine." It was hard to sound convincing with Bailey frozen as a piece of lawn art, her eyes staring sightlessly.

"It's just she's got this ... *condition* ..."

What in the world was he gonna say—?

Melody took a step back and the locket pulled out of Bailey's fingers. Bailey instantly relaxed, sort of sank backwards against T.J.'s steadying hands. Then her eyes cleared and she dropped her hands to her sides.

"Is something wrong?" Melody's voice oozed concern. "Are you alright?"

Bailey looked at her, saw her and made eye contact.

"Yes and no." Bailey's voice was a little shaky. She took several deep breaths, then said, her voice stronger, "Actually, the answers are no and yes. No, nothing's wrong and yes, I'm alright."

Melody took over then, became the penultimate first-grade teacher, leading/shooing/directing them through a doorway into the parlor, clucking as she did so, a soft babble of kind words.

"You just come in here and sit down right this minute … you look so pale … I can get you some ice water … would you like a cool cloth for your forehead?"

Her words weren't really important, it was the soothing tone that propelled Bailey to a velvet settee where she obediently sat. T.J. settled in beside her.

"Now, tell me what I can get—"

A reverberating, two-note *ding-dong* sounded in the foyer, the doorbell they hadn't heard through the thick wood. Melody looked that direction, annoyed, but didn't move to answer it.

"I'm fine, really I am." Bailey managed to sound fine and nodded toward the foyer. "Go ahead and get the door. We've barged in uninvited — please, take your time. We're in no hurry."

"You're sure you're—" The bell sounded again, Bailey produced a pretty good imitation of a real smile, and Melody stood. "I won't be but a moment. I'm sure it's UPS and I'm expecting a package."

Melody left the room and the smile dropped off Bailey's face like the stickpins holdin' it fell out. She reached up and rubbed her temples, shook her head.

"You connected to her, didn't you?" T.J. kept his voice low. When Melody opened the front door, the security alert sounded, like the tinkling of a wind chime, and Bailey's head snapped that way so sharply it was a wonder it didn't yank a crick into her neck. Recognition lit her features … and then faded just as quickly.

They could hear Melody and a man talking but couldn't make out the words.

"Why would you connect touching that locket when Melody shook your hand a few minutes ago and you didn't—"

"I didn't connect to Melody. I connected to *Katydid* in the wrecked camper. She thought her parents abandoned her because she was bad. Then the camper moved … there was a storm and water must have washed it farther down the hillside until it hit a tree, broke out a window. There was a wasp nest in the tree and the wasps were attracted to the empty soft drink cans, food tins, wrappers. And they stung Katydid!"

She swallowed once, then again before she continued. "Flies, too, big fat green ones … I guess the camper landed closer to the car where her parents' bodies were …"

Wasn't no way Bailey coulda said, "decaying."

"The next morning, there was a spiderweb over the broken window — that was the sparkling dew I painted. And the wasps and flies got caught in the web. She thought God sent a spider named Shannuck to protect her, which, I guess, explains Bambi. And the entomology minor at Pitt."

"I s'pose even if Melody don't remember 'em, Katydid's memories is still in there somewhere, maybe come out in subconscious ways." He was thinking out loud, hearing his own thoughts as he spoke them. "Katydid's the little girl you painted so *she's* who you hooking up to."

"… which apparently means Katydid and Melody are … what? Two different people? Like a split personality? She certainly had the childhood trauma to earn one!"

"Oh, I don't think I'd go *that* far, Dissociative Personality Disorder. It ain't like one minute Melody is Melody and the next she's Katydid. That'd be a split personality. If she does have a Katydid personality, it's way down deep in there and it don't get out much."

They heard the front door close and Melody appeared in the doorway to the parlor.

"I'm sorry it took so long. Gardening supplies. The man's taking them around back for me, but I had to sign and the electronic thing for signatures was acting up."

"No need to apologize. We did, after all, show up unannounced," Bailey said.

Melody perched like a small bird on the edge of the wing-back chair facing them. On the coffee table between them was a tea set, an ornate, gold-embossed teapot on the silver tray. Melody must have seen T.J. notice it.

"I just made myself some tea, would you like some?"

"Please, don't go to any trouble for us," Bailey said.

"How could it be trouble? It's already made. And you need something to steady you."

She reached over and actually patted Bailey's hand, then gestured toward the china cabinet beside the door. "Just pick out a cup and saucer you like and I'll be right back."

As soon as Melody was out of earshot, Bailey asked, "Is there something … do you smell—?"

"I sure do!"

"Good, I was afraid it was just me, still smelling that awful …"

"Maybe Melody's one of them people who got no sense of smell." T.J. opened the glass door on the china cabinet and tried to find a cup and saucer that didn't look so fragile it could shatter from the weight of the sunlight on it, one that didn't cost more than his house.

"In the wrecked camper … maybe after she clicked off her sense of smell, she never clicked it back on." Bailey reached out and picked up the first cup she saw. "But what *is* that smell?"

Melody returned with a small pitcher of milk and a sugar bowl piled high with cubes.

"Ahh, that's one of my favorite cups," she said to T.J. as he sat back down, and she poured amber tea into it. "I'd tell you where it came from if I knew." She gestured around the room. "But all of this was here when I moved in."

Melody picked up the little pitcher again.

"No milk for me, thanks," Bailey said. She had mentioned to T.J. once that "in another life" she used to order coffee in restaurants "with a bucket of cream."

He held his hand over his own cup, too, and Melody set the pitcher back down.

"Sugar, then," she said, and without asking plunked a cube of sugar into each of their cups. T.J. stifled a grimace. Neither tea nor coffee should be sweet, in his estimation, though sweet *iced* tea was a staple of Southern dining. Bailey liked sugar, though. She stirred it into the amber liquid of her cup with the tiny silver spoon from the tray and took a sip.

He picked up the spoon, stirred his, and brought the cup to his lips, but only pretended to sip it.

"Mmmm," Bailey said, and he nodded fake agreement. "Some special blend?"

Melody laughed, a musical sound, a little like the giggle of a small child.

"Hardly. Just plain old Lipton teabags. I am a very simple life form." She sat on the edge of the chair, leaning forward expectantly. "Now tell me, to what do I owe this honor — and it really is an honor, I'm serious. I've wanted to meet you for a long time. What can I do for you? Why are you here?"

Bailey looked at T.J. and he tossed the look right back at her. She was the one said she wanted to wing it. This was the part where she'd fall out of the sky on her head.

❧

Brice stepped out onto the Ferriglianos' porch and called Nakamura.

"Lucas Ferrigliano works at Andolino's Pies at the mall," he said without preamble.

"How are we just finding that out?"

The question was as much for himself as it was for Brice, but it stung like a personal rebuke all the same. They had *both* dropped the ball on this. They should have checked, should have known where the boy worked. The fact that it didn't seem important at the time was no excuse. It was their job to check out everything because nothing was important ... until it was.

Brice didn't respond, just continued.

"I found a shoebox hidden in the boy's closet. There were pictures of Riley in it — not lewd pictures, but a bunch of them. His parents said it was the girl who works the drive-up window who told them Lucas was out on a delivery and that he'd be right back."

"I'll check."

Nakamura disconnected. Brice stood holding his phone, trying to keep himself from dwelling on the mistake. There'd be plenty of time for second-guessing later. Players who beat themselves up over fumbles before the final whistle usually lost the game.

It wasn't long before Nakamura called back.

"The manager said Lucas came to work this morning, went out on a delivery and never came back. The manager doesn't know where he is."

"Take a look at the back of that pizza parlor. The security camera only shows a view of the drive-in window. But there's an area on the other side of the drive-in window, back behind it where there were a couple of cars, I assumed employees' cars. That area's blocked from view. The boy's car could have been parked there. If he found some way to get that little girl to the back of the department store, he could have put her into his car and there would be no security camera footage to show it."

"Find out from the parents if they know anywhere Lucas would go, somewhere special to him."

"He's in the wind and knows we're looking for him. His mother left him a message."

"Seal the room. I'm going back to the station, to get Arya to track the GPS in the boy's cellphone."

The parents were obviously upset, but even more so when Brice told Agent Trimboli that Nakamura had instructed her not to allow them to go into Lucas's room.

"Why not?" Tony demanded to know.

"Did you find — what did you find in there?" Francine asked.

Brice ignored them, just climbed the stairs and got the box off the desk in the boy's room and took it back downstairs with him.

"What is that? Where are you going with that?" Tony was borderline belligerent but Brice let it go. Now was not the time to get into a pissing match with the boy's father.

"I need to know where you'd look if you were trying to find Lucas, someplace that's special to him, somewhere private."

Mrs. Ferrigliano started to cry.

"This can't be happening. You can't possibly believe my Lucas has some secret place where he ... took Riley ... No, it can't be."

"We have to find your son *now*. You say he hasn't done anything wrong — then help us prove it. We can't clear him until we talk to him."

The couple looked at each other.

"There are lots of places where ..." Tony shook his head, obviously trying hard to concentrate. Gesturing at the trophies on the wall, he said, "We go hunting in the woods—"

"Where in the woods?"

"Everywhere!" He took a breath. "There's a hunting club, the Mountaineer Sportsmen. About a dozen families. We all have cabins up in the mountains and around the lake."

"You're saying he might go to your cabin?"

"Not ours, we're putting on a new roof. But we have a roving dinner — every month we go to someone's cabin and have a cookout, eat whatever we've killed or caught since the last cookout. Lucas would feel at home in any one of them."

"I need a list of all those cabins and the addresses for them."

"I'll try."

"Do more than *try*, Mr. Ferrigliano."

The father turned pale, went into his home office and returned with a printout.

As he drove back to the station, Brice called Nakamura and told him what had happened at the Ferrigliano house.

"Why did the girl working the drive-up window say Lucas had just gone out for a delivery when he's actually been gone all day?" he asked when Brice got to the station. "Honest mistake?"

"Hardly. Bonnie … something …" Brice knew if Nakamura'd had more than a couple of hours sleep in the past four days he wouldn't have dropped the girl's last name. "She's got the hots for the Ferrigliano kid, admitted he'd asked her to cover for him, said he was upset, had to get away for a while and didn't want his boss to know he wasn't working."

Arya called up a grid map of Kavanaugh County on the big monitor, displaying an area in a fifty-mile radius from Shadow Rock, within which they could trace the location of the boy's cellphone *if he made a call from it.*

Brice produced the shoebox he had found hidden in the top of Lucas Ferrigliano's closet.

"These look real to you?" he asked, pointing to the jewelry.

"Flea market," said Agent Hardesty. Gomez nodded agreement.

Moving the bling aside, Brice indicated the mound of photographs beneath.

"These aren't kiddie porn. Not even borderline. Does this track with you?"

Nakamura studied the pictures, picking each one up in a gloved hand and looking at it thoroughly before handing it off and picking up the next one. When he'd examined them all, he said, "There's nothing sexual here."

"No, but this kid has an unhealthy interest in a boy half his age," Gomez said. "There's *something* not right about that."

Brice and Nakamura joined Fletch and the other agents crowded around the computer monitor. Though he tried to avert his gaze, Brice couldn't control his glance at the accusing clock face on the wall. Marley Ewing had been missing for two hours now.

Tick. Tick. Tick.

"There is no cell service in most of those hollows — walls are too steep for signals to get in," Brice told the agents. "If Lucas is in one of—"

A red light began to pulse on the map.

Arya smiled. "He's making a call. That's him."

Brice consulted the list of names and addresses Lucas's father had provided to him.

"That's Edward O'Halloran's place. It's up on a ridge. It's not just a hunting cabin. He lives there."

Nakamura picked up the displeasure in Brice's voice. "And that's not a good thing because …?"

"Ed owns the hardware store and I'm betting with the personal arsenal he's got in that cabin he could hold off all the blond men in the Norwegian Army."

"Ed's out of town," Fletch said, and everyone turned to look at him. It was the first time he'd said anything since delivering his report at the mall. "I was in the store buying a shovel

the other day and Amanda was working the cash register —
said Ed left that morning to take Hannah up to the Mayo
Clinic for treatments. She's got breast cancer."

"When was that?" Brice asked and saw the look of determined concentration take over Fletch's face that meant he was
thinking hard.

Deputy Tackett stepped into the room. "Just got a call
from a Mr. Andolino," he said to Nakamura. "Said you told
him to call if he heard from Lucas. The boy just called Bonnie
Shepherd … and she started bawling, told him to *run!*"

Brice ground his teeth.

"It was Tuesday," Fletch said, and everyone turned to him
again. "That's when I bought the shovel. Ed O'Halloran hasn't
been in that cabin since the day before Riley Campbell
disappeared."

Chapter Thirty-Seven

BAILEY SMILED at T.J. when he didn't offer to bail her out, but the look in her eyes was sharp as the bristles on a hedgehog.

"Well ... Brice told you, didn't he, that I offered to help him find Riley Campbell?"

At the mention of the child, Melody paled, looked like she had been kicked in the belly.

"Riley!" There was anguish in her voice and her eyes filled with tears. "He was such ... he *is*, he *is* such a sweet little boy! Oh, I know, they're all sweet. But Riley's special, so serious for his age. Solemn. I sometimes wondered if something was bothering him and I made up opportunities to hang out with him — let him clean the blackboards, help load the paperback books in my car. Little things like that, so if he had something he wanted to talk about. But ..."

She fell silent and her next breath sounded a little like a stifled sob.

"What was it Brice thought you could do to help him find Riley? Did going to my classroom the other day help?"

Again, Bailey looked at T.J. Again, he hung her out to dry.

"Maybe you don't know, but police departments sometimes use people with … special abilities to help them find missing children."

"Psychics? Are you a psychic?"

Before she could answer, Melody asked, "Is that what that was, before, when you were looking at my locket? Were you—?"

"No, well, not exactly."

Melody sat back. "If you're concerned that I don't believe in what psychics can do …" She got an odd look on her face. "Things happen sometimes that you can't explain. I *know* that sometimes there just isn't a rational explanation."

"Actually, what I can do … it didn't help in this case."

Again she looked at T.J. and he pretended he didn't notice. He was definitely going to pay for that.

"I paint portraits." Bailey stopped, struggled for words, but stumbled forward. "It's a little like going into a trance and I have no control over what I'm painting. Then I come back to myself and there's this picture. A couple of months ago, I painted a picture of a little girl who drowned."

Melody said nothing, all her focus on Bailey.

Bailey kept going, told her about the portrait of Macy Cosgrove, said the painting had saved the little girl's life.

"So that's why … after I heard about Riley, I offered to try to help Brice find him. He gave me a snapshot of the boy, but the portrait I painted wasn't Riley. It was a picture of … you."

"*Me?* You painted a portrait of me? May I see it?"

"You wouldn't want to see it."

"Why not?"

"Because it's not a picture of you now, today. It's a picture of you as a little girl."

"*Seriously?*"

Bailey nodded.

"But why wouldn't I want to see that?"

Again, Bailey looked at T.J. and this time he took the handoff, figured if he didn't the cost of payback'd bankrupt him. But this whole conversation felt odd, off somehow that he couldn't put his finger on. Melody hadn't blinked at the description of what Bailey could do. Hadn't asked a single question, put up a single protest. Who heard a tale like that and swallowed it whole?

"My mama had the same gift, painted portraits like Bailey's."

He paused for a beat, but Melody asked for no explanation.

"And they was pictures of tragedies. Like train wrecks. Or like that drowned girl. Some awful tragedy that's gonna happen ... *unless you do something to stop it.* That portrait of you, though, it kinda flips the script, don't fit the pattern of the others."

"How so?"

"I painted a portrait of you at age seven when your parents were killed in the car wreck."

Melody didn't respond emotionally in any way to the revelation.

"You knew about the wreck that killed my parents?"

"No, not at first, we didn't," he said. "We just seen the painting of this little girl ... *in the wreck.*"

"I don't remember the accident. The doctors said I'll never remember what happened and why would I want to? Why would anybody want to remember something that horrible, carry those images around in your head?"

"Then you absolutely don't want to see the portrait I painted."

Bailey said the words so forcefully that she sloshed the tea in her cup and a few drips fell on her jeans. She didn't seem to notice, just took another drink and set the cup back down in its saucer.

"Wait a minute ... how did you know the painting was of *me*? If all you did was paint a portrait of a little girl in a car wreck, how did you know that little girl was me?"

"I didn't. We did some detective work to find out."

"We wasn't just being nosey." T.J. felt like he had to put that in there. "We was looking for a link to help us find Riley."

"It didn't help, though, did it? You couldn't find any connection at all, not a thing that linked me to what happened to Riley."

That struck T.J. as an odd thing to say and he glanced at Bailey, but she didn't seem to be focused on the conversation.

"So how *did* you find me?"

"We hired a private investigator. And we talked to the Bartleys, of course." T.J. left it there, hoping she'd offer an explanation of her disappearance. She didn't, so he asked. "How come you vanished like you done, never said a word to them folks after that party?"

An emotion flashed across her face and was gone so fast he decided he hadn't really seen it at all. Couldn't have. The emotion was anger. No, *rage.*

"I needed to become new," she said, as if that made perfect sense.

It occurred to him then — the *spider*? Them boys had ripped the legs off a rubber spider. Since Katydid thought God had sent a spider to save her, maybe—

Melody turned her head and fingered the caramel curls that danced at the end of her ponytail. "Blonde hair is easy to color — like putting paint on a white wall. I almost picked red but I'm so glad I didn't because Darren ..."

Her eyes welled with tears so suddenly they almost squirted down her cheeks.

"I guess you know all about that if you traced me here." Her voice was thick and tear-clotted. "Darren loved the color of my hair, said it reminded him of a chestnut mare. I'd have made it any color he wanted ..." She looked right into Bailey's eyes then, like she figured to find empathy there, and she did. "I'd have done *anything* for him. He was the love of my life."

Bailey's eyes filled with tears, too! It was an extreme

response. Shoot, he'd figured out months ago she'd been married, had a child — that she didn't want to talk about, and he respected that. She was usually so guarded about letting that part of her show, but now she looked ready to cry.

Melody took a deep breath, got hold of herself. Bailey finished off the tea in her cup.

"I had to get away ... Darren's family didn't ... so I reinvented myself."

There was that phrase again. She had to "become new" and "reinvent herself." Well, what she had invented was just about perfect in every way, or that's what the Bartleys had said. The perfect little girl.

"I got a teaching certificate and came back home to West Virginia, settled here. Life was good, and then ... then little Riley was taken. Was *gone*." The word was almost a sob. "I should have walked him and the other boys all the way out to the playground. I shouldn't have just sent ...."

She couldn't continue, put her head in her hands. She didn't cry out loud, but her shoulders shook. He looked helplessly at Bailey. She gave him a blank look in response.

"Wasn't your fault, you gotta know that." Lame, but the best he could do.

She took her hands away, wiped the tears off her cheeks, took a deep breath and forced a tremulous smile. "I know it wasn't my fault." She tried to pull the smile the rest of the way across her face but couldn't manage. "The way you know the recipe for bean dip. Knowing it and believing it are two entirely different things."

Then they sat in silence. T.J. didn't know what to say. Bailey looked kinda dreamy, probably still shook up by what she seen when she connected with that locket. The moment was drawing out toward awkward. And some irrational part of T.J.'s psyche was telling him, no *yelling at him,* that he ought to get up right then, tell this lady it was sure nice to meet her, have a nice day, take Bailey by the hand *and get out of this house.*

"Would you ..." Melody began, firmed her voice. "Would you like to see the ballroom upstairs? It's positively amazing. I feel selfish keeping it all to myself."

"I'd love to see it," Bailey said and stood. In her excitement, she stumbled, must have caught her foot on the edge of the coffee table. T.J. rose and took her arm and steadied her.

"Oops," she said, and burped a little giggle.

Melody rose, crossed to the parlor door and led them out into the hallway toward a right-out-of-a-fairytale grand staircase that wound up to the floor above. It ended in front of big double doors that looked like they was as tall as the front doors on the house.

As they started up the stairs, T.J. became aware of the strange smell again. The stench got stronger the higher up the stairs they went.

Chapter Thirty-Eight

BAILEY CLIMBED the elegant staircase behind Melody, with T.J. bringing up the rear. The house seemed to have acquired a golden glow, with warmth emanating from the hundreds of twinkling lights in the chandelier dangling from the foyer ceiling. What a lovely place! Almost *magical.* She could hear, or thought she could hear, a buzzing sound, too, no — softer than sound. A vibration in the air that seemed to come from behind the huge doors on the second floor that led to the gigantic ballroom T.J. had described as they were approaching the house.

It was all lovely ... except for the smell. Nothing lovely about that. She'd smelled it the moment she stepped into the house. It had gone away while they were in the parlor, or maybe she had just grown accustomed to it, but as they climbed to the second floor, it grew stronger. She tried to identify the smell, but it eluded her. She couldn't seem to focus on it, or on the origin of the buzzing sound, either, which now seemed somehow to come from inside her head.

The source of the aroma, though, became more clear with every step. It was coming from beyond the big doors that now loomed above her at the top of the stairs. They were so tall she wobbled a little looking up at them.

They stopped in front of the doors and Melody asked, "Have you ever been to Pittsburgh?"

Bailey bleated a giggle at the non sequitur and T.J. gave her an odd look.

"When you go up Interstate 79 from the south, you can't see the city." Melody sounded as excited as a little kid. "Then you enter the Fort Pitt Tunnel and when you pop out the other side, there it is — *bam!* — the skyline right in front of you. The skyscrapers and the rivers — the Monongahela and the Allegheny, the fountain at The Point where the rivers merge to form the Ohio — the golden bridges. The surprise is breathtaking."

Her face wreathed in a beatific smile, she was almost bouncing in place in childlike delight.

"I want the ballroom to take your breath away like that — so close your eyes! Don't open them until I say 'now.'"

Bailey obediently closed her eyes. The world swayed when she did.

She heard a gentle rumble as one of the big doors swung inward.

And the stink of — Bailey had no idea *what* —punched her like a fist, staggered her, did indeed *take her breath away.*

"Now!" Melody cried, her voice no longer soft and soothing but ragged, grating and unnatural.

Bailey felt small hands on her back, propelling her violently forward as she opened her eyes, her vision a blur of reddish light. She stumbled, felt T.J. grab her arm, but she was too off-balance and fell to the floor, dragging him halfway down with her.

"What the—?" T.J.'s words seemed to come from a long way off.

Jumbled images tried to connect in her head but thoughts skittered away as quickly as they formed. She heard a thump as the big door slammed shut, felt T.J. lifting her to her feet, but her legs had become bags of water and she couldn't seem to keep them under her.

"Oh my ... dear God!"

That wasn't awe in T.J.'s voice. It was *fear*.

The horrific stink, the *reek* was suffocating. Though her eyes were open, the world swam in front of them. T.J.'s image passed by in a red haze. Then he took her face in his hands, held her head steady, but even then the tumbling and turning continued, the whole world lurched and swayed.

"She drugged you. Musta been in them sugar cubes."

"Drugged?" the word was hard to form, difficult to push out past her lips.

When he let go of her, she crumpled in a heap. T.J. was ... seemed to be *dancing* around. She watched him brush something off his pants leg and then he cried, "Get up! Get off that floor."

She concentrated, tried to see clearly the floor beneath her.

It came into focus then. *They* came into focus. Bugs.

All over the floor. Crawling things. Beetles. Roaches. Something that jumped — a grasshopper, maybe? A cricket? Creatures with tiny whirring wings. Buzzy things — buzzing all around, the air was full of it — cicadas, June bugs — *flies!*

And spiders.

Spiders everywhere!

Shrieking, she lurched to her feet with T.J. steadying her, keeping her upright as he swatted off the creatures crawling up his pants legs and brushed frantically at her jeans.

She swayed and he commanded, "Stand up!" She *tried,* struggled to orient herself, but the whole world pitched and yawed like a ship in a rolling sea.

Ship.

She noticed it at the same time she thought the word. There were ropes above her head that looked like the rigging on a ship, dangling everywhere, hanging down from the balcony boxes on the walls and from the ceiling. There was one piece so large it was secured at both ends and stretched across the whole width of the gigantic round room, from a balcony box on one side to a balcony box on the other.

Then the pieces of what she was seeing coalesced in her head.

The ship's rigging was like a spider's web. A giant spider's web the color of blood.

She heard someone screaming, a horrible sound, warbling and terrified, a sound of horror and revulsion. It went on and on, until the pain in her throat forced her to own the sound, her throat so raw she could only mewl like some small animal caught in a trap.

T.J. held her up and dragged her with him to the door behind them. He banged on it, tried the knob, yanked it.

"Locked."

Then he turned with her back toward the room and she swayed, almost fell, stayed on her feet only by concentrating hard, trying to figure out the nightmare horror around her.

This was no fairytale ballroom with a hardwood dance floor shined mirror bright. The floor wasn't wood at all, at least Bailey couldn't see any — just dirt and mulch and straw and vegetation she couldn't identify. The crystalline chandelier did not cast glittering light in a kaleidoscope of colored flames to sparkle on every surface it touched, either.

This room was dark, gloomy and dank, and a squalid stink filled every breath, like she had crawled into a hole in the earth filled with foul creatures dwelling in filthy darkness. It was as full of crawling life as a jungle, wriggling vermin scuttling across the huge expanse of floor, a twitching sea of multi-legged horror, alive with the whirr and twitter of small wings and rasping legs. Her blurred vision refused to isolate any single thing into clarity out of the living, writhing mass that blanketed every surface. Mounds of something, like a raked-up pile of leaves, dotted the floor and lay heaped up against the walls like ... garbage. Was it rotted-food garbage?

She tilted her head back to get a look upward, though, and the motion made her more dizzy and she staggered. The iron clasp of T.J.'s grip on her arm was all that supported her.

"Stand! You fall and they'll cover you up."

She spread her feet apart, steadied herself against T.J. and peered into the gloom that faded into darkness toward the ceiling. The chandelier was covered in ... in filth. In bugs and she didn't know what else, but the hundreds of thousands of crystals no longer sparkled. They were dull, dirty, the light that shone through them defuse — and no longer multicolored. It was red, only red, like the spiderwebs were slathered in old blood. The chandelier provided less illumination in the huge room than a dim bulb darkened with the phlegm of dusty time in an old attic.

Bailey could see dark openings in the walls around them, the Hobbit-doorway stairwell openings T.J. had described that led to the spiral staircases and up into the concert boxes on the walls. But there was no light in any of them. They glared out into the gloom, black orbs of blind eyes.

T.J. gasped.

"No ... oh, oh no." He shook his head in denial, staggered like something had hit him. But he managed to stay upright and keep her upright, too.

"What is it?"

"There." He pointed up.

Her vision was fuzzy. She tried to clear away the blur by squinting, tried to stand still to relieve the sensation that the room was moving, swaying. There was a thing the size and shape of a golf bag, but wrapped up in something, dangling by a single rope below the web of ceiling ropes. Though it reflected the red light, she thought it was white or silver.

She'd seen something like that before, but she didn't know where.

"What is it?"

"I ... I'm not sure."

But he *was* sure. He knew what it was. She could tell he did. She tried to figure it out on her own, stared at it.

He groaned then, sucked air through his teeth and made a moaning sound in his throat. She looked where he appeared to be looking. Higher up, in a darker corner of the webbing was another one of the silver things, maybe a little bigger than the first.

"T.J., what ...?"

He was looking all around, in the webs above and along the walls, searching for ...

She felt something climb up her ankle and tried to wipe it away, but the motion got her so off balance she almost fell over.

"I'll do it," he snapped, dusted the thing off and kept looking around, searching.

T.J. suddenly began to drag her along the rounded wall to a door. Not huge and imposing like the double entry doors, but larger than a normal door. Either it, too, was made of rough-hewn wood with metal straps or it had been crafted to look like it was. The door wasn't just closed. Some kind of caulking — was that *mortar?* — fastened the door into the door frame, *sealed* it, leaving not the tiniest crack. Even if the door had been unlocked, it would have taken a sledgehammer to open it. Make that a jackhammer. T.J. spotted a couple of other doors on the round wall like it, but he didn't even bother to try the knob.

He continued along the wall until he came to the first of the Hobbit doors on that side. Lying on the floor beside the protruding doorway opening was a silver sack like the two hanging from the webbing above.

"Can you stand?"

"Uh huh."

He leaned her against the wall and she began to slide sideways as soon as he let go.

"Stand up!"

She concentrated as hard as she could, pushed the swirling, swaying away from her consciousness, gritted her teeth.

"I got this. But not for long."

He stepped toward the shiny silver thing — a gigantic turkey leg covered in Saran Wrap after Thanksgiving dinner.

She remembered then where she'd seen the silver thing. In the hallucination after she tried to connect to Caitlyn's portrait. She'd been carrying something silvery white … got a flash of a second one.

T.J. tore at the wrapping, ripped at it frantically, then stopped suddenly, stepped away and made a sound she couldn't define. She looked at the thing where he'd ripped away the wrapping, got a look at what he had seen. And she *shrieked.*

She'd thought her voice was gone, that it was too hoarse to make this loud, shrill wail. T.J. stepped back to her, took her into his arms, turned her body away. But she stared in horror over his shoulder at the plastic-wrapped form. At the small hand and arm sticking out now where T.J. had torn the Saran Wrap off the child's body.

Bailey couldn't stop screaming.

Chapter Thirty-Nine

T.J. Hamilton had seen a lot of awful things in his almost-seven decades of living. Much of it natural horror. Dead bodies, charred unrecognizable in the wreckage of a downed helicopter. That kid from Oklahoma, begging T.J. to help him put his insides back in his belly where it'd been ripped open all the way across.

Some of it'd been supernatural horror that wouldn't nobody but Dobbs have ever believed was real. He'd watched his mama paint one hideous portrait after another all them nightmare years in After.

But even the supernatural horror had made sense! It was beyond human understanding, forces out there he couldn't explain that did things beyond human capacity. *But it had made sense.* Nothing about this made any sense at all.

And it was his fault, too. Him and Bailey stuck here like this, it was all on him.

His "cop's gut" alarm had been clanging ding, ding, ding from the moment he stepped inside this big old house, but he'd ignored it. How many times had he warned recruits against ignoring their intuition, that when they listened to it, the intuition got louder, got clearer as they got older. That if they'd pay attention, it'd tell 'em things wouldn't nothing else tell 'em, warn 'em of stuff couldn't nobody really know was comin'. How many times had he said that and then he went deaf to his own words and pretended he didn't hear that thing clangin' away in his head? Like that stupid robot with the Slinky arms with pinchers from *Lost in Space.*

Danger, Danger, Danger, Will Robinson.

He'd knowed they was something wrong, something *off* about Melody McCallum the instant he laid eyes on her. He couldn't have told you what it was, but the hairs on the back of his neck stood at attention like a class of West Point cadets. He shoulda been on guard. Watchful. Ready to act. A warning like that should have …

But it didn't. He went stupid 'cause she was so little and delicate and 'cause what she'd gone through had been so terrible everybody'd ought to cut the poor little thing slack for the rest of her life because of it.

He hadn't let that stink tell him something wasn't right here. *Had even closed his eyes when she said to.* Only for an instant, but that'd been long enough. And who could have known something like this was comin'? Intuition or not, cop's gut or not, wasn't nothing in this life or the next that'd prepare a man for something like this.

What *was* this?

Why was this?

Well, duh, they had all danced 'round and 'round the issue since they first found out what happened to that little girl whose portrait Bailey had painted. The child had gone *insane.* She'd willed herself into catatonia and re-emerged somebody else, had reinvented herself as the perfect child. Who grew up to be the perfect first-grade teacher … *who thought God had sent a spider to protect her.*

No, Katydid thought that. Melody didn't remember her childhood, didn't remember Katydid.

They all should have acknowledged it a long time ago,

soon's Bailey started having them "hallucinations." She was connecting to a mind gone completely *mad* and wasn't no telling what she was gonna find there. Bailey'd been right — Melody and Katydid were two entirely different people.

And one of them was a murderer, a serial killer, a cold-blooded monster.

Which one?

But a way more important question right now was: What came next?

What'd she drug Bailey for, would have drugged him, too, if he hadn't faked drinking that sugar tea.

She'd kidnapped them kids. All three of them. Riley Campbell. Christi Strickland. And that little girl today from the mall whose name T.J. didn't even know. She'd kidnapped them and then she'd killed them.

And when he and Bailey showed up unannounced at her door, *she musta figured him and Bailey was onto her.*

Which meant she had to kill them, too. Meant she was up there in the shadows somewhere, armed with God knows what kind of weapon, primed to pick them off at her leisure. Or let the creatures she'd stocked this nightmare lair with kill 'em for her. He had no doubt there were poisonous spiders here — of course there were! If both he and Bailey had "drunk their Kool-Aid" like good little victims, they wouldn't have made it two hours.

Any fool could identify the tarantulas, every size you could imagine in your worst nightmare. He could see way more of them than anything else. They was all over everything, likely 'cause they was Melody's *favorites*. But they was crawling across the floor with all kinda other spiders. T.J. wasn't no expert, but just in the area around him he could see in the dim light he spotted ordinary daddy longlegs spiders, wolf spiders, yellow sac spiders, house spiders, hobo spiders, garden spiders and spinning spiders.

Melody McCallum *was* an expert, though, had minored in

entomology in college, knew and understood spiders, what they were like, what they could do and had enough money to … whatever she wanted. And apparently, she'd wanted to build a life-size terrarium and fill it with eight-legged monstrosities. There was dark lumps of … he couldn't tell what it was, some kind of plant life to feed the bugs … lying all around, reminded him of torn-up bales of hay left in a field for cattle. He had no doubt that among the crawly things everywhere, among the writhing sea of predatory spiders and the ordinary bugs that'd been provided for their dining enjoyment, were exotic arachnids even more dangerous than the poisonous spiders he could see.

He knew precious little about the ones he *could* identify. He knew that black widows and brown recluse spiders didn't automatically deliver lethal doses of venom to humans. Depended on the size of the person and the size — and intentions — of the spider. Though the bite of either of them would deliver devastating, debilitating pain — some said the nerve-poison bite of a black widow was the most painful bite of any predator in nature — they delivered different doses depending on whether they intended to eat the prey on the spot or store for future consumption. But either way, the bites of *multiple* black widows and/or brown recluse spiders would most certainly be fatal.

Maybe the bites of the spiders he *couldn't* identify would drop a person like a bullet to the heart.

He didn't know what that soul-less child murderer had planned for him and Bailey, but the only way they was gonna survive it was to *get out of here*.

And if Bailey passed out, he would have to carry her.

~

THE O'HALLORAN CABIN was up at the top of Butterworth Ridge, commanding a spectacular view of the mountainside and the hollow below. No, not spectacular, not anymore. It once had been, and would one day be again … as soon as the woods all around it recovered from the devastating forest fire that had laid waste to thousands of acres of this part of the mountains. The evidence of the forest fire itself was long gone. No charred stumps and blackened ground and bushes. Even so, the recovery stage wasn't pretty. Tangled under-growth had taken over where it could, now that there were no longer hundred-foot-tall trees to shade the forest floor and deny the weeds the sunlight they required. The U.S. Forest Service had planted two or three hundred saplings, maybe more — birch, maple, dogwood, sycamore and oak — about eighteen months ago and most of those had taken root and appeared to be thriving, but it would be decades before there was a mature forest covering the land again.

The fire had wiped out everything in its path in a two-and-a-half-mile swath of devastation, the northwest edge of the blaze just clipping Edward O'Halloran's cabin. He and his family had barely escaped with their lives and in the after-math, he'd built a bigger-better mousetrap on the site of the old one. Now, it sat in a clearing that hadn't been a clearing before the fire. He'd had expensive landscaping done on the house and grounds, but none of it had grown big enough to make the cabin look any less like a shoebox sitting out in the open with no real green vegetation any closer than the tree line to the south about seventy-five yards away. In deference to the fire, O'Halloran had added a fire lookout tower to the top of the house disguised to look like an ornate gazebo where he could see for miles in every direction, able to spot the first hint of smoke from any impending blaze.

From a police perspective, the cabin was a nightmare.

The grounds were totally open and even at the tree line, the trees were too small to offer much cover. The lone front door meant one man could hold off an army. And worst of all was the watchtower on the roof. There was no way to get above the thing to allow a police sniper to shoot down into it. Like the turret on a castle, it was accessible only from inside and offered sightlines in every direction, a firing spot that covered all the land around it, 360 degrees.

As they drove out to the cabin, Brice told Nakamura what to expect. Though he had never attended one of the monthly hunters' feasts, Brice had been to the cabin right after it was completed — to serve a summons on O'Halloran. Some guy was suing him over a traffic accident. After his initial anger at the summons, O'Halloran became a gracious host, showing Brice around. At that time, there was only a smattering of furniture, a kitchen table, a bed in only one of the bedrooms, and gun cases — *lots* of gun cases — but no weapons. O'Halloran showed the sheriff the state-of-the-art security system he'd installed to protect all the firepower he'd eventually load into those cases, video surveillance cameras at all the entrances.

"If he had that kind of equipment, how'd the kid get in there in the first place?"

Brice barked a laugh. "Ed showed that system to everyone he knew. There are probably two hundred people in this county who know how to disarm it. One of them, I'm sure, is Lucas Ferrigliano."

"And the Ferrigliano boy would know how to use all that firepower?"

"As at home with a rifle as a city boy with a skateboard."

Lucas's vehicle with a portable Andolino's Pies Delivery sign attached to the roof was parked at the end of the driveway next to the porch that extended out from the front door and wrapped around the east and west sides of the cabin. He'd gotten the family's old CRV for his sixteenth birthday when his father bought a new one. There was no hope of using the "element of surprise" in this takedown. His mother'd left Lucas a message telling him the FBI was looking for him even before his hysterical not-girlfriend warned him.

Besides, "sneaking up" on this cabin was impossible. If the boy'd been in the fire tower, he'd seen the line of patrol cars as they turned off the highway a mile away. Nakamura spread out his troops, a total of more than two dozen officers, to surround the cabin — five sheriff's department cruisers, four West Virginia State Police cruisers and the vehicle in which Gomez, Trimboli and Hardesty had traveled. They quickly checked out the number of windows and doors on each side of the house, which way the doors opened — in or out — as well as any other potential avenues of escape, and there was none.

Nakamura tried calling the boy's cellphone for the umpteenth time. It wasn't turned off, but apparently the ringer was. They had the telephone number for the land line in the O'Hallorans' cabin and they called it. The boy didn't answer so Nakamura used a bullhorn.

"Lucas Ferrigliano, my name is Special Agent Haruto Nakamura with the FBI. We need to talk to you. We will call you on the land line. Please pick up."

Nakamura called. The phone rang and rang and rang. After two dozen rings, Nakamura was about to hang up when the line opened. The boy didn't say anything, not hello or anything else. But he had picked up the phone.

"Lucas, we need you to step out the front door with your fingers clasped behind your head and walk slowly down the steps."

"No. I'm not coming out."

"You are not under arrest. No laws have been broken here; let's back this down before that happens."

"I won't come out."

"If you refuse this order to surrender, you can be charged with resisting arrest. Let's not go there. You don't want a criminal record, do you? I need you to step out the front door of the cabin with your hands clasped behind your head."

"I said I'm not coming out and I'm not. Just go away."

"We can't do that, son. We have to talk to you. We want to ask you some questions about—"

"About Riley," he said, and his voice broke. "I have nothing to say to you about Riley. You're wasting your time. Go away."

"We're not going anywhere until you come out and talk to us."

"Are you deaf? Didn't you hear a word I said? I don't want to talk to you. I don't want to talk to anybody. Leave me alone."

"Lucas, you're not being reasonable. You're a smart young man. You know we won't leave without talking to you and I know you don't want anybody to get hurt."

"Hurt? What? Are you going to *shoot me* if I don't come out?"

"I didn't say that."

"Yes you did, you said you didn't want to hurt me." He paused as if a new thought had struck him. "*You can't shoot at me!* Please, don't! You know I'm not alone in here and if you shoot at me, you might hit Baby Girl."

Brice exchanged a look with Nakamura.

"Who's in there with you, Lucas?"

"I have guns, too, you know. Did you think about that? I know how to use them. And I can see you but you can't see me. You need to give up and go away. We just want you to leave us alone."

"Lucas, who is it that's in there with you?"

The boy did not respond.

"I would like to talk to whoever is in there with you. Would you put them on the line, please, and let me speak to them?"

The boy barked out a sardonic laugh. "You want to talk to Baby Girl? Riiiiiight. Like I could put the phone to her ear and the two of you could have a conversation. You know better than that. You know I'm the only one here who can talk on a phone, okay. Just me. So, listen to me and go away."

"We are going to stay right here until you come out. Until you both come out. No matter how long it takes. There is nothing to be gained by putting this off. You will have to come out eventually and we will be here when you do, so you need to do it now, before the situation gets a whole lot worse."

"It'll only get worse if you make it worse. I'll only start shooting if you make me start shooting. If I do, a whole lot of people are going to get hurt. Think about that and go away."

The boy slammed the phone down and the line went dead.

"You don't think he's got all three of those kids in there with him," Brice said. It was a statement, not a question.

"If he does, they're all dead."

"Baby Girl ..." said Agent Hardesty. "The little girl taken this afternoon — she's deaf. She can't talk on a phone. Is that who he means?"

"Maybe ..." Nakamura wasn't convinced.

"So he kidnaps three kids, kills the first two and we show up before he has a chance to kill the third," Hardesty continued. "Baby Girl's still alive in there. You think?"

Nakamura shook his head. Brice wasn't buying it either.

"None of it fits," Brice said.

Nakamura stepped away and began to speak into his cellphone, summoning a hostage negotiation team from Pittsburgh.

"Lucas's mother said he was at work at the time Christi Strickland was taken," Agent Trimboli put in. "If the girl at the drive-in window covered for him today, maybe she covered for him then. I suppose if you pulled up to the park with a pizza delivery sign on your car, you might get a little girl to get close enough to it to grab her."

"We didn't see a pizza delivery truck on the video footage from the ATM," Hardesty said.

"Could have turned off before it passed the ATM," Gomez said.

"Nobody reported seeing anything like that anywhere near the park that day," Hardesty said.

"A pizza delivery car can be like a fire hydrant, see it so often you don't see it at all," Gomez said.

Brice shook his head.

"What's his motive — for snatching any of them? We have a box of gifts the little boy hid in a stuffed animal and a handful of harmless — if weird — photos of Riley that Lucas hid in his closet. And this kid has no connection at all to the other two victims — at least none we can find. Why take Riley from school when Lucas had access to him twenty-four-seven right next door? Why take him at all? We don't have any good reasons to support that a sixteen-year-old kid who has barely had a driver's license long enough to get a speeding ticket suddenly goes on a spree and kidnaps three children — that doesn't add up. What for?"

"Then why's he holed up in there with an arsenal of guns and a hostage, refusing to come out?" Hardesty said.

"I'll send some deputies down the road, talk to the neighbors, find out when — or how often — they've seen Lucas's vehicle turn off Route 22 onto this road," Brice said.

Nakamura glanced at the sky and noted the gray storm clouds hurrying across it.

"First, find me a spot to set down a chopper. Hostage negotiation team's on the way and we're on the hook until they get here. Lock it down; we'll wait him out."

Five minutes after they'd settled in to "wait him out," Lucas Ferrigliano started shooting.

Chapter Forty

FROM WHAT T.J. could remember of the layout of The Cedars, there was only one exit from the ballroom other than the doors behind them, which was locked tight, and the handful of internal doors that might as well have been welded shut. There was an elevator and a staircase in the back of the room that led up to a door that opened out into the top turret above the third floor of the house, the part that looked like a lighthouse. From there, another staircase led down on the outside through the roof of the porch and out into the back yard. Would that door be sealed, too? Maybe, but it was his only shot. He had to get them up to that door, and then back down outside — with Bailey barely able to stand.

He didn't let go of her, couldn't or she'd collapse, just turned her toward him, held her shoulders and looked into her face. She was cryin'. She'd started screaming soon's she seen that what was wrapped up in that plastic sack was a child, but she'd stopped in just a few seconds, cut off her own screams like turnin' off a water spigot. She couldn't stop the cryin' like that, though, and she heaved air in and out, tears streamin' down her cheeks.

"You got to help me now," he said. "We got to get out of here. You understand?"

She nodded, but he wasn't sure whether she really did or not.

"Lean on me." He put her arm around his shoulders and held her there by her wrist. Then he half-carried, half-dragged her along the circular wall beside him, makin' for the back of the room. The sound of crunching insects underfoot made his skin crawl. He passed the first of the Hobbit doors that led to a spiral staircase that'd empty into one of the theatre boxes on the wall. Near the next doorway, he heard a sound overhead but couldn't place it. It was scratchy, a little like a cricket but not musical. And a hissin' sound come from somewhere up there in the gloom. Wasn't no bug made a sound that loud, which meant it was Melody, able to see them when they couldn't see her.

The grating *scraaaaaatch* got closer, and suddenly Bailey pulled away from him and stood swayin' in the red gloom.

"Shannuck!" She took in a deep, shuddery breath. "The spider in the camper that protected Katydid …"

Bailey was fighting nausea and dizziness, so it was hard for her to get the words out.

"The spider killed the wasps … *and wrapped them up in shiny silver bags.*"

She turned back the way they'd come, her eyes seeking the body of the child they'd found.

T.J. looked around the ballroom, getting it now.

"That's what this is." He could hear the wonder in his own voice. "A spider's lair. She filled this whole ballroom up with spiders, with bugs for 'em to eat and some kinda plants for the bugs to eat — all 'cause a spider was her *hero.*"

"Where'd she get so many spiders — and poisonous ones?"

"When you's rich—"

The sound came again, the scratchin'-hissin', and the

ropes just above their heads moved. Something was up there in the rigging.

"Melody." Bailey layered the word in horror and cringed away.

"We gotta get outta sight. We sittin' ducks here in the open. No tellin' what she's armed with."

He unwrapped Bailey's arm from his shoulders, grabbed hold of her wrist and pulled her along beside him to the nearest Hobbit door. The interior should have been lit with hundreds of flickerin' colored lights, making the same pattern of sparkles on the walls inside the stairwell as the chandelier made on the walls of the ballroom. But there wasn't no sparklin' lights. No lights at all. It was the black dark of a pipe, not no light whatsoever.

Bailey balked, tried to pull away.

"They's stairs in here and we gotta climb up 'em to the theatre box on the wall. It connects to the next one, and to the next. They's places to get outta sight in them boxes, tables and chairs to hide behind. And them overhanging awnings'll block her line of fire from above. Come on."

He pulled at her arm, but she pulled back, almost fell, would have if he hadn't steadied her.

"Bailey, she's up there somewhere sightin' in on us! The only way out of here's on that back wall. But if we take off runnin' toward it 'cross the dance floor, she gonna mow us down."

She stared at the black hole with eyes open so wide he could see the whites all around, shook her head slowly, refused to budge.

Nothing for it but to force her. He tightened his grip on her wrist and yanked her forward. She'd probably still have fought him, but she couldn't, drugged like she was, and she staggered after him into nothingness.

T.J. put out in front of him the hand not grippin' Bailey's

wrist, a blind man, feelin' around in the empty air. He took one sickeningly crunchy step.

Then another.

And another.

His fingers brushed somethin' solid. Cold. *Metal.* He grabbed it and began to slide his hand along it, feeling his way. Somethin' with scratchy feet like a roach crawled up on his hand and he shook it off, put his hand back down and felt beneath it a crawly — this was a spider! He crushed the spider with his palm, prayin' it wasn't no black widow or brown recluse or some other poisonous thing he didn't know the name of. Tensed for the agonizin' bite pain … that didn't come, he continued forward along what he now knew was the railing, the banister of a spiral staircase. He led the two of them around it in the dark until he found the first step.

Then he began to climb.

One step, two, draggin' a resistant, unsteady Bailey along behind.

Suddenly, she cried out, jerked back and almost toppled the two of them.

"The railing — there are bugs … *things* on—"

"Don't touch it, just hold onto me."

She grabbed the back of his shirt with her free hand and he took another step up. And another.

Something else crawled over the hand he was moving along the banister. Bigger.

"*Aggghhh!*" He couldn't help cryin' out at the sudden stab of pain in his knuckle, shook his hand furiously, knocked the creature off onto the steps. Felt like the whole top of his hand was on fire.

"What—?"

"Danged thing bit me!"

"What was it?"

"I don't know, I don't …"

His hand throbbed in heartbeat bursts of searing pain, but

it was a wasp-sting, bee-sting pain. It hurt like the devil, but it wasn't the agony he'd have felt if it'd been a black widow.

"Musta just been a tarantula."

Bailey went rigid.

"A tarantula *bit* you?"

She began to shake violently.

"They're all over. Everywhere. *I can't.* I have to get out—"

Letting go of his shirt, she tried to wrench out of his grip on her wrist. He held firm, but had to grab the railing with his other hand to keep from being carried off the staircase with her flailing around.

"Bailey, stop it!"

He'd have slapped her to quell her hysteria but he couldn't let go of her or of the staircase railing, and he couldn't have landed a blow on her face anyway 'cause he couldn't see it in the darkness.

"*Be still!*" He squeezed her wrist as hard as he could, knew it hurt, meant for it to! "You gonna knock us off these steps ..." He paused for a beat, thought. "... into a pile of spiders down there in the dark. That what you want — to fall into a *nest of tarantulas*?"

"*Noooooo!*" Lurching forward at him, she grabbed him in a bear hug, sobbing.

"Don't let me fall, not ... please — *tarantulas*!"

"Don't think about 'em. Think 'bout me. Think about holdin' onto me. And look up there."

Above them, probably fifty feet, was the opening into the theatre box seating area. It was only a dim reddish glow against the blackness, but their eyes had so adjusted to the dark that the light was as clear as a beacon.

"Just a little farther. Keep on climbin'."

He put his foot on the next step and the next, slidin' his free hand along the banister, prayin' there wouldn't be another spider on it. The pain on his knuckle had settled into a bearable agony. He felt *jittery*, too, a wiggly feelin' in his belly he knew was the spider venom, like epinephrine in his bloodstream.

One more turn and he stepped out onto the landing of the staircase, Bailey holdin' onto him with grim strength, her face buried in his back. Stretched out in front of them were tables and chairs like in a little cafe, with an awning roof. He recalled them awnings had been white, though this one was an ugly splotched red now. They stayed near the back wall deep under the overhang as T.J. searched for a "sniper" in the intertwined rigging of "spiderwebs" in the gloom. Even up here in the theatre box, they was still far below the chandelier, but he could see it better. The crystals was … was what? No longer shiny, that's for sure. They was dark, like years of time and dust had slathered them in … what was on 'em? What had she poured or sprayed or … he didn't know, but she'd done something to dim 'em, darken 'em.

And the small lightbulbs — hundreds, no, more like thousands of 'em was dark. But there was a few that was still lit — red ones — just enough light to see. Had Melody … unscrewed most of the bulbs? How had she done a thing like that? Wasn't no ladder'd be that tall. It'd take one of them telephone company bucket trucks to lift somebody up that high.

Course, she was light enough that maybe she coulda hung from the struts of the chandelier. But she'd had to a'been a circus trapeze artist in another life to pull off somethin' like that. That little bitty thing couldn't possibly have dangled there, unscrewin' lightbulbs and painting/slathering/whatever-ing all them shiny crystals. And how'd she hang them kids' … *bodies* … up there like that?

The tangled web of ropes moved. Somethin' they couldn't see was climbin' on 'em. T.J. thought he seen a dark shape streakin' across the web, but wasn't nothin', a trick of the light, or the lack of light. Had to have been a shadow. A shadow of what?

BAILEY SWAYED, sick and drunk and nauseous. Whatever Melody had spiked the sugar cubes with was beginning to wear off just a little, but it was still enough to make the world swim, and the floor lurch under Bailey's feet. She couldn't seem to really look at anything because her eyes refused to focus. Everything was just a panoramic sweep, a wash of things past the window of a car traveling at high speed. Everything was moving and wobbly, a mirage.

When she did see something, did manage to focus, it was a horror. Standing beside T.J. as he peered fearfully into the rigging dangling from the ceiling, she looked at the railing surrounding the theatre box suspended on the wall of the ballroom. It was moving. No, *things on it* were moving. It was alive with creatures and as she stared at a spot on it only a few feet away, the smeared images materialized into dozens of small spiders, all about the same size. Maybe they had just … what? Hatched out of eggs? Was that what spiders did? Laid eggs?

The little spiders were crawling all over something. Then the something *moved.*

A tarantula.

Merely looking at the hairy beast horrified her beyond reason. Knowing it wasn't rational fear but arachno*phobia* didn't diminish the terror. It was *a hairy, black tarantula!*

Not a huge one. She knew they could grow to the size of dinner plates. This one was about the size of a lemon, though it probably would have been ten inches across if you spread its legs out from its body flat, instead of bent at the … *knee?* … How could she possibly know the names of the parts of a spider? It wiggled and writhed beneath the baby spiders.

Then she understood. The baby spiders were eating the mother alive.

She began to shudder, gripped by waves of quaking that made her knees so weak she was afraid she — she couldn't collapse! Right now, the only part of her touching a surface were her feet. To get to her, a creature, a *spider*, would have to crawl onto her shoes and up her pants leg. But if she fell down … if her whole body made contact with the floor … *no!*

T.J. turned his head suddenly, looked like he saw something, whatever was crawling around on the spider's web of rigging — Melody up there somewhere above them.

"We got to move … but I'd sure like to get a look at what she's packin'."

T.J. dragged Bailey back toward the wall, as far as it was possible to get under the awning, then he peered around the edge of it.

"Packing?"

"Her weapon. A rifle with a laser sight, if I had to guess. But what's the range? Can she pick us off from way up there where we can't see? Or does she got to get closer?"

The sound came again, the grating sound and the hissing. She looked at T.J. to see if he heard and he did, so the sound wasn't just in her head.

Then they both heard a different sound, a horror *laugh* that mocked humanity in its vulgar corruption of a voice. Ragged and ugly, it was all the more hideous because Bailey knew the throat that made the sound was small and fragile; the lips it passed through were on a face as beautiful and delicate as a china doll.

Suddenly, the world was gone. Bailey was gone. She blinked and her eyes opened on an entirely new reality. Not the horror of the camper, though, with a child trapped inside. This time, it was … there was a ceiling tile above. Not Bailey's BFF, but this was a hospital room.

Chapter Forty-One

From the dark place deep inside herself where she hides, Katydid looks at the distant light. It's dark here because she flipped the switches when she was in the stinky place, flipped them the way Daddy did that time in the garage.

Her eyes are open and light shines in and she could move closer and look out if she wanted to. But she doesn't. She doesn't want to see. She is safer here in the dark where nothing can get to her. No stink. No wasps.

Then a face appears in front of hers, a face with an ugly smile. It looks into her eyes and Katydid can see it from the dark place, the safe place.

Then the man with the ugly face, the mean smile ... touches Katydid.

She doesn't like his touch!

He touches her in that place you're not supposed to touch. Mommy said. Mommy said if anybody ever touched Katydid in that place she was to tell Mommy and Mommy would make it stop because touching Katydid there was a bad thing.

But Katydid can't tell Mommy to make the man stop because Mommy isn't here. Katydid was a bad girl so Mommy and Daddy left her in the stinky place.

*Katydid is afraid of the man and the touches. He's hurting her —
the her who is out there in the light with her eyes open.*

It hurts *and Katydid screams inside her head but she doesn't make any sound because all the switches are flipped. She screamed when the wasps stung her, screamed out loud before she flipped the switches — but Mommy didn't come and make the wasps stop hurting her. It wouldn't do any good to scream out loud now because Mommy won't come and make the man stop hurting Katydid.*

Shannuck stopped the wasps.

Shannnuck … help!

SHANNUCK'S EYES *open and he sees.*

Shannuck is angry!

He will make this man-bug stop hurting Katydid.

The man-bug is fat and ugly, with black hair and a scraggly beard and he is wearing striped pajamas and house shoes. He touches Katydid in that place, the hurting place and he smiles because he likes hurting.

Shannuck rears up on his back legs to be big and scary, a black, hairy spider. He grabs the man by the neck in a rage that completely takes over, that controls everything. Shannuck's fury is fuel that grants strength and power.

The ugly, fat man-bug is surprised. The single black eyebrow above his eyes shoots up. He tries to scream but Shannuck squeezes his throat hard. The man-bug tries to get away, struggles, staggers back, but Shannuck won't let go and the man-bug falls backward onto the floor with Shannuck on top of him. His face is red, his eyes are bulging out. Still Shannuck doesn't let go. He squeezes and squeezes and squeezes until the man-bug lies still and his face is swollen and what was his neck is all squishy where Shannuck crushed it.

Shannuck is angry at the bad things, all rage and killing. Mad at the wasps. And furious at Mommy and Daddy who were supposed to take care of Katydid but they didn't. They went away and left her all alone. Shannuck hates Mommy and Daddy! Shannuck would kill them if he could. Shannuck hates everyone who is not Katydid because they might hurt Katydid. But Shannuck won't let them.

Now, Shannuck gets back into the bed where Katydid is unharmed far back in the dark. He lies down, pulls the covers back up so she is warm and safe. Shannuck is Katydid's protector here just like he was when she was in the awful stinky place where the wasps came. Shannuck will not let anything hurt Katydid.

He will never leave her like Mommy and Daddy did! He will stay with her always.

KATYDID LOOKS out from the deep, safe place inside at the light shining in through the eyes that look out on the world. The man is gone. Shannuck took the man and did to him what he did to the wasps that came to sting Katydid. She is safe here in the dark now. Shannuck is with her, watching, always watching. She doesn't ever have to be afraid again. Shannuck will always take care of her.

BAILEY WAS INSIDE A LITTLE GIRL, looking at the ceiling in a hospital room.

An eye blink later, she was inside a human spider.

An eye blink after that she was back in the little girl.

Another eye blink and she was back here, in the nightmare horror of the grand ballroom of The Cedars.

The fragile boundary of an eye blink was all that separated those realities.

"Bailey!"

It was T.J. She wanted to answer, but … she didn't quite know how. Couldn't seem to translate thought into words.

And then Bailey was suddenly more afraid than she had ever been of anything in her life. More terrified than she'd been of the tarantulas in the darkness. More afraid than she'd been inside the monster spider-person who killed the pervert. More afraid even than she had been when she was hiding with the rats under a dumpster, praying that the men who had murdered her husband wouldn't lean over and see her there.

The fear she felt now was worse! That had been fear of danger. This was *fear of annihilation*. Fear that she would *cease to be*. Not *die* — she certainly didn't want to die, but she'd rather die than cease to exist while she was still alive. Losing who you were, losing your sense of self, your soul, was far worse than dying, and she could feel her grip on her own reality as a person, her Bailey-ness, beginning to loosen.

Felt her sanity … begin to crumble around the edges.

Every time she was yanked out of the here-and-now and into the mind of the insane child, she came back with some of her own reality missing. She left pieces of herself behind when she escaped back into her own mind. And the terror now in her chest was that she would continue to be yanked out of herself into the crazy child, again and again, leaving some of herself behind with each connection until there would come a time when she would come back, but not be all there. Not be all Bailey, with essential pieces of who she was missing.

Or she would simply occupy the body of Bailey but be unable to connect with it. Just living there, like the catatonic child down in the darkness, watching the light above, unable to move the body or think with the mind that was her own.

Or she wouldn't be able to come back at all. There'd come a time when she'd be trapped, a prisoner in the mind, the reality of the insane little girl.

Or maybe … maybe she'd bring some of the crazy child *back with her* to become a part of who Bailey was, on a soul level. Then Bailey, too, would be insane.

She struggled, concentrated, tried to calm the sickening terror, forced her sluggish, drugged mind to *think*.

"T.J.!" She blurted out his name. A single word, but a word nonetheless. *Good!* She clutched at his shirt. "Oh, T.J.!"

He stopped scanning the overhead webs.

"You been connectin' again, ain't you?" He let go of her wrist and put his hands on her shoulders. "Whatever she spiked in them sugar cubes is makin' it worse. It's loosened your grip on the real world." He gestured with his chin to their surroundings. "She's likely put her hand on everything in this room. Then you come along, touch what she touched … With you so susceptible to connectin', might not take mor'n hearin' her voice."

Bailey opened her mouth and the words came.

"It's not just Caitlyn!"

With every word she spoke, she became more herself, more in charge of her own mind. With words, she dragged herself back from the brink and grabbed hold of who she was.

"It's Shannuck. I connected to Shannuck."

In the dim light shadowed beneath the awning, with her vision blurred, she couldn't see his face well, but she felt T.J.'s fingers tighten on her shoulders.

"She's totally insane, T.J. In the wrecked camper, Katydid crawled down into herself and flipped the switches, but then in the hospital she was *molested*."

"How?"

"Some pervert, another patient maybe. It *hurt*. She was scared, cried out inside her head and … *Shannuck came.*"

"Came?"

"She split off, splintered. Her personality. She became two different … she *became* Shannuck."

Now, words gushed out of Bailey in a torrent as she clung to T.J. in the gloom.

"Dissociative Identity Disorder. You said, I remember you said that the shrink told you people with DID *are who they believe themselves to be*."

"If the childhood trauma was … he claimed a diabetic changed his own body chemistry, so—"

"Not just body chemistry, T.J. *Body structure!* Caitlyn didn't just believe she was a spider. She *became* a spider. Shannuck is real! I was inside Shannuck's head."

"You sayin'—?"

"In the park, I touched that rock wall *and I connected to Shan-*

nuck. When Melody grabbed the little girl, she was Shannuck, the spider. Shannuck is the kidnapper."

"You was in ... you connected to—?"

"I saw the world through a spider's eyes. Black and white. And I could see in front and to the sides, too."

She paused to drag in a ragged breath.

"And I've connected to Shannuck other times, too. This afternoon, I smelled roses. I was *here,* inside Shannuck. A spider locates its prey with its sense of smell. I barely remember science class, but I remember that much. And they don't have a nose. They smell and hear with hairs on their legs."

She grabbed the front of T.J.'s shirt, held on with fierce strength, had been so dangerously close to losing her grip, not on T.J. but on sanity.

"T.J., she can *do what a spider can do.* Do you realize what that means?"

He didn't have time to respond because the rope spiderweb wiggled again, vibrated violently. They both looked up at the same time and this time they *saw* what was on the web.

Bailey screamed.

~

DOBBS SAT for a moment after Al Zankoski ended their call, his mind repeating what the private investigator had said about Caitlyn Whitfield a.k.a. Melody McCallum.

Is it possible there was somebody in her life I didn't find, somebody who ... I don't know, kept showing up ... to take care of her?

It was an odd statement, but then there was a whole lot about the man's report that was odd, made no sense. Like the murder victim lying on the floor of a catatonic child's hospital room. Weird, but not totally outside the world of logic and order. Murderers as a group didn't tend to be the most rational people. The fact that this one was never found was strange, but not totally ridiculous.

Taken that far, with only that bit of information, the murder of the crazy person in Caitlyn's room was not totally outside the pale of reason.

But the rest of it.

He sat where he was, opened the document on his computer and read every word of the report, start to finish. When he was done, he was way more confused than he'd been when he started.

Any one of the incidents that had happened in the little girl's life, taken as an isolated occurrence, was strange. Taking them all together, was somewhere on the other side of strange. It was stretching the bounds of reason to believe that all the things that had happened to that child were just coincidences.

They had too much in common. The child, though, unable to defend herself, had been in some kind of danger each time. And every time, someone had come to her defense. Who?

Well, actually, not every time. The gang attack on her and her new husband was unlike the others. In that instance, it wasn't just Caitlyn who'd been in danger. Still, somehow she had escaped with her life even though her husband had not.

Why? How?

Was it possible she had some kind of ... guardian angel? Not some mystical, mythical beast in a fairy-godmother suit, arriving in a pumpkin pulled through the sky by white mice. But a person. Someone in her world who ...

That made no sense, though. How could somebody, *anybody*, have been with the kid 24/7 to rescue her when she was in need — yet nobody *noticed*?

There was something wrong with all of this. Something more than weird. There was something that connected all these dots, some information the private investigator hadn't been able to dig up.

Clearly, T.J. and Bailey needed to know what was going on.

He picked up the phone he had set down after the call from the private investigator and punched the favorites number for T.J. The call went immediately to voicemail. He called Bailey's number then. The phone rang and rang and then went to voicemail. Obviously, T.J. had his phone turned off. Not surprising. The man hated cellphones in general and his in particular. Said it didn't ring when he had an incoming call even when the ringer was turned on but he was so totally technophobic he resisted every urging by Dobbs that he stop complaining about it and take the danged thing to the phone store — either get it fixed or get a new one.

Bailey was another thing altogether. He punched her number again. She seldom had the thing more than three feet from her side, like maybe she was always expecting an important phone call and didn't want to miss it. He suspected the behavior might have something to do with the past she refused to discuss, but — duh — since she wouldn't discuss it, he didn't know.

Bailey's phone rang and rang. No answer.

Dobbs needed to talk to both of them with a sense of urgency not completely explainable by the circumstances, but certainly exacerbated by the fact that neither one of them was reachable.

He knew where they were, though. The Cedars. Melody McCallum's house. He got up and started for the door, only stopped long enough to forward Zankoski's report to Brice.

Chapter Forty-Two

BAILEY'S SCREAMS sounded like bedsheets rippin', filled up T.J.'s head — where his whole being was in rebellion, flat out refusing to translate what he was seein' into reality.

His mind flashed to that shrink, the one he hadn't really believed, tellin' him about the diabetic who had one personality that wasn't diabetic. T.J. believed now! Grasped with growing horror the implications of *voluntary control of body chemistry*.

If you could *think* your pancreas into secreting insulin, what if you could make your adrenal glands produce adrenaline?

His first drill instructor in the Marine Corps had called adrenaline "human jet fuel." The body's response to fight-or-flight situations, adrenaline redistributed blood to the muscles, altered the body's metabolism. The hormone could grant superhuman strength — a mother who was suddenly able to lift a car off her injured child. But an "adrenaline dump" was involuntary and the adrenal gland measured out how much … *unless* …

What kind of mind was capable of controlling the timing and *amount* of adrenaline released into the bloodstream?

Maybe the mind of an insane child who'd turned off her senses by "flipping a switch."

That little girl was above them now in the ship's rigging that'd become a red spiderweb. No, not little girl — an eight-legged … *thing.* A human spider. It was Melody McCallum, of course — though he could only tell that for sure 'cause of the hair, that mane of shiny curls that was the color of a piece of caramel. The woman was clinging to the rigging head-down, in a position no human being could have executed.

She'd put on somethin' on the outside of the black turtleneck and tights she'd been wearin', some kinda bodysuit covered in sticky bristles with a bloated, bulbous belly. Hairy legs hung from the bodysuit. Two legs was up near the top. The next set was her own arms ending in black-gloved hands holdin' onto the spiderweb of rope. Another set of legs dangled from the middle of her back and the final set was her own legs, her feet in black ballet slippers … no, probably rock-climbing shoes.

Her face was a horror, her delicate features so distorted she didn't look even vaguely human. Somehow Melody'd pulled her mouth back 'til it wasn't nothing but a slice across the bottom of her face. Spit dripped in a cascade of drool over what'd been a human bottom lip stretched beyond credibility.

The eyes was … impossible.

Impossible!

'Cept there they was, the eyeballs bugged out beyond the sockets, lidless below faint streaks of eyebrows — operating *independently.* One looking up or to the left while the other looked down. Seeing all around at once. That couldn't be. How could a human being pop out her eyeballs like that? That was crazy!

Wasn't nothing on the face at all you could call a nose, just a ridge of cartilage stretching down it toward the slash where

drool dripped out. The rest of the nose had somehow flat-
tened out, leaving only two small black holes.

And somehow that not-a-face managed to communicate
emotion — arachnid rage and hatred.

The hissing that came from the Melody creature … *from
Shannuck the spider* … was a sound that could not possibly have
come outta her but it did. Then came a grating sound. If
she'd been a real spider, she'd have created the noise by
rubbin' her legs together like a cricket. But she somehow
managed to make the sound with human vocal chords, the
ones she'd used to produce the sick laughter that was not
laughter at all.

She made the sound now. The spider Shannuck made the
corruption of sound. *Laughed.*

"You die. Shannuck kill," said the creature that wasn't a
person anymore, wasn't nothin' like a human being either in
intent or consciousness. Then the spider ran down the web,
head first, scuttled across it toward them at an impossible
speed. Nothing human coulda moved that fast across ships'
rigging.

Bailey's screaming had become somethin' more like a
whine or a whimper. She cowered against him now. T.J. had
absolutely no idea what he would do to protect her from that
thing when it got here.

It wasn't "packin'," armed with a rifle complete with laser
scope. The creature itself was the weapon.

"Die, die, die. All bugs die." The hoary voice erupted like
vomit from the not-human woman racing toward them.

Bailey screamed again, but the sound stopped abruptly
and her face went blank. She had connected again — to the
spider, Shannuck.

~

THE WORLD IS *black and white and divided into segments. She sees the webbing above and below and on both sides at the same time. Out front are the big bug things, the creatures in the theatre box, crawly, nasty creatures, ugly, their forms repulsive. Shannuck must kill them,* will *kill them. He kills any bug that threatens Katydid, the little girl who cowers in the dark, the child he protects.*

Shannuck laughs. He is in charge now, has cast aside the Caitlyn creature he hated, the one who'd appeared when Katydid crawled out too close to listen to the stories the nurse read. Edged out farther and farther and then one day she saw the spider dangling from that black hat and Caitlyn stepped out into the world. Shannuck stayed down in the dark with Katydid, right beside her, ready to come to her defense and keep her safe.

But all that was before the car accident when the Caitlyn creature, the Melody *creature, was trapped in a car just like Katydid had been trapped in the camper. The Melody creature was as frightened as Katydid had been, cried out for help and so Shannuck appeared and saved her! Shannuck ripped the car apart to get her and Katydid to safety and then he killed the bugs in the pickup truck. Shannuck had been a mighty force that day, powerful and fearless, stronger than the sniveling, injured Melody creature — and he'd shoved her aside. Shannuck took control then and ever since, he has ruled supreme. He comes and goes as he likes.* He does what spiders do!

The stupid Melody creature doesn't even know he exists and he uses her to make his way in the world, a world where she is one of the bugs. Mindless, she wonders why there are periods of time she doesn't remember, why things happen she can't explain. She purchased the rope and the rigging and all the other things he used to create his lair, but she didn't know she had done it, found one of the receipts and looked at it in wonder, not understanding where it had come from.

The Melody creature sees the world the way she believes it to be.

Shannuck sees the world the way it is.

The world is a place filled with small bugs for him to kill and store away. Every day he hunts, looks for more little bugs to kill because that is his nature, to kill, to wrap up what he has killed, and store it away.

He runs down the web at the bugs below him, the ugly bugs he will kill — but not wrap around and around in shiny white. He will kill them because they are the enemies of Shannuck, they want to keep him from hunting and killing his prey. They must die the death of all those who oppose Shannuck and endanger Katydid — ripped into little pieces, torn apart in rage.

He laughs at the thought of it, laughs as he runs to kill the wretched bugs.

Bailey gasped. The world spun. She saw the spider coming at them when seconds ago *she had been the spider coming at them.*

She had been inside looking out, now she was outside, looking in.

Bailey was losing herself.

She felt the sliding, the diminished awareness, but she was unable to do anything about it. She could only stare at the monster spider that was really a woman, but really a spider, running down the web at them and she knew Shannuck would kill them both, rip them apart.

Katydid had seen *the real spider* she'd named Shannuck race across the web he'd built to kill whatever was entangled in it. She'd studied how he wrapped up the smaller bugs — little wasps, bees and fat green flies. She didn't know what he did with them and didn't care. Just watched him rolling them over and over until they were small white packages he carried away with him.

Once Shannuck, the human distorted into a spider, was set free, he began to do the same — killed little "bugs" and stored them away. Because *that's what spiders did.* Shannuck would never stop killing. It was *his nature* and he would continue to hunt and murder small children as long as he drew breath on the earth.

The spider racing down the web toward them suddenly paused. Hesitated. It looked around, looked back up the web. It had become aware of something, heard or smelled or saw or sensed something she and T.J. couldn't.

Then it turned, an impossible move for a human. Facing down on the net, it turned and raced back up the net, scuttled so quickly it was gone in an instant, vanished up there in the gloom.

Bailey felt her legs going out from under her, felt herself starting to fall. She was afraid she was going to faint and didn't know what that might mean. Would the person who was Bailey fall into one of the other consciousnesses — live in the significant moments that were pulsing now in the mind of the little girl hiding down in the darkness? The spider? Or maybe Melody? Or would she fall down into her own darkness, into the depths of herself, down into the abyss — and stay there?

"Bailey."

She heard her name called from a great distance.

Then she felt a stinging on her cheek, and her head rocked to the side.

The slap pulled her back, and the darkness converging on her from all sides began to recede.

"Bailey!"

T.J. slapped her again, hard. Tears welled in her eyes and she tasted blood in her mouth.

"Stop it!"

"Come back!"

Back was the nightmare world of spiders and bugs and crawling things.

But back was real. It was where the *real Bailey really was.* And in a strange, desperate way, she welcomed it.

"We gotta move now while she's gone. Cross there."

She looked where he pointed, her vision washing over a small footbridge that connected to the next theatre box, about fifty feet higher on the wall. The bridge looked unstable, as if it merely dangled between the two theatre boxes, like it would sway in the wind if there were one. But when she stepped out onto it, she realized it was solid, had just been designed to look flimsy and delicate — with lattice side rails that were as alive with creatures as was every other surface.

She slid her hand along the top of the railing to keep her balance as T.J. dragged her by the other hand and she staggered along behind him. Something hairy touched her hand, skittered across her wrist and up her arm toward her elbow. She shook it away. But it didn't fall off. It clung to her. She looked at it, focused her blurry attention on it.

A tarantula.

She yanked her other hand out of T.J.'s grip, slapped at the thing … and it bit her.

Bailey shrieked. T.J. turned to her.

"What—?"

She held out her arm, a burning, throbbing agony.

"It bit me. *A tarantula bit me.*"

Just the words were so horrifying she thought she might jump out of her skin. It had *crawled on her!* Bit her! Now her whole arm was on fire, a pounding nightmare of pain.

"A tarantula, not one of the … smaller spiders? Or some kind you ain't never seen before? You sure?"

"Yes," — she shuddered — "a tarantula!"

"Ain't fatal, then. Come on."

He grabbed her other arm and began dragging her along the bridge to the next theatre box.

Bailey was suddenly sick, reflexive heaving clamped down on her diaphragm and she spewed out her breakfast onto the floor of the bridge. T.J. didn't even slow down, just kept dragging her along as she vomited. The world was swimming. Then the world was gone again.

Chapter Forty-Three

She is sitting up in a wheelchair in front of a window. The sun is shining on her face. From far back in the dark, safe place Katydid can see the sunlight shining in through the eyes. She can feel the sun on the skin.

The nice nurse the other nurses call Naomi, who is tall and has big hands and reads her stories every day will be here soon. Katydid likes Naomi. She has a kind face with a big nose, curly brown hair and bright brown eyes that look like the acorns that used to fall out of the tree in the back yard of the house where Katydid lived with the parents she used to have before she did the bad thing and they left her alone in the stinky place with the bugs that hurt her.

When the nurse comes in to read, Katydid moves carefully out of the dark place. Sneaks closer into the edge of the light, so she can listen to the stories.

The hospital room window is open today and the wind is blowing in and Katydid can smell good things. While she waits for Naomi to come and read her a story, she edges closer to the world and smells the good smells. There are flowers and the air is fresh, like it just got washed by rain. She can see through the eyes out into the light, can look over the tops of trees at the clouds and the wires where birds sometimes sit side by side but not today.

The wheelchair is angled so Katydid can see the woman in the bed next to hers, who never gets to look out the window because she is old and sick and can't sit up. Her name is Martha and she talks about her children who aren't there, only she thinks they are. She cries for them sometimes and she yells sometimes and then the nurses come and give her a shot.

She and Martha are alone in the room until the Blaine Thing comes through the door. He's an orderly, but he isn't a nice orderly like the big black man with huge hands who is so strong he just picks Katydid up and puts her in the chair like she doesn't weight anything at all.

The nurses don't like the Blaine Thing. They talk about him, that it's not his fault if sometimes he doesn't understand what they want him to do. They don't really believe that — she's heard them whispering — but they can't say so because he is "mentally challenged" and you can't say bad things about mentally challenged people or you'll get in trouble. The Blaine Thing knows they can't talk about him, knows they can't make him do things if he pretends he doesn't understand what they want and he laughs at them for being stupid. Katydid knows because he talks to himself all the time when the nurses aren't around. He hates them, but he hates the old people more and any time he gets a chance to be mean to the old people he does. The nurses know, but they've never caught him so they can't prove it.

The Blaine Thing does things to Martha when the nurses aren't around. He pinches her hard sometimes and Martha cries out, but the nurses just give her a shot so she will go to sleep and not cry out anymore.

Today, the Blaine Thing has a bent hairpin and he sticks it in Martha's ear. It must hurt because she twists her head and tries to make him stop, but he looks over his shoulder to make sure no nurses are coming and he grabs a handful of Martha's hair and holds her head still and he jabs the thing in her ear and she cries and he keeps doing it.

Then he sees that he has made her ear bleed.

"You old hag! Don't you make a mess and get me in trouble."

He calls her terrible names and says bad words to her as he snatches a tissue from the box and jams it into her ear to stop the bleeding. But when he pulls out the tissue, she's still bleeding and that makes him even madder. "Stop it! Stop bleeding!"

He stuffs another tissue in, pushes it down hard and holds it, but when he pulls it out she's still bleeding. A lot. He jams more tissue into her ear and stuffs the bloody tissues into his pocket.

"You stop that bleeding or I'll fix you like I fixed Granny. I'll get that stuff out of the laundry room that makes the clothes white, and I'll hold your nose and pour it down your throat. Then you'll choke and cough and get sick. And your eyes will roll back in your head and you'll be dead!"

The Blaine Thing pulls the tissue out of Martha's ear and the bleeding has stopped now and he uses another tissue to wipe all the blood out of her ear. But he's still mad.

He glances at Katydid then.

"What are you looking at?" He knows she is not looking at anything but he crosses the room to where she is sitting in front of the window, grabs her by the shoulders and shakes her violently and her head snaps back and forth. "Stop looking at me, you vegetable!" He jabs her forehead hard with his finger and it hurts. "Nothing in there but rotten tomatoes."

He stops shaking her and gets right down in her face, inches from her nose. His breath smells like garlic and decayed teeth and when he speaks, he is so angry he spits on her.

"Want me to stick this in your ear?" He holds up the hairpin with Martha's blood on it. "Poke a hole in your eardrum, maybe poke so far into your head it sticks into your brain and all the rotted tomato juice will come running out your ear."

Katydid is frightened now. There are no nurses around. He can stick that in her ear and they won't see. And he can come back tomorrow and do it again! If he's mad at her, he can do other things to her, too, when the nurses aren't there.

The Blaine Thing grabs a handful of Katydid's hair and yanks her head sideways toward her shoulder. He shoves the hair on the other side away from her ear and—

Shannuck grabs the Blaine Thing's neck and squeezes, roaring rage filling every tissue in the black spider's body. He watches the look on the Blaine Thing's face downshift from shock and surprise to fear. And he is excited by the fear. It makes him feel strong and powerful. Makes him feel good.

"You want to hurt Katydid?" Shannuck rumbles, a raspy, grating voice that sounds like rusty machinery. "You like to make pain? Let's see how you like to feel pain!"

Shannuck rises up to his full height on his hind legs, rises up tall and black and hairy and terrible and beautiful on his hind legs on the bed and holds the Blaine Thing out in front of him like a wasp caught in his web. Then he throws the Blaine Thing to the floor and leaps on his chest. He uses one hairy leg to pin his neck to the floor and with the other, he gouges out the Blaine Thing's right eye. Claws it out of the socket. The Blaine Thing is screaming soundlessly, hysterical, terror granting him strength as he tries to wrench out of Shannuck's grasp but his strength is nothing. Shannuck can lift a hundred times his own body weight, has the crushing power of a trash compactor in a garbage truck. He claws out the Blaine Thing's other eye.

Shannuck hates bugs that make pain, like the wasps and bees that stung Katydid. He grabs the Blaine Thing by the throat with both his hairy, black arms, smells the stink as the Blaine Thing pees and craps himself, smells the feces with the hairs on his own legs. And Shannuck gets his spider face up to Blaine's, who can't see anymore. "Now, you die, hateful, hurting bug!"

Shannuck hurls the Blaine Thing at the screen on the window, which bursts outward with his weight and he drops instantly out of sight.

Scuttling across the room to the sink, Shannuck washes the gore off his black spider legs, wipes away all the Blaine Thing's blood, then just as quickly returns to the wheelchair and sits back down into it.

And Shannuck is gone.

KATYDID SEES out through the eyes, looks at the window. The screen on the window is gone. There is a stink now — feces and other things on the floor in front of the window. But the Blaine Thing is gone now. She sees that Martha's ear has begun to bleed again. It has dripped down her earlobe and is pooling on her shoulder, staining the pink nightgown her daughter brought to her for her birthday.

Then a nurse comes into the room. Katydid hears her but doesn't see her until she comes closer. She looks down at the puddle of stinky stuff in front of the window, then leans out of it to look down. She freezes for a moment before she jumps back so suddenly she hits her head on the window. She backs away, then turns and runs out of the room.

Martha reaches up to feel the blood on her ear. And she smiles at Katydid.

~

A SUDDEN CRACK shattered the air and hunks of bark and wood exploded off a tree two feet from where Nakamura had been standing when he was talking on the phone to the boy.

Nakamura hit the dirt.

"What the—?"

Another shot ripped into a tree about twenty feet from them, where Brice was sure the boy could see that officers were stationed behind a berm of bushes.

Nakamura grabbed the loudspeaker and pressed the button.

"Lucas, stop firing! Nobody's going to come charging in on you. Stop shooting."

Another bullet ripped into the brush a couple of feet to the left of where Nakamura was now crouched behind a burnt stump and a small bush.

"What's he doing?" Nakamura called out to Brice, who had taken refuge behind the door of his cruiser. "He knows we won't return fire. Is he trying to back us up farther away from the house?"

He put the megaphone to his lips and spoke again.

"Lucas, can we talk? I'm going to call on the house phone. Pick up and let's talk."

The boy's response was another barrage of bullets, this

time at the officers on the north side of the house behind a hillock, the shots kicking up tufts of dirt as they plugged into the ground.

Nakamura punched in the number of the phone at the cabin and listened to the ring. The boy didn't pick up, but he did fire two rounds at the officers behind the house.

"Does he think there's going to be a shootout?" Nakamura said.

Brice caught sight of the boy moving quickly from one vantage point in the fire tower on top of the house to another, glimpses of movement, nothing you could get a bead on. Shots rang out again and pieces of tree bark leapt off trees on the west side of the house. Brice took the opportunity to dash across the few feet separating his cruiser from the stump and bush Nakamura was using for cover.

"You a hunter?" he asked, looking out through the limbs of the bush at the cabin sitting in the clearing.

"No, why?"

"I don't know what Quantico trained you on other than your service weapon — AR-15s, maybe, or AK-47s?" He didn't wait for a response. "From the sound of it, this boy's firing a Browning A-bolt .270 hunting rifle, likely has a Diamondback HP 3-12x42 scope. You put the crosshairs of that scope on a deer and if you know how to work the rise on it, you could probably make a shot at seven hundred yards."

Nakamura's face was impassive.

"I was in the Ferriglianos' living room this afternoon and it's full of hunting trophies. The rack of antlers over the mantle — a twenty-two-point buck. The plaque on it said Lucas shot it from four hundred yards — *four football fields* — away."

"And your point?

"The kid has fired nine times at a range of a few hundred *feet.* And *missed* nine times. Not gotten anywhere near a target nine times."

"You don't think he's trying to hit anyone."

"I think he's being very careful *not* to hit anyone. He's goading us, trying to get us to return fire."

"Why?"

"Because he wants us to kill him."

"Suicide by cop."

"Yep."

"So why's he suddenly decided he wants to die? What's changed since we got here and all he wanted was for us to go away?"

As if the question had summoned the answer, Nakamura's phone rang and he spoke briefly and hung up.

"Trimboli said Lucas just called his mother."

"And?"

"And she told him Holly Campbell showed us Riley's hidden treasure, and that we'd found his pictures of Riley."

They'd left specific instructions that if Lucas got in touch with his family, they were *not* to speak to him. They were to turn the call over to the FBI agent immediately.

"Trimboli said she only realized who the mother was talking to, that it was Lucas, when she heard her yelling at him, calling him a child molester."

It was staggering sometimes how stupid people could be.

"Now, he'd rather die than have the world know he molested Riley," Brice said.

"So does that mean he *did* kidnap and murder him?"

Before Brice could respond, the cell Nakamura still held in his hand rang. Caller ID identified "Edward O'Halloran" — the land line in the hunting lodge.

"Hello, Lucas. This is agent Nakamura."

"Okay, I want to give myself up."

His voice was totally devoid of emotion, sounded like the automated attendant in a car wash.

"That's a very good decision Lucas."

Brice mouthed, *stall him.*

"I'll need just a minute, though. You started shooting ... I want to make sure all my men know you're *surrendering*. I'll call back when we're ready."

The line went dead.

"He'll be packing," Nakamura said. "As soon as we show ourselves, he'll reach for the gun and make us shoot him. What've you got?"

Brice explained his idea.

Chapter Forty-Four

BAILEY WHIMPERED, opened eyes she had squeezed shut, and the nightmare world appeared around her. Blood red light. Musky stink. Staggering along beside T.J. He was mostly carrying her because she hadn't been able to move her legs while her mind was … where? There. In the other.

T.J.'s voice … but the sounds were too soft. The great buzzing sound in her head drowned them out.

"… help me … have to try … Bailey, *please*!"

She tried to assign meaning to the sounds but she couldn't seem to make the connections.

T.J. dragged her with her arm around his shoulders off the walkway between theatre boxes and along the back wall of the next one. She could walk better now. The effects of the drug were probably wearing off. But the effect of what was happening to her mind was more debilitating than the drug that had made the constant connections possible. She was losing herself and she didn't know how to stop the process. The path between her and the other, the thing, or the little girl — the walls of self that separated her from them were fading, falling, disintegrating, going from solid to translucent to transparent to … not there at all.

T.J. suddenly cried out, staggered into the wall, dragging her with him until he let go of her arm and she dropped off his shoulder and hit the wall with her back. She balanced there with the wall supporting her. Was parked there. Watched T.J. beat at his pants leg. One of the spiders had bitten him.

She had lost the ability to be horrified by the presence of crawling, biting, poisonous spiders all around. By the bugs on the wall, things that were crawling off the wall into her hair. Beetles. Spiders maybe. Roaches certainly, they were everywhere, so everywhere that the scuttling raspy sound of their movement was so loud it penetrated the buzzing in her head. Or maybe it *was* the buzzing in her head.

She wanted to reach up and dust whatever had crawled onto her head out of her hair, but she didn't. She supposed she could have. But the space between the wanting and the will to respond to wanting was … empty. Like there was no connection. The machine of who she was had been yanked apart, leaving wires dangling, electric wires with sparks flying. She felt something crawl down her forehead and across her nose — a centipede maybe. What she could see of it had lots of legs. Maybe just a caterpillar. Caterpillars turned into butterflies. Butterflies were beautiful, fragile things with delicate wings in the colors of the rainbow. Like the crystals of the chandelier that was supposed to cast multicolored light, fracture into a prism of delight on the walls of the room. But it didn't.

She knew this caterpillar wasn't going to have the chance to become a thing of beauty, not here in this place. Nothing beautiful could live in this place. The caterpillar would be eaten by the spiders first. Did spiders eat caterpillars? She didn't know. Maybe. But even if they didn't, Bailey understood as a foundational truth that didn't need words to articulate — this place was not somewhere butterflies could live, flit from one filthy surface to another. This was a place for ugliness and darkness, filth and poison and pain. Not for butterflies.

She reached up and grabbed the thing on her face. Didn't look at it, didn't want to know that it wasn't a caterpillar but some other multi-legged horror, and flung it away onto the floor. T.J. was groaning, had pulled his pants leg up to reveal … she couldn't see what. She knew it was a bite of some kind because she could see the swelling, but his black skin didn't turn bright red as her arm had when the tarantula bit her.

She thought about the tarantula bite. Waited for the awareness of the pain to return. It didn't. She knew it hurt. Understood that it hurt. But she couldn't feel the pain. That wasn't a good thing, oh no indeedy that wasn't a good thing at all. Bailey had been bitten by a tarantula. Bailey's arm was in agony from the stinging venom of the bite. Bailey hurt. So if she was Bailey, she should hurt, too. But she didn't feel any pain at all.

"… keep goin' … movin' …"

T.J.'s words. He pulled her away from the wall where the crawly things had slithered onto her head and even now crawled down her back inside her shirt. He yanked her forward and her legs carried her along with him as her vision swam in front of her — dark walls, giant spiderwebs. No, ropes. Rope rigging, like on a ship.

No, *spiderwebs for Shannuck.* Shannuck protects Katydid.

Then Bailey was gone again.

~

KATYDID LIES IN HER BED, her eyes fixed on the ceiling tile above it. There is a water stain on one side of it that has an odd shape. Sometimes it looks like an upside-down tree, with a circle of leaves on the bottom instead of the top and a trunk with tendrils of roots on the top. Other times it looks like a clown's face, with kinky hair on the top and a full, brown beard on the bottom.

She looks up at the stained ceiling tile every morning when she wakes up, stares at it until the nurses come in to crank her bed up so they can feed her breakfast. Then they crank her bed back down and she stares at it some more. Sometimes they come and put her in a wheelchair after breakfast. Sometimes they take her gown off her and put her into the special wheelchair that they push into the shower room at the end of the hall where they take the spray and wash her hair. Sometimes the shampoo gets in her eyes and stings, but she doesn't mind. She likes the feel of the warm water on her head and splashing on her body, likes the clean smell when they put a fresh gown on her and put her back into the bed where they have put crisp white sheets that smell like bleach.

Sometimes, when she smells the bleach she thinks of the Blaine Thing who said he had forced his grandmother to drink bleach and killed her. But she doesn't usually think of that. She just thinks the sheets smell fresh and she likes the smell.

She is no longer in the room with Martha. Martha died in her sleep one night. After that, Katydid was moved to a different floor of the hospital, near the craft room, and sometimes the nurses put her into a wheelchair and roll her into the craft room. She liked that. Liked sitting there where she could see the other patients making things with their hands, listen to their voices as they talked, even liked it when one of them began to holler and scream and then the nurses and orderlies would come and the big orderly would wrap his arms around the patient and hold them until the nurse gave the patient a shot and then they stopped making noises and fell asleep.

She liked the smell of the paints in the craft room, the smell of the clay and the smell of wood smoke when they used the wood-burning tool to make things out of blocks of wood.

As she looks at the ceiling tile, she smells the smoke from the wood-burning tool. But it smells different. And she isn't in the craft room, so why does she smell the smoke all the way in here, in the room she shares now with Beatrice, who only breathes because there is a machine making her breathe and when her family comes to visit they talk about unplugging her so she can "die with dignity," and they argue about it and all leave mad.

Beatrice doesn't smell the smoke, of course, but Katydid smells it. And it isn't wood burning. It's something else. The smoke doesn't smell good. It smells bad and then there are bells and alarms and nurses rushing around.

There's a fire!

Katydid is afraid of fire!

Daddy made a bonfire once in the back yard and when Katydid leaned over it to put her marshmallow in the flames, the fire caught her coat sleeve on fire. Daddy grabbed her and rolled her on the ground but she got a burn on her arm anyway that hurt and she was afraid of fire after that.

Katydid smells the smoke thicker now and her heart begins to pound. She doesn't want the fire to get her, to burn her again like it did that time in the back yard.

SHANNUCK LOOKS AROUND. He leaps out of the bed, hurries to the open door and sees smoke in the hallway in front of the craft room. Beside the door of Katydid's room is the opening in the wall where the nurses put the laundry out of the rolling baskets. He climbs inside and scuttles down the slick sides of the laundry chute, holding on with his spider legs, going down head first. He climbs past the opening on the second floor and the one on the first. There is a big opening at the bottom of the chute into the laundry room. There is no smoke here. No fire. Shannuck crawls across the laundry room floor into a corner, where he lies down.

Shannuck is gone.

KATYDID'S not looking at the ceiling tile over her bed now. She can't smell smoke, either. No longer in bed, she is lying on something hard and cold. She smells the good smell around her, the smell of clean sheets and looks up at overhead lights, florescent lights hanging from the low ceiling on strings. She is beside something big and white, a washing machine that is making slushing noises. Then she hears a voice.

"What in the world …?"

She sees a face above hers. It is a woman's face, round and fat, with black hair under a hairnet.

"What are you doing here?" the woman asks her. Then she waves her hand back and forth in front of Katydid's eyes. She turns and calls out. "Juanita, come here! There's a little girl here, a patient from upstairs."

Another face suddenly appears. This one is black, with kinky hair cropped tight to her head.

"How did she get here?" the second woman asks.

"I don't know," says the first. "She was just lying here. I didn't see anybody bring her in."

"Why would somebody bring her here and leave her lying on the floor?"

But neither woman has an answer.

THE PAIN IN T.J.'s leg was worse than the pain in his hand. Way worse. He hadn't seen the spider that bit him, but even if he had … pro'lly wouldn't a'recognized it. Who knew what kinds of spiders Melody's wealth had been able to purchase to stock this nightmare world. He could feel himself reactin' to the new venom, could feel his chest gettin' tight, makin' it hard to breathe, could feel his heart start to hammerin', knew his blood pressure was spikin' so high if there was any weak spots in the blood vessels in his brain he'd have a blowout.

His stomach was starting to ache, too. Like cramps. No, not cramps — one long cramp that tightened painfully and never let go.

Even if what had bitten him didn't deliver a fatal amount of venom, if T.J. didn't get out of here, get Bailey out of here, the accumulation of bites would do 'em in as surely as a single bite of somethin' deadly. How many spider bites would it take 'fore you suffered some kinda fatal reaction, even if it was an allergic one? Half a dozen? A dozen?

He yanked Bailey off the wall where she'd been leanin' in order to remain upright. There was bugs crawling on her —

some spiders, too, but she wasn't even trying to brush 'em off. Just stood there.

"Bailey, you all right?"

She didn't respond. Didn't appear to have heard him.

"We gotta keep goin', keep movin'."

She seemed to really see him for a moment, then her eyes went blank again and he knew she was somewhere else entirely. The constant connections was unhinging her. Wasn't nobody could keep hold of their sanity if they was constantly lookin' into the heads of other people. *Insane* people. Or other *things*.

And he acknowledged the reality that Bailey made an "off-limits" subject among her friends a long time ago. A no-fly zone, nobody was 'lowed to cruise anywhere near it. But truth was Bailey Donahue *had a bullet in her brain*! A bump on the head could kill her. Or not. She'd survived lots of bumps and lumps in the months since she'd put that pistol to her temple and pulled the trigger. But those was physical blows. What about *emotional, psychological blows*? How many of those could she stand?

He had to get her out of here fast or might not be no Bailey left to rescue.

Yankin' her roughly along beside him, he crossed the theatre box, climbed up the slanted walkway to the next one and crossed it, too. He didn't know what it was that'd distracted Melody ... *Shannuck* ... but whatever it was, he hoped it continued to distract her.

"Bailey, you with me, sugar?"

No response.

He dared to pause for a moment, turned to her, took her shoulders and shook her hard as he dared. Her head lolled back and forth on her shoulders like she was a broken doll. He hated to slap her again, but ...

Then present-ness came into her eyes. She focused. Saw him.

"Shannuck killed an orderly in the hospital, then climbed down a laundry chute," she said, spoke like somebody'd just got out of the dentist office and they mouth was still kinda numb. No, it was more like she was havin' to translate her words into a foreign language, conjugate the verbs and recall the words for "orderly" and "hospital."

"Try to stay here with me. Can you do that?"

"Try. Yes. But …" She just looked at him, helplessly, like she couldn't form the words to keep talking.

"We're goin' up in the elevator." He turned to point to the metal cage at floor level below them. He pointed up then, into the gloom of the ceiling. "The elevator opens up in that turret—"

Bailey grunted. Just grunted. He turned back to her and saw a spider on her neck. It was huge, gray and hairy, and he thought it might be a wolf spider. He slapped it off, knocked it to the floor and stomped it out of anger, smashed it under his foot. Then he looked back at Bailey, into her face.

"Bit me." She said it like she was reading the ingredients label on a bottle of hot sauce.

He grabbed her arm, hurriedly dragged her across the last of the box balconies to the circular staircase that led down from it to the dance floor. He plunged into the blackness, scooting his hand along the railing quickly, knocking aside the living things, staggering down the stairs way faster than it was safe to take them, dragging an almost catatonic woman along with him. Around and around. He fell twice. If it'd been a normal staircase, the two of them would have tumbled head-over-heels all the way to the bottom, but the circular railing rose up in a cage around them.

Staggering out into the awful red glow of the ballroom, he took off at his closest approximation of a dead run, hauling Bailey along behind him, toward the metal cage elevator affixed to the wall. He fumbled at the door catch, found it, shoved the door inward and pushed Bailey inside.

Would the elevator work? Or had Melody disconnected it?

He closed the door behind them with a soft clanging sound, dropped the bar across it that prevented it from opening in transit, then turned to the box on the back wall with a green button and a red one. He was about to punch he green one when Bailey squeaked out an incoherent sound. He looked where she was looking — at the big double doors at the other side of the room. One of them had begun to open slowly. The spider thing entered first. She was dragging something across the floor behind her.

Lucas Ferrigliano opened the door of the O'Halloran cabin and stepped out onto the porch. Then he just stood there with his hands at his sides.

"Clasp your fingers together behind your head," Nakamura called out through the bullhorn.

The boy slowly raised his hands in the air in surrender, but didn't clasp them behind his head. Then he started walking slowly across the porch.

"I said clasp your fingers behind your head."

The boy continued in measured strides across the porch and started down the steps.

"You going to arrest me or not?"

He got to the stone walkway and started out across it.

"Lie down on the ground, face down, your hands straight out to your sides."

"Come on, cuff me."

Lucas didn't put his hands behind his head and he didn't lie down on the ground. He just kept walking.

"Stop right where you are. Lie down—"

"You want me, come and get—"

The boy started to reach behind his back to pull the pistol he'd stuck down the waistband of his jeans.

Brice sprang off the porch behind him and tackled him.

After Nakamura'd called Lucas to tell him it was safe for him to come out and surrender, he signaled Brice. It would take the boy thirty seconds — at a dead run — to make it from the fire watchtower on top of the house to the front door, and he wouldn't likely be running.

That gave Brice plenty of time to jump out of the bushes east of the house and bolt across the open grass to the building. He leapt over the railing on the wraparound porch and was waiting at the edge of the house to pounce before the kid had time to draw his weapon.

Brice had six inches and sixty pounds on Lucas Ferrigliano and the boy collapsed under him, slammed into the ground hard, groaned and then began to cry.

Straddling the boy, Brice pulled the pistol out of the waistband of Lucas's jeans and tossed it on the ground out of his reach, then he pulled his hands behind his back and cuffed him. He stood and was pulling the boy to his feet when Nakamura stepped up beside him.

"Where's the little girl?" Nakamura demanded.

"What little girl?" Lucas was sobbing.

"Baby Girl."

"My *dog*?"

Several of Brice's deputies and three FBI agents had dashed into the house as soon as Lucas hit the ground. As Fletcher started inside, Brice called to him. "There's a security camera. Find the playback recorder."

"You're under arrest for—" Nakamura looked at Brice. "How many officers altogether?"

"Twenty-six."

"For twenty-six counts of attempted murder of a police officer."

The number was actually nine times twenty-six, one count for every shot he'd fired.

Before Nakamura had completed rattling off the other charges, Agent Hardesty appeared in the doorway.

"Clear," he said. "Nobody's in here."

As he spoke, an old border collie moved slowly out the door beside him, down the steps and came to sit at the boy's feet.

"Where's Riley Campbell?" Nakamura asked Lucas.

The crying boy lifted his head.

"I didn't touch him. I swear. You have to find him — *ask him*. He'll tell you I never laid a finger on him."

"Christi Strickland — what did you do with her?"

"I don't know anybody named Christi Strickland."

"And the little girl you took from the mall this afternoon — where is she?"

"What little girl?"

"At 2:30 this afternoon you snatched a little girl out of a basket in Your Style Your Way. You slipped her into the back of your CRV parked behind the pizza parlor."

"I was here at 2:30. I've been here all day. When I was leaving for work this morning, I heard the FBI agents on the Campbells' porch saying that when a kidnapper takes a second child, the first … *Not Riley*, oh please no, not Riley. You *have to* find Riley. Please, please find him. If you don't, nobody will ever believe I didn't …"

His tears turned into great heaving sobs then and he stood with his hands cuffed behind his back, tears streaming down his cheeks.

Fletch stepped to the doorway.

"I've got the playback ready."

Brice instructed two deputies to take Lucas to a patrol car while he and Nakamura went into the cabin to a small room off the pantry where a wall-mounted monitor was paused on a frozen shot of the porch on the side of the house and the gravel driveway beyond it.

"I've got it cued up to what you'll want to see," Fletch said and hit the play button. "I fast-forwarded through. The vehicle never moved after it pulled up. This is the last image until we got here."

The camera showed the bottom portion of a red vehicle — halfway down the door and the tires — as it pulled up the driveway. Then feet. Then the boy came into view, walked up the steps to the door. He was alone except for the old border collie that padded along beside him. He stood there, punching in the numbers on the lockbox that held the house key.

Nakamura said something under his breath Brice didn't hear.

"What?"

"Look at the time stamp."

Brice looked more closely at the frozen image and the gray letters on the bottom of the screen: 10:31:40. The boy had arrived at the house that morning. And unless he'd walked into town, he couldn't have been at the mall when the little deaf girl was snatched out of her mother's shopping cart.

Brice and Nakamura stood up from the screen at the same time and the FBI agent nodded toward the window where the boy could be seen in the back of a patrol car, still sobbing.

"Maybe he really hadn't touched Riley Campbell," Brice said.

"Not *yet*, anyway. He would have eventually, though. They always do." Nakamura paused. "We'll probably never know."

An acknowledgement. He didn't expect to find Riley Campbell alive. Neither did Brice.

Nakamura dug at his bloodshot eyes.

"I'll ride back into town with Hardesty to brief the other agents."

Reinforcements from Pittsburgh. They would intensify the investigation, question every human being in the lives of all three children. Go down every conceivable rabbit hole, however unlikely. Maybe someone only wanted one of the children and the other kidnappings were a smokescreen.

Maybe there was more than one kidnapper. Stranger kidnapping was rare, despite all the cop show plots to the contrary. But more than one stretched the bounds of possibility. Still …

Of course, Riley Campbell blew all the theories out of the water. If a stranger had somehow fixated on that particular little boy, there were dozens of easier places to snatch him than off a school playground. *Why at school?* And *how* at school? The other kidnap locations were difficult; the school was impossible. Brice was convinced that the missing piece to all the puzzles was there. The thought triggered the feeling he'd had before all else was shoved aside in the pursuit and capture of Lucas Ferrigliano. A niggling itch, a feeling in his gut that he had missed something at the mall. But he couldn't grab hold of it before it vanished like smoke from a dying campfire. He was too tired. Perhaps the best thing the new phalanx of FBI agents could provide was fresh eyes on what they already knew. Every mother's child who'd been working on this case was fried.

Nakamura looked at his watch, and when he looked up at Brice their eyes locked. Understanding passed between them that needed no words.

Marley Ewing had been missing for almost three hours.

Brice's tired mind didn't want to do the math, but the numbers appeared anyway.

Christi Strickland had been missing for more than twenty-four hours.

And Riley Campbell … three days. Three. *Days.*

Brice walked slowly to his cruiser, inhaling the fresh smell of coming rain as he pulled out his phone to check his messages. He stopped where he was when he spotted the voicemail from Bailey.

"The private investigator found her, found Caitlyn Whitfield." Her voice was full of excitement, awe and wonder. "She's alive! Dobbs'll forward you the whole report and you better be sitting down when you read it. Brice, Caitlyn Whitfield grew up to be ... Melody McCallum. No, I am not making that up. Melody McCallum. I plan to have a loooong talk with that woman!"

He hit replay, listened again, certain he'd misunderstood—*Melody McCallum.*

He stood dumfounded, trying to get his mind around it, then listened a third time as he got into his cruiser.

... Dobbs'll forward you the whole report ...

Scanning down through his emails, he clicked on one that had come in from Dobbs, opened the attached report and read it.

Then he read it through a second time.

Chapter Forty-Five

T.J. WATCHED Melody McCallum scuttle spider-like across the open floor, her body distorted and misshapen, hunched over, her arms and legs double-jointed. She was draggin' a silver package like the other plastic-wrapped pouches that held the bodies of three murdered children sealed inside. This one was a lot bigger, though he couldn't get a good look at it from here.

Slippin' a loop of the rope attached to one end of the package around her shoulder, the Melody-spider thing grabbed the lowest-hanging piece of rigging and started climbin', a spider skittering 'cross a web, carryin' a sack of—

T.J. froze.

Bailey screamed — shock and terror and grief like he woulda screamed, too, if he could have. If his mouth hadn't suddenly been welded shut, his jaw froze like he'd been hit by a taser.

The body the woman spider was draggin' across the webbing wasn't wrapped up all the way like them kids' bodies, head-to-toe like leftovers in the refrigerator sealed in a silver glaze of the Saran Wrap. This body was only wrapped from the shoulders down. Above that was visible.

It was Dobbs.

"Is he …?" Bailey whispered voice was anguished.

"Dead?"

He couldn't believe he'd said the word. 'Cause wasn't no way Dobbs was dead. That was as impossible as the sun fallin' into the ocean with a *sizzzzz* sound. Couldn't happen.

Yeah, it could. T.J. was a Marine. A soldier. He'd gone into battle with many a friend who didn't deserve to have his head blown apart by a sniper or his gut ripped open by an IED.

But … *Dobbs?*

Then T.J. saw movement.

Dobbs was dangling upside down from the rope as the spider creature hauled him upward into the web and T.J. seen his head turn! Seen him look around. He was alive.

Alive *right now.*

But for how long?

Raymond Dobson weighed 270 pounds if he weighed an ounce and if Melody McCallum weighed more than 110 T.J. was a dill pickle. But there she was, carryin' Dobbs's body up rope spiderwebs like he was made outta paper mache.

T.J. had to do something.

What?

Clearly, she'd overpowered Dobbs, not that that was much of an accomplishment. Though Dobbs was big, he wasn't particularly strong. But even if the man coulda bench-pressed a Buick, no human could match the strength of a spider. Unarmed, all of 'em together wouldn't stand a chance 'gainst the beast. T.J. had to get outta here and get a weapon. He had a "Colt 1911" pistol, a favorite of Marine old-timers, in the glove box of his car. A bullet between the eyes would drop the creature — whether it was a first-grade teacher or a human spider.

That was the only hope for Dobbs or Bailey, the only chance *all three* of them had to survive. T.J. had to shoot that *thing.*

He turned and punched the green button on the back wall

of the elevator. It lurched, but made no sound, just started risin' slowly up the wall toward the opening at the top that led outside. Unless she'd sealed that, too.

The elevator had been designed to give the occupants a panoramic view of the ballroom, where ladies in evenin' gowns and gentlemen in tuxes whirled 'round and 'round in the sparklin', kaleidoscopic light show of the big chandelier. To make that view last as long as possible, the metal box literally *inched* up toward the ceiling.

The spider creature stopped halfway up the web rigging and 'tached the rope tied to the cellophane capsule holdin' Dobbs.

Left him there hangin'.

Upside down.

The human body was designed for the heart to pump blood from the legs up the body, but not in the opposite direction. Hangin' upside down 'lowed the blood to pool in the brain. T.J. had read 'bout triathletes and the like decidin' to dangle themselves upside down for various periods of time — for hours even. Dobbs's overweight body couldn't take that kind of trauma. The increased pressure of the blood would eventually cause swelling severe enough to do brain damage. Or kill him.

Every moment that he just *dangled there* …

As soon as the spider creature'd secured Dobbs to the netting, it skittered up into the gloom above and vanished. Had to be an entrance up there somewhere into the ceiling, some way to get outta here when she'd heard Dobbs at the door.

How did she hear the doorbell in here? He hadn't heard it. Did the thing — she, Shannuck, Melody, whatever — have all the faculties of both species? Human hearin', but on the degree of magnitude granted by the spider part of a "blended species"? It could think like a human, speak, laugh — if you could call the sound it made laughter.

What else could it do?

Better questions: where had it gone and when was it comin' back?

He looked around for it, tryin' to look everywhere at once which resulted in seeing nothin' at all. His heart was hammerin' a hole in his ribcage, part from his own terror, part courtesy of the venom in his veins. If he got bit again, a coronary could very well be in T.J. Hamilton's immediate future.

He turned to Bailey. She was looking around fearfully, too. *That* was a good sign. She was aware enough, human enough, Bailey enough to be scared spitless about what might happen next.

Then she went blank, left the building. Only for a moment this time, though. When she blinked back into reality, made real eye contact with him, she grabbed his arm and tried to speak. But she couldn't, could only look up.

T.J. followed her gaze.

Chapter Forty-Six

Segmented reality. Color gone, just shadows — black, white and gray. The buzzing sound. Hissing. Angry, furious. The bugs are down there waiting for Shannuck.

With both his eyes focused forward, he sees them right below him in the cage, looking around, trying to find him. He crawls quietly down toward them, stops to jam a piece of the web into the elevator cable housing. He will kill them, twist their heads off their bodies and watch the blood pour out their ragged necks onto his legs where he can smell it, warm blood. He will rip them apart, tear them into little pieces.

Bailey was standing beside T.J., watching the horror descend on them.

No, no, she couldn't look at it for another second or she would go mad, so she focused on T.J. instead. He'd looked up when she grabbed his arm, saw what she saw coming at them, and was staring transfixed at the monstrosity climbing head-first down out of the web overhead and onto the top of the elevator cage.

Bailey grunted. In her mind, she screamed, shrieked, but the only sound she could make was a grunt. She felt her head turning, her eyes moving almost against her will away from T.J.'s face to behold the thing that could not possibly hold onto the elevator cage like that but it did, the same way a spider held on. Then it turned and righted itself and she was looking out through the bars at the horror of a human face that had been transformed into a spider — not three feet away.

The mouth opened and the stink of the breath was so disgusting Bailey felt bile rise instantly into her throat and she was unable to swallow it back. But she had already vomited up everything in her stomach, so she merely stood gaping at the creature, dry-heaving into the back of her throat.

"You die. You bleed. I crush, kill." The hoary words came from the ruin of a mouth and she felt T.J. shudder beside her.

"Stab your eyes, rip your head, crush your brains."

Then the set of spider legs that belonged to the human Melody McCallum, the ones with hands in black gloves grasping the bars of the cage, began to spread the bars apart. Bailey heard the metal groan as the creature bent them. It seemed to take no effort at all. In moments, the spider creature would pull the bars far enough apart to crawl inside the cage with them and rip them to pieces. It would—

Bailey fell out of the world.

And into the spider.

Maybe it was the state of mind of the spider — its whole being gearing up for slaughter — that caused the kaleidoscope of images, no scene, no consistent narrative, just images swirling around and around in a frenzy, moving faster and faster like some manic merry-go-round with demon horses and monster riders.

FRACTURED VISION.

Black and white.

Out front, a small bug. A little boy. Riley smiling as he runs across the hallway from the bathroom. He walks along beside the spider talking, but there are no words in the silence of the spider's head. The boy holds a sack of books and stands waiting as the trunk of the car opens. Then the spider reaches out and grabs the bug, snaps his neck in a single flash of movement, tosses him like a doll into the trunk and closes the lid.

Jagged images.

A black-and-white landscape out a car window. Trees, bushes, bugs crawling, children-bugs, crawling over the landscape. Hate the bugs, kill the bugs.

The car stops, the spider beckons. A little girl gets up from beside other bugs and approaches. She is smiling. The spider lunges out the car window, puts one hand on the top of the wall and uses the other to grab the bug. It snaps her neck and hauls her off the ground and in through the car window in seconds.

Walls and floors and racks of clothing. The spider crawls, hunting, seeking prey.

A small bug sits in a shopping cart. The spider takes it, breaks its neck, jams it into a bag and zips the bag shut.

Bugs in a cage, Shannuck is filled with loathing and rage and power and strength. He will kill the bugs — now!

BAILEY BREATHED STINK. Her head swam, the ache of spider bites on her arm and neck was a faraway, distant pain she didn't attend to as she watched Shannuck spread apart the bars of the elevator cage.

Seconds, just seconds and it would be over.

Then the spider stopped, froze in place, and an instant later it was skittering away, up off the cage of the elevator and into the rigging. It scuttled in seconds up the web into the shadows and vanished.

A breath carrying something like a strangled sob burst from T.J. beside her. She turned to him. Only she didn't turn. She had come loose again, the wires yanked apart. She was inside Bailey, but it felt like a temporary thing. Her *self* didn't live here anymore. It was not attached to this body, to these senses. She had no more control over these arms and legs … or thoughts or memories … than she did over Shannuck. She was just along for the ride.

T.J. turned back to the button on the wall and punched it. Nothing happened. He punched it again and again. Held it in. Nothing. The cage didn't move. He looked around, above the cage.

"She jammed the cable up there." He pointed to the piece of rigging that had been dragged over to the cable and stuffed in around it so it wouldn't move. "It won't go up or down. We're stuck."

The words were only sounds without meaning. Bailey looked at him, watched him from inside the Bailey body. Felt nothing.

BRICE PULLED his cruiser off the road and drove slowly down the winding lane to The Cedars, through stately trees that had begun to sway slightly in the growing wind. He'd been here a couple of times before, once answering a call when two of the tenants got into a brawl. A second when an Italian man named Tony *Something* had gotten drunk and was chasing his wife around the ballroom on the second floor, threatening her with a broken wine bottle because he had found texts on her phone from another man. Gratefully, Tony Something had been very drunk, his wife sober enough to dial 911. Then she'd managed to stay ahead of him in the ballroom, climbing up the spiral staircases and crossing the bridges between the theatre boxes on the walls until help arrived.

Of course, she refused to press charges. That happened way more often than most people would believe. The man had been threatening to kill her, *tried* to kill her, would likely have succeeded if he hadn't been so drunk and clumsy. But he blubbered his apologies, said he was sorry, he loved her, he didn't mean ... yada, yada, yada. The couple had moved away shortly after that and Brice didn't know what had happened to them. He sincerely hoped Mrs. Tony Something had managed to keep her abusive husband drunk enough to stay out of his grasp.

Pulling to a stop under the portico of the stately home, Brice sat looking at the residence. T.J.'s car was parked beside Dobbs's Jeep in the paved area under the overhanging roof.

Bailey hadn't actually said she was on her way to Melody's, but it wasn't hard to deduce this was where she'd come. She was here, now. So were T.J. and Dobbs, though they hadn't traveled here together.

On the way into town Brice had tried to call all three of them. Tried several times. None of them answered.

Why not?

He almost read through Zankoski's report a third time, as if going over it one more time would make sense out of all the things that didn't make sense. Coincidences? Seriously? Three men dead — a mental patient, an abusive orderly and Melody McCallum's husband. All killed with extreme violence. *By whom?* Not a shred of evidence in any one of the murder cases. Nothing close to a suspect.

And what possible connection could murders years ago — one in Ohio, one in West Virginia and one in the Bahamas — have to the kidnapping of *three* children here, now? The only connection of any kind that hooked all the disconnected pieces together was the little girl named Caitlyn Whitfield a.k.a. Riley Campbell's teacher, Melody McCallum.

He started to get out of the car but stopped.

Teacher.

Then he did open the report again but didn't read the whole thing. Just scanned down to the part where Zankoski described Melody's employment history. After she graduated from Pitt, she got a job in Shadow Rock at *Madison Elementary School* — the school where Christi Strickland was currently a fifth-grade student. Three years ago, Melody McCallum had been a *second-grade teacher* there.

That little girl had *smiled* at whoever it was who'd beckoned to her from the other side of that rock fence yesterday afternoon.

He sat for a moment, trying to figure out where he was going with all this. Then he placed another call.

"Twice Told Tales, can I help you?" said a gruff voice on the other end of the line.

"This is Sheriff McGreggor. I want to double check something. It's about some books that were dropped off there on Wednesday—"

"More than two hours! That's how long the street was blocked in front of my store when all the parents went barreling down to the school. It was a mess, customers couldn't—"

"Melody McCallum brought some books to your store right after lunch—"

"One of your deputies already talked to me about that — a nice fellow named Fletcher. He wanted to know if she'd brought the books like she said, and I told him yeah, showed him — two boxes full of paperbacks and a few more in a grocery sack."

Brice let out a breath he didn't realize he'd been holding. That's what Fletch had reported. And Brice didn't *really* believe Melody—

"She did it the same as she did last year, but there were more books this time."

"Did what the same?"

"Left the books out back, but I haven't gotten around to counting—"

"She *left* the books? She didn't *give* them to you?"

"No, I got a voicemail saying she'd dropped them off. We did the same thing last year. There's a drop box by the back door we check every morning to see if somebody's donated—"

"So you don't know *when* she left the books?"

"Doesn't matter to me. They were *clearly* marked, a first-grade teacher's printing is perfect."

Brice thanked the man and hung up.

Then he sat. Melody could have dropped off the books at the store during second recess just like she said she did. But she *could* have deposited them in that drop box some other time — late Wednesday afternoon, even Wednesday night — anytime before the owner checked the drop box the next morning.

And If she didn't go to the bookstore, where *did* she go for thirty minutes right after Riley disappeared?

Brice put the car in park, pocketed the keys, and inhaled the sweet smell of roses as he climbed the steps and rang the bell. He heard no sound, so maybe the button didn't work. Or maybe the door was so thick it was soundproof.

No one answered. He punched the button again. About to ring it a third time, he heard a noise inside and the big door opened to reveal a small brunette woman with a smile as warm as a spring morning.

"Is this about Riley? Have you found him?"

Her face was an anguished mixture of fear and hope that seemed totally genuine. But she must have at least been acquainted with Christi Strickland even if the little girl hadn't been one of her second-grade students. Was it possible she hadn't heard Christi had been kidnapped, too? Possible.

"No, I'm sorry. We still haven't located the boy." He paused for a beat. *"Or the other two children."*

She didn't seem to hear him. He watched hope whoosh out of her, saw her grab hold of her emotions. "So, Sheriff—"

"Brice, remember."

"Brice, yes. Please come in."

He stepped inside, holding his hat in his hands.

Chapter Forty-Seven

THIS TIME, when Bailey fell out of reality, the world didn't fracture into misaligned pieces. It didn't drain of color to black, white and shades of gray. There were no side views to try to process with a human brain designed only to see forward.

THE EYES through which she looks see the foyer of The Cedars, the mirror there. The mirror reveals the image of a beautiful woman with hair the color of a square of caramel candy, dazzling blue eyes, wearing a black turtleneck. Melody!

She is looking out through the eyes of Melody McCallum/Caitlyn Whitfield. Not Katydid. Not Shannuck. Another person altogether.

This is a person who split off from the other two. Life began for Caitlyn/Melody two days before Halloween when she was nine years old. That's when she left Katydid hiding deep inside herself and came out into the world because a nurse had read to her, made her feel safe, a nurse who'd had a spider dangling from her witch's hat.

Melody pauses in front of the mirror, runs her fingers through the curls of her ponytail. She takes a deep breath, smiles broadly, steps to the door and opens it.

Brice is standing on the porch with his hat in his hand.

"Is this about Riley? Have you found him?"

Hope blossoms in Melody's chest. Maybe the little boy is going to be alright after all. She has felt so terrible about his disappearance, would do anything, anything *to help police find him. What could possibly have happened to him?*

"No, I'm sorry. We still haven't located the boy."

She's so disappointed she struggles not to cry, misses what he says about some other children, fights back emotion, trying to get herself together. She is glad to see the sheriff, no matter why he has come. She likes him a lot.

"So, Sheriff—"

"Brice, remember."

"Brice, yes. Please come in."

He steps inside.

"I don't know why you … stopped by, but I'm glad you did."

He has a nice smile. A kind smile.

Images flash into her mind. A man, tall and good-looking with curly blond hair, smiling at her. It is Darren, her husband. They are walking hand-in-hand on a deserted beach, joking about the lousy service they'd just gotten at a fancy restaurant.

And then he hits her!

It was the night they were attacked — the police said it must have been a gang. Right before Darren was murdered, she'd jokingly suggested he'd been flirting with the waitress, and he'd turned on her in a fury, hit her with his fist. Knocked her unconscious. When she woke up in the hospital, Darren was dead. Gone. And she had no way to frame what he had done in the final few moments of his life, couldn't even bring herself to tell the police about it. Her questions about Darren would never be answered. She had loved him so much, had been so devastated by his loss, that she hadn't so much as looked at another man since that horrible night.

Until the day Brice came to the school to ask her questions about Riley.

"Actually, Miss McCallum, a couple of things have come up that I need to ask you—"

"Wait a minute. I thought we settled this. Brice and Melody — right?"

"Okay, Melody, I was wondering—"

"About your friends? They're here, you know."

"Yes, I saw their cars parked outside, but they're not answering their phones."

How kind he is to be so concerned about his friends! She knew he'd be kind. That first day when he was asking about Riley, she knew he was a good, kind man.

"Of course they're not," she said with an engaging smile. "I can tell you why. In fact, I'll show you. They're upstairs in the ballroom."

She indicates the staircase winding up the side of the wall to the double doors in the center of the second-floor balcony overlook.

"Come with me." She takes his right arm, as if she were a bride and he were walking her down the aisle. She likes the feel of him next to her, so tall and strong. As they ascend the steps she tells him all about what T.J. and Bailey had said to her.

"... and she said she paints pictures of, well, of what hasn't happened yet, and I'm sure she didn't expect me to believe her, but I know there are unexplainable things in the world."

Like the blank spots in her memory. Almost all of yesterday is gone. She got up, dressed, got into her car to go to the grocery store. Then nothing. The next thing she knew, she was standing at the top of the stairs and it was evening. She went into the kitchen and saw that she hadn't gotten the groceries she'd left to get hours before. And this afternoon ...

"Bailey said she offered to paint Riley and you gave her that snapshot I gave you, but instead of painting Riley, she painted my portrait."

Brice wrinkles his nose, as if he smells a bad odor.

"Is something wrong?"

"You don't smell ...?"

"Smell what?" She looks at him, uncomprehending.

"That ... never mind." Then he changes the subject. "The morning Riley was taken, you said you delivered the paperbacks to the bookstore. But the manager said you just left—"

She doesn't want to talk about that. It's another hole in her memory.

After she watched the boys walk down the hallway to the playground …
her mind is blank. So she directs the conversation back to the painting.

"Bailey said the portrait she painted of me wasn't one I would want
to see. Have you seen it?"

"As a matter of fact, I have. And she's right. You don't want to
see it."

They have arrived at the double doors.

"You have to do the same thing I made Bailey, T.J. and Dobbs do,"
she says, as excited as one of her first-graders.

"And that is?"

"Close your eyes. I want the grandeur to hit you all at once when you
open them — just like it did the others."

She turns her head, then glances back at him. His eyes aren't closed.
They're open — wide open, in fact, and there's a strange expression on
his face. He's looking — staring, really — at her hair, her ponytail.
She opens the big door on the right and steps into the room still holding
his arm.

Even now, after all these months, she is stunned by the beauty of the
room. The parquet floor, so shiny it reflects the sparkling light from the
chandelier like a pool of still water. The chandelier still takes her breath
away and she stares at it in awe. Thousands of shiny pieces of perfectly
cut glass, each a prism, refracting the light, casting hundreds of thousands
of rainbows into the air all around, a waterfall in brilliant color.

On the far side of the room, the elevator carrying T.J. and Bailey is
almost to the top. But … T.J. is not inside it. He has climbed out of it
and now stands on top of the cage. Why on earth …?

"My God!" Brice stammers and his whole body tenses. She looks up
at him, but doesn't see stunned delight on his face. She sees horror.

Then Melody was gone, blinked out like a snuffed candle.
Bailey's vision dimmed, as the light in the room — so bright
through Melody's eyes — became the putrid haze of red. She
tried to cry out to Brice, to warn him, but she couldn't make a

sound. T.J. yelled from above. He was on top of the elevator cage, and he called out, "Brice. Look out! She's—"

In Bailey's swimming vision, what happened next seemed to crank down into slow motion. Melody's back hunched, her head drooped. She was holding onto Brice's right arm and she grabbed it with her other hand ... *and Shannuck broke his arm.* Like it was a brittle stick. Just snapped it. Brice screamed in agony, staggered away, reaching for his gun with his other hand. But the holster was on his right side. The spider creature was on him instantly, grabbed his shoulders and threw him twenty feet, where he hit the floor on his back and slid across it. Brice fumbled for his gun with his left hand. Shannuck leapt across the distance between them — leapt in one jump — yanked the pistol out of Brice's holster and threw it away. Bailey could hear it clatter on the hardwood floor. Then Shannuck stood hulking over his prostrate form and Bailey knew the spider was going to kill him. Crush him, mutilate him just like the orderly, maybe tear his eyes out of their sockets.

T.J. swung down off the top of the elevator and jumped into the cage through the open door, swinging it shut behind him and fastening the metal bar in place across it. He punched the green button, must have pulled the jammed rope free because the elevator began to move upward again.

Shannuck never turned his head toward them, but Bailey knew the spider could see not only what was in front of him but what was on both sides as well. Stepping away from Brice, the human spider leaned over and scooped up a handful of creatures — bugs, roaches, spiders — off the floor and threw them into Brice's face.

He batted at them with his left hand, his right useless, lying at an odd angle to his body. Then he screamed, a shrieking howl. He'd been bitten. He slapped at his face, tried to rise, screamed again. Shannuck lifted his head and made the sound, the horror noise that passed for laughter. He turned toward them then, just as the elevator clunked into place at the top of the shaft. T.J. shoved on the back panel of the cage. The panel swung out and T.J. grabbed her hand, yanking her forward toward an open corridor. He shoved Bailey in front of him, then paused for a heartbeat, looking back.

Dobbs hung upside down from a human spiderweb. Brice writhed on the floor in agony.

No one left behind. T.J. was a Marine.

Turning to Bailey, he cried, *"Run!"*

A short hallway.

A door.

Something that looked like rubber weather stripping was fitted all the way around the door, sealing the multi-legged horrors inside.

Game over. They were trapped.

T.J. grabbed the doorknob, turned it and pulled and the door opened. The seals slid along the floor with a rubber scrapping sound and sunlight blinded her. A fresh breeze ruffled her hair and she took great gulps of clean, pure late-afternoon air. The shock of the air and the light steadied her, washed away some of the dizziness, and her mind cleared.

T.J. hauled her along beside him across a width of planking to a staircase. She grabbed the railing and with T.J.'s grip on her upper arm, the two of them ran down the stairs, crossed a landing, ran down another, longer set of steps.

The wind was gusty with the smell of rain in it. Thunder rumbled in the distance. Another landing. Another set of steps, shorter this time. They passed through the roof of the surround-porch and down to the flagstones of the path leading away from the house toward an opening in a hedge.

Bailey was gasping for breath but could feel her full senses returning with every intake of clean air.

She and T.J. raced down the flagstones to a tall gate in the ornate metal fencing that ran from the staircase above, along the railing of the wraparound porch, across the path and ended in a tall hedge twenty feet ahead. T.J. was gasping, too, his face flushed dark. He was as fit as a man half his age, but she could see the blood vessels in his neck bulging, pulsing with every beat of his racing heart.

T.J. turned the handle on the gate. It was locked.

"If I boosted you up, could you climb over—?"

But even as he suggested the idea, it was clear it wouldn't work. The thin metal struts of the fence were only about two inches apart and granted no purchase. The first cross bar, for a foothold or handholds, was eight feet off the ground. The fence was capped by a bar featuring ornate spikes each a foot tall, making the whole structure fifteen feet tall. Unclimbable even with a boost.

"Only way out is through the maze. *Her* maze."

Bailey remembered then. T.J. had told her the back yard of The Cedars was a gigantic hedge maze that reminded him of *The Shining*.

They both heard it at the same time. Someone, some*thing* was coming down the stairs they'd just descended.

T.J. grabbed her arm and shoved her in front of him down the flagstone path and through the opening in the hedge. The hedge itself was as impenetrable as a four-foot thick wall. It stood at the height of the fence — fifteen feet. Once through the opening, there were corridors leading left, right and straight ahead. T.J. turned right and ran down the corridor, dragging Bailey along beside him. Though still slightly unsteady, she was much more sure-footed than she'd been before. The drug in the sugar cube had apparently worn off. And the fresh air, the *glorious* fresh air …

They got to the end of the corridor leading right from the maze opening and turned right, then left, then right again.

Bailey was hopelessly confused and suspected that T.J. didn't know where he was going either, wasn't running *to*, just *away*, from the spider creature that surely now stalked the maze behind them.

Chapter Forty-Eight

BRICE HAD NEVER FELT pain like he felt now in his right cheek. It was a searing, burning agony that took his breath away in its ferocity. The tortured nerves in his cheek screamed daggers into his whole face and it was all he could do to keep from wailing.

What just happened?

Melody had turned her head and he'd noticed her ponytail. Started to make some sort of mental connection ... as she opened the door and the horrible stench ...

And then *she broke his arm.* Threw him across the room. Grabbed his gun. Dumped ... *bugs* in his face. And was gone.

What *was* this?

Nothing made any sense at all and he couldn't concentrate, focus, with such agony in his face. A spider bite. A black widow? Maybe. He'd only caught a fleeting glimpse of black legs before it ... his eye had almost instantly swollen shut. Another pain suddenly stabbed into his neck on the left side, but it was wasp-sting pain, bearable. His face, though ...

He ground his teeth hard, trying not to shriek.

He'd been shot in the leg in Kosovo, suffered shrapnel wounds in Afghanistan and had been badly burned as a volunteer fireman — a three-inch-wide swath of puckered tissue across the length of his lower back testified to the severity of the third-degree burn that required months of painful skin grafting to heal.

But none of his previous wounds had been anything like this. The torment stole his breath, made it impossible to think. He had to think, had to figure out …

He could feel things crawling on him. Bugs … he saw a roach. Certainly more spiders. More black widows! He had to get up off this floor. Couldn't just lie here and let … He couldn't stand another bite like this one!

Horror gave him the strength to roll over on his side. The movement shot daggers of agony up from his hand to his shoulder when he moved the broken arm and he cried out then in spite of himself. He rose to his knees slowly, looked around, understood nothing about his surroundings. It was a monster room out of a horror movie made in hell.

He didn't dare stand, knew he wouldn't be stable enough to remain on his feet, but kneeling like this he could dust the creatures away.

Help. He had to summon help.

Keying the shoulder mic was an awkward movement. It was on his left shoulder and he would ordinarily use his right hand, which now hung useless at his side. He lifted his left hand to the switch, tried to …

A tarantula the size of a saucer skittered across the floor not a foot in front of him and his instinctive backward cringe threw him off balance and he tumbled down onto the floor again, banging his head painfully and landing on his broken arm. Lightning bolts of pain fired up the arm to his shoulder and down to his fingertips.

You're going to die here.

The thought materialized in his consciousness like an instant message on a cellphone screen.

His muddled thinking … it was so hard to think with the

pain shrieking in his face. He knew it was horribly swollen, could feel the tightened skin spreading. If his other eye swelled shut, he would be blind. He had to move now while he still could.

Gritting his teeth against the agony, he rolled again onto his side, used his uninjured left hand to shove himself upward and made it back up to his knees. That's when he saw the silver thing hanging in the rigging.

A man. Was that …?

Dobbs?

Was he hallucinating? Was it possible that was Dobbs hanging upside down from a rope around his legs, forty feet off the ballroom floor? Wrapped up in something shiny … Saran Wrap?

Where was Bailey? T.J.? Were they hanging …?

He looked around frantically, searching … oh, please, no.

Another silver package, but small. *Too small.* And another. Smaller. Those couldn't have held Bailey or T.J.

Those were children.

Oh, God.

What was this?

How had Melody snapped his arm? And her face. That had to have been a hallucination. It couldn't have contorted like that, couldn't have changed—

A bullet of pain shot into his ankle like a fiery arrow. Agony so intense he couldn't even shriek. He turned awkwardly, hammering his pants leg, screaming then, howling. Off balance, he tumbled onto his back, crying out with such force he was instantly hoarse.

You're going to die here.

He screamed and screamed and …

Get a grip or you are going to die here!

His left hand trembling, he reached up, used his chin to steady the shoulder mic and managed to push the button. Then he spoke a single phrase that would light the fuse of every police officer who heard it. Two words that would send any human being with a badge running through walls to respond.

"Officer down!"

That's what he *tried* to say. But his swollen lips — and swelling tongue! — garbled the words.

Concentrating. *Oh, God it hurt!* His face, his ankle, his arm. *You're going to die here.*

"Of-fi-cer down!" The words were barely intelligible. "Repeat, of-fi-cer *down*! At The Cedars."

Was there a response? He didn't know, wasn't even completely sure he had transmitted. His hearing was … was the swelling in his face affecting his hearing, too? His phone was in his pocket, but there was no way he could get it out or use it if he did.

Something else bit him. But he was wrapped in cotton now. His face and ankle shrieking in agony, everything else … becoming numb. The sensation of creatures crawling on him faded. The world was graying out.

He supposed he really was going to die here.

Then the darkness took him.

Chapter Forty-Nine

T.J. WAS PANTING, soaked in sweat, his black face flushed almost indigo.

Bailey was gasping. Terror. Exertion. Spider venom.

But T.J. no longer had to drag Bailey along beside him. The fresh air and movement had cleared her head — the effects of the drug were gone. Adrenaline had taken its place, granted her strength, erased her pain.

When they got to an intersection of hedge passages that opened out in three directions, they paused and Bailey looked down. Fresh scuff marks in the dirt. They had already come this way!

"Do you know where you're going?"

"No."

"Is there a way out, or just twists and turns that go nowhere?"

"A way out."

"You sure?"

"No."

He dashed off down the corridor on the right with Bailey on his heels, made another right ... and came up against a solid hedge. Dead end.

He turned, froze and she read horror on his face. She heard a hissing sound behind her, saw that T.J. heard it, too, so it wasn't just in her mind.

Please, no. Not in the spider's mind. If I have to die, not while I'm in there!

But she didn't plunge out of reality into the insanity of the not-human.

"I tear your head off!"

The hoary voice came from behind *and above* her. She turned to see what had drained the color out of T.J.'s flushed face. Shannuck was on top of the hedge, perched fifteen feet above them. There was no way out of the dead-end corridor without passing beneath where the spider watched them with impossible eyes.

It was a spider. A woman, yes, but even without the dangling legs and hairy belly of the spider suit, what crouched above them was a spider.

"You die!"

The spider hopped down from the top of the hedge, off a fifteen-foot hedge like stepping off a footstool, and landed in the dirt thirty feet from them, hunkered down there, coiled to pounce.

T.J. moved in front of Bailey, between her and the spider. The gesture was touching. And futile. There was not a thing the man could do to protect her. Nothing any human could do. Shannuck was going to kill them. It would be over in seconds. Then he would kill Dobbs if he was still alive. And Brice, too, if the poisonous spiders hadn't already done the job for him.

Bailey's fear began to morph into anger. Last-breath, death anger, a sudden, burning rage in her chest. She clenched her teeth, found her hands involuntarily balling into fists.

"Call her," T.J. suddenly hissed over his shoulder. "Talk to her!"

"Talk to—?"

"The little girl!"

It took a heartbeat or two before Bailey understood. Then she cried out, "Katydid!"

The spider froze.

"Are you there, honey? Can you hear me?"

The spider remained as motionless as a statue. Bailey stepped slowly around T.J.

"Katydid, I want to see you. Please come out and talk to me." She paused, trying to think what else— "You were afraid the glue holding up the sky would let go, remember, like the glue Daddy used on the horn of your unicorn. So you asked Mommy about it."

Nothing happened for a few seconds. Then the change was like watching wax melt. The hunched form of the spider straightened. Arms and legs pulled back into their sockets. The face relaxed and features formed on it. Innocent features, somehow much younger than Melody McCallum. Achingly young.

"Mommy called me Katydid," said the little girl dressed in black tights and a black turtleneck standing in the dirt in dusty satin ballet slippers — they *were* ballet slippers. Her voice was soft and musical, sounded like the ringing of tiny bells. From the same throat that had produced — *don't go there!* Her ponytail had come loose and when she shook her head, strands of her tangled hair fell into her eyes. "You're not my mommy."

"No, I'm not, sweetheart, but you *know* me. Don't you?"

Macy Cosgrove had recognized Bailey as a friend or she never would have gone running up the mountainside with her. Maybe—

"Uh huh. I know you."

Bailey had been there with Katydid, knew how terribly, terribly wounded she had been and somehow, on some level, Katydid understood that.

The fingers of a fitful wind reached out from the

approaching storm and harried small funnels of dust and leaves along the ground at the little girl's feet. She looked down at them. Then she *saw* them, registered and connected. Her head came up and her eyes caught Bailey's and lingered for a second before she looked around, turning her head in wonder.

She took in a breath.

"It smells ... *good.*"

Bailey was the only person in all the world who understood how significant that simple statement was, the only one who knew the horror that had filled every breath this child had taken — hour after hour, day after day. Bailey knew because she'd been there, too, smelled it as Katydid had.

"The roses ... I like how they smell. So ... *sweet,* almost like you can taste it."

It took Bailey a moment to figure out what roses she meant. The ones around the front door of The Cedars. The ones Shannuck smelled with the hairs on his legs.

But this little girl wasn't Shannuck. She wasn't a kidnapper, a murderer. How could she be held responsible for what the monster had done?

The rain came then, only a few drops at first, each making a tiny meteor-crater circle in the dust around Katydid. She put out both hands, palms up to catch the raindrops, turned her face toward the sky and opened her mouth. A raindrop splatted on her nose and she giggled — a musical sound — and looked at Bailey. She was smiling.

"It's nice here."

Then the smile faded, drained slowly off her lips and out of her eyes.

"It's dark there, where I am."

"Don't go back there, Katydid. Stay here with me in the light." There had to be a way to control the Dissociative Identity Disorder. Drugs or therapy or something. Some way to fasten the fragile Katydid to the real world, a way to keep out—

"Shannuck does bad things now." The child's tiny voice was so soft even the gentle breeze almost carried her words away. "I've seen. I've *watched* him. He has to stop hurting people … little kids."

Then she gave Bailey a look of such utter sadness and loss, it broke Bailey's heart.

"He's not my protector anymore." A single tear appeared and slid down the child's cheek. "I have to flip the switches. Turn off … everything."

It took Bailey a moment to realize what—

"No!"

She started toward the little girl but a strong hand grabbed her arm and T.J. whispered in her ear, "You got to let her go."

Bailey tried to wrest her arm away, struggled to free it, but the old man's grip was iron.

The little girl stood perfectly still, her eyes locked on Bailey's.

"Sweetheart, don't! Oh, please *don't* …"

The child lifted her hand to her face, curled her finger over her nose and put her thumb into her mouth.

"Katydid, *no!*"

She only sucked her thumb for a moment, then folded up and collapsed into the dirt.

T.J. let go of her arm and Bailey rushed to the child lying in a fetal position on the ground. She was as limp as a rag doll when Bailey gently eased her onto her back. Her eyes were not staring in sightless catatonia, though. They were closed. Bailey felt the little girl's neck searching for a pulse. There was none.

Katydid had flipped a final switch and stopped her heart. She was dead.

In the distance, Bailey heard the wailing cry of a massive

symphony of sirens painted on a low rumble of thunder. It began to rain in earnest then, a heavy, punishing rain that pelted the bushes, soaked the dirt and drenched Bailey as she tenderly lifted the lifeless child into her arms and cradled her there, rocking slowly back and forth.

Chapter Fifty

Dobbs's face had just the suggestion of a smile, the not-smile he used to hide by ducking his head when him and T.J. was ten years old and his mama was going on about how he hadn't ought to be out there makin' friends with "a colored," when all the time T.J. was sittin' right on the other side of the mulberry bush, waiting for the woman to stop jawin' so him and Dobbs could go fishin'.

The big man was watching Bailey cut up the last of Brice's steak for him because his arm was still in a cast after the surgery required to mend the "greenstick fracture" of the ulna he'd suffered when Melody/Shannuck snapped it.

Bailey and Brice were seated with Dobbs around a table on the wide back porch of the Watford House, dawdling over the dinner T.J.'d whipped up with his near magical ability to transform a piece of meat into ambrosia with an outdoor grill. He had left the grill turned up high while they ate to burn off the grease and now he turned it off and closed the lid. Soon's it cooled, he'd scrub the grates with a wadded-up piece of aluminum foil.

Taking off his apron, a manly garment — black and gold, with a Pittsburgh Steelers' logo on the front — T.J. sat back down at the table where Bailey was talking about Senior FBI Agent Haruto Nakamura.

"… think his friends call him Harri?" she asked.

"That would imply he has friends," Brice said.

"He might have been an emotionless robot around you," Bailey said, "but no way was he a Sphinx when he stepped into that ballroom — maybe a tarantula crawled over his shoe! I bet he turned as white as a gym sock."

"Or looked like he'd just swallowed one."

In truth, all the law enforcement officers who'd responded to Brice's *officer down* distress call that Saturday evening more than a month ago had been shocked beyond any description by what they found in the grand ballroom of The Cedars.

Just getting Brice and Dobbs out of there and into ambulances had been a harrowing experience not a member of the Kavanaugh County Sheriff's Department would ever forget. T.J. hadn't seen it, but he'd heard that Fletch refused to wait for a hazmat suit, just went barreling in, picked Brice up, threw him over his shoulder in a fireman's carry and beat feet out of that house like somebody'd yelled "run, Forest, run!" Of course, they couldn't even load the sheriff into an ambulance until he'd been "decontaminated," stripped down to his skivvies to make sure he didn't have a black widow spider in the cuff of his pants.

Even with the combined efforts of the rescue squad and the fire department, it took almost two hours to get Dobbs down from the ship's rigging. They *did* wait for hazmat suits.

Wasn't much of an exaggeration to claim that the ambulances bearing Brice, Bailey, T.J. and Dobbs had barely made it to the hospital before the first of the phalanx of news media descended on the horror like crows tearing at roadkill. Within hours, it was an international story beamed all over the world.

Behemoth white news vans, wearing satellite dishes like some rapper's ball cap, backed up traffic on the narrow mountain roads. Fox News, CBS, NBC, MSNBC, BBC, even Al

Jazeera sat bumper-to-bumper for hours to earn the privilege of filming stuff their viewers'd take one look at and be so horrified they'd switch channels to roller derby.

Then an alphabet soup of state and federal agencies grappled with what to do with the contamination ... the *infestation*.

The NIH (National Institutes of Health), ATSDR (Agency for Toxic Substances and Disease Registry), the CDC, the EPA, even the Department of Agriculture — and those was just the ones T.J. knew what their initials stood for — they all wanted a piece of the action. Until they seen what the action was. Every mother's child of 'em had been briefed on what to expect, all thought they was prepared for what they'd see, but there wasn't no way to prepare a person for a thing like that. More than a couple of the first responders balked and refused to go into the room — even wearing hazmat suits.

T.J. didn't know what they'd done — or who had done it — to get rid of the plague. He could have asked, but what difference did it make? Didn't matter who done what, not a living soul in Shadow Rock, West Virginia would ever willingly set foot in that place again.

The footage they'd shown on national news was so horrifying, in fact, that when the Shadow Rock Town Council proposed burning the still-quarantined building to the ground, the Historical Society Nazis actually agreed to consider the proposal.

The various agencies cataloged eighteen different varieties of spiders among the thousands in the house along with an untold and uncounted potpourri of miscellaneous bugs that'd been provided to feed them. Many — not all, but a good-sized number — of them spiders was poisonous. Black, brown and red widow spiders, hobo spiders, yellow sac spiders, wolf spiders, funnel web spiders, brown recluse, even deadly Brazilian wandering spiders. How the fragile little teacher had come by such exotic creatures had still not been determined.

Seemed proof to T.J., as if he needed it, that if you had enough money, you could buy anything off eBay.

The doctors suspected Brice had been bitten on the cheek by one of the widow spiders — black, brown or red — and possibly by a wandering spider on the ankle. But it was an allergic reaction to the venom that had come very close to killin' him. He'd been unable to breathe without a ventilator — his diaphragm paralyzed — for three days.

The right side of his face was still puffy, with a healing wound that'd likely leave a good-sized scar. All evidence of the tarantula bite on T.J.'s arm was gone now, but he'd had outpatient surgery earlier in the week where — judging from the necrosis of the skin — a brown recluse had bitten him on the left leg. He had a bandage the size of a baby's diaper where they'd removed the last of the ulcer and skin lesions there that refused to heal. He was sure multiple skin grafts awaited him.

Fang marks on Bailey's neck indicated she'd been bitten by a wolf spider there, a huge one — horrifying, but no more poisonous than a bee sting — in addition to the tarantula bite on her arm. She and T.J. had been pumped full of antivenom and hospitalized for a couple of days, with symptoms that ranged from severe abdominal pain and rigid muscles to vomiting and — in Bailey's case — shock. Dobbs had been kept overnight for observation as well, but suffered no ill effects from hanging upside down. He had suffered no spider bites, either, but whatever she'd hit him on the head with had created a goose egg the size of … well, a goose egg. He was so hard-headed wasn't no concussion, though.

Brice had got the worst of it — at least physically. But it was Bailey who'd taken the biggest hit mentally. Flashing in and out of the mind of a *murderous spider*! T.J. had been terrified she'd suffered massive psychological damage. That she'd be haunted by debilitating, *permanent* post traumatic stress disorder. That all that mind-numbing horror would chew up her soul.

Truth was, Bailey could barely remember any of it! And what she could remember was fuzzy and indistinct. Melody'd spiked the sugar cubes with an as yet still unknown concoction of psychotropic drugs, hoping to render both Bailey and T.J. groggy and disoriented. The drug-soup did just that to Bailey, with the added side effect of removing her inhibitions, leaving her defenseless against mind connections. But when the potion was flushed completely out of Bailey's system, it carried the images it had enabled along with it. Bailey could distinctly recall touching Melody's locket, connecting with Katydid. Her next clear memory was running through the backyard maze. Everything in between was mush.

In actual fact, all four of them was lucky to be alive. Which was more than could be said for the three kidnapped children, whose funerals were held one after the other in three different churches with uncounted thousands of people attending. The devastated community was still staggering from the blows. The parents would never recover. Lucas Ferrigliano had been voluntarily committed to some fancy psychiatric facility in Pittsburgh and would face all kinda criminal charges — *as an adult* — when he was released.

It had taken the combined confirmation of all four of them to convince Agent Nakamura that the diminutive first-grade teacher had done the things they had seen her do.

"I believe you because I don't have any choice," he had told Brice when he'd returned to Shadow Rock to interview the sheriff, who was still in the hospital a week after Melody McCallum's death. "It has to be true. The physical evidence bears it out."

Evidence that included a review of the surveillance camera videos at the mall, where Brice pointed out what he had missed, what he'd put together in his head a split second before Melody'd turned on him — the ponytail of the woman in the baseball cap exiting the mall carrying an apparently empty gym bag was unmistakable, clearly Melody's distinctive caramel-colored brown. And Christi Strickland had, indeed, been a student in Melody's second-grade class at Madison Elementary School. There was a mountain of other forensic evidence, of course, traces of fiber and hair in Melody's car and in the gym bag, but given that the children's bodies had been found at The Cedars, none of it mattered.

"The history of unexplained murders during Caitlyn's hospitalization ... the testimony of four *reliable* eyewitnesses ... and ..." Then Nakamura had shaken his head. "I'm sorry ... I just can't ..." He'd stopped, finished in a whisper. "She *became* a spider?"

Of course, Nakamura was only given the sanitized version of events, one that left out any mention of the portrait Bailey had painted, or how she had gotten involved in chasing down Melody McCallum's true identity in the first place. A reasonable lie sufficed — that Bailey was a friend of Brice's and she had suspected Melody from the beginning.

"I don't know ... call it woman's intuition," she'd said, and shrugged.

That was a more plausible and certainly more palatable explanation than reality — that Bailey had painted a picture of a little girl trapped in a wrecked camper while her parents' bodies decomposed nearby, and then fell into and out of a spider's mind, watching him murder three adults — a pervert, an orderly and Melody's husband — and kidnap three children.

The autopsy of Melody McCallum's body revealed no apparent cause of death. Her heart had simply stopped beating.

"I'm really looking forward to explaining my reports to my superiors — even with a mountain of physical evidence and eyewitness testimony," Nakamura had said, weary astonishment still written on his face. "That woman *willed* herself to die."

T.J. could tell Bailey was struggling to assimilate it all. To reconcile her pity for the pathetic little girl and her loathing terror of the spider. *That* would take time.

As Brice and Dobbs talked about — what else? — Pittsburgh Steelers football, he caught Bailey looking at him. He gestured with his chin toward the kitchen, she nodded and the two of them began gathering up plates and hauling them into the house.

Once inside, she set the dirty dishes on the countertop, reached down and picked up Sparky, who'd been busy as a one-armed paper hanger ever since they'd all got home from the hospital. First, he'd lick T.J.'s whole face, then he'd lick Bailey's. Then back to T.J. He'd been hanging tight to Bailey today, though, could sense in his Sparky way that she was troubled.

She cuddled the ball of fluff close.

"We didn't do any good, T.J.," she said, keeping her voice low. "I painted that portrait … and Riley Campbell still died. So did Christi Strickland and Marley Ewing. In fact, the portrait almost got the four of *us* killed."

T.J. turned on the hot water tap and began to fill one side of the double sink.

"And you think you'd be better off to treat your *gift* like Mama done hers. Ignore it. Destroy the paintings. Don't get involved."

"And you *don't* think that would be better?"

"Depends. Maybe you'd ought to ask Macy Cosgrove." Bailey stopped petting Sparky, her face expressionless. "Or all the little kids in this town who's outside playing in the sunshine right this minute, riding they bicycles — or more likely in a dark room somewhere sitting glassy-eyed in front of some stupid video game — little kids who *ain't dead bodies* wrapped up in cellophane hanging upside down in Melody McCallum's ballroom!"

He hammered the next words like nails into a plank.

"You think Shannuck woulda stopped at *three*? If we hadn't

caught Melody McCallum, who would have? The sheriff's department and the FBI — they was both clueless. Who'd ever have suspected that sweetheart first-grade teacher?"

He looked around the countertop, spotted a sponge and held it under the running water.

"Maybe somebody would have ..." — Bailey was scrambling — "I don't know, stumbled over the bodies somehow and ..."

"Even if a plumber come to fix a leak had accidentally wandered into that ballroom, Melody'd still have got off. 'Cause ain't no way a little bitty thing like her coulda done what she done. No jury on the planet'd convict her, especially since she coulda passed a room full of polygraph tests."

Picking up the top plate off the pile of dirty dishes, T.J. wiped it with the wet sponge and set it in the other side of the double sink.

"When Melody's car got run off the road and Shannuck saved her — and replaced her as the dominant personality — first thing he done was *kill* the men in that pickup truck. And he woulda gone on killin'. 'Cause that's what spiders do. Maybe for years!"

Horror stole Bailey's voice so she could only whisper. *"Years?"*

"How many kids you think Shannuck woulda murdered — *and got away with it?* — if you'd walked out into your back yard and set that painting on fire?"

She folded inward emotionally, sank down into one of the chairs at the kitchen table, all the air gone out of her. Sparky hopped out of her arms to the floor and stood up on his hind legs with his paws on the cabinet. He wasn't quite tall enough, though. His little pink tongue fell an inch short of the crumbs on the countertop beside the dirty dishes.

"Last time, there was Macy — *alive.* But this time—"

"—was different from last time." T.J. turned off the tap, set the plates in the sink full of hot water and began to wipe his hands on a towel. "And next time will be different from this time. Ever time this thing happens to you, you gonna have to decide what to do about it, case by case."

"I don't want to decide. I want—"

"Bailey girl, listen to yourself. *I want. I don't want.* How's that workin' out for you?" T.J. made a *humph* sound in his throat. "I'm having deja vu all over again here 'cause I done had this conversation."

"With Dobbs?"

"With *Brice.* When you 'nounced all confident that you wasn't never again gonna paint a portrait like the one of Macy Cosgrove."

Bailey got that awful haunted look in her eyes.

"You think there'll be more of them, don't you?"

"I told Brice then and I'm tellin' you now — we ain't the ones get to decide that."

"Then *who* does?"

Fear passed between them as real as a gust of wind. T.J. reached out and patted Bailey's shoulder, but his own hand was unsteady.

"Sugar … I ain't got no idea."

THE END

A Special Request

Thank you for reading *Red Web*.

If you enjoyed this book please consider writing a review of it on your favorite bookseller's website so other readers might enjoy it too. Just a couple of sentences would mean a lot to me.

Thank you!
Ninie Hammon

Author's Note

If *Red Web* totally spider-creeped you out, (and if it didn't, you weren't paying attention) you might have trouble believing what I'm about to tell you.

I am arachnophobic.

Arachnophobia is the fear of spiders. No, it's more than just fear. It's not merely somebody who's spooked by spiders or who gets the creeps when they see one crawling up the wall or who hates those gigantic spiders in people's yards at Halloween.

Arachnophobia is a *phobia*, which Webster's defines as "an extreme or irrational fear." Two key words to note here: *extreme* and *irrational*. That'd be me — *extremely, irrationally* afraid of spiders. I had a close encounter with a huge tarantula when I was five years old and I have been arachnophobic ever since.

I once ran through a plate glass door when a kid put a rubber spider on my shoulder. (I have the scar of 23 stitches to prove it.)

If I see a spider in a room, and nobody kills it, I will never set foot in that room again. Extreme? You betcha. Irrational? Busted.

This is the point in the narrative where you're wondering:

If you're arachnophobic, whatever possessed you to write a book like *Red Web*?

Actually, my arachnophobia is the main reason I decided to write the book in the first place. I can't think of anything on the planet more horrifying that a spider. My favorite author, Stephen King, has said on multiple occasions that a spider is the true embodiment of evil.

I couldn't agree more.

I go all out to give my readers the best I've got. (My husband says there's a sports phrase for that: *I never leave anything on the field.*) When I decided to make the second book in the *Through the Canvas* series reeeeeally horrifying, I wanted it to launch my readers into another whole dimension of goosebumps.

And there's nothing more horrifying than a spider. Decision made.

But between *deciding* to write a story with hundreds of spiders in it and actually *writing* a story with hundreds of spiders in it there's this little thing that has to happen called "research."

You can't write about spiders unless you know a whole lot about them.

I knew *nothing*.

But Google is your friend, right?

Want to know the ten most poisonous spiders in the world?

Want to know which spider has the deadliest venom?

Want to know how the human body reacts to a bite from a tarantula?

… a black widow? … a wolf spider?

Just Google it.

Let's back up to that arachnophobic thing. Remember the *extreme* and *irrational* part.

That's *me!* I cannot *look* at a spider!

I can't even look at a *picture* of a spider.

And therein lies the problem with "Google is your friend."

Every time you Google spiders, they post a picture beside the information!

And sometimes there's even a video that starts *automatically* — suddenly you see the thing crawling across a rock or engaging in some charming and endearing behavior like eating its young.

My effort to research spiders left me in tears — literally.

My husband walked in on the tears and offered to help.

And so began the strangest research experience of my whole writing career. (Yes, even stranger than crawling through a coal mine on my hands and knees.)

My husband sat in front of the computer monitor. I sat where I couldn't see it. He'd look up a spider, like Australian wandering spider or Brazilian jumping spider, read the blurb and then describe the picture to me while I took notes.

The system quickly degenerated into conversations like:

"What color is it?"

"Black. Well, mostly black. The stuff sticking out of its body is brown."

"So black spider, brown hair?"

"I'm not sure the brown stuff is hair."

"If it's not hair, what is it?"

"Fur maybe?"

"Spiders don't have fur.

"How would you know? You've never looked at a spider for more than a second before you start making that sound."

"What sound?"

"You know what sound. That squeak you make."

"I do not squeak."

"Yes, you do. You sound like a baby rabbit that got run over by a hay baler."

"Fine, black spider, brown *fur.* What does its face look like?"

"I might not be looking at the face. I might be looking at the butt. It's hard to tell."

"It looks the same coming and going?"

"No, this side's got black dangly things hanging down with bristly hair. "

"Fangs?"

"Maybe. But the jumping spider didn't have hairy fangs. Maybe these are antennae."

"What do the eyes look like?"

"I don't think this one has eyes. I can't find them."

"It has to have eyes or it'd bump into trees and rocks and other spiders."

"Maybe it sees with those dangly things."

"How can you see with dangly things?"

"I don't know. I'm not a spider."

After several enlightening conversations like that, I started writing, figured I'd just have to wing the descriptions. And I quickly realized I didn't have to describe the spiders. Nobody cares what spiders look like. A spider's a spider. Readers can picture them looking any way they want.

Besides, if I described the spiders reeeeally well, my readers might start making that squeaky sound …

Ninie Hammon
February, 2020

About the Author

Ninie Hammon (rhymes with shiny, not skinny) grew up in Muleshoe, Texas, got a BA in English and theatre from Texas Tech University and snagged a job as a newspaper reporter. She didn't know a thing about journalism, but her editor said if she could write he could teach her the rest of it and if she couldn't write the rest of it didn't matter. She hung in there for a 25-year career as a journalist. As soon as she figured out that making up the facts was a whole lot more fun than reporting them, she turned to fiction and never looked back.

Ninie now writes suspense--every flavor except pistachio: psychological suspense, inspirational suspense, suspense thrillers, paranormal suspense, suspense mysteries.

In every book she keeps this promise to her Loyal Reader: "I will tell you a story in a distinctive voice you'll always recognize, about people as ordinary as you are--people who have been slammed by something they didn't sign on for, and now they must fight for their lives. Then smack in the middle of their everyday worlds, those people encounter the unexplainable--and it's always the game-changer."

Also By Ninie Hammon

Cornbread Mafia

Fire In The Hole

Blown' Up A Storm

Ridin' For A Fall

So Shall The Tree Grow

Nowhere, USA

The Jabberwock

Mad Dog

Trapped

The Hanging Judge

The Witch of Gideon

Blown Away

Nowhere People

Through The Canvas Series

Black Water

Red Web

Gold Promise

Blue Tears

The Taken Saga

The Taken

The Changed

The Hidden

The Saved

The Unexplainable Collection

Five Days in May

Black Sunshine

The Based on True Stories Collection

Home Grown

Sudan

When Butterflies Cry

The Knowing Series

The Knowing

The Deceiving

The Reckoning

The Fault

Stand-alone Psychological Thrillers

The Memory Closet

The Last Safe Place

9 781629 551548